LEAVING NEVERLAND

LEAVING

NEVERLAND

JAMES SAFRENO

Library of Congress Control Number: 2021917710

HARDBACK: 978-1-955955-82-9
PAPERBACK: 978-1-955955-81-2
EBOOK: 978-1-955955-83-6

Ordering Information:

For orders and inquiries, please contact:
1-888-404-1388
www.goldtouchpress.com
book.orders@goldtouchpress.com

Printed in the United States of America

CONTENTS

X

PROLOGUE

THE HOOKER FAMILY TREE goes back many generations. With the many Hooker family records that the family has, the Hooker name goes back more than three thousand years. The Hooker name is mentioned many times in these family records. The trouble is all Hookers are not related by blood. The Hookers are of the royal linage of Great Britain, my father being a Baron and having a large estate in Preston, England. Before Great Britain, the Hookers were from Naples and part of Britain's invaders during the Roman Empire invasion. Before Naples, the Hookers were from Kalamata, Greece.

And before Greece, the Hookers were from the island of Santorini or what was then called Atlantis, where they became great seafarers with excellent knowledge in sailing and navigating. They all had great wisdom and erudition in all the sciences far beyond all people who populated the earth. The Hookers got their knowledge from the many discoveries they found doing science experiments and what they did not discover; they got their knowledge from others around the globe and beyond.

The British Captain Samuel Wallis found the island of Neverland in seventeen ninety. He entirely wrote off the island as being of no value.

It is a desert island with no signs of life or water and surrounded by an impenetrable reef and man-eating sharks, so his ship's journal said. What the Captain did not know is the Hookers discovered the island more than two thousand years before. They also found a narrow channel through the reef and a river through the dry mountainside that led to a tropical interior teeming with life and water. It is here where the Hooker family hid their great wealth and knowledge. It was here In Neverland that some of the Hooker family was when Atlantis disappeared. The island of Neverland got all but ignored and forgotten because the island was thought of as of no value and had dangerous waters, and it was far from the shipping lanes.

As was said before, the Hooker family has not been related by blood for centuries. The Hookers, for the most part throughout the centuries, didn't have relations with females opting to concentrate on their studies and research and other family business. There were times that a few Hookers did take a wife and did have sex one way or another. How the Hooker name went on with the lack of relationships was to kidnap male children from various cities, towns, and villages worldwide. They then brainwashed, surgical, and medically changed them so that the children would think they were always a Hooker. The brainwashing, surgical, and medical treatment would all be done on the ship The Black Pearl, also known as the Jolly Roger, and on the island of Neverland at the family compound. The captain and patriarch of the Hooker family did all the brain washings, surgical, and medical treatments.

On May eighteen, nineteen fifty-six, the Baron James Hooker, captain of the Black Pearl, the last of the Hooker family, sailed into San Francisco Bay. He docked at Alameda rented a vehicle to search for the next boy to kidnap so the Hooker family would survive.

ONE

KIDNAPPED

CAPTAIN JAMES HOOKER LEFT the Black Pearl at the dock in Alameda, rented a GM pick-up truck from Hertz, and pulled out his Alameda and Oakland maps. It was seven o'clock in the morning, and he was looking for a good place to hunt for a child. He found a park in Oakland called Sanborn Park. It was wooded and had a creek that went to the bay. The Park also was next to a school and was near a freeway. It seemed perfect to find what he was looking for, and he headed for it.

"Ma, I'm going over to the park; Charlie isn't at home," seven-years-old James Reno said. Charlie Kahler was my best friend; also, seven-years-old with blond hair and with brown eyes. We were about the same size; I had brown-haired with green eyes and a few freckles across his nose. "Maybe I'll play with Cathy or Barbie Sweeter or just go to the park." Cathy was a blond-hair girl a few years older than me, and her sister Barbie was a year younger than me with darker hair than her sister.

"Alright, if you go down the creek, stay out of the water and watch out for poison oak," my mother said.

"Ma, you know I've never gotten poison oak." I have never gotten poison oak, but I have gotten wet playing in the water.

James Hooker checked out the park by looking for anyone and finding concealed places to abduct a boy. He was happy there wasn't anybody in the park, and there were many places of concealment. He also looked for roads for escaping and then checked to see if he had all he needed to succeed with his abduction. Satisfied with everything, he waited with his car parked on east seventh street, which dead-ends next to the school and, more importantly, the creek and park.

After finding out that the Sweeter family was going out of town, so there was no one to play with me, I went to the park to the swings. As I walked towards the park, I casually looked over and saw a pick-up truck with a man in it but did not think much of it.

What caught my attention was the truck was parked backward with the back end close to the wooden fence to the creek. As I walked across the wooden bridge over the creek, I heard the pick-up door open then close, but again, I did not pay much attention to it as I headed to the swings.

James Hooker walked over to a clubhouse that was next to the swings. As he was walking, he glanced at me and then looked into the clubhouse through a window, then looked at me again and then walked around the side of the building out of my sight but in view of the walkway to the bridge. There was a bench on the side of the building, so he sat and waited.

After about forty-five minutes to an hour, I got bored and headed to the creek. As I was walking towards the creek, James Hooker followed me. James Hooker was going to drag me into the bushes but decided to wait to see if there was a better place to nab me. To James Hooker's delight, he saw me climb the fence of the creek. James Hooker looked around, not seeing anyone; he climbed the fence and headed down to the creek after me.

I was squatting down, looking for frogs and minnows with my back to James Hooker.

I happened to look behind me and was startled by the man behind me, he is about to grab me when I got out three words in fear, "what do you." Then he put his hand on my mouth, and I felt a needle in my arm, and everything went dark.

James Hooker put a large canvas bag over me and carried me up the bank and into the truck's back. There he placed a tarp over me and drove off towards the pier where the Black Pearl was moored. No one was around when we got there, so he untied the tarp, grabbed the sack I was in, and carried me into the ship's bowels. He laid me on a table in one of the rooms, strapped me down so I could not move, and placed an I.V. into my arm, which contained something to keep me asleep for at least a day. Finally, he put the tarp on the ship, locked everything, and headed for Hertz to turn in the truck. On the way back to the Black Pearl in a cab, he was pleased with himself that no one suspected anything was going on. After paying for the taxi, he waited until the cab was out of sight. He then released the ropes then headed out of the bay and into the Pacific.

He headed southwest at more than 15 knots an hour. After about four hours, he stopped and dropped the sails and went below to check on me. I was still out, and he added another I.V., put up all the sails, started the motor, and headed out again south at more than seventy knots an hour. He was heading to an island called Genovesa, which was uninhabited.

It took about two and a half days to reach Genovesa, and the Captain dropped anchor in a hidden bay just in case someone else came to the island. All this time, I was kept unconscious with a medication placed into my I.V.

After a few hours of rest for my new father, he came into the room I was in and stripped me of all my clothing, and he destroyed them. He then washed me and started to place many medications that altered me over time from what I appeared. The first thing that changed was my hair, which changed to a golden blond, and my eye color changed to aqua green. He injected my brain with chemicals over the next three days to make me forget who I was. He injected into my muscles chemicals that gave me the strength over time of ten Olympic athletes. It also increased my intelligence, so I had an I.Q. of two hundred and fifty. Anything I saw or read, I understood it and remembered it. The medications went on for three additional days. Then my father started to alter my appearance surgically by changing my ears so they were more pointed, and he did things to my face that gave me a little elf-like feature. It took three days for the swelling to go down. Then he placed probes into my brain, put headphones over my ears, then opened my eyelids. He played a movie with the sound of a nuclear holocaust and my new father saving me from destruction. He also somehow changed my speech from an American accent to more of an English accent.

All this brainwashing went on for more than a week before I came out of anesthesia. When I was fully awake, I was sick and confused. "You were very ill, and you won't feel better for a few more hours." "Do you know who I am?"

"No."

"Do I look familiar?"

"Yes, but I am not sure who you are."

"I am your father, James Hooker." "Do you know who you are?"

After thinking a few seconds, I said, "No."

"Your name is Peter." "I call you Peter the Pan because of your mother." "I'll carry you to bed; you rest for now, and we will talk later." He went and got some pills told me to take them. He said they would make me feel better and help me to rest.

Shortly after taking the pills, I fell asleep and was out for about three hours. When I woke, I tried to sit up, and I saw the man who said he was my father sitting at a table. He spotted me and said, "How do you feel?"

"Much better than I did."

"Good, you will be weak for a while, then you will be able to give me a hand around here like you use to." "Are you hungry or thirsty?"

"Yes, very much so."

"Come off the bed and come over here; make sure you hang onto the walls until you get your strength back into your legs."

I did as he said, and I was wobbly trying to make it to the table. He got up and grabbed my arm, and as he did, I looked at a mirror hanging on the wall and said, "I don't recognize myself."

"It is the sickness; sit down here at the table, and we will talk while you eat." He fixed me some food that had fish in it, but it did taste good. He also gave me something to drink that tasted a little sweet, but it quenched my thirst and made me feel better.

"What else do you remember?" my father asked.

"Not a lot." "There was fire, explosions, buildings collapsing, people dead or dying, and blood all over the place." "I saw a woman with long blond hair; you were talking with her; was that my mother?"

"Yes, she was."

"There was another man with her, wasn't there?"

"Yes, your step-father." "He didn't treat you very well from what you told me."

"I didn't like him, your right." "He resented me because you were my father." "What happen to my mother?"

"She wouldn't leave your step-father." "She told me to take you with me and that if you stayed with her, your step-father wouldn't treat you very well." "So, we left on the Black Pearl."

"Why was there all the death and destruction?'

"Most of the world was at war, and it is a nasty one." "There is chaos everywhere." "Don't you remember?"

"No, do you think my mother is still alive?"

"I don't know." "Do you remember that large flash of light when we were three hours out to sea?"

"No, I don't remember much about this ship or any flash of light."

"I can understand your memory loss." "That flash was a nuclear explosion." "Even though your mother and step-father left, they couldn't get far enough away to survive. We did survive because of how far we were away."

"This ship can move at a speed of seventy knots, away from all the chaos."

I was silent for a few minutes, then said sadly, "I suppose you are right." I was quiet again, then said, "Why do I speak like someone from Britain when I lived in America?"

"Your mother and step-father are English." "Because of your step-father, you spent a lot of time with me on this ship and Neverland." "Don't you remember?"

"No." I became more comfortable with my father after talking to him. I finally asked him, "You said my name is Peter the Pan; the Pan was because of my mother; why my mother?"

"Your mother thought that you look like a Pan because of your pointed ears, like in the book." "Your mother was from England, but your mother's ancestors came from a country where some people look like elves." "Do you know what a Pan is?"

"A mythical person from Greece."

"Yes, your right." Again, I was silent, but I accepted what my father said. "Do you remember how to operate this ship or anything else?"

"No."

"Do you remember Neverland?"

"No."

"Alright, Neverland is where our home is." He was quiet for a moment, then his whole demeanor change. "For now, on you will call me captain when we are on this ship." "At Neverland, you may refer to me as your father." "You will do everything I tell you without argument." "You must learn your chores fast; we can't stay here long." "Now, get outside and get some sun." "Your training will start tomorrow." "Any trouble from you, you will be severely punished."

Without a word, I went outside to the back end of the boat. I looked around at my surroundings, and not seeing anything important to me, I sat down on the deck. My father or the Captain stayed down below. I was wondering what I did to make him angry. I also wondered what he would do if I did something wrong. The warm sun on my body was making me sleepy, and I started to doze.

I do not know how long I was sleeping when my father came out of the ship's bowels. It was getting cloudy, and the boat was swaying back and forth. My father was scurrying around the deck, tying things down. I got up and went to him, and he said, "Storm is coming."

"What can I do to help?"

"Nothing for now; I will get finished shortly." When he finished, he said, "You better go down below."

"Alright, I have to go to the bathroom anyway."

I started to go when he grabbed me hard and said, "You don't go down there unless you don't have any alternatives." "I'll show you where to go." He took me to the boat's side, which was upfront, flipped out what looked like a half basket, and said, "Get in."

I nervously looked at how far the water was down from the deck and said, "I don't need to go now."

He smacked me across my face and bottom and forced me into the basket. He left, and in tears, I relieved myself. The water from the waves coming up cleaned my bottom. When he returned, he jerked me off the basket and tied my arms together; he threw a rope over the main mast and hoisted me up about two feet off the deck. He got a whip and started whipping me several times, and I cried out in pain. "I told you to do everything I told you." "If you defy me again, it will be worse." He whipped me some more then went below deck, leaving me hanging and crying.

I hung there for what seemed hours. My whole body hurt, and I was bleeding. The ship was swaying more, but the wind felt good against my body. Finally, the rains came, and the water washed the blood off my body. After a while, the Captain came on deck, lowered me down, untied me, and told me to get below deck. As the Captain came down with me, I stood out of his way, not saying anything; he threw me a towel and said, "Dry yourself." He then grabbed a book and said, "Get up on the bunk." He handed me a book and said, "Read and study this book; I expect you to know everything in it by tomorrow."

I opened the book and started reading, and I was surprised that I could read so fast. What surprised me more is I understood everything I read. The book was about sailing. It told the parts of the boat and what each part does, and how it is maintained. It was a thick book, but I got through it before the Captain finished dinner. "How far through the book did you get?" the Captain asked me while we ate.

"I finished the book."

"Good, where and what is a jib?

"A jib is a triangular sail that sets ahead of the foremast of a sailing vessel." "It's tack is fixed to the bowsprit, bows, or to the deck between the bowsprit and the foremost mast."

"Good."

"Jibs and spinnakers are the two main types of headsails on a modern boat."

"Yes." "What kind of a knot do you use to tie down a sail?"

"A bowline."

"Yes, do you know how to tie a bowline?"

"I've never done one, but I believe I can."

He grabbed a cord and a cloth napkin and handed it to me, and said, "Tie this up in a bowline knot." I did as he said and gave it back to him. "Very good." "Don't ever forget it; you will have to climb up and tie the sails." It made me nervous about what he said, but I didn't say anything; he would just beat me.

"Why don't you and I have any clothing on?" I asked.

"Does it bother you?"

"No, you are my father, but it would be awkward if someone else came by."

"We won't be seeing anyone." "You and I don't have any clothing on because it is easier and faster to move around." "If you have to relieve yourself while your working can't leave your post, you have to relive yourself where you stand and clean it later." "Do you understand?"

"Yes."

"You will get used to it and won't want to wear anything."

The storm was coming down heavy. Wind and lighting caused flashes of light to come into the cab every time it flashed. It was getting late, and the Captain sent me to bed while he was writing in the ship's log. He finally locked the log into a locker that he had warned me never to get into it. He turned off the lights and climbed into the bed next to me. As my father called it, the bed or bunk was large; three more people could have slept here. I scooted over to the bed's far side, but he grabbed me and pulled me next to him. I was too tired to move back, and I did not want to anger him, so I stayed, anyway, at first, it was nice. I liked the way he smelled and the feel of his warmth. He put his arm around me, and I liked that too, but then his other hand started wandering over my body; I was confused about it; in part, it felt good, but then I did not know. He grabbed my hand and wanted me to do the same, and I did; this went on for a long time until we both fell asleep.

The next day the Captain was up before me making something to eat. I went outside to relieve myself. The storm had passed, and it was nice out, which surprised me because of the storm we had. I threw a bucket into the water and drew it up. Then I bathed by washing my hands and face, then throwing the rest of the water over my head. After drying a bit, I went down below where my father was; he glanced at me and said, "Sit down." I sat, and he dished up some potatoes, vegetables, and fish again, but I did not complain.

"I'm going to need a brush to clean my teeth," I said.

"I'll get you one and one for your hair; it's going to grow long." He looked at me and said, "Like it used to be."

I nodded and said, "Are we leaving port today?" "It's nice and clear out?"

"Yes, and you will watch everything I do to move out." "I'll only show you once you better learn it, understand."

"Yes." He reached over and handed me another book, but it was in another language. I looked up at him, confused.

"It's a book about battle tactics." "You will need it someday when we must go into battle."

"It's in another language."

"Yes, German." "Try to read it."

I looked at it, and somehow, I knew what the words were. It was by Admiral Hans von Koester, and its title was "Tactics of Naval Warfare." The Captain didn't give me a time-limited, which I was happy about, and it was a short book. I figure it would take me a day to finish it.

"Can you read it?" the Captain asked.

"Yes, I'll have it finish tonight." "I didn't know I could read German."

"Yes, German, Greek, English, and Latin." "You will learn more languages." I nodded and finished my breakfast, then went outside to wait for my father.

When he came out, I could tell he wasn't happy, so I said before he blew up, "Did I do something wrong?" "You look like your angry with me?"

He stared at me and snarled, "Don't you ever leave me unless I dismiss you, not down below, on the deck or at Neverland." "Do you understand?"

"Yes, sir."

"You will learn to do everything on this ship and at Neverland." "We will share doing the chores; that includes cooking and cleaning." "Do you understand?"

"Yes, sir." I was shooked up, but at least he didn't beat me.

"Watch; you will have to do it the next time." He started cranking up the anchor, and then he hoisted the sails, and we started moving. He ran to the ship's wheel, and we headed out of the bay. "Peter, climb up the main mask and perch yourself up there." I looked up there nervously and headed for the shrouds, and he said, "Grab that rope hanging from the mast; if you slip, you can use it to swing down."

"Yes, sir." I grabbed the rope and climbed; it wasn't hard getting up there, but it made me uneasy when the ship would swing from one side to the other. I found a spot where I could both of my feet down and hang onto the mast; it wasn't much larger than a stool's seat. I was up there several hours when I spotted another ship. I yelled down, "Captain, I see another ship."

He yelled back, "Where?"

"About two points starboard."

He looked steered portside and yelled, "Swing down here." I grabbed the rope and jumped and swing out over the ocean, and then as I let the rope slip through my hands back onto the deck. "Grab this wheel and keep it on the same course," he snarled. He grabbed a spyglass and looked at the ship until it was out of sight. He then grabbed the ship's wheel out of my hands, tied a rope on it so it wouldn't move, then grabbed me, and I knew I was in for a beating. He tied my arms again, hoisted me up, got a whip, and started whipping me. As he beat me, he said, "The next time you spot something, you tell me everything." "What it is and where it is." The pain shot through me as I scream in pain, and tears streamed down my face. The beating went on until I passed out.

I don't know how long I was out when I woke, I was still hanging, and the Captain was at the wheel. I just stared at him, and he took notice. After about thirty minutes, he came over to me, untied me, grabbed my arm, and took me over to the ship's wheel, and said, "It's your shift; you keep it on that heading." "Keep an eye out for anything." "I'll relieve you in eight hours."

I took the wheel, did not say a word to him, and I do not think he cared. After he left, tears streamed down my cheeks again, but I kept on course and kept a lookout for anything. After a few hours, I was thirsty but did not try to get some water. I was wondering if it was not better to be with my step-father. Then again, he and my mother were most likely dead now, and maybe there was a good reason for the beatings. I know my father didn't have much patience. He expected perfection all the time. It seems to me he could be a little more tolerant and be more of a teacher than a disciplinarian.

It was dark out about nine o'clock when the Captain relieved me. "I left you some food on the table; eat then get some rest." "I'll come and get you for your next shift." "Before you go in, grab a bucket of water and clean the blood off you."

"Yes, sir." I did what he said and went down below. I started eating, and to my surprise, it wasn't fish; it was pork with vegetables and some beans. I drank a lot of water, grabbed my book, and started reading as

I ate. I finished eating in about a half-hour, and an hour later, I had finished the book. I went outside to relieve myself, not saying a word to my father, and then went to bed.

I was woken at about six by my father. He had breakfast waiting for me, and he said, "Eat, relieve yourself, then start your shift."

"Yes, sir." I grabbed my book and left it on the table while I ate and then went outside and relieved myself and took the wheel.

After a few minutes, the Captain came on deck, angry, and said, "Why did you leave your book on the table?"

I stared at him, then said, "I finished the book." He looked at the book and then me and went down below.

Ten minutes later, he came back, stared at me, and said, "Do you know why I am so hard on you?"

"I would assume because I made mistakes."

"It's part of it." "It's just not the mistakes, one mistake could kill you or me or both of us, so I will always be hard on you." "It was the way I got raised, and it will be the way you will get raised.

I put my head down and said, "I understand, sir." After my shift, I went down below, drank some water, and notice my father had left me another book, "A general outline of the Hooker family." It talked about our ancestors, the Black Pearl, or the Jolly Rodger, and of Neverland. I went on deck and to my father with my book in hand, hugged him without saying a word, then went downstairs, hopped on the bed, and read the book.

For the next two weeks, everything went well. I didn't make any mistakes, and I had finished several books. We made many course changes as we moved west. One day the Captain said, "Peter, go up the main mast and keep watch."

"Yes, sir." I knew we were near Neverland. I was getting excited to see the island. I had read about it in one of my father's books, but the book did not go into very much detail. "Captain, I see what looks like a storm straight ahead."

"Peter, come down." "Take the ship's wheel." He grabbed a spyglass and checked out the pending storm. He then said, "Go back up, tie-down all the sails except the flying jib and outer jib, also the spanker." "Then come back down here."

"Yes, sir." I flew up the main masked and started tying up the sails with a bowman's knot. I was surprised how fast I could move, but within less than forty-five minutes, all the sails got tied up, and I used the rope to swing down to the deck.

"That is not a storm, but there will be rough waters." "Go to the bow and look out for rocks and dangers." "I don't believe you will see any but check anyway."

"Yes, sir." As we got closer, the water did get choppy, and I couldn't see very far. It was like a thick fog, so we were traveling slow. This fog went on for more than a half-hour before it started to get lighter. Then we popped out of it, and there was an island in front of us.

T W O

NEVERLAND

"**P**ETER, COME OVER TO me."

"Yes, sir."

"That island is Neverland." I was disappointed by the way it appeared. It was a desert island with no sign of water and not much of a beach. It had a high steep mountain near the shore and rocks and boulders all over the place. We sharply turned portside and traveled for some time; the whole island looked the same to me. Finally, the Captain turned starboard heading directly towards the island. "Peter, do you see on the ridge of the mountain there looks like two horns sticking up?"

"Yes, sir."

"There is a reef all around this island; if you head straight in the middle of the two horns, you shouldn't hit the reef if you are careful."

"Yes, sir." "I read about the reef." I went to the starboard side of the ship. I could see the fins of what I assume were sharks as we moved forward. I looked upon the ridge and thought I saw movement on top, but I could not determine what it was. I looked in the water again and saw the reef; we were about two feet from it.

I walked over to the Captain and said, "I saw what look like sharks and then the reef."

"Yes, the sharks won't come down the channel because of the water's temperature and the salt content." "There is also fish on the other side of the reef that will attack them." We were about thirty feet from the shore, and the color of the water changed to a lighter blue, and we turned sharp portside. We turned starboard again, and there was a hidden channel, and we headed down it. As we traveled down the channel, the rocky brush changed into many different colored bushes, trees, and vines. The landscape was also teeming with life. It wasn't long when I spotted something white that looked like a cross of an ape and man; I pointed it out to my father.

"Captain, what is that?"

"They are called Pongo." "Part ape part, man." "They are intelligent, so I've read, but they won't have anything to do with me." "I don't know much else about them other than they got brought here a little more than two thousand years ago."

"Could I try to meet them?"

"If it doesn't interfere with your studies and chores." "They don't appear to be dangerous, at least not to us." "There have been battles between different groups of them." We came into a small interior bay, and the Captain headed for a dock on the opposite side. "Peter, do you know how to swim?"

"I don't know, sir."

He latched the ship's wheel down, came over to me, picked me up, and threw me into the bay. I went under the water and came up shocked at what happened. "Swim over to the dock." To my surprise, I swam to the dock with no problem. I got there as the Jolly Rodger came up to the pier. My father threw me a rope and told me to tie up the ship to the dock with a bowline knot. I had to tie the ship's bow and stern, and then my father shoved a gangplank out to the pier. "Come on, board Peter." I did as he said, and he pressed a button, and a large hatch open and a crane popped up. "Unload everything in the cargo hold and take it up to our home." "There is a cart up on the bank."

"Yes, sir." At that, he took a few things from the quarters down below and left for the house. I took a deep breath and started to unload the hold. It wasn't as hard as I thought it would be, I didn't know I could lift such big boxes, but I had no trouble. I completely emptied the hold within two hours and loaded the first of many loads on the cart. Then, I pulled the cart down to the house and went in, calling for my father. He came out of a room, and I asked, "Where do you want the boxes?"

"Place them on the porch." I did as he said and made many trips back and forth until everything was stacked. He then said, "Go back to the ship check to make sure everything is locked down and tied up." "Then dive into the water and check under the hull to make sure there is no damage or anything attach to the hull."

"Yes, sir." I headed back to the ship and took care of everything on the boat. Then I dove under the water and checked out the whole hull, and it was clean and undamaged. As I walked back to the house from the trees about fifty meters away, I saw a few of those Pongos looking at me. I stopped then walked over to them, but they disappeared into the jungle before I got halfway. When I got to where they were standing, I saw some tracks that looked like human footprints, but I didn't see any Pongos. I had a strange feeling though they were still looking at me. When I got back to the house, I found my father and said, "Father, I saw some of those Pongos near the jungle, but they disappeared into the jungle when I approached them."

"I'm surprised they came this close to the house; they must be curious about who you are." "Let's go take a walk around the property so I can show you everything." He held my hand, which I liked as he showed me the huge house. The house had an extensive library and a laboratory. The house had a room with a lot of electronic equipment in it with microphones and something that looked like radars. The house had a few rooms that got used for medical purposes. Then, of course, the house had a big kitchen, sitting room, dining room, six bedrooms, and three full bathrooms. It also had a gym and a large conservatory. Out of the back door, there were many shops where you could build anything. Next to the shops, there were two large warehouses, one full of food items with freezers and the other full of hardware you would need from day to day. There is a path next to the warehouses that went back a kilometer to three caves with doors. It was apparent all three caves were man-made, with the walls and ceiling of concrete. The first cave went back further than I could see, and it was full of gold. The next cave was about the exact size of the first cave, and it was full of gemstones and jewelry stacked in boxes of all types. The last cave again was the same size as the other two caves, full of scrolls, books, paintings, and statues made from several different kinds of materials from all around the world. What was different about this last cave, this cave was temperature-controlled and had a system where moisture and dust got removed. After the three caves, my father showed me another smaller cave. We didn't go into this cave. My father told me that there was material in there that was very dangerous. If you do not handle the material properly, it could harm you, so he would show me how to manage it when I was older. As we walked back to the house, my father said, "The valuables in the first two caves were found around the world and under the waters." "The third cave, almost everything was attained in Atlantis and Alexandra's libraries." "The books were from private owners and different libraries." "The paintings and statues got commissioned from the artist and private collections." "They also from art galleries from around the world."

"Father, have you ever read any of those scrolls and books in the third cave?"

"No, my research is in medicine." "Each of our ancestors had their specialty that they have researched in." "I'm hoping that you will be the first Hooker that is more rounded in your studies."

"I will, father."

"You will find all the information you need in the house library."

"Yes, sir."

I went to the library to find a book to start with while my father started cooking. As I looked at the rolls of bookshelves, I wondered to myself where to start. I finally decided to take the first book on the shelf and start reading books until something interested me, then concentrate on that subject. I was in the sitting room reading when father said, "Dinner is ready; come to the dinner table."

"Yes, sir." We had soup first, then a salad, and after the salad, we had chicken with rice and carrots.

"You are going to have to start cooking."

"When do you wish to start, sir."

"We will wait a few days, but tomorrow morning you will come into the kitchen and watch how everything works." "I will also have a schedule at what to cook for each meal."

"Yes, sir."

"There are cookbooks in the kitchen for each meal."

"Yes, sir." I was quiet for several minutes, then asked my father, "May I ask you a question?"

"Yes."

"Am I your only child you have, or do I have other siblings."

Now it was his turn to be quiet, but after a few minutes, he said, "You have one other half-brother."

"Shouldn't we go get him before he dies?"

"I don't know where he is yet." "It took me some time to find you."

"Will we go when you find him?"

"Yes," he said, troubled.

After dinner, I went back to reading, and I finished the book, placed it back into the library, and grabbed another book. I was reading it when my father said, "It's time for bed." He took me to the bedroom, and I climbed into bed, and then he joined me. I snuggled next to him; then, he put his arm around me. Then, after a short time, he started doing the same thing he did on the ship but more intensely. I did everything he said; I didn't want to get beat. I didn't know what I could do about it, but I decided to stay away from my father as much as possible.

The next day I was up early with my father in the kitchen; he showed me how to operate everything and the precautions when using the equipment. After breakfast, my father didn't have any chores to give me, so I took off into the jungle looking for the Pongo.

I found a trail that I went down, looking all around. The canopy of the jungle was so thick the sun seldom came through it. Many beautiful birds were flying around and making all sorts of noise. I could hear animals breaking through the brush near me, but none attacked me. Then, as I was looking up, I caught sight of a white flash flying through the trees. I kept on going when three feet in front of me, a spear hit the ground. I froze and stared at it, then finally walked over, and I grabbed and examined it. It had a wooden shaft with a stone head, much like an arrowhead. The spear was taller than me but had an excellent feel to it. I decided to carry it with me as I walked through the jungle. Screams were coming from the treetops, but I kept going figuring they wanted to scare me, which they did. I was walking for about two hours when I came out to a grassy field. There were herds of what look like different types of antelopes. I saw smoke from what I assume were campfires across the valley, and I headed towards it. As I got closer, I saw what looked like dwellings. Suddenly several of the pongo rushed up to me with spears in their hands, making all sorts of noise.

THREE

PONGO

I WAS FRIGHTENED; THE ONLY thing I could think to do is to fall on my knees and offer the spear to them with my head down so I couldn't stare at them. They all quieted down, and one of the Pongo approached me. He took the spear, but I kept my arms up, and he ran his finger over one of my hands, and I looked up. Then he said to his comrades, "Meek tock zouk tie." I didn't know they could talk, and I didn't know what he said, but two Pongo came and grabbed me and drugged me to the village. When I got to the village, a female Pongo that looked angry pushed the two Pongo away that had me, and she took my arm pulled me to a hut saying something to me, but I didn't understand her. I sat on the ground and waited to see what would happen next. I already decided if I ever get back to the house, I will search the library to see if there is a book on the Pongo language.

Some ancestors must have researched the Pongo. She tried to feed me something. I smiled and took it, and it tasted nutty; I liked it. Then, another Pongo came into the hut, stared at me, and sat down. The Pongo was a male and pointed to me and said something not too happy to the female. The woman gave him something to eat, but as he ate, he kept staring at me. After eating, she took me down to a stream, and she carried a leather cloth with her. We went into the water, and she washed me. I placed my hand affectionately on her face, and she smiled, another thing I didn't know she could do. We got out and sat on the bank to dry. Another younger female Pongo sat down beside me, and I smiled at her, too, and she grabbed my hand. I let go of the younger Pongo, grabbed a stick, got the older female's attention, and started drawing on the dirt. I drew a picture of the bay and house and then the jungle and village of the Pongo. I pointed to myself and indicated I must go back to the house. She wasn't happy, so I placed my hand on her face again and then drew a sun and then indicated I would be back the next day. She smiled and said something to the other female Pongo, who looked happy, and I got up and left. I got to the jungle without being stopped and went down the trail, and in about two hours, I made it back to the house.

"Where have you been?" My father asked.

"With the Pongo." "They are a peculiar species." "They can talk, but I don't know what they are saying."

"I'm surprised they let you go," my father said, concern.

"I am, too; some of the males weren't happy I was there." "An old female took me into her hut and fed me, then bathed me."

"Well, I can't be bothered with them." "You be careful around them." After my father talked to me, he went back to the lab, and I went into the library. I was looking for anything on the Pongo, especially in the area of language. I didn't know where to begin as I was looking around confused. My father happened to walk past the library and saw I was looking for something, so he said, "What are you looking for?"

"Something on the Pongo."

He came and sat at a table where three things looked like a picture frame with a microphone in front of them. He pushed a button, and the picture frame lit up, and then he said, "Pongo."

Three titles with their location came up, and I said, "Thank you." He left, and I found the books, grabbed all three of them, and then went into the sitting room to read. One of the books was on the history of the Pongo. The next book I looked at was on the culture of the Pongo. The last book, fortunately, was the Pongo language. The first two books were not very long, so I read them first and finished them by dinner. They both gave me a greater knowledge understanding of the Pongo.

We had fish for dinner, and my father said as we ate, "You will cook all three meals a day after tomorrow."

"Yes, sir." "I will do the dishes after dinner if you wish."

"That would be helpful." "I want to get busy on some research I was doing."

"I've read the first two books about the Pongo." "The third book is a language book of the Pongo." "After I clean up after dinner, I'll start learning it."

"Alright, but don't let your other studies suffer."

"Yes, sir." "I'm surprised I can read so fast and understand and remember everything." "For someone, my age I'm surprised I could do this."

"Well, your very smart; just be grateful."

"I am grateful." After I finished cleaning everything, I went into the sitting room and started studying the Pongo language.

I studied for several hours when my father came into the room and said, "Time for bed." I didn't finish studying, but what I plan to do when my father was sleeping, I would go to the loo to read and study the rest or most of the book. That night my father groped, fondled, and did other things again but not as long as he did the last time. I could tell he was tired, and he fell asleep quickly. I quietly got up, grabbed my book, and went to the loo. I was there for about two hours and finally finished the book. I was tired when I went back to bed and fell asleep quickly.

My father was not in bed when I went down to breakfast; he was already there, and he said, "Your kind of late."

"Yes, I put the books back into the library."

"I thought you said you didn't finish the language book?" my father said with anger.

I had to think fast and said, "I was a bit constipated, and so I went to the loo." "While I was sitting there, I finished the book."

I don't think he believed me, but he let it go and said, "Tomorrow, you will do the cooking."

"Yes, sir."

"Can you speak, Pongo?"

"I think so." "I will find out later today."

"I want you to learn another language." He thought for a few seconds and said, "I think German would be good for you to learn."

"Yes, sir."

"You will have to learn it at the same time as you do your other studies."

"Yes, sir." After breakfast, I left at a fast pace to the village of the Pongo. I knew as I went that the Pongo saw me traveling down the trail. When I got to the grassy valley, some male Pongo was staring at me; I do not think they trusted me at all.

I walked into the village, and the same old woman greeted me with a smile, and she said, "I knew you would come back to me."

I understood her, and I said to her surprise, "I do not lie; I told you I would come back, and here am I."

"You speak our language." "I am overjoyed; come to my home, and we will talk." She wasn't the only one who heard me talk; all that did hear me came to the older woman's home.

"Do not fix me too much; my father fed me not long ago." She nodded and gave me something sweet. "Thank you."

She ate with me the same thing and asked, "How many seasons are you?"

I assume she meant years, and I said, "Seven."

"I am called Mussel; what are you called?"

"Do you mean, name?"

"Yes, name."

"I have two names, Peter the Pan Hooker." "What is the name of the girl I sat down next to the water called?"

"Tinker." "She likes you very much."

I smiled and assumed turned red, then said, "She is very nice."

"My people are call Kelpie."

"I thought you are Pongo?" "That is what my father told me."

"All like me are Pongo." "This village is Kelpie."

"I understand."

She smiled and said, "You have a father, the one by the water with salt?"

"Yes."

"What of your mother?"

I put my head down and said sadly, "I believe she died in a faraway land."

She came over to me and hugged me and said, "I will be like your mother."

A tear fell down my cheek, and I said very emotionally, "I am not like you or the Kelpie." "They will never accept me."

"Do not let this bother you; we are more alike than you think, and I will talk with the elders if they accept you; everyone will." "Let's go down to the water; it is cooler there."

"Alright." As I left her hut, many Pongo was outside, and I said, "Hello." They all gasped with surprise and followed Mussel and me to the river.

We sat at the bank and as we talk someone behind me said, "How is it you can speak to us?"

I said, "I learned your language from a book."

"What is a book?" someone else asked.

"They are symbols that are drawn that tell me your language." That seemed to satisfy them, and there were no more questions. After a short time, most got bored and wandered off, and as I was talking to Mussel when Tinker came and sat down beside me. I grab her hand, which she liked, and said, "Hello, Tinker."

"It is true you can speak our language," she said, pleased.

"Yes," I replied with a smile.

Just then, out of the corner of my eye, I saw the same male who came into Mussel hut yesterday, charging me with his stone knife drawn. I stood up, and he knocked me into the water, saying, "You are not wanted here; you must go, or I will hurt you."

I got up and drew my knife, and he was about to attack me when a shock Mussel said, "Tox, you will not harm him."

Tox did not lower his knife but said with much anger, "He is not part of our people."

By this time, a large crowd had gathered, and an old male came and grabbed Tox's knife and said, "The elders will say if he will be part of our people like your father was."

I lowered my knife, then Mussel grabbed Tox with anger and said, "He is your brother; it is I who have said this." Then he lowered his head and walked off without saying a word.

I got out of the water and asked, "Why does he hate me?"

"We have never had one such as you have anything to do with us, and Tox doesn't like change." "I will leave you alone with Tinker." "I think she would like that," she said with a smile.

About an hour after this incident, there was a lot of commotion with a person I assume was a village crier calling people to a meeting. Mussel came to me and said, "We must go to this meeting; it is about you."

All gathered in front of six male elders, and Mussel started talking to them about me, letting them know she wanted me to be part of her people. The same elder that took the knife out of Tox's hand asked me, "Why has one such as you come to my people?"

"There are many reasons." "I was curious about the Kelpie." "I was also lonely; I do have a father, but he is busy with his studies, and at times he has beaten me." "My father told me you are intelligent and wise, so I wanted to learn from you."

There was much discussion about me from all the elders. Then the same elder asked, "You did not feel afraid when you first came here?"

I hesitated, didn't know how to answer that, then said, "I don't know how to answer that exactly." "I was afraid, I would say, but I knew I was strong and smart and could take care of myself, so I took a chance and came anyway."

One of the other elders asked, "Are you violent?"

"No, but I will protect myself or someone I care for."

The elders talked amongst themselves, then Tox said with anger, "Maybe he isn't violent, but his father is what if his father goes to war with us."

The elders stared at me, and then Mussel said, "Tox doesn't worry about his father; he is just jealous of this one called Peter the pan."

"This is not true; I have nothing to be jealous about," said Tox.

"Then why are you angry with me, Tox?" "I've done nothing to you," I said.

"I am not angry with you," he replied.

"Then why did you attack him with your knife drawn Tox?" said the same elder that disarmed him.

He held his head down because he knew the elder was correct, and I said, "I wish to be your friend if you will let me."

"I would have to think about it," Tox replied to me.

The elders talked again, and then the one elder that was doing most of the talking said, "Our concern is your father, he is a violent man, he has never been kind to us."

"I am not like my father." "He is what he is, but if it helps, my father said to me he is not interested in any Pongo, and he is too busy to deal with you."

"We all know you are not like your father, and perhaps your father won't bring violence to us." "I'll tell you what we have decided we will let you stay with us, but since your father has no love for us, you must spend some of your time with him." "If things go well, you may become Kelpie." "Will you agree with this?"

"Yes, sir."

At that, the elders got up and left, and the crowd went back doing what they were doing except for Tox. Mussel and I went over to Tox, and Mussel said, "Peter the Pan is a good person Tox; he has a lot of love in him."

He nodded, and I said, "Tox, will you show me how to be Kelpie?"

"When I have time."

At that, he left, and I went off with Mussel. After walking a short time, she asked, "Will you be staying here tonight?"

"Tomorrow, I must do work at my father's home." "I do not know how long I will be gone, but I will come when I can." "Then, when I return, maybe, Tox will teach me."

"We will all teach you."

For the rest of the day, I walked with Tinker. At one time, when we were next to the river, I notice that all the Kelpie stayed near the shore, not getting in or near the deep water. I asked Tinker, "Does the Kelpie know how to swim?"

"What is a swim?"

"Be able to move on top of the water."

"No, can you?"

"Yes, do you think all Pongo is this way?"

"I would think so."

I thought this was odd and wondered why. Then, Tinker pulled me into a wooded area, and she started getting very friendly with me, much like my father at night. I didn't understand why she was doing what she was doing, but I let her.

It was getting late, and I said, "I have to head back to my father's house." So, we headed back, and I told Mussel I had to go back to my father's house after hugging her and left. I got back to the house several hours before dinner, so after informing my father that I was back, I went into the library and got a book on the German language. I got another one on physics, then went into the sitting room and studied. I studied German for about an hour and a half; then, I got started on physics.

At dinner, my father asked, "What are you studying?"

"German as you asked me to, and physics."

"What is your opinion of physics?"

"So far, it is fascinating."

"If you like physics, you better start your study in mathematics." "I will get you a book after dinner on that subject." "I will also show you how to use a computer to help you with your studies."

"Computer?"

"Yes, that machine that tells you where to find the books."

"That would be helpful, father."

"How was your visit to the Pongo village?" "Could you talk to them?"

"Yes, I could talk to them." "As I used the language, I was able to become more fluent." "The day went very well with them." "The elders said they would let me stay, and if everything went well, they would make me a member of their tribe."

"If everything went well?" "What did they mean by well?"

"They are afraid of you." "They think you might do them harm."

"You can tell them I won't harm them and that I am not interested in them." "I'm too busy to deal with them anyway."

"Yes, sir, I've already told them that." "I found out their species is called Pongo, much like we are called human." "Their tribe is called Kelpie." "Each individual has their name and personality." "I believe they are more intelligent than we both assumed."

"Intelligent, that is a bunch of poppycock." "They may be smarter than most apes, but intelligent nonsense." I didn't say more about the Pongo nor intend to anymore in the future unless asked. "Tomorrow, you will cook all three meals." "I put everything in the fridge."

"Thank you, father."

"It's all right; you will do the cooking every third day so you will have time for your chores, studies, and to visit your Pongo friends."

"Thank you." After dinner, I went back to studying and then went to bed.

The next day I got up at about five-thirty and showered and got ready to cook while my father slept. For breakfast, we had scrambled eggs, sausage and bacon, and toast. I also made coffee and hot water for tea. For lunch, we had sandwiches and soup with sweet tea. At dinner, I cooked baked chicken with mashed potatoes and peas. I did get some studying between meals but not much after cleaning up dinner; I started studying again.

My father came into the sitting room and, while handing a book, he said, "That is an algebra book; study math books first will help you understand physics better.

"Yes, father."

As the weeks passed, I read and studied more and more books, and my relationship with the Kelpie had significantly improved, and I learned a lot. Tox hadn't shown me anything; he stayed away from me as much as possible. Tox's behavior made me sad there is much I could learn from him. I did talk to my mother Mussel, and she said, "Your brother makes me sad also, and I've talked to him, but he is stubborn." "He is not a bad person; I believe he will change in time."

I had been spending a lot of time with Tinker. I found out from Tinker and many others in the village that females and males have relationships very young. That explained why Tinker was so amorous. I told Tinker and my mother that I was not like the Pongo I couldn't be like until I was a lot older. They laughed but understood; however, it didn't slow down Tinker's affectionate endeavors.

Tinker and I were sitting on the bank of the river talking, and I asked her, "Tinker does this river have a name?"

"Yes, it is called the Bolu, and it is the largest river on this land."

As we talked and chucked rocks into the river, I noticed Tox was with some of his friends across the river. They were horse playing; I asked Tinker, "How did they get across the river?"

"Far up the river by the mountain, the river is not as wide as here, and trees are over water Tox, and the rest must have swung over to the other side."

I looked at him, and he spotted me even though it was a considerable distance across the river. As he stared at me, one of his friends, who were swinging over the deep part of the water to impress the females, accidentally slammed into Tox, who flew into the water. The whole village went crazy, not knowing what to do. Tinker went to tell Mussel; I dove into the water and swam out to Tox, who was fighting to keep his head above the water. By the time I got to him, he had swallowed a lot of water, and he was about to drown when I grabbed him, dragged him back to the shallow side of the river. He didn't fight me; he was too exhausted to do much of anything. When I got him near the shore, two male Pongo came into the water, grabbed Tox, and laid him on the ground. Mussel was a healing woman, which I did not know; she took care of Tox. I went to Tox, concerned he might be worse than he was. He smiled at me and grabbed my hand and pulled me down, and placed his hand on my face as a sign of affection.

Now I knew everything between Tox and me would be good, and the next day this became true before I got to the village. He came out of the trees and grabbed me by the arm, and said, "I am going to show you how to move faster." He went up a tree-like he was running. I looked up, the first limb was very high, but I tried jumping anyway. I not only made it to that limb but to the limb above, with ease, which had to be more than twelve feet about the ground. I scurried up to where Tox was and waited to see what he was going to show me. "You grab this and swing this way if this is leaning that way."

"What do you do when you get to the other side?"

"You grab another or a limb or anything you can grab on to."

"Suppose what I grab on to is too weak to hold me."

"Then you will fall, but don't worry, it doesn't happen too often," Tox said with a smile. We started moving through the trees and moving fast. I was nervous at first, but I became comfortable with it and did it with more confidence after a while. That afternoon when I went back home, I made it to the house in less than thirty minutes.

"Father, do you know how to fight?"

"Yes, I know several methods."

"Will you be teaching me?"

"Yes."

"When?"

"Tomorrow, we will talk, and I will show you."

FOUR

A KELPIE WARRIOR

THE NEXT DAY MY father handed me three books on fighting; they called Judo, Kyudo, and the last called Kung Fu. "After you read these books, you will go to the computer, and there are three movies on the fight styles," said my father.

"Yes, sir."

"When you have read and watched the movies, and you understand them, I will work with you with these fighting styles."

"Yes, sir." I told the Kelpie people I would be gone for a while to learn something, and they were sad but accepted it. From time to time, I did see the Kelpie, especially my brother watching me from the jungle next to the house. I had all three books read in two days, and in five days, I saw all the movies demonstrating how to fight even though I had to cook two of those days.

When I was confident that I understood everything, I went to my father and informed him. "Go to the grassy area between the warehouse and the jungle, and I will join you." I did as he said, and the lessons started, and he wasn't very gentle with me. Over the weeks, I received many injuries, but I did learn and learned fast. The one advantage I had even over my father was I was extremely fast and strong. One day when my father came, he joined me with a bow and a quiver of arrows in his hands. He gave them to me and told me how to use them, then said, "When you can hit dead center every time, I will show you what to do next this them.

After a week, I never missed my target, so I went and talked to my father, "Father, I never miss a target."

He grabbed twelve pieces of paper and said, "Follow me." I did as he said, and he posted the twelve pieces of paper ten feet apart. "Step ten feet back from the first paper, then run as fast as you can and shoot arrows at the paper as you run when you can hit all of them all the time, come talk to me."

"Yes, sir." This exercise took me more than a month to achieve, but I could do it; approaching my father, I said, "Father, I can hit the paper every time."

"I saw you; swinging through the trees in the jungle; take those pieces of paper and put them in the trees and see if you can hit the target up there."

"I use both of my hands to move through the trees."

"Find a different way; adapt, and overcome."

"I will try, sir."

I was up in the trees when my brother Tox and some of his friends approach me He showed me some affection then said, "What is it you are doing, and what are those things you carry?"

"This is a weapon; it is called a bow and arrows." "My father has been training me how to fight so that I can be a great warrior and hunter like you."

He smiled then said, "I see by the marks on your body he has been beating you too."

"Yes, he is not gentle when he trains me."

"Maybe we should not be gentle with him."

"No, this would not be good; besides, he didn't harm me in anger." "When you go back home, tell mother I love her, and I hope to be coming soon."

He laughed and said, "I will tell her and Tinker too."

I smiled, and he and his friends took off, and I went back to placing the paper throughout the trees. Over the next few weeks, I tried several ways of flying through the tree without my hands; then, I figured out a way by using my feet, legs, and body to shoot the bow and still swing through the trees. I was not as fast as I could by using my hands, but I knew I would get faster as time went on. I let my father know of my progress, and in the next few weeks, he showed me how to use the knife. "You will have to learn how to use a rifle soon and the weapons on the ship and this island."

"Yes, sir."

After training for many months, I visited the Kelpie village with my knife and bow. I got a warm welcome from all, and as I was spending time with my mother and Tinker, my brother approached me. "It is time you learn how to hunt." "We will see how well your weapon works."

"Yes, we will." We traveled for a long time, and I asked my brother and his friend, "What do we hunt?"

"The striped Kannutu," said one of Tox's friends.

"How many do you want?"

My brother and his friends laughed at me, and my brother said, "Three would be nice, but we will be lucky to get one." We came upon a herd of striped antelope; at least, they look like antelope to me. Tox and his friends went after one Kannutu, and I ran past them towards the running herd. As I passed the first Kannutu, I hit the animal with an arrow behind the front leg, and it went down. At the second Kannutu, I hit that one; also, I stopped and look at Tox and his friends who were far behind me, still trying to kill their Kannutu; which they finally did. Tox asked, "Where have you been?"

"You said you wanted three Kannutu, so I shot the other two; they are up above."

Everyone looked at me in disbelief, and Tox asked, "Did you clean them?"

"No, I don't know how to clean them."

"Good, you must be careful when you approach the Kannutu, or they may kill you because they are just wounded." "You will learn today how to clean them."

Tox showed me how to approach the animal and how to clean it. As I was cleaning the Kannutu with Tox, one of his friends asked Tox, "How are we going to carry three Kannutu back to the village."

Tox was shaking his head thinking when I said, "I can carry one myself if you all can carry the rest."

Tox's friends looked at me disbelieving, and my brother said, "If he says he can, then he can." He left two of his friends with the knife to cut the Kannutu up. The rest of us went to my kills. Tox made me clean the next two Kannutus, and I did just fine. I hefted the kill on my shoulder and went down to Tox's friends. The rest of the meat got divided up, and we carried it back to the village.

The whole village got stirred up over the kill, and some of Tox's friends told everyone, including the elders, what happened. The elders came together for a meeting; they asked me, "Let us see this bow," the head elder asked, and I handed him the bow and arrows. He pulled back on the string with an arrow and let it go. The string snapped on his arm, and he threw the bow down. Tox picked it up, and he tried the same with the same results.

I picked up the bow and arrows and shot at a target on a tree and said, "It is not easy; it takes a lot of practice."

"Your bow is a great weapon for you, but not for us." The elders were about to leave when Tox said, "Wait, what my brother did was a great thing; why not make him part of the Kelpie."

"It is not time, yet we will wait a little longer to decide."

I was disappointed, and it showed, but I didn't say anything. My brother came up to me and said, "I'm sorry, Peter, I do not know why they wait."

"It's alright, Tox; my heart is Kelpie." I then headed back to the house and to my studies.

At dinner, I told my father about the hunt and my kill. He stared at me for some time then said, not too happy, "What did this antelope look like."

"Something that you would see in Africa with stripes." He was quiet again, and I said, "Are you angry?"

"Not at you; that animal is endangered; this island is the only place to find them."

"They don't look endangered to me; there are several huge herds of them that I've seen."

He stared at me again and finally said, "Perhaps you are right; it was a long time ago when they got brought here." He then changed the subject.

It had been more than a year and a half I was on the island; when I sat down for breakfast, I had something on my mind and said, "Father, have you found my brother yet?"

"No, but I am getting closer," he said with much hesitation. He looked at me and said, "I have to go to another place, and you can't go with me; it's too dangerous, so you will stay here." Then, as I stared at him, he continued talking to me, "Perhaps I will get information on your brother."

My head popped up, and I said, "I will be alright here."

"I'll want you to keep up with your studies and keep this place clean."

"Yes, sir."

"You will give me a hand preparing and loading the ship."

"Yes, sir." "How long will you be away?"

"Six to ten weeks."

"That would be fine, sir." Four days later, he left, and for the first day, I stayed home, then went to the Kelpie village. I told my mother, Tox, and Tinker about my father and that I could stay for the next five days, and they were thrilled. On the second day at the village, I talked to one of the elders and asked him, "I have never seen another Pongo village." "Are there others, and if there are, are they bigger?"

"Yes, there is some bigger or about the same, and there are many smaller." "Some of them are, our enemy and we have been at war with them, especially the Migos who are terrible people and have a much larger village."

"When have they last attacked?"

"It has been a very long time; they are very far away; do not worry about them." What he said still concerned me, but I put it out of my mind. I spent the next two days at my house then went back to the Kelpie.

I was with Tox, we had finished hunting, and just came into the village when we noticed that the elders were meeting with the village, so we joined them. "We have heard that the Migos are preparing for war against who we don't know." "What we do know is some of the smaller villages have joined them," said an elder. "It is not the time for panic, but it is time for caution."

I looked at Tox and asked, "What weapons do they have?"

"The same as you have seen here, and they will use rocks too."

More than a week passed, I was with my mother when a woman came into her hut, upset, and she said, "My two of my sons are hurt and also one of their friends." My mother grabbed something and left to help, and I followed her. The whole village was abuzz with the preparation of war.

I went over to Tox, who was repairing two spears, and said, "You are going to war."

"Yes, I must." I looked at him worried, and he noticed, and he said, "If I don't go to war, I will get shamed, and my people would suffer."

"I will go too."

"No, you are too young."

"I am almost the same age as you; besides, I am skilled in battle."

"You are not Pongo."

"You're right, so the elders can't stop me."

He stared at me, then said, "You will use your bow."

"Yes, and knife."

"Your father would not let you."

"My father is not here; it is my decision."

Just then, the elders called a meeting, and Tox and I joined the meeting and were standing in front of the crowd. Tox had told me how battles got fought, which was head-on, and I knew that would be very bad for the Kelpie. So, when the elders said what the attack plan would be, I stepped forward and said, "The attack plan is bad."

"What is bad?" "It is the way we have always gone to battle."

"Yes, and you have lost too many." "I am skilled in battle; know a better way."

"What is this way?"

"May I show you?"

"Yes."

I got four people and placed them together. Then I got six more I put two in the middle, two to one side of them, then two to the other side. I then explain to those I choose what I wanted to do. I walked over to the elders and said, "These four represent the Migos; these six represent the Kelpie." "These two will attack as always, and the Migos will become sure of themselves because they think they are stronger." "The rest will sweep around to the side and attack, which will confuse them, and many Migos will die and run away in fear." As I talk all those Kelpie, I chose moved the way I said. So impressed the elders were that they got up all excited.

When they calmed down, they said, "Peter the Pan, we will do this plan of yours."

"Good, we will have less injured with this plan."

"We?" "You will not be going; you are not Kelpie and are too young."

I got angry and was about to say something when Tox said, "You know my brother should be a Kelpie; there is no reason why you haven't made him Kelpie." "He is stronger and faster than any here; ask any of my friends." "With his bow, he is a better hunter than any here." "Since you say he is not Kelpie, then you cannot stop him from going."

The elders talked amongst themselves and then said to Tox, "We know your love for your brother and his love for the Kelpie." "You are right; we should have made him Kelpie, and we will before we leave." "We do know he is a great hunter, but he is young, and if he were hurt or killed, his father would go to war with us, so we can't let him go."

"You all are fools; perhaps we need new elders," said Tox with much anger. Many agreed with him.

I went up to Tox and put my arm around his shoulder, shooked my head, and said, "I have much respect for the elders." "They have much wisdom, and they only what they think is best for me." "I am not that much younger than Tox, and what he says about me is true." "I have never lied to anyone." "Tox is also right; I am not Kelpie, and if it means I can't go, I don't wish to be Kelpie." "My father has left this land and won't be back for a long time." "So, it is up for me to decide if I go or not."

The elders talked about themselves then said, "We know you do not lie, and we will make you Kelpie; you can go, but you must be in the group that your brother is in."

I nodded and stepped back into the crowd, pulling my brother with me. The meeting broke up, and I went and got my bow and quiver; I already had my knife. Tox and I went to our mother, and Tinker joined us. They were both worried we were going, but they understood. Tox turned to me and said, "Are you ready to go?"

"Yes."

"I will get both of you some food." We thanked our mother, and I stroked both my mother's face and Tinker's face and then left.

Tox and I were in the group that would sweep right, and there were sixty in our group. The elders made me Kelpie before we left, just like the elders said. We headed out; we hugged next to the jungle at times, swinging through the trees. It took us three days to get to the place the Migos were, and we hid in the wilderness and waited for everyone to get into position. I could see the Migos. They were different from the Kelpie; they had a black mane that went over their head and down their back; it made them look fierce. Tox said they dye their hair with the black grunge berry. The center Kelpie advanced when the sun was in the Migo's eyes as I said they should. The Migos were acting overconfident and laughing when they spotted the center group, just as I predicted. Just as each was about to pounce on each other, both groups on both sides attacked. As I expected, the Migos were in chaos. Many of Migos were killed or wounded. The Migos tried to kill me, but I was too fast for them, and my arrows hit true, killing many Migos. When I ran out of arrows, I flew into the Migos, knife drawn, with the power of a charging bull. I was slashing and tossing Migos all over the place, but it didn't last long; twenty minutes later, the Migos who weren't too wounded or dead were running off to save their life. We lost two Kelpie and thirty wounded, including Tox and me. Tox and I were not severely damaged; we just had a few bleeding cuts; Tox called them honor marks. As we sat, rested, and tended our wounds, the elders called for a meeting. "By the hands of our brave warriors have destroyed the Migos." "If it weren't for Peter the Pan's plan and his great ability in battle, this battle would have been lost." "For this Peter, the Pan, you will be rewarded when we get back to the village where all the Kelpie will honor you." "We will be leaving soon back to the village, so you should get everything together."

I gathered my bow, quiver, and arrows while Tox got our food, and we headed back to the village. I asked Tox, "What do you think they will award me?"

"I don't know, but they don't reward people very often; in fact, I don't remember them ever rewarding anyone anything." "Mother will be happy when she finds out."

Runners were sent ahead of us to the village to tell them of our victory. When we entered the village, there was a grand celebration. After a short time, Tox and I were brought into our hut for mother to attend to our wounds better than we had. The celebration went on all night, and after a few hours' sleep the next day, the elders had called a meeting. "Peter, the Pan should get most of the credit for our success." "We wish to reward him for his efforts, with the agreement of the Kelpie, by making him an elder and leader of our people." "Do all agree to this?" the elders asked the people. All wholeheartedly agreed, and I got pushed up to where the elders were.

I was surprised, and I thanked the elders and the rest of the Kelpie. I then said, "If I am your leader, I wish to tell you something I believe you need to do." "If you don't want to do it, I will respect how you feel and will not force you; I love you too much to do that." I was quiet for a few seconds, then said, "Someone told me, all Pongo were one people at one time, and in those days, all were at peace." There was much agreement amongst the Kelpie. I continued, "We must send a large force of Kelpie to every village, that includes the Migos and their friends, and tell them to meet here or where ever you wish to talk peace" "I will tell you what to say to them."

"I have a question," shouted someone.

"What is it you want to know?"

"What if we get attacked?"

"Then you shall destroy the village and its people." There was a lot of talk amongst the people, and I said, "If you have a fear of the Migos and their friends, skip them, and I will go with you." That seemed to satisfy them, and we had a vote, and everyone agreed. The ones who were going gathered, and I said, "We shall meet at the great falls with those from the other villages." I told them what to say and what to do with the other elders' help, and they left with my brother Tox. I knew they wouldn't be back for more than a week. I decided to go back home and get busy with the chores and lessons that I had neglected for a while. I caught up with all my chores and lessons in about a week and then went back to the village.

The day after I arrived at the village, the Kelpie warriors came back with great news. "All villages agreed to meet, including the Pukui and the Ika." "We even went to the enemy villages except for the Migos, and they agreed to meet." "I think you should go to the Migos with us, brother," said Tox.

I nodded and said, "I will do this after you rest." "How did these villages treat you?"

"Stories of our battle with the Migos, and you have spread throughout all the villages; we got treated with respect and fear, said Tox.

Again, I nodded and said, "Perhaps this will help with the talks with the Migos."

The next day we flew through the trees towards the Migos village. It took nearly a week to get to them, and when we got there, we waited outside of their village. The Migos were armed, thinking there was going to be a battle. I stepped forward and yelled, "We come in peace, wishing to talk; will you send one in authority to speak to me?" After a few minutes, one did come forward at old Migos by the look of him. I said, "We wish to meet in peace to talk to you about ending hostilities and about uniting our peoples."

"You are not Kelpie."

"I am Kelpie; I am not Pongo." "Should this matter?"

"We do not trust Kelpie, nor those who float on the water in the house; you are not Pongo."

"It is I with the help of the Kelpie who fought and defeated you." "When was the last time that this has happen?"

"It has never happened and never will again."

"Were you at the battle?"

"No."

"You would not be saying this if you were there." He looked nervous, and I said, "Will you come and talk peace and to get united as one?"

"We will not agree with this."

"Then all your people will die, and there will be no more Migos."

He stared at me in disbelief, and I turned to leave. He shouted, "wait," I turned around, and he said, "We will come."

"No." "You must have a vote; all your people must agree."

"It is not our way the leaders decide for the people."

"It must be a vote of your people, or there will be trouble for you and your people." "We will wait for your answer." At that, I turned and left, and he went back to his people. It was more than an hour we waited when we got approached again.

"It has been decided that we will come."

"By all your people?"

"Yes," I explained to him where to meet and how many people could come; I also explained what would happen if they did not show or caused trouble. The Kelpie and I then left for home happy at what just happened.

Ten days had passed, and the Kelpie and I met at the assigned place with the other villages, including the Migos. The meeting got heated at times, but in the end, everyone agreed that there would be peace, and the Pongo would unite under the Kelpie if I led them, and I agreed. All the people went back to their villages to know that they would be attacked and destroyed if they broke the agreement. We entered our village with great excitement and celebration that went on for two days. Afterward, I had to go back to my house because my father was due soon.

F I V E

IN SEARCH OF MY BROTHER

I WAS HOME FOR FIVE days when my father came into the bay on the Black Pearl. I waited for him on the pier. He threw me the rope to tie up the ship, and then he joined me on the dock. He didn't look good, and I asked, "Are you ill, father?"

He stared at me and said, "Yes." "Unload the ship and bring everything up to the house." "Secure the ship and check the hull."

"Yes, sir." He then went up to the house. I unloaded the ship and then secured it. Afterward, I dove under the water and checked out the hull. It took me about an hour to bring everything up to the house; then I went to my father. My father had been drinking; I could smell the liquor as I stood in front of him. "I got everything done, father."

He stared at me and then asked, not too happy, "How did you get those scars on your body?"

I was nervous to answered him but said, "The Kelpie and Migos had a war, and I got wounded."

He screamed angrily, "Who are Kelpie and Migos."

"They are Pongo villages; I belonged to the Kelpie."

"They are animals; you belong to no Pongo group."

"No, you do not understand; I am Kelpie."

At that, he grabbed me, tied my arms together, and hoisted me up, and began to whip me. This time it was different; I never screamed out; I just stared at him without emotion. This reaction from me frustrated him, and he tried to whip me harder without success. He finally gave up and said, "You can just hang there."

"If you only let me explain, you would understand."

"What is it you want to say?"

"The Kelpie are passive people; they are not violent." "The Migos are terrible people; they have attacked and taken over many villages." "They would have done the same to the Kelpie, and after they took over every village, they would have attacked us." "The Pongos are different, but they are not like any animal I know of." He stared at me then went into the house, leaving me hanging.

I was hanging about forty-five minutes when he came back and let me down and said, "I don't want you to go back to those Pangos."

"I am now the leader of all the Pangos." "I've never disobeyed you, but I will go back to the Pangos; you won't be able to stop me." He was surprised I was defying him, but he didn't say anything. He turned around and went back into the house.

I had made a lot of stew, so when father went into the kitchen to cook something, seeing I had already cooked, he sat down at the dining table to get served at dinner time. I served my father and myself a small salad and then stew with homemade bread and wine to drink. As we were eating, my father said, "I know where your brother is."

My head popped up, and I asked, "Where?"

"He is in England, at or near a town called Wigan." "It makes sense we have an estate near there if it still exists."

"When are we going?"

"A few weeks if I feel better."

"What is your ailment, father?"

"It's a rare disease that there is no cure."

"You are a doctor with more talent than anyone on earth." "Can't you do something?"

"I am going to try, but I could die from it."

"How did you get this disease?"

"The same way as you got sick." "It comes from the dregs of the world."

"If you want me to do anything to help you, I will."

"I know you would; you have a kind heart."

After dinner, I went on the computer and found out where Wigan was and was excited about going. I waited to go to the Pongo for a week so that my father would not get too angry. When I did go, I talked with the elders. "I will be going away for a long time." "My father and I go on the floating house to find my brother, who is very far away." The Kelpie were very upset that I would be gone for so long, but not as much as my mother, brother, and Tinker was. I continued talking to the elders, "I believe that we should add another to the elders."

"Who and why Peter, the Pan?" everyone asked.

"It doesn't matter who as long as it is a female." "The females of the Kelpie are not represented in the village."

"Do you think we do not care for our females?" asked an elder.

"I know you do, but you and I are not female, and there are things about females that males do not know or understand." Most of the females agreed with what I said, and the elders decided they would let a female be an elder. I then said, "Tox and an elder should take my place while I am gone," the elders agreed. On the last visit to the village before we left, the elders chose my mother to be an elder, which made me happy, and three days after I returned home, we sailed off to England.

I thought I would have trouble working on the Black Pearl because I hadn't been on the ship for so long. However, I found out quickly that I had no problems; in fact, it was easier for me than the last time I was on the ship. We headed southeast, we were going around Cape Horn, and I understood that it would be a cold and a rough ride. I notice that my father was doing alright, but he would have a day or two of sickness with seven to ten days where he felt just fine. I only hope when we went around the horn that he would be alright. We had a fair wind with either clear skies or cloudy skies.

We anchored on the west side of Islotes Motu Lti Motu island. A rocky island suited more for birds than humans. I believe it would be tough to get on the island. My father got some clothing out and said, "When it gets too cold, or I tell you, you will put this clothing on to keep warm."

"Yes, sir."

After we left the island, we went more south than east on a course to the Cape Horn. Two days out from the island, my father got sick again, and I was getting worried that he wouldn't be well when we got near Cape Horn. On those days he got ill, I did most of the work on the ship. My father was only below one day, and about noon the next day, he came on deck and said, "Peter go below and get dressed."

"Yes, sir." I was glad he told me to get dress because it was getting cold.

When I came up to the deck, I got told to drop the sail and stow them. It took me but a few minutes to do as I got told, and then my father started the engines, and we moved much faster. I offered to take the ship's wheel, and my father let me have it. I had figured that it would be better for my father to rest. Six hours later, he came back and said, "Go down below and get something to eat." "Two hours from now, you will have to do your normal shift."

"Yes, sir." He had left food on the table for me, and after I cleaned up, I tried to get some rest. A little less than two hours, I went on deck, relived myself, and took over the wheel. The water was getting really choppy, and the sky darkened as we got nearer to the cape.

Eight hours later, my father relieved me and said, "Try to get as much rest as you can; I might have to call you on deck; we are very near the cape, and the weather will get worse."

"Yes, sir." I don't know how long I was sleeping when I got thrown out of bed. The ship was being tossed all over the place, so I went on deck to check on the Captain. Waves were crashing on the deck; I noticed my father was having a hard time at the wheel. I yelled because of the noise of the storm, "Go below and rest; I'll take the wheel."

It was not easy steering the ship, but I was strong and able to keep it on course. "Keep it on the same heading," The Captain yelled. About dawn, the storm started to quiet down. About an hour later, the Captain came on deck and said, "I'm going to fix something to eat, and after I eat, I will relieve you, and you can eat and get some rest."

"Yes, sir." A little more than an hour later, the Captain relieved me, and I went to eat and rest. I was sleeping at least eight hours when I woke and went on deck to relieve myself and talk to the Captain. We passed the South Sandwich Island, which I thought we would stop, but the Captain continued, so I asked, "Why didn't we stop at the island?"

"It's too cold, there is disease there, and too many hostiles go there." He was silent for a moment and then said, looking at me, "I don't want you to get a relapse and get sick again."

"Where are we going?"

"Edinburgh of the Seven Seas." "It's not the greatest port, but the island is warmer, and there aren't that many people." "We should get there in two days." On the second day, Edinburgh of the Seven Seas came in view. It was a rocky, grassy place we dropped anchored in an area that didn't have much wind, and it was about seventy degrees out, much warmer than the cape. We stayed there for two days, slept, and bathed. My father brought books with us and insisted that I study when I could. While we slept together, he did as he always did, and I didn't fight him. After two days, we hoisted anchor and headed north under full sails.

I was up in the rigging when I spotted a ship, so I yelled, "Captain, ship, five points portside."

He checked the radar and turned on the engines, and yelled to me, "Hang on." He then slammed it in full throttle, and the ship's speed significantly moved faster, and within thirty minutes, there was no sign of the boat, and I let the Captain know.

After we were out of sight of the other ship, the Captain cut the engines. Things went back to normal, and after about three days, we dropped anchor in a bay at Vila Do Porto. It was hot when we dropped anchor. That night we went to sleep, and the next day when I woke up, I told the Captain, "My head is spinning, and I don't feel good."

He got his doctor's bag and checked out my heart, and took my temperature. He gave me a shot and placed an I.V. in my arm, and said, "You rest, I think you will be alright." he then got another machine and passed it over me, and said, "You're having a relapse; you will most likely get worse." "Captain, how did I get this relapse?"

"Probably something in the air or something in you don't worry about it."

"How long will it last?"

"It could be more than a week."

"Captain, you need me; you can't do it all by yourself," I said, getting sleepy.

"I'll be alright; now, no more talking; I want you to sleep." Soon I was sound asleep, and the next day my father headed to Preston, England. It took him two days where he moored the ship at an obscured peer. He made sure I would be unconscious for two days, lock everything, and place a forcefield around the Black Pearl so no one could get on the ship. He then found a place to hire a car in Preston and headed to Wigan. He had looked for a victim for some time, then he saw what he wanted, a boy with blond hair going to his shoulders. The boy whose name was William Clearfield was perhaps a year younger than me. I was a few inches taller and, of course, tanner because of being exposed to the sun. He lived in a run-down house, he didn't have a father, and his mother, when she wasn't drinking, she was using drugs. It was a miracle that he was growing up so well, and he wasn't a wild boy but more of a meek child. My father waited until midnight and found an unlocked door in the backyard; he went into the messy house, and he saw the boy alone in his room. My father put his right hand over his mouth and gave him a shot that knocked him out.

My father stripped the boy and started to place him in a bag when he heard behind him, "Who the hell are you?" It was a sloppy-looking woman who it was evident that she was either high or drunk. My father was on her with a flash, knocking her to the ground. When she hit the ground, there was a snapping sound like a twig stick. There were no vital signs; my father knew her neck was broken she was dead. He dragged her into another room and then checked out a window, and no one was aroused or on the street. He finished putting William in a bag, picked him up, went outside through the back door, then placed William into the car and drove to the ship. When he arrived, he got out and looked to see if he was alone. He was always careful he didn't want to get caught, there would have been trouble, and someone else would have died. He brought William down below and placed him on the floor. My father came over to me and checked me to see if I was still out, and I was. He added more medication to my I.V. that would keep me asleep and then tended William. My father unlocked the medical room and then took the bag off William. He placed him on a table and inserted an I.V. into his arm, and gave him the same medications that he gave me. After checking me one more time, he left the ship and headed to the car hiring business, where he got the car, dropped it off, and walked back to the ship. He hoisted the anchor and set sail south, out of the Irish Sea, towards the Isles of Scilly to rest and get started on William. He stayed there about a day and a half, then headed towards Ilhéu De Baixo, part of the Portuguese Azores. He dropped anchor at a lonely desolate bay on the east side of the island. He came down below and looked at me, and he knew he had to revive me soon. However, he got some sleep first, hopped on the bed next to me, and fell asleep.

After doing some work on William, he came out and locked the door.

My father was doing just about the same to him as me, then William's name got changed to John. My father came over to me and removed the I.V. and gave me a shot of something that would flush the drugs that he had in me out. He then cleaned me up and let me sleep. I woke up about two hours later and wasn't feeling very well. "Captain, I feel horrible."

"I know you do, but you are getting better." "You need to start eating something."

"I feel too sick to eat."

"I know you feel this way, but you will eat." "We will start with just a little and something soft." He fed me something like baby food, and I was able to eat it. After I ate, he told me to sleep for a while, and I did drift off to sleep. After he ate, he went into the room with William, and he worked on him for hours. When he came back, I was already awake. "How are you feeling?" my father asked me.

"I feel much better."

"Good, I want you to go on deck during the day and get some sun; it will do you some good."

"Yes, sir."

"Take something to eat and drink too."

"Yes, sir." I was on deck until dusk when I went down below and sat on my bed.

About thirty minutes later, my father came out of the medical room and said, "Are you up to making dinner?"

"Yes, sir, I can manage." I fixed dinner, something simple, and my father sat down and ate with me. "You spend a lot of time in the medical room." "Did you get my brother?"

"Yes." "He has the same medical problem as you had when I first got you except, he is in worse shape."

"Will he live?" I said, worried.

"I don't know." "I don't want you to try to see him before he comes out of it; you might catch what he has again, and you could die."

"Yes, sir." "What happened to his mother?"

"She, unfortunately, died when I got him; he almost died." "His name is John."

We stayed at Ilhéu De Baixo for five days, and I got my full strength back. Then, we headed to the island of Ilhéu Branco, and in two days, we dropped anchor. "How long will we be here, Captain?"

"We will be here until your brother comes around, or he passes away." He saw the worry in my face, and he said, "The chances are in his favor to live." "I want you to stay on deck and watch for other ships or people while I take care of your brother."

"Yes, sir." I felt better at what he said, but I was still worried. As the days passed, I did the cooking when my father wanted to eat, and when he didn't, I just made a sandwich for myself and ate some fruit.

On the seventh day, my father came on deck and said, "He is waking up; I think he will be alright."

"Can I see him?"

"Not now, maybe tomorrow." "I'm going to get some rest; then you will cook."

"Yes, sir."

When I woke up the next day, my father had food on the table, and he was with John. Our father was at John's side when he opened his eyes, and our father said, "How do you feel?"

"I feel sick, sir."

"Do you know who I am?"

"No, sir, but you look familiar."

"I am your father; my name is James Hooker." "Do you know who you are?"

He thought for a minute, then said, "No, sir."

"You're John Hooker." "You will feel better in a few hours." "You have been very sick; do you remember the war?"

"I remember explosions and smoke, sir." "As my head clears, I do remember you."

"Good." "You have a brother outside the door who is very worried about you." "Are you strong enough to see him?"

"Yes, sir, I would like that very much."

Our father went to the door and told me to come in, but before I went in, father said, "He doesn't remember much, and he is confused."

I went over to John and said with a smile on my face, "Hi, I'm Peter, the Pan, your brother." I then kissed him.

He stared at me for a few seconds and asked, "Are you the real Peter Pan?"

"I'm the only one I know."

"I didn't know he was real."

I looked confused, and our father said, "Peter, there is a book by the author James Matthew Barrie called "Peter and Wendy;" most people call it Peter Pan about a boy much like you." "Well, not you, although the story is much like you."

"I don't understand, Captain."

"James Barrie wrote it about your grandfather, whose name was Peter." "You are more like the character in the book than grandfather was." "So, you are the real Peter Pan."

"My Kelpie mother is called Mussel, which means Wind."

"Maybe she is Wendy in the book." "The original book is in the library back at home."

"Can you fly, Peter?" asked John.

"Sort of, I guess."

"I wish I could."

"You will; I will show you how."

"We better go and let John rest." "John, in a few hours, I will carry you to bed, but you rest here for now."

"Yes, father," he said with a smile.

"You don't call me father when you are on this ship." "You say yes, sir, or yes, Captain." "You only call me father when we are off the ship."

"Yes, sir, but what ship?"

I said before the Captain did, "I will explain later."

I kissed him again, and we left, and the Captain locked the door and said, "We head home tomorrow."

"Yes, sir."

I was on deck when the Captain put John on the bed. I had been getting the ship ready for departure the next day when the Captain came on deck and said to me, "Your brother is in bed." "I want you to feed him the same food as I fed you; also, bathe him." "When he is strong enough, I want you to train him with everything, including how we sleep at night."

"Yes, sir." "Captain, you don't look very well."

"Yes, I'm getting sick again." "You will have to take the ship out tomorrow morning; you think you can do it."

"Yes, sir, I shouldn't have any problem." After I finished preparing the ship, I went down below to check on John and to study. The Captain went on deck with some cushions to lay on and rest. John was still sleeping when I looked at him. He was very beautiful, but he was dirty. I looked into a mirror and then look at him, and he did look like me. I was studying when I saw John move, so I went to him. "How do you feel?"

"I feel sick."

"I'll feed you, and then I will bathe you." "You will feel better after, and in a few days, you will be alright. I fed John two bowls of food, which he ate, and then I hopped on the bed and placed John on my lap and fed him a bottle of milk, which he resisted at first but then drank. As he was drinking, he closed his eyes and leaned his head into my chest, and I kissed him, which caused him to open his eyes and then close them again. When he finished the bottle, John snuggled next to me and felled back to sleep. I gently laid him down and went back to studying. When John woke next, I went over to him and asked, "How do you feel?"

"Better."

"Good, I'm going to bathe you."

I got a tub of warm soapy water and started washing John, first his face, then the rest of his body. As I was washing him, he said, "You love me, don't you?"

I smiled and said, "Of course I do; you are my brother."

"Is that why you kiss me?"

"Yes, I love you very much, maybe more than you can understand."

"I love you too."

I smiled and gave him another kiss, and this time he kissed me back. "I'm going to start cooking for the captain and me." "I will feed you again and give you a bottle." "Maybe I can give you some fruit, but I will have to ask the Captain first."

He nodded, and as I finished washing his hair, I gave him another kiss, then started cooking.

I made some clam chowder and fried fish with potatoes and peas and tea to drink. The Captain came down below as I set the table; he looked at John and then said, "How is he?"

"He is feeling better, but I think it will be a few days before I can start training him."

"I'll get some books down, and he can start studying along with you." "I also want him to get some sun."

"Yes, sir." He had been drinking. I could smell the liquor on him, but I didn't say anything. "How are you feeling, Sir?"

"I'm getting better; maybe I can relieve you tomorrow."

"That would be helpful, Captain." "I could get some rest and help John." That night I crawled in bed with John while the Captain slept on deck. John snuggled next to me, and I kissed him and caressed him, and he did the same until we both fell asleep. The next day before light, I went on deck, hoisted the anchor, unfurled the sails, and headed south towards the Cape Horn; I did all this without waking the Captain.

About an hour after sunrise, the Captain woke and came over to me; he adjusted the direction I was going and said, "Stay on this course; I'm going down below."

"Yes, sir."

He looked a John then went into the galley and got something to eat. After eating, he hopped into the bed with John, and John snuggled next to him. After a short time, the Captain started doing the same thing to John as he did to me.

After twelve hours, my father relieved me, and I went below. John was awake, and he told me about our father, and I let him know he does the same thing to me. I ate and offered food to John, but he refused any. I hopped in bed, and he sat up and leaned into me and said, "I need to relieve myself."

"You think you can walk?"

"I can try." I Jumped down then helped him down. He was wobbly, so I helped him walk; we headed for the deck." "Where are we going?" "I have to go to the loo?"

"You will see."

We went on deck, and I took him to the bow and showed him how to get on. "You must be joking," John said, concerned.

"Come on, get on; you will get used to it."

With my help, he got on, and he relieved himself, and boy did he go. He giggled every time a wave hit his bottom until a big wave hit him, and he got soaked. He got off and said, "That was interesting."

I laughed and said, "Yes, now bend over."

I threw a bucket of water on his bottom, and he said, "Thank you."

All this time our, father was staring at us. "I'm going down below to sleep."

"I'll join you," John said.

"No, you will not; you go down below and study," said the Captain.

"Yes, sir."

I was doing my shift at the wheel when John came on deck and over to me. "Did you finish your lessons?" I asked John.

"Oui, enfin."

"You sound like you're speaking French."

"Yes, father wants me to learn it."

"When we are on the ship, don't refer to him as father; you will get into trouble."

"Thanks, I forgot."

"Did you find your studies hard?"

"No, which surprised me." "They weren't hard, but they were sure long."

"I study a lot also and do my chores." "I will help you when I can." "I must also teach you how to run this ship and do other things."

"Do you speak French?"

"No, German, Latin, Greek, and Pongo." "If I know the Captain, he will most likely make me learn French too and you, German, Latin, and Greek."

"Is Pongo a native language?"

I smiled and said, "Sort of." John looked around the ship, and I said, "This ship is called the Black Pearl." "Years ago, when our grandfather was our age, it was called the Jolly Roger."

"Like in the book Peter Pan."

"The name of the ship in the book Peter Pan and Windy is called the Jolly Roger?"

"Yes."

"I'm going to have to read that book." "This ship is the fastest ship ever made." "It has a special hull, that's the bottom of the ship, it is made from a special material." "Its engines are also special, and with the sails, it can go over eighty knots or maybe faster." "The next fastest ship can only go one hundred and seven-point six kilometers an hour or fifty-eight point one knots." "We also have an advance radar system and a force field system." "Our weapons are more powerful than any in the world."

"Are you going to show me everything?"

"Yes, by the time we get back home, you will be able to work this ship as well as I can."

"Where is home?" "Is it far?"

"Home is a large island called Neverland." "It's not in this ocean; it's in the Pacific; it will be a while before we get there."

I looked at John, and he had his mouth open, and I said, "What's the matter?"

"Neverland is where Peter Pan lived in the book."

"Yes, I'm going to have to read that book." We talked about the ship for hours and what he must learn. He wasn't thrilled about working in the rigging and the sails, but I told him how I felt and how I learn to love it.

The Captain came on deck and said, "I've come to relieve you, Peter." "You two boys go down below and eat."

"Sir, after we eat, I plan to start training John."

"That would be fine." I went to the bow of the ship and relieved myself. Then we both went down below to eat.

"John, have you studied in the books about sailing yet?"

"Yes, the Captain gave me some books."

"Good, that will help." We went on the deck, and I said, "You watch me, and then you will try."

"Alright."

I few up the main mask and stood where I looked for ships, "This is where we stand to look for ships." I then got on one of the sails and yelled down, "When we tie up the sails, we come out here." I then swung down to the deck on a rope.

"Peter, that was marvelous." "You looked like you were flying."

"Yes, and so will you." "Grab the rope if you slip, which I know you won't; you can swing down on it." "I'll be right behind you." "Now, scamper up the Jacob's ladder."

He started up going up alright, but as he got higher, he got slower. Finally, he got to the crow's nest, and we stood there for a while. "We are high up," he said nervously and hanging on for dear life.

"You need to relax and have confidence in yourself."

"I'll try."

"There are thirty-two points on a compass." "If you were to spot a ship, let's say over there." I pointed to the right of us, "You would say Ship, eight-point from bow to the person steering the ship." "Do you understand?"

"Yes."

I pointed just a little low from where I pointed and said, "What would you say if a ship was coming from that direction?"

"Ship ten points off the bow."

"That's right." I then pointed to the other side of the ship, "What would you say if a ship was coming from there?"

"Ship twenty-four points from the bow."

"That's right." "I'll test you again tomorrow."

"We will swing down now." "Grab on to the rope." "Lean back and push off as you go out; let the rope slip through your hand a little at a time, and you will go down to the deck." "Don't worry if you swing over the water; you will come back to the deck."

"Peter, I'm terrified."

"I was too, just like you." "You will see how much fun it is, and you will get better every time you do it." "John, just have happy thoughts, and you will fly."

He smiled at me, took a deep breath, and pushed off. He did go out over the water a little, but not as bad as me the first time. He did everything I told him, and he landed on the deck. He let go of the rope, and I grabbed it and joined him down on the deck. "Did you see Peter?" "I did it," John said excitedly.

"Yes, you did very well." "We will go up again tomorrow, and I will show you how to get on the sails." "After we eat tonight and I go out to my shift at the wheel, you will join me." I looked over to the Captain, and he smiled and nodded his approval. We then went down below and got our books and hopped on the bed to study. We helped each other, and I started learning French and John the other languages.

It was getting late, and I jumped off the bed and started dinner. John asked, "What are you cooking?"

"Pork chops with mash potatoes and carrots, also red wine to drink." "Do you want to help?"

"Yes."

He jumped down and joined me, and I said, "You stay here and peel the potatoes." "I will ask the Captain if you can eat this."

"Alright."

"Captain, can John eat a regular dinner tonight?"

"How is he doing?"

"He is doing fine, Sir."

"He can eat with us then."

"Yes, Sir."

"When will we eat?"

"About an hour, Sir." "I'll eat then relieve you, Sir."

"That will be good, Peter." I turned to go down below when he said, "You're doing a fine job with John, Peter."

"Thank you, Sir." I went down below and finished cooking with John's help.

"Did the Captain say I could eat regular food?"

"Yes." John smiled, and he started to set the table while I was whipping the potatoes. I poured John a little wine and some for myself, and we ate.

"Tell me about Neverland."

"I want it to be a surprise to you, but I will tell you this, don't be fooled when you first see Neverland." "It is wonderful there with things you have never seen before."

"Because of my memory loss, I don't know what I've seen and what I haven't."

"You have a point there." We finished dinner, and I fixed the Captain's plate and went on deck. "Sir, as soon as I relieve myself, I will relieve you at the wheel." "Your food is on the table."

"Peter red or white wine?"

"Red, Sir."

"That's correct." I took over the ship's wheel, and the Captain went down below after telling me to maintain the same course.

"John, how do you feel?"

"I feel very well, Sir."

"Sit at the table with me while I eat."

"Yes, Sir."

"How are your lessons coming along?"

"Very well, Sir." "Peter has been helping me, and I have been teaching him French." He stared at John and then nodded.

"We are going to be getting into some cold weather soon." "I'll have special clothing for you to wear."

"Yes, Sir."

"The seas will get very rough too." "I want you to stay down below when this happens." "You're still too weak to handle the rough seas."

"Yes, Sir."

"Did you drink some wine?"

"Yes, Sir."

"What did you think of it?"

"I drank it, Sir, but I'm afraid I am not a wine drinker."

The Captain poured him a big glass full and said, "Drink it."

"Yes, Sir." John lifted the glass and started drinking it slowly, but the Captain lifted it higher, forcing him to drink faster.

"How do you feel?"

"I feel peculiar, Sir, and a bit nauseated."

"I wanted to show you just how it feels when you drink too much."

"Yes, sir."

John started to clean the table, and galley and when he finished, he came on deck. But instead of coming to me, he went to the ship's rail and heaved several times. "Grab the ladle and rinse out your mouth and drink some water." He did as I said, and I asked, "What is the matter with you; are you sick?"

"Father made me drink a large glass of wine."

"Don't call him father while on this ship he will beat you if you do." Tears streamed down his cheeks, and I said, "I'm sorry I yelled at you." "I'm just trying to protect you." "Do you see the scars on me?" "It was from the Captain punishing me."

"I know." "Why is he so mean?"

"I don't think he is a bad man." "He did the same to me with the wine." "He felt it was a lesson I needed to learn." "I think he is the way he is because of the way the Captain got raised, and I think he is very ill." "When he is very sick, he starts drinking, and I think this makes him mean too."

"I think you are right."

"I'll show you how to steer this ship." For the next hour, I explained how to steer, what to expect, and how the radar works. I also told him what to do if you are alone and need to relieve yourself.

He wasn't too thrilled about that. "Have you gone on the deck?"

"No, I go before I take the wheel and after I am relieved." "It has been closed at times, but I was able to hold it." After a few hours, I asked John, "Do you want to give it a try?"

"Yes, please." I gave him the wheel, and he was surprised at how much muscle you needed to keep on course.

I let him steer for about three hours, and then I took over, and he was tired. "You better go down below and get some rest." "We will go up into the sails tomorrow." He kissed me and went down below.

After I ate the next morning, John and I went on deck. "Peter, come over to me."

"Yes, Sir."

"It's going to get cold; when you relieve me, put on your cold-weather clothing." "When you spot the South Sandwich, Islands wake me."

"Yes, Sir."

I went over to John and said, "Grab the rope and go up the Jacob's ladder." John did go up faster than yesterday, but I knew he would have to get faster. He waited for me at the crow's nest. When I joined him, I grabbed the rope and said, "Watch what I do." I swung out to the sail, grabbed a rope on the sail, and placed my feet on another rope below. I looked back and then swung back. "You want to give it a try?"

"Alright." He flew across and grabbed the sail's rope, and he placed his feet on the same rope I put my feet on." He was a little shaky on the sail, but he did alright.

"Swing back." He did as I said and stood beside me. "You did well; just remember to have confidence and think happy thoughts." He giggled, and I said, "You giggled yesterday; why?"

"In the book Peter Pan, Peter told Windy to think happy thoughts so you can fly."

I rolled my eyes and said, "Swing across again, then swing back."

He did as I said and then asked, "What happens if the swinging rope slips out of my hands once I get on the sail?"

"Watch." I swung across, let go of the swinging rope, and then I leaned way back and grabbed the rope again and swung back to John. "We will practice this another day when you are stronger and have more confidence." "Now, swing down."

He was about to swing when he yelled, "Ship, off the stern."

The Captain looked and then checked the radar and yelled, "Hang on." I grabbed John tight, and the Captain started the engines, then we began to move fast. We were up there for nearly an hour as the Captain made course changes. It wasn't long when the other ship disappeared; then, after we traveled for a time, the Captain turned off the engines.

"John, now you can swing down." He did as I said, and when the rope came back to me, I swung down.

I went over to the Captain and looked at the radar. The Captain also did and saw the other ship was changing course away from us. The Captain went back on course to South Sandwich, Islands. John and I went down below, and I went to bed while John studied.

I was on the deck at the wheel with my cold weather close on for several hours when I looked at the radar and saw an island. I called down below for the Captain. "Ahoy, Captain island on the radar."

The Captain lifted John off him and placed him on his back, and John woke. "John, get your cold-weather close on and go back to sleep."

"Yes, sir," said a sleepy John.

The Captain came on deck and looked at the radar. "Keep the ship on course."

"Yes, Sir." As we got near the Island, the Captain took the wheel. "Is the Island the South Sandwich Island?"

"Yes."

"How long will we stay here."

"A little more than a day." We went into a bay and dropped anchor. "Lower the sails, Peter."

"Yes, Sir." Forty-five minutes later, the sails were down, and we went down below. The Captain made some hot water, and we had tea and biscuits and then went to bed with John on one side of the Captain and me on the other.

When I woke up, John and the Captain were at the table eating. "Peter, come join us at the table."

"Yes, Sir, I'll need to relieve myself first."

"Alright, but make it quick." I went out and relieved myself, then joined everyone. "We will prepare the ship for going around the cape today."

"Yes, Sir." We made sure everything got latched down, and the sails got secured the rest of the afternoon, and then we rested.

The next morning, I hoisted the anchor just before dawn, and the Captain started the engines, and we set out for Cape Horn. John got told to stay below again unless called on deck. I got told to go to the bow and watch for rocks and icebergs. I didn't see any, but I sure got cold and wet from the waves crashing on deck. The waters were rough, but I don't think as rough as the last time. After we traveled three-quarters around the cape, the Captain said, "Peter, take the wheel." "I'm going to the bow."

"Yes, Sir." As I held the course, I wondered how John was doing. I could imagine he was frightened.

After we passed the cape, the Captain came over to me, adjusted our course, and said, "We are heading to Easter Island to rest." "I'm going down below to put something dry on, and then I will relieve you."

"Yes, Sir."

He was gone for more than an hour and a half when he finally came on the deck with John and said, "Go down below and put on the dry clothing I left for you." "Eat the food I left for you, then come back on the deck." "We need to get the sails up."

"Yes, Sir." I was afraid he would have John do it, so I moved fast, got dressed, and ate. When I got back on deck, John was at the wheel, and the Captain was talking to him.

"Keep it on this course while your brother and I set the sails."

"Yes, sir."

"Let set the sails, Peter."

"Yes, sir." All the sails got hoisted up, and I went up the main mask and unfurled them. This unfurling took a little more than an hour. I stayed at the crow's nest for about a half-hour, looking for any ships that might appear. The Captain went down below, and that was the last I saw of him for some time. I swung down to the deck and went over to John, who was squirming and said, "What's the matter you have to relieve yourself?"

"Yes, will you please take the wheel?"

"I told you to relieve yourself before you take the wheel." I smiled and said, "Go." He ran to the bow and stripped out of his clothing, and he went. I could see the relief on his face as he went, and I started giggling. After checking the radar, I gave the wheel back to him and said, "I'm going down below." "Keep an eye on the radar for any ships, I'll be back in a few hours, or so I'm getting some rest." "Call down below if there are any troubles."

"Alright."

Father looked up when I came down, "Are you going to sleep?"

"Yes, Sir, then I will relieve John."

"I might join you in bed." I nodded and took off my close, and went to bed. It wasn't long when the Captain joined me as he put his arm around me. I could smell the liquor on him, and it worried me because of how he gets when he is drinking. I drifted off to sleep and woke several hours later with the Captain's arm still around me. I got up, dressed, and went on deck.

"I'll relieve you as soon as I relieve myself."

When I finished, I took the wheel, and he said, "I'm glad you're back; I was getting tired."

"How long was I gone?"

"At least four hours."

"Well, you did well; you can go down below and either sleep or study." "I will be at the wheel for another eight hours or more."

"Alright, if you need me, just call."

I smiled and said, "I will." After four or five hours after John left, I had noticed it was warmer. Perhaps I could take my clothing permanently off at Easter Island.

The Captain finally came to relieve me after ten hours. "Go down below, get some rest, and do your lessons."

"Yes, Sir."

I relieved myself first, then went down below. John was at the table studying; he looked up, smiled, and went back studying. I undressed and crawled into bed. After about three hours, I went out and relieved myself without saying anything to the Captain. Then I went down below again, this time to study. I sat down beside John and studied, helping John as he needed it. I finally was studying French while John was trying to learn German, and we were helping each other as we were learning. "Peter, fix me a sandwich and bring me some rum," demanded the Captain over the intercom. I fixed him a large sandwich and got him a mug of rum, and brought it to him on the deck.

"Are you feeling ill, Sir?"

"A little bit, I am hoping the sandwich will help, and the rum will dull the pain." "You will relieve me in a few hours; go down below and start dinner; have John help you." "Eat before you relieve me."

"Yes, Sir." I went down below and told John, "We have to fix dinner now." I decided to fix a beef stew, "John, cut up some potatoes and carrots and throw them into this pot." I added some water to the pot and set it on the burner. I then started cutting up some beef and added it to the potatoes that John put in the pot. I then put some spices in with the leftover peas we had. Finally, John put in the carrots, and we let the stew simmer adding water as needed. After about forty-five minutes, I tasted the stew and thought it was missing something.

I let John taste it; he smiled and got the leftover bottle of wine and added it to the stew, waited a few minutes, and tasted it again, then had me taste it. "It just needed a bit of wine Peter."

"You're right." We had plenty of French bread and butter. I made some sweet iced tea; then we sat down to eat. It was a little early for me to relieve the Captain, but I relieved him anyway, figuring he wasn't feeling well, and he needed to eat. It was almost the end of my shift at the wheel when I spotted an island. I got on the intercom and said, "Island three points on the port side." A few moments later, the Captain and John came on deck.

The Captain took the wheel and said, "That's Easter Island." "I know a safe place on the east side of the island to drop anchor." We dropped anchor nearly an hour later in a small bay. It wasn't the best place, but it would do for us to get a little rest. "We will be here about a day and then head for Tahiti; there is a protected bay there that I know." "We will stay there for about a week, then head to Neverland."

We all went down below after securing the ship and lowering the sails. We went to bed to get rest, and I was out before I think my head hit the pillow. I got up before everyone else, the Captain and John snuggling together. I went into the kitchen to start dinner and made clam chowder and baked fish with vegetables and scallop potatoes. The smell of the food must have awakened the Captain and John because from behind me, I heard, "What are you cooking Peter," said John."

"Fish, with clam chowder soup." "It will be ready in about twenty minutes."

"I'll set the table," said the Captain. "I'll also get an appropriate wine." It was light out still, so, after we ate and cleaned up, we all went on deck to get the ship ready for the trip to Tahiti the next day.

On the deck, I asked the Captain, "Sir, we always check the ship for damage and problems." "We never find any; the ship seems to be indestructible; why do we check it so often?"

"We can't take a chance of breaking down." "There is no protection on the high seas." "This ship is supposed to be indestructible, as you say, but I feel it is better to play it safe than to be sorry if something does happen." "Besides, it doesn't take that long to check the ship."

"Yes, Sir." We headed the next day northwest towards Tahiti; we all took turns at the wheel and up in the crow's nest except the Captain. John's time at the wheel increased more and more as he did his shifts until he was doing an eight-hour shift the same as the Captain and me. We did see a ship a couple of times, and we made course shifts to avoid them.

After about five days, John was on the crow's nest and yelled, "Captain, island four-points starboard."

The Captain called me on the intercom, "Peter, come on the deck." I was on deck in less than a minute, and the Captain said, "Go up above and send John down here."

"Yes, Sir."

I went up and told John to swing down below, and John did as I said and went over to the Captain. The Captain gave him the wheel and went to the bow of the ship. As we got nearer to the island, the Captain yelled to me, "Drop the sails." I swung down and brought down the sails, and the ship started to slow. Meanwhile, the Captain took over the wheel, and John came over to help me. After the sails were down and the ship at a certain speed, the Captain started the engines and said, "Peter, John, go to the bow and watch for rocks and dangers." We were going around the island. At a certain point, we went through a reef and towards a cove with a beach. "Drop anchor," said the Captain.

John and I ran to the anchor release and dropped the anchor. We then went to the ship's rail to look at the island. "John, do you know how to swim?"

"I don't know."

The Captain overheard and picked up John and threw him into the water. I watched and saw he was having trouble, so I jumped in and went over to him. "Let him do it himself, Peter," said the Captain.

"Don't panic, relax, think happy thoughts, pull with your arms, and kick with your feet." He did as I said, and he started swimming poorly. We headed towards the beach, "You are doing fine." I swam behind him, and when I knew the water was shallow, I stood up, but John kept swimming. "John, stand up." John looked back at me, and seeing me stand, he stood up.

He was breathing hard and said, "I almost drown."

"No, you didn't, you did just fine; you just need to relax and have more confidence."

"Well, I'm glad I'm sitting on the beach."

"You still have to swim back to the ship." John sighed, and I said, "You can do it." "The Captain did the same to me." We explored our area of the island and then came back to the beach. "You ready to go back to the ship?"

"If it means swimming, I'd rather not."

I laughed and said, "Come on, let's go; I'll be right behind you."

He swam better back, and when we got there was a rope that John and I climbed on deck.

We went down below, and the Captain said, "I want both of you to swim back and forth to the beach at least twice a day."

"Yes, Sir," I said as I sat at the table with my books.

The Captain got up, and as he was going up to the deck, he asked John, who was lying on the bed, asked, "How well did you swim, John?"

"I did better as I swam back to the ship, father."

My head popped up, and I could see the anger on the Captain's face. He grabbed John's arm and pulled him off the bed and up onto the deck. I immediately got up and followed him. A frightened John was trying to apologize to him by saying, "I'm sorry, Sir, please forgive me." But the Captain wasn't listening to him. He tied John's arms together and hoisted him up a meter, and grabbed his whip.

He was just about to whip a crying John when I rushed him and grabbed his arm and said, "You will not whip John; it's not his fault." He tried to pull his arm away from my grip, but I guess I was too strong for him.

"Then who's fault is it," an angry Captain said.

"It's mine; I didn't train him well enough."

He lowered his arm and growled, "You're right; you will take John's place." He tied my arms together and hoisted me up, and said, "I'm going to beat you not only for not training well enough but for mutiny, which is worse." He beat me more than he usually would, but like before, I did not say a word. John could only watch me crying even louder. When he finished, he went down below, letting John and me hanging.

"I'm sorry, Peter," said John, sniffling. I didn't say anything; I wasn't happy with him. It was late at night when the Captain came on deck and let John down, but he left me hanging.

John looked at me; a tear dripped down his cheek, and he went down below. The sun had been up for hours when the Captain came on deck to let me down. "I hope you learned your lesson."

I just stared at him and didn't say anything, and that disturbed him. He turned and started to leave when I said, "I will never allow you to whip anyone anymore for minor mistakes." "I am your son; I'm not an animal." He quickly turned around, angry, and I got into a fighting stance with my knife drawn. He stared at me for a few minutes, turned around, and left. I put my knife back in its sheath, dived into the water, and swam to the island. I went into the jungle, climbed into the trees, and found a comfortable place to lay and fall asleep.

It was late in the afternoon when the Captain said, "John swim to the island and tell Peter to come back on the ship."

"Yes, Sir." John made it to the Island and went into the jungle. I saw him, but when he called for me, I didn't answer him. I didn't want to talk to anyone, and I still wasn't in a forgiving mood to speak to John. After searching for about an hour, he swam back to the ship and told the Captain he couldn't find me.

The Captain lowered the skiff and, with John, rowed to the island. I saw them come into the jungle, and I watch as they called for me. The Captain yelled out, "You're right, Peter; the punishments will only happen for major things." "I won't beat you or John anymore."

"Please come back with us, Peter; I love you," said John.

The Captain wondered if I climbed the mountain, but after he thought for a while, he didn't think so even though he knew I could do it. "Come, John, let us go back to the ship." "I'm sure he is hiding in the trees, he heard us, and he is thinking about it."

They went back to the skiff, and I came out of the trees, and when they made it to the ship, I walked out to the beach. They climbed up on the ship and started to hoist up the skiff. I went back into the jungle to think. I knew I would have to go back some time; if the Captain is truthful about not beating anyone anymore, I would have to put that out of my mind too. Then there was John; did I genuinely hate him. No, I loved him; why would I protect him and take his punishment. He got told many times how to act on the ship, yet he still made a mistake, but then again, we all make mistakes; we are only human. I walked out to the beach again and paced back and forth. It had been more than an hour since they returned to the ship, so I decided to swim back to the ship. There was a rope hanging over the side of the ship. I'm sure they put it there in case I decided to come back. As I grabbed it, I saw a fin in the water. I knew it was a shark, so I climbed up on the ship real fast before it attacked. When I got on deck, there was no one there. I assume they were down below. I was hungry, but I wasn't in the mood to join them, so I went to the stern and laid down. I figured that if I slept, the hunger pains wouldn't bother me as much.

I was asleep when John came on deck to relieve himself, and he spotted me. He went down below and got the Captain. The Captain picked me up, and I awoke but didn't say anything when he placed me on the bed. Seeing me awake, he asked, "Are you hungry?" I nodded yes, and he went into the galley and fixed me a large sandwich and some iced tea. I went to the table and ate. John came back and sat next to me, and I looked at him and continued eating, not saying anything. I saw a tear seep from his eye; I knew he was anxious that I would hate him forever. I put my arm around him, and he snuggled into me. I finished eating, and the Captain said, "Get on the bed." I did as he said, and he rubbed a salve on my back and front. "This will make the scars go away." When he finished, he turned out the lights and told me to slide over; he got on the bed and then called John on the bed. Before I had fallen to sleep, he put his arm around me, and it was there when I woke up the next day.

I was on the deck when John approached me and said, "Are you mad at me, Peter?"

"No, not now."

"I was worried you would never talk to me again."

"No, I love you too much to do that." "You do need to remember what you're supposed to do." "You saw what happens when you don't."

"I'm sorry."

"I know you are."

The Captain came on the deck and said, "You need to practice swimming out to the island and back, John."

"Yes, Sir."

"There are sharks out there; one tried to attack me when I came on the ship yesterday." He went to the ship's rail and looked, and John and I joined him. I pointed at one about thirty feet from the ship.

"We better not go onshore unless we take the skiff," said the Captain.

"Yes, Sir," I said. We stayed at Tahiti for five more days and then headed for Neverland.

SIX

DEATH

I WAS IN THE CROW'S nest when I spotted a fog bank that I assume was around Neverland. John was at the wheel, and I called down, "John, fog bank in front of the bow; call the Captain."

John got on the intercom and said, "Captain, fog bank front of the bow."

The Captain came on deck and yelled up to me and said, "Peter, come down and take the wheel."

I swung down and took the wheel from John. "We are near Neverland; it's just past the fog bank." John stood next to the Captain at the ship's rail.

After about ten minutes, the Captain came over to me and said, "Take down the sails and then come back and retake the wheel."

"Yes, Sir." John helped me, and just before we broke out of the fog, I took over the Captain's wheel after the Captain started the engines, and John joined the Captain again at the ship's rail. Then when the island came in view, I seen the expression on John's face, which was about the same as it was with me, he looked over to me, and I smiled.

The Captain came over to me and said, "I want you to take it into the dock."

"Yes, Sir."

I lined the ship up with the two peaks that looked like horns on the ridge. I slowed down as we went through the channel, and when we were about thirty feet from the rock beach, I turned the wheel hard portside. I found the river that went to the inter bay and our port and turned starboard. John became excited when the scenery started to change, and then he spotted the Pongo. John ran over to me and said, "Are those the Pongo?"

"Yes, from the Kelpie people, I know them." I waved to them and yelled to them in the Pongo language, "My brother and I will come to the village soon."

I came into our bay and headed to the dock at a reduced speed. When I came up to the dock, the Captain said, "John, go out on the dock and catch the mooring rope."

"Yes, Sir."

I cut the engines, and John caught the rope and tied the ship up to the dock. The Captain put the gangway out on the dock and disembarked the ship. He turned to both of us and said, "Unload the ship and bring everything up to the house." "Also, secure and check out the entire ship."

We both said, "Yes, Sir," and got busy unloading the ship. John and I carried everything up to the house.

Then we took care of the ship, and it was time to dive into the water when John asked, "Are there sharks in these waters, Peter?"

"No." "The sharks don't go past the reef; they don't like the fresher water and its temperature." "There is also a fish that will attack them if they try." "Those fish won't attack us?"

"We jumped into the water and checked out the hull, and then got out and walked back to the house. Father had gone to bed with a liquor bottle, and John and I went to see him. "Are you ill, father?" I asked. John stared at me when I called him father.

"Yes, I took some pills with the liquor and rest." "I will be alright, Peter."

"Would you like us to feed you in bed?"

"No, if I need something to eat, I will go to the kitchen and fix me something." "Did you do everything to the ship?"

"Yes, Sir," we both said.

After we left our father, I said, "Don't forget when we aren't on the ship, we don't call our father, Captain; we call him father." I started showing John the house, and when we got to the library, I showed him how to work everything. He typed up "Peter Pan" and got the book for me. I then showed John the buildings on the grounds and the caves then explained the defense system for the island. The following day, John and I worked in the kitchen, making breakfast when father showed up at the table. I gave him tea while we finish making breakfast, and then we all sat down at the table. "Father, we need to add sonar to the radar system on the ship."

"I know I will be working on a system today and have it installed in the ship by the end of the week."

"Yes, Sir." "John and I would like to visit the Pongos."

"Well, if you two want to go, go."

"What about lunch and dinner?" I asked.

"If I want to eat something, I can fix something."

After we cleaned up everything, John and I went to the jungle and climbed one of the trees. I showed him how to swing through the trees. He was excited to try, and although he was slower, we were moving faster than if we walked to the village. About halfway through the jungle, some of the Pongo joined us until we made it to the grassland. John and I jumped down with the other Pongos. "Are they friendly, Peter?"

I smiled and said, "Yes, I am their leader." "This one is Koa; he is the brother of Tinker."

"This is Mana, and this one is called Ipo." "Koa is all good with the Pongo?"

"Yes, especially with my sister when she sees you." "Is this your brother?"

"Yes."

"The girls will like him, maybe the boys too."

I giggled, and John asked, "What did he say?"

"He was talking about his sister and you."

"What did he say about me?"

"He said you are pretty." The Pongo's left, and we went to the village to a warm welcome. As predicted, one female Pongo hooked onto John; her name was U'i, and she drugged him upstream into the jungle. John cried out to me, and I said with a smile, "Good luck John, just do your best."

About two hours later, John came back and found me and said, "Do you know what she did to me?"

"Yes, this has happened to me." "How did you do?"

"I would guess as well as you."

"You will have to learn the language better, at least well enough to talk to them."

We stayed in the village until late afternoon and headed back to the house. When we got home, father was working on some electronics; I assume the ship's sonar. John was relieving himself when I went into the lab and asked father, "Do you wish me to fix something for you to eat."

"That would be good," Father said without lifting his head.

"You are sweating a lot, father, and you don't look good; you need rest."

"I'm the doctor, and you're not." "Peter, I have a sickness that is going to get worse no matter what I do."

"Are you going to die?"

"I don't know for sure, but I know I will do everything to prevent it."

I nodded and left to the kitchen, and after a while, John joined me. "I found the language book on the Pongos."

"Good, I'll help you if you want me."

John nodded; I could have told John about father's health but didn't. I decided he didn't need to be troubled about it. I had finished the book about Peter Pan and saw many similarities between me and the book. John could speak Pongo well, and I knew he would get even better. When we went to the village the next day, John was having trouble with U'i, but at least he could talk his way out of anything he didn't want to do. When she found out about John's mother's death, my mother Mussel adopted him too. Tox took a liking to John and taught him how to fight and hunt with the spear, and he was happy to go with him to get away from U'i. I would train him later with the bow and other kinds of fighting. We took turns going to the Kelpie village; I going to different villages when I went. John liked Tox a lot, and U'i well, sometimes successfully fended her away and sometimes not. I was the same with Tinker and me, but I didn't let it bother me as John did. Why they wanted John and me, I don't know it's not like we were adults we couldn't do much. "Peter, come with me down to the ship." "I want you to install the sonar and test it."

"Yes, Sir," but you will have to tell me how to do it."

He nodded, and I installed it. He told me, "Swim out to the edge of the river with this decoy, and we will see if it works."

"Yes, Sir."

I did as he said, and when I pulled the decoy slowly, the sonar worked, and Father said, "I've calibrated it some here, but when we go out to the high seas, I'll do a better job."

"Yes, Sir." We walked back to the house without him saying a word. He grabbed several books on medical treatment and sat in the sitting room reading.

About a year had passed since we came back on the Island; John and I had made several trips to the Kelpie people and other villages. With a large force of Pongos, John and I had to go to the Migos village because some had gone back to their old ways. There was a battle, and many of the Migos that were giving many villages trouble got killed. John proved to be a great warrior gaining great respect in the Kelpie village. We took the remaining Migos, moved them to other villages, and burnt down their old village, and there was no more trouble.

Father's illness was getting worse, and even John knew and was worried. One rainy day when John and I were studying in the sitting room, Father came in and said, "Peter, John, we need to talk." "I'm assuming both of you have notice I'm getting sicker." John and I both put our books down and gave father our full attention.

"Yes, Sir," said John. "We are anxious about you."

Father nodded and said, "We must make a trip to Brazil far up the Amazon to a people called Gavião." "They may have medicine that may help me if they still exist."

"Father, are you strong enough to make the trip there?" I asked.

"I hope so, Peter." "I have no other choice but to go."

"Do you speak their language?" I asked concerned

"I speak Portuguese and some native languages in Brazil, but I will try to get an interpreter."

"When do you want to go, father?" asked John.

"In two days, you boys will have to do most of the work. I will help as much as I can."

"Yes, Sir," we both said.

It was dark out but still early when father went to bed, "I will go to the Kelpie village and inform them of our departure," I said to John.

"It's too dark out; going by trees, you will get hurt," John said.

"I know I will go by ground." "I'm a faster runner than you; that's why I'm going."

John nodded, and I took off to the village. I got to the village in about an hour, and I went to my mother's home where she and Tox were. I let them know what was happening, and my mother said, "We have medicines that might help."

"I know, but my father will not take your medicines, at least not now; maybe if the medicine we get doesn't work, he might try yours." After telling the rest of the elders, I left for home and got home late. I crawled into bed next to John, and I was asleep within minutes.

Two days later, I took the Jolly Rodger out through the channel and headed to Cape Horn. We rested a day at Pitcairn island for a day and headed to the cape. Father came on deck once while I was at the wheel, and he worked on the sonar and then went below. I made sure that everyone was in the cold weather clothes before we went near the cape. It was I who was at the wheel when we went around the cape without a problem. We dropped anchor at Ascension Island, and I talked to Father, "Sir, we are at Ascension Island."

"You and John have done well." He pulled some charts out and showed me where to sail up the Amazon River. "Use the engines when you go up the river." "When we go up the river, have John stand watch at the bow." "Then inform me that we are on the river." "Be careful, Peter; there are those who will try to kill all of us."

"Yes, Sir." "When do you want to leave, Sir."

"Tomorrow."

Before the first light, we headed for Brazil and the Amazon River. We made it to the river in about four days, and we went up the river with engines only. I had John at the bow watching for hazards, and then I called Father. "Sir, we are going up the river."

He came on deck with a chart of the river. He showed me the chart and said, "We want to go here to Barcelos." "We will get an interpreter there."

"Yes, Sir."

It took us three days to get there, and we dropped anchor. "I'm taking the skiff; you two stay on board, don't talk to anyone," said father wearing shorts.

"Yes, Sir," we both said.

"I'm setting the force field also."

"Yes, Sir," John said.

John and I went down below and slept; Father was gone for hours when he finally returned with an older man who didn't speak a language we understood. When he spotted us, he stared for a minute and started to giggle, then went back talking to Father. I asked Father, "What did he say, Captain?"

"He said, "You two not wearing anything will fit in well with the tribe we are going to." "I told him I don't wear anything myself." "We are going to a people called Korubo."

We headed out, moving slowly northwest, moving up one river then another. The man pointed where to turn as we went; the water looked very muddy as we went. We went down several different rivers for three days. Then, we couldn't go any further with the Black Paerl, so we took a skiff and traveled another two days, then we walked through the jungle. We crossed into a valley and got surrounded by many naked natives who had bows and arrows. The man who was with us said something, and we got guided to a village. Many of the village boys and girls were interested in John and me; as we went to a hut, I thought there was a chief or elder. The man that came with us said something, and then Father said something in Portuguese, and the man translated it. There was a conversation for some time, then Father turned to us and said, "These people will take care of you while I'm getting treated."

We both said, "Yes, Sir." He nodded to one of the natives, and he got taken away. John and I were taken by some of the other village children and guided to a hut for sleeping. They fed us something that tasted like yams and a green vegetable. They also gave us some meat; it had a smokie sweet taste to it. After we ate and rested awhile, some of the children took us to play a game with their bows and arrows. They were shooting at some target; the last one was moving. When it was John's and my turn at the bow, we both looked at the bow. They were a little different than my bow; their bow was about the same but made from a different material, and this one didn't have leather wrapped around it. My arrows were shorter than the ones the Korubo people had. I tested the bow's pull and then took my shot at the first target and hit dead center with much approval of the Korubo people. John did the same with the same results. For the following three targets, John and I did the same. Many hunters of the Korubo tribe became interested in our abilities. They came over to watch as we went to shoot at the moving target. John and I shot simultaneously, hitting it with ease, much to the rest of the people's jubilation. We went back to the sleeping hut with the rest of the people. We communicated with the Korubo people with sign language; it seemed to work, but it was frustrating. We never paid much attention to their language because we figured we wouldn't understand anyway. However, some of the men approached John and me and tried to talk to us, and we did pay attention this time because they used the word Pongo. We notice their language was like the Pongo language at home. So, I said to John in Pongo, "They sound like Pongo, don't you think so, John?"

"I didn't pay much attention before, but they do."

By this time, the once chattering Korubo people stopped talking and came over to us. An old man in what sounded like broken Pongo said, "Many rains past long before I was born there were a people called the Pond." "They were very smart and strong but kind." "They taught us their tongue, and it got passed down to father to son and daughter." "They were a hairy people and had hair the color of a Gwalch." "Where did you learn this tongue?"

"The Pond lives where we live; we call them Pongo."

"This cannot be there are no more Ponds." "It is said other people took them and killed them."

"Where I live, they are many, and I am their leader," I said. There was much talk among the Korubo, and finally, one said, "Can you bring them back?"

"They live far away beyond the great water." "They have forgotten about the Korubo; they won't come back; they like their home now," I said.

"There was talk again among the Korubo, and finally, the old man said, "At least they are still alive; this makes us happy." "We ask you to speak to them of the Korubo."

"We will both talk to them of you," John said. Korubo went back to what they were doing. Before he left, I told the old man that my father didn't speak Pongo, and he went to tell the ones that were tending to him. The next day a hunter came up to me and asked, "Would you and your brother like to go on a hunt with us?"

"I know I would; I will go ask my brother."

He nodded, and I went to find John. I found him by a stream trying to spearfish with some other boys. "John, do you want to go hunting with me and some of the Korubo?"

"No, you go."

I went back to the hunter, and he gave me a bow with some arrows; then, we headed into the jungle with some more people. We traveled about twenty minutes then spotted some large monkeys in the trees; one of the men pointed to them and shot at them but missed. I shot and hit a monkey, but it hung up in the trees, so I jumped up ten feet, grabbed a limb, and started climbing. I reached the monkey and freed it, and let it fall to the ground. I then found a vine and swung down to the ground. The hunters were amazed at what I just did. I didn't think there was no big deal about it. After about an hour of hunting, we went back to the village. The next day I was down at the river with John and the other Korubo boys trying to spearfish. I got bored and went into the jungle and up a tree. I was resting on a limb, looking at everyone trying to spearfish, playing, or working by the river. When I heard a scream, I looked and seen a girl running from a large spotted cat. I swung down between the girl and the cat with my knife drawn. The cat pounced on me as I drove my knife into him, then pulled it out and shoved it into him again. The cat was strong, but so was I, and as I stabbed him, he got weaker, so I kept on stabbing him until he went limp. By this time, many from the village came with the hunters with their bows. Two men took care of the cat, and I was taken to the sleeping hut and treated for the wounds the cat gave me. They put a salve on the wounds from the cat and had me drink a sour liquid. I got sleepy, and I fell asleep when I woke, it was near dark out; I got up and relieved myself and returned to the hut where a woman gave me something to eat. Another woman came to me with red paint; she grabbed my chin and started painting my face with a design. She then said, "Do not touch your face for a while until it dries."

"Why did you paint my face?"

"What you did was a great thing." "You are also part of the Korubo now too."

"What about my brother?"

"He is Korubo too." At that, she got up and left.

John came over to me and asked, "Are you alright?"

"Yes, I'm fine." "By the way, you are part of the Korubo people now like me."

"I know this, Peter." "You might have gotten killed; you scared me."

"There is nothing to worry about; I'm alright." "If I didn't do anything, that girl might have gotten killed."

"Peter, there is something else to worry about; we haven't seen or heard of Father for two days."

"I'm worried about Father too." "If we don't hear from Father by night tomorrow, we will start questioning how he is."

"Alright, Peter."

The following day, I stayed in the hut while John was out with some other boy. The same woman who put the salve on my wounds came over to me and looked at my wounds and said, "You are healing very good, and the marks are fading." "I will put some more on you, and you will be alright."

"Thank you." It was late afternoon, and I was in the hut leaning against a post, daydreaming as I watched everyone outside when I felt someone grab my arm and lift me. "Father, are you alright?"

"I'm fine; I was going to ask you the same thing, and why is your face painted?"

"I'm alright they put medicine on my wounds." "It's not as good as your medicine, but it is slowly working."

"I will work on your wounds when we get back at the ship, and we are out into the ocean." "What about your face?"

"I fully don't know why they painted my face." "I do know John, and I are accepted as part of the Korubo."

"Does John have a painted face?"

"No." "I think it also has something to do with me saving that girl from a big cat."

"Yes, I heard you killed a jaguar that was very dangerous but brave."

"Are you strong enough to go back to the ship tomorrow?"

"Yes, Father, I'm strong right now." "Did the Korubo help your trouble with the sickness Father?"

"Yes, I'm much better, but I got told although what they have given me will help with the pain, it will not cure me, and there will be a time when it doesn't help with the pain either." "They gave me enough medication to last a long time; perhaps I can improve on it."

"Yes, Sir."

Father stood just outside the hut, and John spotted him, and he came running. Father gave him a kiss and hug and told him of our departure.

After saying our goodbyes to everyone, we left for the skiff and headed downstream towards the Black Paerl. We will miss the Korubo, but I'm also glad we are heading home. After two days, we dropped off the interpreter in Barcelos and headed down the Amazon and out into the ocean. The Captain said to me, "Head for Ascension Island and drop anchor." So, John and I took turns at the wheel and in the crow's nest. We did see a couple of ships but made course changes, and in three days, we dropped anchor in the same place we were in Ascension Island.

"Sir, we just dropped anchor at Ascension Island," I said. I didn't get any response from the Captain, nor did he come on deck. I yelled to John, who was in the crow's nest, "John, go down below and check on the Captain while I secure the ship." He flew down to the deck and went below.

A few minutes later, John returned and said, "Peter, the captain is asleep on the bed." "He has a strong smell like liquor on him."

"Alright, we will rest and then start dinner." John nodded, and after the ship got fully secured, we rested on deck.

We started dinner, and while we were cooking, the Captain never woke when dinner was ready; we brought it to the table, and John woke the Captain by shaking him then said, "Captain dinner is ready, Sir." "Would you like to come to the table or eat in bed?"

A groggy Captain woke and said, "I'll eat at the table; help me up." John helped him to the table, and I served him, and he asked, "Where are we, Peter?"

"We are at Ascension Island, Sir." "How long do you wish to stay here, Sir?"

"Use your best judgment, Peter." "Is the ship alright?"

"Yes, Sir."

After he ate, he went back to bed, and John said, "We will sleep on deck, Sir."

He waved his approval to John and rolled over to sleep. John asked me, "What's the matter with him; I thought that medicine the Korubo was supposed to help him?"

"I don't know, but I think the medicine makes him sleepy, and mixing it with liquor makes it worse." John and I grabbed a blanket and books, and when we weren't sleeping, we were studying.

As we woke up the next day, the Captain came on deck to relieve himself, and John asked him, "Are you hungry, Captain?" "We are about to cook breakfast."

"I'm a bit hungry, John."

"Good, I'll make a hearty meal, Sir."

John and I went down below to the galley after we relieved ourselves and started cooking. When we all sat down to eat, I said to the Captain, "I thought when you used the medication, you didn't need to drink?"

"Every time I take the drug the Korubo gave me, it doesn't work as well as it works the last time I take it, so I drink to help me get through the pain." "I also don't want to use too much until I can find out how it was made." "For that reason, you and John might have to do most of the work on this ship." "Do you think you can go around the cape by yourselves?"

"Yes, Sir."

"Good, the less I work, the better I will be."

"We will leave tomorrow, Sir."

He nodded, and when John and I went on deck, John asked, "Is he dying, Peter?"

"Yes, I think so."

We all had our cold-weather clothing on, including the Captain, when we went around Cape Horn. The weather was about the same as it seems it always is when we traveled down there. We sailed up to Easter Island to rest and check out the ship. We dropped the anchor in a small isolated cove, and I informed the Captain. Then, John and I stripped out of our clothing and took a bath. The Captain stayed down below most of the time, either on the bed or in the medical room. "John, I think we need to check out the ship, and then if everything is alright, we need to be heading home tomorrow."

"We aren't going to drop anchor in Tahiti?"

"I don't know; I will decide tomorrow and let you know."

"Don't you think we should ask the Captain?"

"I suppose so, but he doesn't seem very interested in the ship."

The Captain was reading something as he ate at dinner, and I said, "Captain."

He lifted his head and said, "What?"

"I intend to leave Easter Island tomorrow." "I don't think we should drop anchor in Tahiti."

"Why?"

"Too many people in the area."

"Perhaps you're right." "There is a smaller island called Oroatera; check on the charts; you will find it." "You have to be careful; it is shallow there."

"Yes, Sir."

He went back to reading for a few minutes, then raised his head and said, "Peter, John, you are both captains now; take turns." "Whoever is at the wheel will be the Captain or do it the way you want." "I am no longer the captain I just your father; do you both understand?"

"Yes, Father," I said as John nodded. He went back to reading and picking at his food.

We made it to Oroatera, and I found a channel into the deeper water. I had John at the bow watching for shallow water we made it through, but I thought we might have scraped the bottom at one time. When we dropped anchor and secured the ship, John and I decided to rest first and then the next day check out the ship. We also kept watching for anyone coming near us; we were only three miles from where there might be people. The next day both John and I jumped into the water and checked out the ship, especially the hull. There was no damage; it was as if we never scrape the bottom. When we were at Oroatera, we didn't see anyone and left the same way we came in. Several days after leaving Oroatera, we arrived home. I decided that John should take the ship through the channel and to the pier. He did just fine, and I secured the ship to the dock. Father left the ship without saying a word carrying a few things. John and I unloaded and secured the ship and brought everything up to the house.

Father mainly stayed in the lab eating little or nothing, but what primarily concerned me was he hardly ever slept that I knew.

John and I went to the Kelpie village and gathered the elders, "While we were gone, we met a people called the Korubo," I said. There was no reaction when I said Korubo. I asked, "Have you ever heard of these people?"

"No," they said.

Then John said, "They said the Pongo use to live with them; that some other people killed some of the Pongo and took others away."

"We know nothing of this," the elders said.

"The Korubo wanted us to bring you back to them but understand if you don't want to go," I said.

There was talk among the elders, and they said, "We don't know the Korubo." "We are happy here; we will stay here."

Both John and I nodded, "It is alright." "I have told the Korubo you would say this, but I told them we would tell you anyway," I said. Then John started telling them about the Korubo, and later that night, we went back to the house.

A year and a half passed by, and Father looked terrible, but he would not listen to us when we tried to talk to him. One day while John and I were about finishing up making dinner, I went into the lab to ask Father to come to the table, not thinking he would. When I got there, he was lying on the floor, and I ran over to him and shook him, asking, "Are you alright, Father?" I yelled for John and felt for a pulse, and I found one.

When John came running, he asked, "Is he alive?"

"Yes, give me a hand putting him on the bed."

He wasn't breathing very well, so John gave him oxygen while I gave him an I.V. of fluids. Then I went to the computer in his room and research what else we could do for him. I gave him some painkillers and some nutrients so he wouldn't starve. John and I took turns watching him bring each other food as we ate. It was the second day at night, while John watched him, he woke, and John called for me. With difficulty, he said, "Peter, John, there are keys in my desk; get them."

John ran and got them, "Here, father."

He held them and said, "These keys open all my files of my secret writings and also my logs on the Jolley Rodger." He handed the keys to me, then said, "When you read these papers and logs, don't be too angry with me." "I love you both; all that is here on Neverland is yours." Then, just before he passed out again, he said, "Bury me with our ancestors on the ridge."

I said to John, "I'm going after mother." "Maybe she can do something."

John nodded, and I ran out of the house and into the jungle. It was starting to get light as I went up a tree and swung towards the village. When I got to the village, I ran to my mother's hut and told her what was happening; she gathered some things, and she and Tox joined me going back to my home. When we got to the house, and we went into the room that Father laid. Mother went and check on Father and started shaking her head. She walked over to us and said, I am sorry; there is nothing I can do; he is gone. John and I were in total shock. We sat down with tears streaming down our cheeks. Tox came to us and said, "I and others will help you with your father's body." I nodded, and he left and went to the village.

SEVEN

RETURNING HOME

MOTHER CAME OVER TO try to comfort John and me. About an hour and a half later, what looked like the whole village showed up. Tox came in and asked, "What can we do to help?"

I got up and said, "Build something to carry my Father; he wanted to be buried in a cave up near the top of the mountain." The Kelpie made a litter to carry him, and as he got put on it, they shower him with flowers. They took him up the mountain while John and I followed him from behind. When we got to the cave, I opened the door, then he was brought in, and John and I followed. I was amazed at all the past relatives that got buried there. We showed those who had carried Father where to put him, which was a niche in the wall. They placed him in and then went out as others came in and placed flowers on him and around the grave, then left. Finally, John and I left and shut the door, and we walked down to the house. "John, I will talk to the Kelpie people." He nodded, and I said to the people, "Thank you for all your comfort and help." "The loss of my father is deeply hurting John and me." "We will be here mourning for some time until the pain of our lost is gone." "We wish to tell you we love you all." At that, John and I went into the house. Tox and mother joined us, hugged us, and then left.

I snuggled next to John when John said, "Peter, what are we going to do without father?"

"I don't know, John; my mind isn't very clear." "Father said we should read his logs and papers, so that is what we will do, that is for sure." "Mother said the pain would go away in time; I hope she is right." We both drifted off to sleep as troubled our mind was.

The next morning, we were melancholy; we both weren't in the mood to eat, but John said, "We should eat before we get sick, besides maybe we will feel better."

"You're right, John." We ate, but we didn't eat that much. After breakfast, we sat in the sitting room, staring out into space. Finally, I said, "I'll open up the cabinets with Father's secrets papers, then you take then bring them in here, and we both will read them together." "While you're getting the papers, I'll get the logs."

"Alright, Peter." We got everything in the sitting room, and John sat down next to me asked, "How are we going to do this, Peter?"

"You sit next to me, and we will share reading out loud." We started with Father's logs on the ship. Everything was going fine until we got to when we sailed to get John from England.

"October fourth, I gave Peter a drug to knock him out and gave him an I.V. to keep him out." "I couldn't let him find out what the condition of England was."

"October ten, "I found a male child by the name of William Clearfield, and I got into his house where he was alone and gave him a shot to knock him out." "Unfortunately, his mother showed up and in a struggled fell and broke her neck and died." "She was a trashy drunk who never took care of her son." "I had to change William's name to John so he would disassociate who he was like I did with Peter." "I also altered John's brain and gave him medication to enhance his abilities, the same as I did with Peter." "I didn't alter John physically as I did with Peter because I didn't have to." John was distraught at what I read. He was crying when I said, "What he did was terrible, John, and he did it to me too."

"I don't remember any of my past, and he killed my mother." "My name is William Clearfield, but I don't know William Clearfield." "I have no one."

"You have me." "I love you; that will never change." "I am your brother; that will never change either." "What do you wish to be called John or William?"

He thought for a moment, then said, "I know you love me, and I love you." "You are my brother; you can call me William or John; it makes no difference to me."

We read the rest of the logs and found out how twisted his mind was, but he also expresses his love for us and why he did things the way he did. Then we got to the log about me.

"April fifth, I find myself very lonely, especially after these last three years since Father had died." "I must face it; I am not getting any younger; I need someone to carry on the Hooker name."

"April twelve, I've been on the high seas for twenty-one days, and I am nearing San Francisco Bay in the United States."

"April thirteenth, after checking the charts, I docked near Alameda Naval Base." "I secured the ship and headed to a place to hire a vehicle."

"April fifteen, I found a park next to a school where I could obtain a child." "I walked the neighborhoods and found a young boy who lived next to the school." "His name was Jimmy or James, and I found out his last name was Reno." "His mother was hanging clothing when he told her he was going to the park." "I quickly went to the park before he went." "I saw the boy come from the school and across the road to someone's home." "I thought I lost him, but he left the house and crossed the bridge to the park; I got out and followed him." "I took a chance that he would go down the creek, and it paid off he went." "I quietly went down to where he was and gave him a shot that knocked him out."

"April seventeen, I have the boy with an I.V. in the medical room on the Black Pearl." "I am partial to long hair blond boys, so I changed his brown hair and altered him physically to look more like an elf." "When I finished him, he reminded me of Peter the Pan, so I named him Peter."

"April eighteen, I have been filling Peter with drugs to enhance him; he is recovering quickly from the brain operation."

"April twenty, Brainwashing is almost complete; I had made a movie of mass destruction, and I forced his brain to absorb it." The log and papers went on and on about what he did to John and me. John and I also found logs of past ancestors; when we finished reading everything, we were both shocked. John went to bed; I'm sure to cry, and I went out onto the porch to stare out into space.

The next morning, we were both stressed and upset, and it showed. John asked, "What do you want to do, Peter?"

"I don't know." Some tears seeped and fell from John's eyes. "Nothing has changed, John, you are my brother, and I love you."

As the months passed, the food supply started to get low, and my interest in Neverland wasn't there anymore. "What is the matter, Peter?"

"We are getting low on food, and I'm losing interest in Neverland."

"What do you want to do?"

"I don't know; we do have to get food."

"Perhaps you should try to find your relatives."

"They would be your relatives too."

"Suppose they don't want me," John said.

"Then I won't go with them; we stay together as brothers, or we are orphans." "Besides, you and I don't look the way we should have looked."

"Especially you, Peter." "I'm willing to go, Peter."

"John, will you go to the village and asked the elders to meet here and also mother Tox and anyone else you think should be here."

"Yes." John left, and I went to get the charts to study them.

Everyone showed up, and John and I explain to them what we plan to do. "I am your mother, and Tox is your brother."

"You are and always will be, but we are not Pongo, and there are those who like to mate with us, and we can't do this." "We love all Pongo, especially you and Tox," I said.

"Someday, Neverland might get found, and many will fight to possess this place and will harm the Pongo as they did before." "We must go and make sure this doesn't happen," John said.

"Will you come back someday?" asked mother.

"Yes," I said.

"Then go," Mother said.

They left sad, which upset John and me, but we had to sail back to my origin for the sake of Neverland, John, and me. We studied the charts and maps and decided that going to the San Francisco Bay would be the best thing to do and dock in Alameda Naval port. We eliminated going to England for two reasons. One, if we must leave quickly, going around Cape Hope or Cape Horn would slow us down too much. Two, According to the papers and logs we read, John had no relatives in England anymore. Before we get to America, John and I decided to demand a government representative from England and the United States. We also will ask for a representative from the Barristers Thomson Snell & Passmore of England and a reputable Barrister from the United States. We planned to transmit a message to both the United States and Great Britain before we left.

We studied all the charts and maps and placed them on the ship. We loaded the ship with all the food we had, and then we readied the ship. "John, don't you think we should give them a gift to impress them?"

"Yes, but two gifts, one for the United States and one for Great Britain."

"What shall they be?" I asked

"No, weapons for sure, maybe something in the medical field or space."

"I don't feel space at this time would be good." "Perhaps cures for two different types of cancer." John nodded, and we prepared a transmission to the two countries.

It was the end of May when we got everything set up. We plan to bounce a signal off the Moon so no one would be able to find us until we wanted them to find us; it would interrupt their television and radio. "Peter, I don't trust any country," said John.

"Neither do I, John; we will be cautious." "I think I will start, and you can jump in as you wish; is that alright with you, John?"

"Yes." "Are we going to record before we transmit?"

"Yes, then we can review it before we transmit it." John sat next to me, and we started to transmit. "I wish to apologize for interrupting your entertainment" "My name is Peter the Pan Hooker, also known as James or Jimmy Reno."

"My name is John Hooker, also known as William Clearfield. "I'm the brother of Peter."

"We were both kidnapped, physically altered, and brainwashed by a man by the name of James Hooker." "He convinced us that he was our father, everything else about him we will tell you when we see you in person except for he has passed on."

"We will be traveling to San Francisco by ship." "A very advanced ship," John said.

"We should be in San Francisco sometime in June." "You should know we do not trust any country." "If you mistreat us, we will leave and go back from where we are coming from, and I assure you we can do just that." "Our ship was called the Jolly Rodger, but now is called Black Pearl." "It has enough armaments to destroy any navy; I suggest you don't try us."

"We are peaceful; we don't want to sound violent; we just don't trust anyone." "Please have government representatives from England and the United States when we come into port." "Also, a representative from the Barristers Thomson Snell & Passmore of England and a reputable Barrister from the United States," said John.

"Understand we have enough knowledge to advance mankind centuries into the future if you don't mistreat us," I said.

At that, we ended our transmission. We finished prepping the ship, and we sailed towards the United States. We made sure we were off all sonars and radars for two days so that no one could track us back to the island. We made it to Kiribati island and dropped anchor in about three days without any trouble. We rested for two days and then went to the Hawaiian island of Kauai on the deserted side. This time a ship did spot us but couldn't catch us, and we made many course changes. We stayed in Kauai overnight and then left for San Francisco. Less than halfway to San Francisco, we were surrounded by two destroyers, a frigate, and an aircraft carrier. They tried to signal us with flags that John and I understood but preferred talking by radio. We had put our force field on long before the ships came for our protection, and it was just as well because two jets flew over us. So, I radioed and said, "This is the Jolly Rodger or Black Pearl." "I am Peter the Pan Hooker; we can read your flags but prefer to speak by radio." I then waited.

"Black Pearl, this is Admiral Billingworth; where is your Captain?"

"Admiral Billingworth, my brother and I share the Captain's chair." "I am Peter the Pan Hooker."

"Peter, you sound like a child."

"I am Admiral, but it would be a mistake to underestimate my brother or me."

"Is there an adult on your ship?"

"No."

"We must board you, young man."

"No one will board this ship unless we allow you."

"If we have to, we will board you by force."

"Try it at your peril." "We will be leaving you now." All sails got raised, and we started our engines, and we started to pull away from the other ships. "John, get ready on the weapons."

John hopped on the weapon system, and a destroyer tried to cut us off, but John fired a round across their bow, and they backed off. The other destroyer wouldn't back down, so we place a round in its bow after firing a warning shot. Then all the ships and the jets tried to fire on us as we went by them, but their rounds bounced off our force field. I got on the radio and said, "I warned you, Admiral, what would happen." "We could have sunk all your ships with ease; if your jets attack us, we will knock them down."

"You're in big trouble, young man."

"No, Sir, you are the one who attacked us in international waters; it is you who is in trouble." At that, we pulled away and out of sight of the other ships. As we neared the San Francisco Bay, we spotted on sonar a submarine approaching us. John got back on the weapons, and I radioed and said, "Submarine, I have spotted you, and I have a shield all around this ship, including the hull." "We are not violent and mean no harm, but if you attack me, we will attack you."

"Black Pearl, we just can't let you into the bay; we don't know your intentions."

"We are two boys on this ship; we aren't even teenagers." "I am also an American citizen who hasn't harm anyone."

"What is your intention, Black Pearl?"

"Dock in Alameda and find my parents." "If it doesn't work out, we will leave."

There was silence for a few minutes, then the man in the submarine said, "Black Pearl, two Coast Guard ships will escort you to a dock in Alameda."

As we went under the Golden Gate Bridge, two Coast Guard pulled in front of us. We had to slow down for the ships to be able to stay ahead of us. It took about forty-five minutes to get to Alameda. "Black Pearl, this is the Coast Guard dock at pier six." We slid right into the dock and dropped anchor. Several men came onto the dock with rifles, and they demanded to go onboard.

"We will only talk to the admiral of this port," said John. At that, we put away our weapon system and started to secure our ship.

The soldiers were getting frustrated with us and tried to board our ship but found out quickly that wasn't going to happen. We needed to moor our ship, so I said, "Please move off the dock." They refused, and I said, "I warned you." I slowly expanded the shields over the dock, and they got pushed back. The ones who didn't run off the pier got pushed into the water. I shoved the gangplank out to the dock, and John threw me the ropes to moor the ship.

John went to the bow of the ship and said, "Please have the admiral meet us at the ship."

"Admiral Mc Donald is on his way," One of the sailors said.

The Admiral and another man came to the dock. "Are you Admiral Mc Donald?"

"Yes."

"Do you have identification?"

"Yes." He pulled out a card and said, "How am I going to get it to you?"

"I'm enhanced; hold it up, and I can see it from here." "You check out, Sir." "Who is that other man with you?"

"He is from the FBI." "I will vouch for him."

"Alright, Admiral, have your men move back, and I will let you two on to the ship." The men moved back far enough to let the two men in, and I lowered the shields in front of the dock. "Walk forward, Sir." Both men walked to the gangplank, and I raised the shields. As he walked on the ship, he saluted our colors first before stepping on the deck, and I liked that; it showed respect. John and I had hand weapons that we trained on the Admiral and the FBI man.

"Young man are you going to shoot us?" asked the Admiral.

"Not unless we must, Sir," I said. "Will you both remove your weapons and throw them down below?"

"I don't have a weapon," said the Admiral.

"I believe you, Sir." I looked over to the FBI, and he wasn't happy, but he gave up a weapon. Then I said, "Now your other weapon, Sir." He removed a gun from around his ankle and threw it down below. Then John and I threw our weapons down below. "Gentlemen, would you please sit," I said as I pointed to four chairs. We sat, and John brought some refreshments. "My name is Peter the Pan Hooker, also known as Jimmy or James Reno." I pointed to John and said, "This is my brother John Hooker also known as William Clearfield."

"I'm Admiral Lenard Mc Donald, and this is Mister Jack Sonders of the FBI." "We have some questions to ask both of you; would that be alright?"

"Yes, Admiral, you may ask anything, but be aware there may be answers to my brother, and I may not be able to answer, at least for now."

"Alright, why are both of you not wearing clothing?"

I looked at John, and he said, "We don't wear clothing because it is our custom, and when sailing on this ship, it makes it easier to work." "We do wear clothing during cold weather."

"You two said someone kidnapped you who and why?" asked Mr. Sonders.

"Captain James Henry Hooker as we knew him was our Kidnapper." "He kidnapped us and raised us as his sons to carry on the Hooker name and not to be lonely." "I should tell you his name may not be correct." "I believe he got kidnapped also." "It is a custom of the Hooker clan to kidnap boys and raise them as their own." "This custom goes back for thousands of years," I said.

"Mr. Sonders asked, "What did he do to you?"

"He operated on our brains, and in my case, altered my look, gave us chemicals, and brainwashed us, and..."

I hesitated, and John said, "He beat us and had relations with us."

"Tell us about this ship and the place you come from?" asked the Admiral.

"We cannot tell you at this time about this ship or where we come from other than the name of the place, we come from is Neverland, and this ship is hundreds of years advance than any country has." "Gentlemen, we have the knowledge that would advance humankind thousands of years," I said.

"You two will tell us everything, including where this Neverland is," demanded Mr. Sonders.

I lost my patience and said, "I'm trying to be patient, but I'm losing it." "You don't know who you are threatening." "I may be a citizen of this country, but we are leaders of a sovereign country too." "I told you if it didn't work out here, we would go back to Neverland." "I've told you we wish to see representatives from both Great Britain and the United States." "We also told you we wanted to meet with our solicitors from Great Britain and the United States." However, you had shown us nothing but disrespect since before we were in your waters." "Now get off our ship; you fools will lose everything."

Mr. Sonders tried to grab John and me, but I grabbed his throat and lifted him off the deck, and threw him into the ship's rail. Meanwhile, John step between the Admiral and me. The Admiral yelled, "That is enough, Sonder; you will get off this ship before I have you arrested." Mr. Sonders got up shaky, and without a word, walked on the deck, I lowered the shields, and when he walked through, I put them back up. John and I looked at the Admiral, and if looks could kill, he would have been dead. "Boys let me apologize to you; we aren't all like him." "I'll report him to his superiors." "Your government representatives and solicitors are coming; they should be here in less than an hour."

"And what about our relatives?"

"We need to examine both of you first; they know you were coming; you will see them tomorrow or the next day, depending on their schedules."

"There is nothing wrong with us."

"We would still like to examine you first, and it wouldn't be appropriate to meet these people without some clothing on." "Will you come with me?"

John and I looked at each other, and John said, "We will go with you, but first, we need to secure this ship a little more, and we want you to keep that man away from us."

"Good, and I'll keep that man away from you." "I'll wait for you to secure the ship."

John went below got the two gifts and documents saying Neverland is a sovereign nation. I got all the weapons put ours away, and gave Mr. Sonders to Admiral Mc Donald. Then I dropped the shields on the pier, and we all walked through. Then I said, "Computer raise shields."

"Admiral, if some scientists find a way to go through our shields, this ship will blow up, taking more than half the United States with it." "Do you understand, Sir?" said John.

"Yes, I understand. As we left, John and I noticed armed sailors with other people behind them with what looked like cameras. The Admiral yelled, "Bring those blankets down here." A sailor brought two blankets, and the Admiral said, "Rap these around you, boys." We put the blankets over our shoulders but didn't try to hide our bodies. People were trying to ask questions to us as we went into a vehicle and got taken away. "We are going to Oak Noll Naval Hospital."

"Do our representatives know where we will be?" asked John.

"I believe so, but if they don't, we will get them to both of you."

"May I ask you when you think you can tell us about Neverland, your ship, and its weapons?"

"Admiral, First, let me tell you the weapons on our ship is nothing compared to the power we have at Neverland." "We will tell you what we have when we feel that we are getting treated correctly, and we know you will handle what we have properly." "We will tell you how things work little by little so John and I can benefit from these items first." "For example, you know how to split an atom, am I correct?" I said.

"Yes."

"If you didn't, we would give you that knowledge for a price and for shared use of that knowledge."

"You want to get paid for what you have and have use of what you have?" he asked.

"Yes, but the cost won't be as much as you would expect," I said.

"We don't need a lot of money from you, Sir; we already have a lot of money," said John.

"The money you will pay is the price for our knowledge," I said.

"Alright, boys."

"Admiral, I haven't talked to John about what I am going to say, but I believe he will agree." "When all representatives are present, we will not only make a deal with the United States but with Britain also."

We could see the Admiral was uptight about this because he bit his lip but then said, "Alright, boys." "What are those things you are carrying?"

"Copied documents, proving that Neverland is a recognized sovereign nation." "We also have gifts for the United States and Great Britain that will demonstrate our great knowledge," said John.

"Let me see them then."

"No, you could be present when we give them to the Government representatives, and you can see them then," I said.

Oak Noll Naval hospital was up on a hill. Many navy nurses and doctors greeted us when we left the vehicle while we left our blankets. They tried to take what we were carrying away, but we refused to release them, and by order of the Admiral, we were able to keep them. We were taken to a room with two beds and told to bathe first and then get into some loose clothing. John washed and got dressed first while I watched our things, then I did the same while John had our things. John and I both hopped on a bed and waited to see what would happen next. A doctor followed by two nurses came into our room, and the doctor said, "You two are supposed to be in separate beds."

"We have always slept together," John said.

"It's hard to work on you when you are together; besides, this bed is made for one person," he said.

"We have enough room; you can only work on us one at a time; when you need to work on us, we will hop off the bed when you do," I said.

"Alright, boys." "Nurse, have housekeeping bring a wider bed in here."

"Yes, Sir."

I hopped off the bed as the doctor examined John and when he finished, I jumped up on the bed, and he examined me. When he finished with me, I asked, "Where is Admiral Mc Donald?" He was supposed to bring our representatives here."

"They are here now." "They were just waiting for me to finish examining both you boys." "I'll let them know they can come in now." We nodded, and everyone left.

Ten minutes later, four men and one female came into John's and my room. Admiral Mc Donald introduced everyone, "This is the ambassador to Great Britain, Mr. Henry Blackwell." "From the state department of the United States is Mr. John Brown." "Your solicitors from Great Britain, Mary Witherspoon, and Arthur Greenfield." "Your solicitor from the United States, Jack Bryant."

"Miss Witherspoon and Mr. Greenfield, are you from the Barristers Thomson Snell & Passmore of England?" I said.

"Yes, we are," said Mr. Greenfield.

"And you know you represent the Hooker family?" I questioned.

"Yes, we have represented your family for years," Mr. Greenfield said.

"I've asked for an American solicitor to help you here; do you think you can work with Mr. Bryant?" I asked.

"We didn't need him, we have had dealings with the American government before, but he will be helpful, so we welcome him," said Miss Witherspoon.

"Very well, we first have gifts for the British and American governments that we wish you to let the Admiral know what they are," said John. "This is for Britain, and this is for the United States; in giving these gifts, it is our wish that both the United States and Britain will not only share it with themselves but the world too."

John handed both dossiers to the two governments. When they looked at them, they had a shocked look on their face; the American representative said, "Is this real?"

"Yes, ask any of your scientists they will confirm it," I said. The American and British representatives told Admiral it was a cure for two particular kinds of cancer.

"We also have a copy of a document stating the Neverland is a sovereign nation." "I will give it to the representatives of Thomson Snell & Passmore," John said.

"We also have a copy of this document; said Mr. Greenfield; we will give this copy to Mr. Bryant."

"That would be acceptable," I said. I looked at John, and he nodded. I said, "We possess many things and knowledge on our ship and on Neverland that will advance humankind perhaps hundreds of years into the future." "We wish to negotiate with the help of our solicitors and perhaps our parents a deal where your two governments can obtain the knowledge we have."

"That is very generous," said Mr. Blackwell of Britain and the American Mr. Brown.

"When will the boy's parents be here?" asked Mr. Blackwell.

"Tomorrow at three in the afternoon, I've already sent word to them," said Admiral Mc Donald.

"Sir, have you informed them that my features have changed?" I asked.

"Yes."

"We will be here at four to discuss the negotiations," said one of our solicitors.

All left, but the Admiral, and he said, "Do you think I can be at these negotiations."

"That would be fine, Sir," said John.

"Don't you think you should disarm the ship now that everything has gotten set up?"

"No, not yet." "Not until the end of the negotiations, and everything is signed and taken care of through our solicitors."

"Alright."

Just then, a nurse came into the room and said to the Admiral, "Sir, there are a lot of reporters wanting to interview the boys."

"How many journalists are there?" I asked.

"About thirty or more," said the nurse.

"That's alright, boys, I'll take care of them," said the admiral.

"No, if we don't talk to them, they will harass us until we do," said John. "Perhaps Admiral, you could talk to them and have them pick two or three Journalists to represent all of them."

"Alright, if that is what you want." The Journalists took pictures and asked many questions about who we were and why we were here. They also asked many questions about things we told them we didn't want to talk about at this time.

The hospital housekeeping brought in a larger bed and took the other two beds away. We were bored about six o'clock that night, so John and I snuck out of our room and did a little exploring. We went down the hall and noticed that we were in the place where children got treated for illnesses. We came to one room where there were four children, and we walked in. "Hello," John said. "My name is John Hooker, and this is Peter the Pan Hooker."

The four boys started to giggle, and one boy who was about nine said, "If you're Peter Pan, then where is Tinker Bell?"

"Back in Neverland," I said.

They all laughed, and a boy said, "If you are the real Peter Pan, let me see you fly." I looked at John and shrugged my shoulders and jumped up, nearly hitting the ceiling, and went over one of the boys to the one who wanted me to fly. All the boys were shocked, and the boy who asked me to fly saw my ears and said, "You are the real Peter Pan."

I smiled and said, "I'm the one and only."

"Are all the stories I read about true Peter?" asked another boy.

"I've read a book that is called Wendy and Peter." "Although there are some similarities, there are some things that are different too."

A nurse came into the room and said, "You two boys aren't supposed to be here; let's go."

We followed the nurse back to our room; as we went, John said, "We were bored."

"Well, you could watch television," the nurse said.

"What is television?" John asked.

"I will show you."

She turned the television on, and we just stared. She showed us how to work this television, and after she left, I said, "It's kind of like a computer, I think." John nodded, and we climbed back into the bed and watched.

The Next day after we ate lunch, the Admiral came and started talking to us. "I wish to talk to you about your parents before they get here."

"Alright," John and I said.

"Frist, John is not blood-related; you must realize that, Peter."

"You're right, but he is my brother who I love, and my genes aren't the same anymore either; John's genes are more like mine now." "If they accept me and not John, then that will be a major problem with me, and I will act accordingly."

"Are you saying you will try to leave and go back to Neverland?"

"Admiral, there won't be a try; we will leave if we choose, but if you mean will we leave, John and I would have to talk about that." "I will tell you this that if these parents of mine don't accept both of us, we both don't accept them."

"Alright, let's talk about something else." "I don't know how your parents will react to you; you don't look like anyone in their family; expect them to be shocked."

"We understand," I said.

"They will be with you for an hour before your solicitors join you." "I'll leave now and will meet with your parents when they come." We both nodded, and he left.

John and I hopped up on the bed and laid down, and John said, "Peter, they are your parents, you should go with them, don't worry about me."

Tears seep from my eyes, and I said, "No, you are my brother, and I won't get separated from you." "I don't want to talk about it anymore."

In waiting, we both dozed off to sleep, and while we were sleeping in walked a man and woman with two boys followed by Admiral Mc Donald. Seeing John and me sleeping, the Admiral shooked our feet, and we both shot up awake. When my eyes cleared, I saw the other people in the room. "Peter, this is your family," said the Admiral.

I looked at them, and I could see their emotions were in turmoil, "You know we didn't name you Peter," said the one who was my father.

"It is my understanding you named me James or Jimmy."

"Do you know us?" my mother asked me.

I went over to my mother first and looked closely, then sniffed her and stepped back, then asked, "Have you been to Africa?"

"No."

"I remember a woman with a red African hat holding clothing."

She started laughing and said, "I use to wear a red hat like that to hang, clothing to dry."

I went next to my father, who I sniffed and grabbed a cigar out of his top pocket, and looked at it and said, "King Edward or Roi-Tan."

"Yes."

I then went behind my parents and looked at my brothers. I started getting dizzy, had flashes of pictures in my head, then everything went black, and I collapsed. John yelled, "Peter."

He ran to my side in tears, and I woke up as nurses and doctors ran into our room. My family stepped out into the hallway with the Admiral. "I'm alright, John." With John's help, I stood up and looked for my family. "Where is my family?" I asked.

"In the hallway," the doctor said.

I went out there and said, "Please come in." Then I told the nurses, I don't need you right now, and after giving me a quick look over, they left. I went over to my brothers and said, pointing to the bigger one, "You dropped a toilet seat on me and caused me to bleed."

"Your name is David." He was giggling and said, "Yes."

I looked at Jerry, who was acting shy, and said, "Don't be nervous, Jerry, I won't hurt you."

I looked at all of them and said, "Small things are coming back to me, but I have to tell you it may be some time before I can remember everything." "I assume the Admiral told you about John." "He is my brother; that will never change, and if you want me to go with you, you will have to adopt John too and love him as much as you do me." "If you don't or can't, then I am as dead to you as you thought I was."

"You don't give us much as a choice adopting and raising another boy is very expensive," said my mother.

John and I giggled, and I said, "John and I are giggling because our wealth is greater than you could understand." "Look, if you don't want us, that is alright; we can live by ourselves; we don't need an adult."

"No, we will take care of both of you," said my father.

"No, you don't understand; you all have to agree; I won't live in a house with animosity in it." "I would suggest you go back home and talk about this."

"Alright."

"I would like you all to stay and talk with our solicitors."

"What's a solicitor?" asked my father.

"It's British for a lawyer, Sir," said Admiral Mc Donald.

"Alright, we will stay; when will they be here?"

"About ten minutes."

I could see my mother was uptight and didn't want to be here. I didn't know if it was just John or both of us, but it didn't make any difference. My parents went out into the hallway, and David came over to me and said, "Don't worry about your mother; she will come around; she just has to get used to you again."

"She may not have to; John and I are a package deal; if she can't get comfortable with us, then we will go back to Neverland or our estate in England," I said.

"Where is Neverland?"

I looked at John, smiled, and said, "Second star on the right and all the way till midnight."

He shook his head and went out to the hallway soon after the Admiral came in and said, "John Peter, we are going down to a conference room; come with us."

We went on a different floor then into a conference room and joined our solicitors who were already there. After introductions, the solicitors asked, "What is it you want us to negotiate."

"We have a list of things," said John. "We both want dual citizenship in the United States and Great Britain." "We will allow both countries to be a protectorate of Neverland, but the people of Neverland and we have total control of the country."

"There are people in Neverland?" asked Mr. Bryant.

"Yes, they are not human, but they are sentient and very intelligent," I said.

"We want a price for the knowledge we have, not too much, but something also a royalty and rights to use and have any items we let them buy," said John.

We talked to the solicitors for some time and told them to add anything that would benefit John and me. Then I asked my parents, "From what has gotten said to the solicitors, do you think it was good, and would you add anything else?"

My father answered and said, "Everything sounds good; I can't think of anything else to add."

"I think it would be better if you let us deal with the government officials, and then we will report back to you for your approval," said Mr. Greenfield.

"Alright," John and I said.

As we left, I said to my parents, "I guess we will hear from you in a few days?"

"Yes," my father said.

"Then goodbye," both John and I said.

John and I went back to our room and hopped up on the bed. We were silent for several minutes, then John said, "I'm not sure even if your parents want us."

"I know what you mean, John." I was quiet for a few seconds, then said, "Perhaps they acted the way they acted because they were shocked, confused, and disappointed at the sight of me."

"Perhaps."

The next day John and I felt melancholy over the previous day. We got taken on a trip to a residential neighborhood. And stopped in front of a house we got out, and a doctor said, "this is where you lived." I looked at the house and the one next door. Then I walked to the alley on the other side of the house, and I walked down it with John at my side. Tears fell from my eyes as I saw the school behind the house. I ran back out to the street and looked up the road, and started running as John ran with me. The doctors followed in the automobile. I came to a white house, stopped, and went up the steps to the front door and rang it. A lady came to the door, and I asked, "Is there a blond hair boy here about my age." To the door came a boy; I stared in shock and only got the name, "Charlie," out as I started crying again.

He stared at me and said, "Jimmy." "You're Jimmy Reno?"

"Yes."

His mother was standing there, and the doctors started to explain who I was. "Do you mind if they talk alone, it may help with his memory?"

"No, Charles can talk to him as long as he wants." John and I went into his backyard, and we talked for over an hour, and my memory was coming back. What was great Charles acted like I never was kidnaped, and I felt this love. We told him a lot about Neverland and sailing our ship and, of course, the Pongos. We also told him we would be back at the first chance we got. We had to leave, and we said our goodbyes and left.

In the afternoon, the next day, four men came into the room and said, "You two are Peter and John Hooker?"

"Yes," John said.

They grabbed our arms and told us to put our arms behind our back which we did, confused. They then place handcuffs on us, and I said, "Why are you doing this?"

"Shut up," they said. The men then took us out of the room and down the hall.

"Where are you taking us?" John asked.

"You will see when you get there."

"Does Admiral Mc Donald know about this?" I asked

"He is the one who told us to come and get you."

I looked at John and said, "Not now." As we left, the hospital doctors and nurses tried to stop these men from taking us, but the men showed their badges and brandished their pistoles. We got placed in a back vehicle, and they drove off.

It wasn't long when we came to a compound with a very high fence. I saw other children behind the fence and said to John in Pongo, "John look at that fence."

"I see it, Peter," John replied in Pongo. We came to the front of a large tan building with a sign next to it that read, San Leandro Juvenile

Detention Center, Alameda County, California. "This is a correctional institution for children, Peter," John said.

"Yes, I believe you're right." We came to a stop and were taken out of the automobiles rather roughly, then brought into the building. There standing in the large room amongst many guards was Mr. Jack Sonders of the F. B. I. with a snide smirk on his face.

"Well, boys, now we will do it my way." "You will answer all my questions starting with that ship of yours," Mister Sonder said threateningly.

"You have made a big mistake, Sir; you will get nothing out of us," I said. He slapped me on my face a couple of times, and I just smiled.

"You can't do that here," said a man in casual clothing.

"We can do anything we want; we are from the F. B. I.," said Mister Sonders annoyed.

"Not here, not with these boys," the man said.

"Lock them up then; I'll question them in a few days."

"What is their charge?"

"Enemy of the state."

"What, that's not a charge."

"I don't care, then failing to cooperate with the F. B. I." "They have information vital to the United States," said an infuriated Jack Sonders.

"Okay, how old are you, boys."

"Twelve," said John.

"We can put them in pod four," said a guard.

"No," said Jack Sonders. "Put them with the teenagers."

"They will be hurt there," said the man in casual clothing.

"They will answer my question quickly, then won't they." "Put them with the teenagers."

"What do we have with the teenagers?"

"Pod six, Sir."

"If they leave that pod, make sure they have handcuffs on, understand," said Mister Sonders.

"We know what we need to do."

"Have fun, boys," said a sarcastic Mister Sonders. We got taken to a room, and our handcuffs got removed. Then we got told to strip out of our clothing, and we got some underclothing and warm grey pants, and a shirt. We got some sandals and stockings which we hated. They gave us a sack full of more clothing, blankets, sheets, and hygiene.

We got taken down several halls accompanied by four guards and the man in the casual clothing who said, "I don't want to lock you boys up, but I don't have a choice." We didn't say anything but gave him a disbelieving look. We passed a window to that yard with the high fence, and the same man noticed us looking and said, "You will be able to go out there tomorrow, boys." We both smiled, and we finally came to a room with many older boys in it. "Just keep to yourselves and don't mix with those boys." "If they bother you, let us know, and they will get punished."

"We can take care of ourselves," I said.

We went in, and the man yelled, "Listen up, you are to leave these two boys alone." "You bother them; you will answer to me."

He then nodded to a guard, and the guard said, "Boys in room seven and nine, come here." They came, and the guard said, "Stockwell, you're moving into cell nine with Parker; clean your cell out of your things, Stockwell." He wasn't happy but did as he got told, and we went into the cell.

EIGHT

ESCAPE TO NEVERLAND

WE SAT ON THE bottom bed and looked at each other, and John said, "Are you alright, Peter?"

"Speak, Pongo; I'm fine but angry."

"What are we going to do?"

"When we go to that yard, we will scale that fence and escape."

"Hey, come to the door," said some boy. We got up and walked to the door, and that same boy asked, "How old are you?"

"Twelve," said John.

"Why are you here?"

"Does it matter; we are here; what does it matter," I said.

"It matters according to what you did to get in here."

I looked at John, sighed, and said, "The F. B. I. want some information from us, and they feel if they put us in here with all of you, it would scare us to tell them." He looked at us for a few seconds and left.

"I don't think he believes us, John."

"Yeah."

It was about four-thirty, our door popped open, and other boys lined up for dinner, so we joined them. We got eyeball by a lot of the other boys, but we ignored them. We found a table and sat down, and started to eat. Four boys came over to us, and one of them said, "Give up your cake." We both looked up and ignored them, which got us a slap to the head.

We didn't say anything but kept eating anyway, and they took the cake from our tray anyway. I said to John in Pongo, "Let them have it; it's better that they have it than get in trouble for hurting them, and we can't go outside."

"Alright, but I'm losing my patience."

"If they do one more thing we don't like, we will take care of them." "Just try to do it where the guards don't see it."

John smiled and said, "Yes."

We finished our meal, which wasn't very good, and put our tray away. As we were going back to our cell, a boy with black skin came up to us and said, "You need to tell the guards you need to be moved out of this pod before you get hurt." "Those four white boys mean to do bad things to both of you."

"We can't move from this pod the F. B. I. won't let the guards move us," John said.

"We can handle ourselves when we have to." "We would have done something to those boys." "We didn't because we didn't want to hurt them, and the guards wouldn't let us go out to the yard but thank you for telling us," I said.

"Why is that yard so important to you?" he asked.

"We plan to escape," John said.

He started to laugh and shook his head and said, "The only way to get out of that yard is to go over the fence." "If you tried, the guards would be on you before you got five feet."

We smiled, and he left laughing. We headed to our cell and got cut off just before we went in. "You two little shits need to go talk to my friends over by the shower, now."

We smiled, and I said to John in Pongo, "They are going to try something." "Be careful; the guards don't see you."

"Yes."

We walked down to the shower and waited to see what would happen. The boys threw John in one shower stall, pulled the curtain, and did the same to me in another shower stall. Two boys pulled down their pants and said, "You are going to do us both." I started laughing, and they grabbed me, and I grabbed them by the throat and threw both out of the shower stall, and they flew over the tables and into the glass window. John did the same with the same results, and we both walked down to our cell while everyone stared at us.

A bunch of guards came into the pod, yelling at everyone to get into their cells. They came into our cell and demanded to know what happened. John said, "They slipped on a bar of soap when wanting us to give them a bath."

"Give you a bath, you say?" "Let's not bathe with them anymore."

"I don't think they will want to bathe with us anymore," I said with a smile.

The guard left, and we went to bed sleeping together; the guards knew we were brothers and didn't bother us about sleeping together. The next morning, we showered, and no one bothered us, and when we ate, no one took anything from us. We had to wait until three in the afternoon to go outside. "I'm sorry, boys, but I have orders to handcuff you two." We nodded and presented our hands, and we got handcuffed.

Some of the boys watched as we were handcuffed but didn't say anything. When we went onto the grass, the boy with black skin came over to us and said, "Try climbing that fence with those cuffs on." We surveyed the fence and chose a place to go over the fence, and I turned my back to the guards, and John stood in front of me, and I grabbed his cuff and pulled the chain between them, and the cuffs broke apart. He did the same to me, and we could remove the rest of the cuffs off our wrists.

We looked up at the fence, and I said, "It looks like thirty-five forty meters high." "You think you can jump that high?"

"With no problem, Peter." We looked around; some of the other boys looked at us. The guards were smoking over by the door and carrying on a conversation.

"Let's go," I said.

We jumped and made it near the top of the fence. Without a problem, we were over the top and down the other side. The guards dropped their cigarettes and came running at the same time radioing for extra help. The other boys in the yard came running to the fence. Shortly after that, the guards were there, but all they saw was two boys running extraordinarily fast down the street; when the guards got to the street side of the fence, we were nowhere in sight.

We dashed in and out of cars as we went over or down streets. We headed north. We figured we had about thirty to forty-five minutes before the guards would inform other authorities of our escape and or would come after us. We ran down east fourteenth street and came to an apartment complex that we went into to rest. "John, no one will stop us from going back." "We will do everything and anything to stop them."

"I agree, Peter." We started running again down east fourteenth street; we could hear sirens as we went but didn't know if they were for us. As we ran down the road, we attracted many stares because we were two blond hair, white boys, and the speed we were traveling. Unfortunately, as we traveled, we passed a police station, and we got spotted; the police gave chase, but we left them in the dust. By the time they got their automobiles out, we were nowhere in sight. We got to twenty-eighth avenue, and we headed down it, and when we got to seventeenth street, we went down to the end of that street where there was a wooded brook. We went down and hid in the woods until it was dark.

"I think we will go now and see if Charles will come with us, John."

"Is it far, Peter?"

"No, but it is dark out, so we will have to go slow." We found his home, and John and I hopped the fence and made our way to the main house through his backyard.

As Charles's siblings grew, Charles moved downstairs, where there was a room with a bath. John and I looked through the window and seen Charles in there. So, we tapped on the window to get his attention. He spotted us and signaled to us to go around to the other side, to a washroom under his house.

He invited us into his room and asked, "What are you doing here?

"The authorities have mistreated us." "They locked us up at a juvenile detention center where we were maltreated, so we escaped," John said.

"Charles, we are going back to Neverland." "We want you to come with us," I said.

"I don't know." "I would have to talk to my parents."

"No, Charles, you can't tell them, they are good parents, but they will turn us over to the authorities."

"I don't think I can go."

"Charles, you don't have to stay there forever, just stay at least a week, and if you want to go back, then we will take you back," said John. Charles was having a struggle making up his mind.

"Charles, I would guess your parents are not wealthy?" I asked.

"No, my father works hard, but we don't have a lot of money."

"You come with us, and no one in your family will ever have to worry about money for the rest of their lives; John and I will make you very rich."

"You have that much money?"

"What John and I would give you; it won't even get noticed," John said.

"It's mostly in gold, silver, jewels, and other valuable things, so your family will never have to work; come with us."

"Why are you doing this for my family and me?"

"I love you, Charles; I thought you knew."

"And so, do I, even though I haven't known you as long," said John.

"I have feelings for the both of you too." "You said I could come back when I want?" We both nodded, and he thought for a moment, then said, "Alright, but I want to leave a note for my parents."

"That's alright with us," said John. He wrote a letter saying where he was going that would come back, and he would make them very rich. He changed out of his clothing, and about nine-thirty, at night, we headed to the brook.

We all hopped the fence, and I whispered to Charles, "We will follow this brook to the bay and then go to our ship; no talking unless you have to." "Charles, if you get tired, tell John or me, and we will rest."

"Okay." We headed out down the brook going through several tunnels. We had to take it slow because it was dark, and Charles couldn't go as fast as John and me.

After several hours we made it to the bay. We headed north after I whispered to John and Charles, "There are likely to be many more guards around the Black Pearl than there normally would be." "They will think that is where we are heading. "We must be extra careful and quiet." "Charles, we all are going to get wet, but not to worry, we can dry everything out."

"Alright." It took us several hours to get to the ship, and we quietly swam up to it, and I was able to drop a shield panel and climb up to the ship without being seen. I dropped a rope latter down to Charles, and with help, he climbed up to the deck, and I turned the shield back on. We went down below, and I told Charles to take off all his clothing and wrap himself in a blanket to keep warm and stay down below. John and I stripped naked, much to the shock of Charles, and went on deck. John went on to the dock and released the moorings, and when he pulled in the gangplank, he got noticed, and all hell broke loose. I had raised the anchor and started the engines while John raised the weapon systems, and we moved out as they shot at us. John took over the wheel and headed for the Golden Gate while I raised the sails. We weren't halfway to the Golden Gate when the Coast Guard came after us. They weren't able to catch us, but what I didn't know they tried to blockade the exit from the bay.

I yelled to John, "Give them a warning shot." He did that, and we scooted right between them and out into the ocean. We went west for about five hours, then headed south, heading to the island of Jicarita off Panama to pick up supplies.

When we were off the coast of Mexico, John said, "Peter, if you want to go below and get some rest go ahead; I'll watch the sonar and radar."

"Alright, John, I'll fix something to eat before I relieve you." "If you get tired, let me know, and I will relieve you."

"Alright." I went down below, and I saw that Charles was sleeping on the bed. I got some water to drink, crawled into bed, kissed Charles, who stirred, then laid down, and went to sleep. I don't know how many hours I was asleep, but I woke because of Charles's stirring. "Did you get enough sleep, Charles?"

"Yes."

"Good, are you hungry?"

"Yes, a little." "Where are we?"

"We are most likely off the coast of Mexico." "I'll get busy cooking, and we can eat." At that, I got up, and he stared at me because I was naked.

"Don't you and John wear clothing?"

"No, why should we; it's hot outside."

Just then, he was about to get up but remembered he had nothing on himself. "Where are my clothes?"

"I don't know; why do you want them?"

"Well, I'm used to wearing clothing."

"It's best that you don't." "Are you bashful?" "You look no different than me, and we slept together." "If I remember right before I got kidnapped, I saw you with nothing on." He didn't say anything, so I added, "I know you feel awkward, but after a few hours, you won't, but if you still want your clothing, I'll find them for you." "I love you." "I don't want you to feel uncomfortable." He had his head down for a few minutes, then threw the blanket aside and got up. I looked at him and said, "You look normal to me."

"Did you kiss me before you went to sleep?"

"Yes."

He was quiet for a few seconds, then said, "That was nice of you."

I smiled and said, "John and I kiss each other all the time."

"Do you want me to help you?"

"Yes, that would be helpful."

"What are you cooking?"

"Soup and sandwiches." "John or I would cook something fancier, but we are both tired." We cooked and set the table and got ready to eat, and I asked, "Charles do you want to drink wine?"

"Real wine?"

"Yes."

"No, I don't drink wine."

"Alright, we will have tea and biscuits."

We ate, and just about halfway through our meal, he said, "I thought you said we were going to have tea and biscuits?"

I smiled and said, "I forgot biscuits are cookies to me, and after dinner, John will get them for you." "Would you bring me some on deck?"

"Yes."

"Good, I'm going on the deck to relieve John." "Will you help him clean up too?"

"Yes."

I went on deck and asked John, "Are you tired?'

"Yes."

"There is food down there." "Would you make some tea and bring out biscuits."

"Yes."

"Charles will help you clean up, and he will bring me some tea and biscuits."

"Good."

"He doesn't have anything on; he is still having a hard time getting used to it."

John giggled and said, "He shouldn't wear anything; it's going to get too hot."

"Yeah." "You have any problems?"

"No, but I know they are searching for us."

I nodded and said, "You better get something to eat and get some sleep." He nodded and went down below.

About an hour later, Charles came on deck with tea and biscuits. I locked the ship's wheel after I checked for any nearby ships. Then I had some tea and biscuits while Charles asked, "How much longer is it going to take to get to where we are going?"

"We should be there tomorrow, but we will only stay until we load this ship."

"I wonder if my parents saw my note yet?" "If they had, I wonder if they are upset?"

"I would think so, and I would think they would be upset, but they will be happy when they see all that money they will have."

"I hope they don't get too mad at me."

"If they get mad, it will be the mad, that means they love you."

"I suppose."

"After you go back, they will think of it as you went to summer camp."

"I guess they would." He smiled then and said, "They will most likely be madder at you and John than me."

"Yeah." I had one more cup of tea and a biscuit and went back to steering the ship. I had noticed that Charles, who was next to the ship rail, was acting like he had to relieve himself. "Charles, come here." Charles came to me, and I said, "Do you have to relieve yourself?"

"Huh?"

"Do you have to use the loo?" "I mean the toilet."

"Yes, I do."

"It's a little different on the ship." I locked the wheel, and we went to the ship's bow, and I showed him. He wasn't too happy, but he went, and

I said, "We have a regular toilet down below, but we don't use it unless it is bad weather."

"What do you use on Neverland?"

"That depends if we are in the Jungle or at the Pongo village, we dig a hole and go and wash ourselves down at the river." "We do have facilities much as you have at your home." About six hours into my shift, I noticed a ship getting too close for my comfort. I started the engines and slightly changed course. I kept an eye on the ship to see if it got any nearer, but it didn't, and it finally faded from the ship's radar.

Charles had gone below little more than an hour ago, and it had been more than nine hours since I started my shift when Charles came on deck and said, "John got up late and made dinner." "He; said he was sorry." "He will relieve you when he got finished eating." "Are you mad?"

I looked at Charles, surprised he asked, and I said, "No, why would you say that?" "I love John."

"I thought you would be mad because of the way you look."

"No, I'm just tired." "What did John make for dinner?"

"Pork chops, they were good." "Had wine, too; I don't care for it." I giggled, and after a short time, Charles went down below, and about fifteen minutes later, John came on deck.

"Keep your eye on other ships; one got uncomfortably close, so I started the engines."

"We should be at Jicarita about sunrise," John said.

"Yes, we will only stay long enough to rest and load the ship." John nodded, and I went down below.

I was asleep for about seven hours when John came on the speaker and said, "Land ho." I got up, and as did Charles, and we went on deck. Charles and I relieved ourselves; I climbed up to the crow's nest and yelled, come two points starboard and hold it there."

"Aye, Aye," John replied.

I swung down and joined John. "There should be a wide channel between the two islands; there should be a place to hide when we get there."

"Do you want to take the wheel while I go to the bow and watch?" asked John.

"Sure, but drop the sails first; we will go in using the engines."

"Alright."

Charles came over to me and asked, "You think there are any people there."

"No, we don't go into port if there are people." I smiled and said, "If there were any people, we still wouldn't be wearing any clothing." "Besides, we threw your clothing overboard some time back." Charles gave me a shocked looked, and I laughed. In about forty-five minutes, I cut the engines, and John dropped anchor.

Charles asked, "When are we going on the island?"

"After we eat and sleep and check for any other ships near," John said. We were all eating breakfast when John said, "I love how Charles is funny."

"Yes, he puts a smile on my face all the time." Charles's face blushed, and I put my arm around him.

Before we all went to bed to sleep, Charles asked, "If we all sleep at the same time, how will you know if a ship approaches?"

"The radar and sonar are left on; if a ship is within a hundred miles, a loud alarm will go off," I said. After about six hours, Charles was the first one up; then, I got up, letting John sleep. Charles and I were on the deck, getting the skiff ready and a floatable raft to go onshore. After we got the skiff and raft ready, we went down below and cooked. It was too late after dinner to go to the island, so we decided to go the next morning. After an early breakfast, we all loaded up in the skiff and headed to the beach with a device that will tell us where the supplies were. The same device opened the concealed doors, and we started loading the skiff and raft. We found our supplies, and it took us nine trips to the ship to get everything on deck.

Charles and I walked on the beach while John stayed on the ship. "Where do we go to next?" asked Charles.

"The island of Fernandia for more supplies, and after we load the supplies, we head to Neverland." "We may stay a couple of days to rest; it has more protection than this place."

"How far is it?"

"About a thousand miles, we should be there in one day."

"Tell me about Neverland."

I smiled and said, "Neverland is a large island." "It got discovered centuries ago; no one thought it was of any worth, and it had no access to the island, but they were wrong." "It got discovered years before anyone by a Hooker ancestor, and he found a way to the island." "It has a reef around the island and man-eating sharks on the ocean side of the reef but none on the island side." "A strange fog bank also surrounds the island." "It's off the main shipping routes and all but forgotten by all nations." "Everything else about the island, I want it to be a surprise for you." We fooled around on the beach for a while and then went back to the ship. We all moved the supplies into the cargo hold; then I made dinner, we ate, cleaned up, and went on deck until late. We stayed another day to rest and checked out the ship, and then we left for Fernandia.

I was at the wheel when I spotted the island, and everyone came on deck. "This island is completely different than Jicarita," said John. Jicarita was tropical, where Fernandia is volcanic.

"Yes, and a couple of those volcanos are active," I said. "I hope we had enough rest because I don't want to stay here long."

"I agree," said John.

"It smells too," said Charles. "It must be sulfur or something."

"Yes, well, we can pass gas, and no one will notice," I said with a smile.

After checking if anyone was around, we went onshore. It took some time to find the supplies because they got covered with a thin coat of lava, but we were able, with some effort, to open the doors. It took us more than twelve hours to bring everything on board. What we couldn't store in the cargo hold, we lash it to the deck with a water-resistant tarp on it. We don't know how it happened, perhaps when we were busy with the cargo, but we got spotted. "John, Charles, we better get out of here."

"You're right, Peter, let's raise the sail and go," said John.

We had just raised the anchor and got the sails up when two jets flew over our ship, circled, and flew back over. We turned on our engines and went out into the sea. We raised our, weapons and I yelled to Charles, "Charles get below; it's going to get nasty." Just then, an Ecuadorian patrol ship came after us, followed by a helicopter. We raised shields and, on our radio, came someone speaking in Spanish. "No, hablo Español," I said.

In broken English, he said, "Stop boat, we come on."

"No," I said.

There was nothing for a few seconds, then he said, "You in our water; we shoot if no stop."

"No, you shoot, we shoot." The Ecuadorian ship fired at the stern of our ship, I assume, for a warning shot, but some of their rounds hit our shields. John fired a round over their bow, and they swerved out of the way.

A radio message came over the radio in English, "Black Pearl, this is the United States Cruiser Leahy stop your shooting."

"Cruiser Leahy, if we are fire upon, we will fire back." We were fired upon by the helicopter, and John knocked it out of the sky. The cruiser said something in Spanish; I assume for them not to fire on us. It didn't work because two Ecuadorian jets fired on us, and we knock them out of the sky. The patrol ship didn't try to follow us, opting to pick up the men from the aircraft. The American ship which came into sight said, "Black Pearl, do you have a Charles Kahler on board?"

"Cruiser Leahy, yes, we do."

"We want him; his parents want him back."

"No, tell his parents if he wants to go home after he gets to Neverland, we will get him home."

"Kidnapping is a serious charge; can we talk to him?"

"One-moment Cruiser Leahy."

"Charles, come on deck." "We never kidnap Charles, Leahy he came with us with his own free will."

Charles came on deck, and I gave him the microphone. "Hello, this is Charles Kahler."

"Charles, this is the Cruiser Leahy." "Did you volunteer to go with them?"

"Yes."

"How is your health?"

"I feel better now than before."

"Your parents want you back."

"I know; tell them I will be coming back."

"Black Pearl, is Peter available?"

"This is Peter."

"Peter Admiral Mc Donald wanted you to know that he had nothing to do with your and John's arrest." "He said Mister Sonders of the F. B. I. and some of his men have gotten arrested." "He wants you to come back."

"Cruiser Leahy, tell the Admiral no for now; John and I will have to think about it." "We have been treated poorly and not taken seriously."

"Also, my parents are having too much of a hard time deciding about John and me."

"You and John will have a problem with Ecuador because of what happened."

"Cruiser Leahy, they attacked us; we don't worry about them." "This will be our last transmission until we want to talk to the United States and Britain again." I stayed at the wheel another six hours before I was relieved by John. John and I decided that we would not stop to rest at any other island but push it to Neverland.

I was at the wheel one afternoon when Charles wasn't on the deck for the last two days, he was reticent, and I knew something was on his mind. Charles was to the left of me when I said, "What's wrong, Charles?" "You have been quiet for the last two days."

"I'm just thinking about things."

"Your parents." He nodded, and I said, "I'm sure once you get to Neverland, you will feel better."

"Maybe."

"You know that John and I love you and would never do anything to hurt you."

"Yes, I know this." "Do you think I can steer this ship?"

The seas weren't stormy, so I decided to see if he could handle the wheel. "Alright, but it is harder than it looks, so I will stay with you just in case you have a hard time." He grabbed the wheel, and he was surprised how the wheel put a lot of stress on his arms.

After ten minutes, he looked at me and said, "This steering makes your arms tired."

I took the wheel back and said, "That is why we rest as long as we do when we are dock." "You did do very well, though, for your first time."

"I was only steering for a short time."

"You must remember John and I were enhanced, and we have been steering this ship for a long time."

We were on the seas for three more days, and on the morning of the third day, John yelled down from the crow's nest, "Fogbank, to the bow."

Charles walked to the bow to take a look while I yelled to John, "Drop sails." He swung into the sails and started tying them up. Then he swung down and put them away.

After he finished, he joined Charles at the bow to watch for rocks. I had turned on the engines about two miles from the fogbank, and I could see Charles was getting excited.

After we entered the fog, Charles was getting impatient, waiting to get through the fog, and he came over to me, saying, "How much longer we will be in this fog?"

I pointed to the bow and said, "Do you see it getting lighter." He ran to the bow, and we popped out of the fog, and I turned to the port side, going around the island. I saw that Charles was disappointed at what the island looked like, and I had to laugh.

He came over to me, disappointed, and said, "Neverland isn't what I expected."

I giggled and said, "I felt the same way, but this island is more than what you see." I could see he didn't understand, and when I saw the horns on the ridge, I swung the ship starboard side and lined the ship on the horns. "Charles, do you see on the ridge that it looks like two horns up there."

"Yes."

"We go right between those horns, and we will go down the channel in the reef." "If you look in the water on either side of the ship, you will see the sharks." He did, and he was fascinated by what he saw. We got through the channel, and I turned the port side and continued around the island. He came and stood by me, and I said, "Watch what happens." I turned the ship starboard and entered the river that went to the inner bay and our dock. Charles was totally in awe at the changing landscape.

"Then he spotted the Pongos, and he pointed to them while saying, "Peter, are those Pongos?"

"Yes." We entered our bay and headed to the dock. John dropped anchor and then Jumped on the pier, and I threw him the mooring ropes.

NINE

DIVULGENCE

WE UNLOADED ALL THE supplies and brought them up to the house to get stored in the warehouses. We then cleaned the ship and secured it after we checked out the hull. John and I showed Charles the house, and he was impressed; then, I told him, "We will show you the rest of the compound tomorrow morning."

"When am I going to meet the Pongos?"

I smiled and looked at John, and John said, "There are things about the Pongos you need to be informed about; we will take you to the village in a few days." We all fixed something simple for lunch and dinner and went into the sitting room after cleaning up.

John looked over to me to do the talking about the Pongos. "Charles, I am going to tell you about the Pongos." "The Pongos are not homo sapiens like us, but they are sentient sapiens."

"I don't understand," said Charles.

"If an alien from another planet came to earth, they would be sentient sapiens."

"Are the Pongos from another planet?"

"We don't know." "We do believe that they are not native to Neverland but came to Neverland by a Hooker ancestor perhaps hundreds of years ago from South America." "Charles, you need to know the females, and at times the males are amorous."

"What does amorous mean?"

"They are affectionate; they may try to mate with you."

A shocked Charles said, "I'm too young for that."

"So were we," said John.

"It doesn't happen all the time," I said.

"What happens when they find out I can't do anything?"

"They will still try."

"Why would an adult Pongo try?"

"I'm not talking about an adult Pongo." "The Pongo can have babies at a very young age younger than us." "Having relations is common to them."

"Can a human mate with them and have a child?"

"I don't know and don't want to find out."

"How do you and John handle it?"

"We just let them do what they want; we can't have babies yet."

"It won't be long when you can." "I thought you are their leader; why don't you just make it a law not to do this."

"I'm afraid a law like that might disrupt the population of the Pongo." "We don't have to worry about it for a while." "Maybe I can come up with something else by then." John and I told him about all the different animals and plants that most thought were extinct but aren't. When it was time for bed, I said to Charles, "John and I prefer sleeping together." "You can sleep with us if you want, you're like a brother anyway, or you can have your bed."

Charles thought for a minute, then said, "I like sleeping with both of you."

The next morning, we stored our supplies in one of our warehouses. Then John said, "Let's show you the rest of the compound, Charles."

The first cave we went into was the precious metals, minerals, and jewels cave. Charles was shocked at what we had. We went into the next cave, which was paintings, books, and sculptures, and again he was surprised at what we had. The next cave had documents, scrolls, tablets, writings, and other things from antiquity. We explained to Charles that many of the books in the library are signed first editions. Inside the lab was an underground vault with all discoveries and inventions since the first Hooker. At the last cave, I told Charles, "We won't be going into this cave; there were toxic materials in them that you had to wear special protection to enter."

"What are they for?"

"Weapons, energy, medical purposes, and other things."

The next day I was making dinner when Charles came running into the kitchen, "Peter, there is something wrong with John."

"What's wrong?"

"He's crying in the library."

I dropped what I was doing and went to the library and found John at a computer crying. "What is wrong, John?" "Why are you crying?"

He looked up at me and said, "I remember who I am." I picked him up and started kissing him, and I took him to the sitting room and held him tight. What surprised me, Charles got on the other side of him and tried to comfort him. He cried for about forty-five minutes more, then Charles and I were able to calm him down.

"John, I'm hurting too." "As time goes on, that pain becomes less." "You must keep telling yourself that I love you and now by Charles; you're not alone." He laid his head on my chest, and Charles and I wrapped our arms around him.

After dinner, we all sat in the sitting room, and Charles said to both John and me, "Do either of you want to be called by your real name?"

"It doesn't matter to me; call me what you want," I said.

"But if someone asked you who you are, what will you say?"

"I'm comfortable with Peter, and everyone calls me Peter, so I guess Peter."

"What about you, John?" I asked.

"I feel the same as you, Peter." "I suppose if someone always calls me William, I would change it."

"I think I would change it too," I said.

We didn't do much the next day, but we went swimming in the bay and sunned ourselves in a grass patch. We were all cuddled up in the bed at night when John and I were woken by Charles screaming. John and I shot out of bed; it was Kuna, an elder of the Kelpie. "Kuna, why are you here?"

"Your brother Tox was killed by the hand of three Migos." "When this happened, your mother collapse; she is dying." "We sent out a war party and found those foul people, and we killed them."

"John, I'm going through the trees; take Charles down the path, please."

"Alright, Peter." John told Charles what happened as we left.

When Kuna and I got to the village, we went right to mother's hut where there were people outside, and I went in; mother was lying down, and next to her was Tinker with two other women. I kneeled next to her and said, "Mother, it's Peter."

"Peter, I hoped you would come, and where is John?"

"He shall be here shortly; he is walking here with our new brother Charles."

"Charles, is he like you and John?"

"Yes."

"You know about Tox?"

"Yes, it saddens me." "Why are you ill, mother?"

"The loss of Tox is too much for me."

"You have John and me, and if you want, Charles will be your son too."

"I know I do, and I love you and John very much, and I would love your new brother Charles too." "You must understand you and your brothers are not from me, Tox was, and I am too old to have another from me." I held her hand until John and Charles showed, and John knelt beside her while Charles stood. I translated what was getting said between sniffles.

Mother felt John's face as tears fell from his eyes. "John, I love you and your brothers, do not be sad for me."

"I do not want you to die, mother."

"We all die; it is my time." She looked at Charles and said, "Come near me, Charles."

I told Charles what she said, and he knelt next to her, and I knelt next to Charles. "Charles, you are very much like your brother's." "I would love you too and adopt you too if I could." When I translated what mother said, Charles, whose eyes were already tearing, lost it. We were with mother for a long time, and about sunrise, the whole village must have felt her death coming because they started a rhythmic chant, even those inside her hut were chanting.

John and I've heard this chant before. It wasn't long after the chanting started, mother's eyes opened wide, and she looked at all three of us and closed them for the last time. All three of us hugged and kissed her and left the hut while the women prepared her for burial. The burial was much like fathers with flowers that smelled like Neverland. They also carried her up to the mountain's ridged to a cave for Pongos. They laid her next to Tox as our father got laid next to our ancestors. John, Charles, and I followed them up the mountain and into the cave and said our last goodbye. When we got are back to the village, I told Kuna, "The elders need to pick another for the council."

"Yes, we have chosen Filtra to take your mother's place."

"I wish to meet with the council tonight." He nodded and left.

All three of us were quietly sitting at the riverbank, sad over what happened. Tinker came over to me and grabbed my hand; she wanted me to go with her. We went into the forest. I know what she wanted, and sure enough, we fooled around. We were there for a while when we headed back to the village, we saw Charles with a Pongo female, and it was funny seeing him struggle. John was nowhere in sight, and I figured he was with another Pongo. I talked to an elder, getting ready to meet with the rest of the elders when John came into the village and joined me. John and I sat down where the meeting was going to get held, and we spotted Charles coming towards us, stumbling as he approached, and we laughed. He sat next to me, and I asked, "Did you have fun?"

"Yes, I think so." We laughed again, and finally, all the elders came.

"Peter, why have you called us together?" asked elder Kuna.

"I want runners sent to every village." "Villages are to send two people representing their village to live here." "You are to pick two to represent this village too." "When all are here, come and get me."

"Why do you want this? An elder asked.

"I do this to stop what happened to my brother to happen to someone else." "Also, it is not right to lead the Pongo because I am not Pongo, and I am not here enough; we must discuss this."

"We will send out runners tomorrow morning."

We headed back to our house, teasing Charles all the way. We were at our home three days when word got to me to meet with the elders. We all went to the village. While I was with the elders and the villages' representatives, John and Charles disappeared with some Pongos. "Each village will have its elders to say what happens to their village." "The representatives will decide what will happen with all Pongos and will punish those who don't follow your laws." "You will pick who will lead you by a vote of all pongo; I cannot lead you no more." "I do want to be able to be heard amongst your elders."

There was much talk between the elders and representatives that went on for hours. Finally, they came to an agreement, and they turned to me and said, "Is this alright with you, Peter?"

"It isn't up to me for it to be alright; it is up to all of you." They all talked amongst themselves and agreed it would get done as they said. The meeting broke up, and I walked over to the river.

"It wasn't long before Tinker came to me, and we walked off toward the forest."

We stayed overnight and headed back to the house. We had been at the house for about three weeks, and at dinner, Charles said, "I think it is time to go home."

John and I looked at him; we felt crushed, but John said, "I think we should talk about this after dinner in the sitting room; Peter, there are things I have troubles with too."

I looked at both of them and said, "Alright, I'm troubled about things also."

After dinner, we all met in the sitting room; I looked at John to say what he wanted to say. "We said Charles could go back anytime he wanted, so if he wants to go back, he should."

"Do you want to go back, Charles?" I asked.

"Part of me says no, part of me says I should, and that side is a bit stronger."

"The trouble is if we take him back to Oakland, they will arrest us, and I sure you and I will get in a fight with the authorities someone would likely get killed," said John.

"You're right, John," I said.

"Then what are you going to do?" asked Charles.

"We could drop him off in another country and inform the authorities he is there," said John. I struggled with this whole conversation about him leaving and staying, and both John and Charles notice.

"Something is bothering you, isn't it, Peter?"

"Yes." I was quiet for a bit, then I said, "I don't want to see Charles go; I love you, Charles." "I also know if Charles wants to go then, he needs to go." "When he goes, where does that leave us." "Mother and Tox are gone, and I don't lead the Pongo anymore."

"We have Tinker and U'i," said John.

"They want to mate; you know soon we will be able to, and we mustn't, so they will take another."

"Yes, your right," John said. "There are also many other problems."

"Like what?" I asked.

"I am losing interest in Neverland, and I believe you are too." "We don't study anymore." "There is going to be a time when we will need more supplies." "I think we have ten years or less when other countries will discover Neverland." "And in the meantime, what happens if we get sick or injured." "Father was the one who knew medicine, not us." "Then there is the problem with Charles not only getting him home giving him and his family money."

"Everything you said is true." "I feel much as I did when our father died, and we went back to the United States." "You know this could be a good thing for everyone, but we must be smart about it," I said, a bit more optimistic.

"I don't understand?" said Charles.

"Neither do I," said John.

"We can go back and make a life for all of us, but not the way we did last time."

"What do you have in mind, Peter?" asked John.

"I don't trust any one country, especially the United States." "As a whole, one country will make the other country abide by the agreement we will get." "I feel we need to bring in a third country, perhaps Australia or New Zealand." "I think we will bring everyone to Neverland that includes our families." "In that way, the government people will take us seriously." "We will know if my birth parents will accept both of us, and Charles's family perhaps won't be as angry with Charles or you and me." "We can also bring in people who will take care of the Pongo, such as Jane Goodall and other scientists who will protect all of Neverland." "We will have to come up with the details before we do something, but what do you both think?"

"I think it will work, Peter, at least better than before," said John

"It sounds good to me," said Charles.

"It may take a little time to get everything organized before we can get everything done," I said.

"How long?" asked Charles.

"Maybe a week, then the time to get everyone here."

"That's alright; when do we start?" asked Charles and John.

"Now," I said. We worked late into the night, only stopping to eat or relieve ourselves. We continued to work the next day; we wanted to make no mistakes this time. That night, we thought we had a good plan and decided to set everything up the next day.

We set up the cameras so that we can transmit to Australia that night. "They will see us naked," said Charles, concerned.

"Does it make a difference to those who see you?" "Those who you don't know you will never see again." "Those that you know, such as your family, has seen you with nothing on." "Even my parents had seen you with nothing on when we were little." "Besides, after a short time, they won't remember how you are."

"I guess you're right," Charles said, not so happy. "Why are we going to transmit at night?"

"Because if they see the plants, they may be able to find us, and I'm not ready for them to find us yet."

"Peter, it is several hours till dark." "I feel we should use the telephone link instead of cameras at least until we talk to the British and American ambassadors," John said.

I thought about it for a few seconds and said, "You're right, John let's set it up."

"How long will this take?" asked Charles.

"About ten minutes," replied John.

Our computer had the telephone number of Australia's prime minister, so we called it again by bouncing a signal off the moon. "Prime Minister Robert Menzies office Henrietta Mayfield speaking."

"Hello, this is Peter the Pan Hooker, John Hooker, and Charles Kahler speaking." "I wish to speak to the Prime Minister, please," I said.

"Is this a joke, young man; you could get into big trouble?"

"No, this is no joke; please don't make the same mistake Britain and America made, madam," John said.

"Hold on, let me talk to his aid."

She was gone for a few minutes when a man answered and said, "Who is this?" "I am Clarence Barkly, the Prime Minister's aid."

"I'm Peter the Pan Hooker; I'm with John Hooker and Charles Kahler." "As I've told the Prime Minister's secretary, don't make the same mistake as the British and Americans did; get us the Prime Minister."

"First, tell me your birth names, so we know this isn't a crank call."

"I'm sure you have tried to trace this call you won't be able to, but my name was James Reno, my brother John was William Clearfield, and I'm using Charles Kahler's real name."

"Wait a moment; I will get the Prime Minister."

We waited for about five minutes; finally, a man came on the telephone and said, "This is Prime Minister Robert Menzies."

"We are voice checking you, Prime Minister, and you check out." "I am Peter the Pan Hooker; we wish to negotiate a deal with the United States, Britain, and Australia." "Through the ambassadors of Britain and the United States with you representing Australia."

"Let me talk to Charles Kahler first."

"He can hear you talk."

"Charles, is he telling the truth?"

"Yes, Peter and John never lie; you can trust him."

"Okay, Peter, I just wanted to see if Charles had an American accent." "What do you want me to do, and what does Australia get out of it?"

"There will be three meetings; this is the first meeting." "For the next meeting, I wish you to find a large secured room that can accommodate a large number of people." "Then put a large screen television in it with an antenna and camera." "Let me know where it is, and we will transmit a live picture of us to you and the ambassadors." "The last transmission will have all the people in that same room, and we will negotiate." "In doing this, Australia will reap some of the knowledge we have." "How much depends on your ability to negotiate with the other two nations."

"Alright, I will get the two ambassadors here tomorrow; how can I contact you, and is it alright if I and the others bring other people with them."

"You all can bring who you wish, and I will contact you at about ten a.m., and you can give us the location of the meeting goodbye."

We turned everything off, and John said, "That went fairly well."

"Yes," I said as Charles nodded.

The next day we called and got the same lady as before, "Prime Minister Robert Menzies office Henrietta Mayfield speaking."

"This is John Hooker." "I wish to speak to the Prime Minister."

"This is the Prime Minister."

"This is John, Sir."

"Give me the location of the meeting." He gave John the location, and I fed it to the computer and nodded to John. "Sir, how long will it take all to be there."

"About ten minutes John."

"We will give you thirty minutes; then, we will transmit."

"Very well, John."

Thirty minutes later, I had a remote control in my hand and started to transmit. We had blocked the window with tarps so they couldn't see outside when we could see a clear picture of the meeting room, and I assume they could see us. "Can you see and hear us?" I asked.

"Yes, we see you," said a man who looked like the Australian Prime Minister.

"Please introduce yourselves, and I will introduce us."

We all introduce ourselves, and the American Ambassador said, "So we know this is not a hoax; tell us what happened off the coast of Ecuador."

John and Charles looked at me, and I said, "Sir, our patience is starting to fray." "Let this be the last test as to who we are, or we won't negotiate with you but with the People Republic of China or/and the Union of Soviet Socialist Republic." "I believe you are talking about the downing of an Ecuadorian helicopter and two jets and our conversation with the American Cruiser Leahy."

"Alright, Peter, what do you want to talk about?" asked the American Ambassador.

"We don't wish to talk about anything to you." "Each one of you will bring to the next meeting Australia either the heads of your countries or someone who can decide for your country." "Failure to do this will mean we will go to another country." "Also, you will bring with you noted scientists of all fields, including Jane Goodall." "If she gives you trouble, tell her we can give her all research on Chimpanzees that would take a lifetime to go through." "Tell her what we have to offer her here will be even more interesting than her Chimpanzees." "You will contact

Charles's family and my immediate family and bring them all also to the next meeting." "We also want Admiral McDonald to be in the meeting." "Three of the most important people we want at the meeting are Miss Witherspoon and Mr. Greenfield, of Thomson Snell & Passmore of England." "Also, Jack Bryant, they are our solicitors." "John, Charles, do you want to add anyone?"

Charles shook his head no, but John said, "You should ask our solicitors to bring an army of accountants and compilers of what we have." "We will pay all costs of what we want." "Everything else will get discussed at the next meeting. "How long will it take to arrange all of this?"

"It will take about three weeks."

"Good, we will contact Prime Minister Robert Menzies in about a week and a half." "Good-Bye," I said, and we cut the transmission.

"How do you think it went, and is the timeline alright, Charles?" I asked.

"I'm satisfied with everything," said Charles.

"It's fine with me, also Peter," said John. "We will have to contact the Pongos and let them know what is happening."

"Yes," I said as Charles shook his head in agreement.

Over the next few days, we let the Pongos know what we were up to; they were somewhat confused; they excepted what John and I said and would go along with what we wanted. At about a week and a half after the last meeting, we called Prime Minister Menzies. "Sir, has there been any progress to bring the people we requested to Australia?" I asked.

"Yes, all have agreed to come; they should start coming in about a week."

"Charles's family and my family too?"

"Yes, your mother doesn't like to travel by plane or boat; however, she is coming."

"Yes, I remember that." "What about heads of state?"

"Representatives from both countries will be coming." "I don't know who they will be yet."

"Have you heard from Jane Goodall yet?"

"Yes, she is coming."

"Do you have enough room for everyone in your conference room, Sir?"

"It will be a little crowded, but we do have enough room."

"Then, we will contact all of you on the twenty-seventh about this time."

"That would be fine, Peter." At that, we cut communication.

On the day of the video negotiation, we all bathed together, I wanted to swim in the bay, but John said we should jump into the tub. When we got out, we brushed our hair and checked each other to make sure we looked right. We sat on the couch, John, with the remote for the camera. We still had the windows covered for the time being. At ten-thirty, John turned on the camera, and everyone in the Australian conference room could see us, and we could see them. "Ladies and Gentlemen, I need to tell you all these negotiations and conversations are getting broadcast around the world." "Let me set a few ground rules that John, Charles, and I have agreed on." "Do not talk over us." "Some of you might get emotional; please don't; this is not the time or place." "Do not try to threaten us like what happen last time." "Don't bother lying; everything will be written down and sign, and as I told you, the world is listening." "Prime Minister Menzies would you be a mediator in these negotiations, so there isn't chaos," I said.

"Yes, I will do that."

"I see four groups here, our families, the scientist, our solicitors, and the government negotiators, which includes Admiral Mc Donald." "I don't see why we need everyone to have to be in these negotiations for hours; we will leave the governments and our solicitors for last." "When we get finished with you, you can enjoy Australia until you are brought to Neverland if the negotiations go well," said John. "Are there any questions about what I have said?"

"What if things don't go well?" asked Mr. Kahler, not too happy.

We looked at Charles, and he said, "I assume you are referring to me." "If things don't go well, John and Peter will find another way to send me home." "However, we are confident that negotiations will go well."

He sat down, not convinced, and I said, "We will start with the parents." "I've gotten elected to make an opening statement, and you may ask any question, but where we are." "I am Peter the Pan; you knew me as Jimmy or James, but I don't look like him, I don't think like him, and even my DNA has changed as it has with John." "Mr. and Mrs. Kahler, there is no reason to be angry with my parents, John, or me." "We did not kidnap Charles; we told him he could leave when he wanted." "We did offer him a ride to Neverland and more wealth than he and your family can understand." "There is no reason to be angry at my parents or John and me." "I am surprised that my family is here; John and my memory has come back." "John and I realize there will be bumpy roads ahead, and some are getting used to." "Do you wish to ask us any questions?"

"I would like to know why you don't have any clothing on?" asked Mrs. Kahler.

"We don't have clothing on because it is the custom here." "My clothing got destroyed getting here, and we have no clothing to wear." "I am comfortable without close; besides, you have all seen me without anything, even the Renos had seen me without me when I was in diapers." "Those I don't know I'll never see again, and most will forget about our nudity in a few months."

"You said you would get Charles back home if these negotiations don't go well; what about you and John?" asked my father.

"John and I haven't decided we will go with you." "You, being here, goes a long way in persuading us to go with you." "We will make that decision when we see you." "If negotiations don't go well, we can't go back to England or the United States; we would get arrested."

"Charles, how have you been treated?" asked Mrs. Kahler.

"I've been treated well, mom." "They had protected me whenever there was a danger." "John and Peter love me, and I love them and always will." "Everything they have told you is true; they don't lie."

"What did that man who kidnapped you do to you and John?" asked my mother.

"Ma, you don't want to know; it's too graphic to tell you at this time." "Wait until we see you, and you can examine us, and we will tell you." "Mrs. Kahler, we do love Charles very much to us; he is like our brother." There were no more questions, and I said, "If there are no more questions, then you may leave, or you can stay." "We will next talk to all the scientists, in particular Jane Goodall." "Do any of you have any questions?"

Jane Goodall got up and asked the first questions. "How much information do you have on the Chimpanzees and describe your Pongos?"

I looked at John, and John said, "Miss Goodall, you could spend the rest of your life studying Chimpanzees here and not be able to study everything." "I'm embarrass to say we don't have any photographs of the Pongos." "What I can tell you if you crossed a Chimpanzee with a human and the human part is more dominant, you would have a Pongo." "Most are about our size or smaller a few, maybe a couple of centimeters taller than us." "They are highly intelligent and sentient; they have a language."

"What do you want from me regarding the Pongos?" she asked.

"To protect our friends," I said.

The rest of the scientists asked many questions until one asked, "When will we be going to Neverland?"

"Everyone will come at the same time as everyone else." The scientists left the meeting, and I said, "The accountants and compilers are here to make an accounting of our great wealth and knowledge." "Unless you have any questions, you may leave this meeting." There were no questions, and they left. I saw my father and Mr. Kahler still at the meeting sitting next to each other. Also, I saw Miss Witherspoon, Mr. Greenfield, and Jack Bryant, our solicitors. "To our solicitors, you are here to protect us from arrest and any other legal trouble." "Also, to prove our sovereignty, then to get a great deal with the three governments in question." "I also wish to say we are all happy to see our fathers here and sitting next to each other." "To the three governments and Admiral Mc Donald because of what happen the last time, it won't be as cheap or as easy as before for you to get a deal." "We will negotiate, but we trust our solicitors more than we trust you." "We also wish to hear the feelings of our fathers; I include Mr. Kahler because Charles is part of this and will share in with our wealth also." So, it started the solicitors showed all the proof of Neverland and our status regarding England and the United States. The negotiations went on for more than three hours. The solicitors said it was a good deal, and our fathers were happy also.

John then said, "We are cutting transmission to the world as to where we are for security reasons." John looked at me, and I nodded; he continued, "We will need you to get a large enough cruise ship to bring everyone to our home." "You will need a transport to come into our port; your ships won't be able to drop anchor in our bay." "You will need to bring at least six cargo ships; perhaps more will get needed; you can determine that when you get here." "You will need enough tents, toilets, beds, and bedding for everyone." "We do have food, but we will need more because of the time you will be here and the number of people you have." "We have all the power you need, but we could use help to string power to all the tents." "We have room in our home for both of our families and maybe a few other people also." "You will need hazardous protection uniforms because one of our vaults has materials in them that are dangerous."

"What is in them that are dangerous?" asked Admiral Mc Donald.

"We have never gone in them, but I believe it has to do with radiation and chemical."

"Are they weapons?" he asked.

"We don't know." "If I had to guess, it is materials for medical, science, and possibly weapons too." "I know our weapons we do have are more than powerful to destroy the earth." "Now, this may concern you, but with our agreement, you will have control of them when we sign the agreement," I said.

John continued and said, "We will need a large naval force to protect our land and perhaps some ground troops too." "However, when you first come on our land, there will be no weapons until we sign the agreement." "We will talk to you about this when you get near us." "We are capable of knocking down any aircraft, blowing up any ship, or repel any invasion that gets thrown at us." "We will do just that if another country attacks us."

"We would prefer you tell us first," said the Admiral.

"We will, Sir," said John.

"How long will it take you to get everything together?" I asked

They all looked at each other and said after a few minutes, "About a week."

"Is that alright with you, dad, and Mr. Kahler?"

"Yes," they both said.

"Because of the large force that you are sending, we won't give you a straight route to our home." "You are to head west from Sydney; we will give you several course changes to get to us; we are doing this for security reasons."

"We understand," said the Australian Prime Minister. The meeting ended, and we shut everything down.

"I think everything has gone well," I said.

"I think so too," said Charles and John.

"I think we should take all the tents in the warehouse and set them up with beds and lights in them," said John.

"You're right, John, and maybe we need to set beds in the house also then decide who is going where."

"Yes," both John and Charles said. Over the next three days, we set everything up in the field next to the house. We also brought beds, linen, and blankets into the house. We had both our radar and sonar on around Neverland as far out as Sydney. It was a little more than a week when we saw a sizeable naval force leave Sydney.

A day after they left, we radio the fleet. "Neverland fleet, this is John Hooker, come to five points to portside." The fleet was moving at about seven knots an hour. We kept them on that course for two days, then we said, "Neverland fleet, this is Peter Hooker, come to three points portside." "Neverland fleet, can you go faster?"

"Peter Hooker, we can go about twenty knots."

"Speed up to twenty knots."

Four days later, we contacted them again and told them to go ten degrees portside. It was Charles who spotted other ships coming towards us. "Peter, John, something is coming towards us."

We all looked, and I said, "They are too far out to know just who they are." I pressed a button, and it showed when we had to act. "We have a few days yet; we will watch them in the meantime; we will talk to our fleet."

"Perhaps we should give them a more direct route Peter," said John.

"We might as well, especially if those other ships don't change direction," I said.

Two days later, we were able to identify the ships; they were Russian, two cruisers, two frigates, and an aircraft carrier. There was also a submarine that concerned us. "Neverland fleet come to three points starboard." "Neverland fleet, do you have a secure line?" I asked.

"Yes, we have just scrambled the signal."

"Get me your commanding officer; it's an emergency."

"Admiral Mc Donald here."

"Admiral Mc Donald, you are on a direct route to Neverland." "There is a large Russian fleet heading our way."

"Peter, can you give us the longitude and latitude?"

"Yes, one seventy-three degrees longitude and fourteen degrees latitude."

"We will do our best, Peter."

"Admiral, we have two lines, one for warning and one for an attack; if you can't get to them and they cross that second line, we will strike, and they will not survive."

"I understand." "How far away are the Russians from your first line?"

"At the speed, they are going a day or a day and a half."

"Peter, how far are we away from you?

"You have about three days of travel at speed you are traveling." "Sir, I have a strong feeling that there is someone amongst you feeding information to the Russians."

"Why do you think this?"

"Their movements are shadowing you." "Sir, we will keep communications open to you so you can hear what is going on with us."

"Alright, Peter."

We let the Pongos know what was happening. "Peter, I set up the voice translator to our computer," said John.

"Thank you, John."

"We can raise the weapons system and shields anytime you wish."

"Alright, John."

"I feel we should use a lightning bolt on the lead ship first." "Not as many will get killed if we use a less powerful weapon."

"I am concern about killing too many also, Peter," said Charles.

"Alright, we will try it your way; perhaps you're right; those sailors can't help it if they are from Russia," I said.

Three hours later, the lead ship, a cruiser, hit the warning line. "Russian cruiser, we can see your fleet, and you are entering Neverland waters change course due east or west," said John. There was no answer after five minutes, so John said, "Russian cruiser if you and your fleet do not change course, we will attack."

That got their attention, and they finally said, "We are in international waters; we do not recognize your right to these waters." "Besides, we do not listen to little children."

"Russian cruiser, we do not wish to kill you." "There are British, Australian, and American warships coming to protect us." "This is our last warning before we attack," said John.

"Raise shields and weapons," I said. Five minutes passed, and there was no answer or change in the direction of the ship. So, I said, "Target and fire on the lead ship." There was a thundering sound and a flash of light, and under two minutes, the Russian cruiser got hit in the bow section. All chaos broke out with the other ships, five Russian jets few off their aircraft carrier heading for us, and all five got shot down. "John, fire a lightning bolt into the aircraft carrier's bow." John did as I said, and the bow of the carrier got hit. The last thing the Russians did was fire a missile towards us from their submarine, but we could jam the missile controls, and it crashed into the ocean. John fired a low-yielding harpoon at the submarine, which fried their electronics, and it was disabled. The rest of the Russian fleet stopped coming towards us, and I radioed them, saying, "Russian fleet, I'm sorry for your losses, but you had gotten warned." "Any further aggression will get met with destruction." "The British, Australian, and American warships have gotten notified of your damage; they are the nearest ships to you."

Less than a minute later, they said, "Neverland, what you did is an act of war." "We have notified our authorities back in Russia."

"Russian fleet, we have broadcasted everything you and we said and the damage we did to your ships to the world, including Russia." "What we did to you was nothing compared to what we could do to Russia." "If your country attacks us, there will be no more Russia." We didn't hear any more from them, and I contacted the Neverland fleet. "Neverland fleet, did you hear what we had to do?"

"We did Neverland." "Can you tell us where they are?" We gave the Neverland fleet their location, and after several hours we lowered our weapons and dropped our shields.

The time came when the Neverland fleet came into view of the fog bank, and we radioed the fleet. "Neverland fleet slow to nine knots." "Neverland is on the other side of the fog bank," I said.

"Are there any hazards in the fog bank, Neverland?"

"There are, but we will make sure they don't harm you, just follow our instructions." "You should be out of the fog in about forty-five minutes," I said. Then ten minutes after the fleet entered the fog, I said, "Neverland fleet, when you exit the fog, make a hard-portside turn and cut your speed in half." "There is a reef all around Neverland, and the waters a full of man-eating sharks."

"Neverland is an island, is this correct?"

I smiled as Charles and John giggled, "Neverland fleet, have you never read the story of Peter Pan and Neverland?" "Yes, Neverland is an island, a huge island." When they broke out of the fog, they all turned portside and reduced their speed just as I asked. I then said, "Get ready to drop anchor Neverland Fleet." "Drop anchor," I said.

"Neverland, when can we come onshore?"

"Now, if you wish, we will give you instruction on how to get through the reef." "Look on the ridge of the mountain in front of you." "You will see two spires that look like horns." "Do you see them, fleet?" John asked.

"Yes."

"Take your transports between those horns." "Do not put your hands into the water; the sharks will attack you." "You can't bring your bigger ships through the channel because the draft of your ships a too deep." "I would request in your first transport to bring our solicitors, Admiral Mc Donald, and whoever else you want, but no weapons." "When do you think you will come?" asked John.

"About an hour Neverland." Charles was getting excited as the transport came through the channel without incident; we gave instruction to turn portside and then starboard, where the river to our bay was. We all went out with a device that can detect a weapon and if a person is lying, amongst other things. We had put the Black Pearl in the middle of the bay to give room for two transport boats at the dock. We all approached them with weapons as they moored their boat to the pier. We had those in the boat line up. There were fifteen of them, and when John scanned the third one to the end. He found out that he had a weapon, and we trained our guns on him. "Get out of your clothing," I said. He didn't move, and I said, "Admiral if he doesn't take his clothing off, I will kill him."

"Sailor, take your clothes off."

"No, Sir." "I'm not going to take off my clothes in front of these boys."

"These boys are naked, and we are used to seeing people without anything on," I said.

"You two sailors strip him." He pulled out a pistol, and I shot him in the arm, knocking the gun out of his hand. "Take him into custody."

"Wait," I said. "Question that sailor, John."

"What country are you working for?" He wouldn't answer, so John shoved a finger into his wound, and he screamed. "What country are you working for?"

He still wouldn't answer until John started to move his hand towards his wound again, and then he cursed us in Russian. "Looks like he is your leak, Admiral."

"Tie him up." "Can I use your radio, Peter?"

"In a minute, Admiral, I want to test all these people to see if they are lying." Everyone else checked out, so I took the Admiral to the house to use the radio. He called for some people to take the sailor into custody. "We will need to check every person who will come here, Admiral, but they can start to come onshore."

"Alright, Peter, but there might be a few who I can vouch for."

"Alright, Admiral." Charles and John gave our weapons to the cleared sailors and joined us.

"What would have happened if the Russians or we came here with force?" the Admiral asked.

John smiled as did Charles and I, and John said, "We do have the capability of putting a forcefield around this island, but if someone got through anyway, follow us, Admiral." We walked towards the jungle, and Peter yelled out in Pongo, and out came over a thousand Pongos with spears. "The Pongos are deadly with those spears and would have killed all that came ashore," John said.

"I hope you have larger transports than the one you brought, or it is going to take a while before you get all the supplies and people here," I said.

"Yes, they have tender boats which carry about one hundred and fifty people," said Admiral Mc Donald.

"Well, as you can see, we have several tents with beds and bedding." "We also can accommodate about thirty people in the house." "Our families will get housed in the house; the big problem will be bathing facilities and loos." "We do have food for several months, but we will be loading the Black Pearl with food and other things," I said.

"We will be bringing more tents, and we will take care of the toilets and showers." Just then, two transports full of sailors and supplies came into the bay, and the Admiral said, "Show me how that device works that you use on us when I first got here." I showed him, and he got the men lined up as he cleared them. Over the next couple of hours, things were being erected all over the fields, and our solicitors approached me.

"We will need you and John to sign some documents as soon as possible," said Mr. Bryant.

"I thought it wasn't legal for someone our age to sign anything?" I questioned.

"Normally, it isn't, but since we are here on Neverland, it might be, and we don't want to take any chances," said Mr. Greenfield.

"Peter, your parents will also sign we have already talked to them," said Miss Witherspoon.

"We also want to go over your holding back in England," said Mr. Greenfield.

"Yes, Sir." "We will want you to set something up with the Kahler's also." "Since they are Americans, I would think Mr. Bryant will handle them and my parents." "He nodded, and I said, you all will be staying in the house; perhaps you are willing to share a room." They all agreed, and I showed them to their room. John and Charles came over to me, and I said, "I think we should start cooking something, don't you think?"

"Yes, but how much?" "Maybe we should talk to the Admiral first," John said.

"Admiral, we should start cooking to feed those who will be staying at the house," John said.

"There is no need; professional cooks should be here in about an hour and thirty minutes." "They will do the cooking for the house, and military cooks will be cooking for people outside." "Well, for the time being, it looks like we won't need to do much then," I said. John, Charles, and I were sitting out on the porch when the first tender boat from the cruise ship docked. Charles got excited when he spotted his family, and then I spotted my family. We walked out to them, and for some reason, my heart was pounding. I guess I was afraid that they were going to get angry. They came up to us with my siblings and Charles's siblings giggling, I assume, because we weren't wearing anything, and Mrs. Kahler said, "All three of you need to put something on."

"We have no clothing except cold weather clothing, and it's too hot for that," I said.

"Couldn't you have worn a loincloth?" asked my brother David.

"We never thought about it; why do we need to wear anything?" I asked.

"It's just not proper," said Mr. Kahler.

"It is on Neverland," said John.

"No one except you all seems to be concern about us not wearing anything," said Charles. "I don't mind not wearing anything."

I could see our families were not happy about what was getting said. I said, "I can see you are uncomfortable with us not wearing anything; we have cloth, so if someone can sew, we will wear a loincloth or anything else you can make."

"There is no need we bought you clothing while we were in Australia," said my Father.

"We will wear them, at least during the day, when we sleep, we wear nothing," said John.

"Ma, you don't look good," I said.

"I had a hard time on the ship; I might have seasickness."

"Let me take you to your rooms; you will be staying in the house, and I have medication for you, Ma." On the way to the house, I asked Mr. Kahler, "Mr. Kahler, are you mad at John and me?"

"I'm not happy with all three of you."

"Do you know why Charles came with us?"

"No."

"You will after you rest, and perhaps you won't be so angry." "You need to know John, and I love Charles, and I believe he loves us."

"I know you love Charles, you always did, and I know he loves you and John."

We showed them to their rooms and showed them our room. Charles was allowed to stay with us; I was worried he wouldn't be able to. I went up to my parents' room with medication for my mother. "Ma, drink this; it will make you feel better in about an hour." "You should sleep for a while; you will feel more refresh."

"What is this medication you gave me?"

"It's a compound from some plants on this island." "It's safe, John, and I have some medical knowledge, and John has taken it before." She took it, and I said, "I would like to talk to you about John."

"Alright," said my father.

"Are you going to adopt him?"

"Yes, we are."

"Are you both agreeing to this, and will you love him as I hope you love the rest of us."

"Yes," said my Father.

"Ma?"

"Yes, but you and John are very different than what your brothers look and speak."

"Yes, your right, I don't know how much we can adjust, but we will try." "You need to know John's real first name is William."

"Yes, we know," said my father.

"Well, if it bothers you, John nor I care what you call us." I started to leave when I said, "Later, I will show you and Mr. Kahler something that will make it so you and my brothers will never have to work again."

I went outside when the cooks for the house approach me, "We just settled in, where is the kitchen, and I got told you have food for us to cook."

"Yes, follow me." I took them to the kitchen, and they were impressed. I then showed them where the food stores were. Before I left, I asked, "Do you have a set menu?"

"No, we will cook anything you wish," said the head cook.

"I will eat anything, but my sibling and perhaps the Kahler children also are poor eaters." "You should talk to either my brothers or my mother, also Mrs. Kahler."

"We will do that."

John and Charles were on the porch, and I joined them. "How is your mother, Peter?" asked John.

"She is fine; she is sleeping." "She is your mother too; they are going to adopt you."

"They told you this," he said, surprised.

"Yes, the only trouble our mother has is we are so different than they are."

"Well, they are right about that you are different than when we were little," said Charles.

"We can't help that; that was James Hooker, who did that to us."

"I know that."

Mrs. Kahler heard us talking and came out and said, "Charles, you need to come to our room and get into some clothing." "James, William, your father, wants you to go to his room to change also."

"Yes, mam," both John and I said.

We went upstairs and knocked at the door. "Come in."

Our mother was on the bed sleeping or trying to sleep. "You wanted us to come," I said.

"Yes," my mother got up and grabbed two white briefs with two short blue pants. "Put those on." We did as she got two shirts, both blue also, and handed them to us.

We put everything on, and luckily, they fit fine, and we both said, "Thank you."

"We would have bought you shoes and socks, but we didn't know what size you were."

"It's just as well we need to be barefooted when we need to sail the ship back to America," John said.

"Did the cooks talk to you yet?" I asked.

"Yes, I know what Jerry and Dave eat but didn't know what you two will eat."

"We eat anything," John said.

"I've already told the cooks," I said. "Are you feeling any better?" I asked.

"Yes, I feel alright." Admiral Mc Donald gave out the other rooms to the dignitaries. Both the scientists and our accountants and compilers asked us for a place they could work from, and John, Charles, and I went to the warehouses to see if there was room there, and there was room. John, Charles, and I got told that dinner would get served at five pm.

We were in our room when five o'clock came around. We washed up and went downstairs; we were about to sit down next to our parents when Queen Elizabeth and Prince Philip came into the room. John and I, with a few others, immediately bowed. "Please sit; we can be informal here," said the Queen.

"We are sorry, Your Majesty, Peter, and I did not know you were here," said John.

"That is alright, John." "You and Peter are family; did you know that."

"James Hooker, our Neverland father, said he was an earl and that we were lord," I said.

"He was right, and now both of you are earls, which means we are cousins."

That surprised us, and I said, "Your Majesty, our family, and many other people here do not know the customs of England and the Royal Family."

"It's alright, Peter," she said.

The Queen and her husband sat next to us, which pleased me greatly. We got served according to our likes, and as I was eating, I asked in German, "Prince Philip, you speak German."

"Yes, French too," he answered in German.

"I switched to French and said, "That is wonderful; John and I would like to visit Europe someday."

The Queen answered in French and said, "I hope Great Britain too."

"Oh yes, we will, your majesty Great Britain will be the first place we will go," said John enthusiastically in French.

"When you come, you will come to Winsor to visit me," she said in English.

"Yes, we will, your majesty," we both said together.

"If they are earls and I am their brother, does that mean we have a title?" David asked.

"No, it doesn't work that way." "However, we will treat you as part of the royal family."

After dinner, our parents and Charles's parents went on the porch with the Queen and Prince. They seem to prefer each other's company. I showed Jane Goodall the library and how to work on the computer. I also gave her the book with the Pongo language and told her it would benefit her if she learned the language. She asked again, "When can I see the Pongos?"

"I think it would be better if you learn the language first, but I will go to the village called Kelpie and see if one will come back to me."

"That will be wonderful," she said. I warned her one more time about the Pongo's amorous behavior.

The next day after breakfast, I went to our room, stripped out of my clothing. I ran to the jungle, jumped into the trees to the amusement of many people, then swung towards the Pongo village. Less than thirty minutes later, I was at the village and talking to the elders. They agreed to send Tinker as their representative to the house. I got back to the house by eleven in the morning; I showered and got dressed. We were on the porch with both our families. There was a commotion in the field near the jungle, and I knew what it was. "John, I think Tinker is here." "Would you get Miss Goodall and bring her to the jungle." "I'll go to meet Tinker."

John nodded, and David asked, "Can I go with you?"

"Yes."

"Me too," said Jerry.

"Yes, you too," I said. We walked out to Tinker, and when we reached her, she was laughing at me. "What is so funny?" I asked her.

She grabbed my pants and tried to pull them down, and said, "You have this wrap around you."

"It is the custom of these people and my birth mother." She looked at David and Jerry, and I said, "They are my birth brothers."

Just then, John came up with Jane Goodall, "Tinker, this is Jane Goodall that we told you about she wants to learn from the Pongo," said John.

"She wears wrappings also," Tinker said.

"It is my custom; does it offend you?" Miss Goodall said in Pongo.

"No, you speak pongo," Tinker said, surprised.

"Not very good; I am still learning."

"I will teach," said Tinker taking her hand.

"Miss Goodall, I'll leave you in the hands of Tinker," I said in English.

"Thank you; I will be alright with Tinker," she replied. We all left towards the house except Jane Goodall and Tinker, who went into the jungle.

At two o'clock, we had the agreement's signing, but not until our solicitors look at the agreement one more time. It got televised worldwide, and John and I said a few words, as did the three countries' representatives. After the signing, both families and the solicitors went to the dining table I said, "After we finish this meeting with the solicitors, we will go to the warehouses to see our wealth. "I've talked to John, and we both decided that Charles and each of his siblings will get ten million American dollars." "The money will get put into trust until their twenty-first birthday." "Mr. and Mrs. Kahler will also get ten million for them to use as they wish." "All my brothers will get ten million put into trust until their twenty-first birthday." "Our parents will get ten million to do as they wish." "In addition, if Charles needs more money, if it is a reasonable reason, he will get it." "Our parents will get an additional fifty million in case a relative need it." "Our solicitors will write up the papers guaranteeing this."

"You have that much money, Jim?" asked my mother.

"Let me answer that, Peter," said Miss Witherspoon.

"The boy's estate in Britain is worth many billions of pounds, which is much less than they have here."

"An English pound is worth more than an American dollar," I said.

"The accountants just did a superficial look in one part of the cave section, and they are guessing it is in the trillions of pounds," said Mr. Greenfield.

"Peter and I would like to take you down to the caves now if you are up to it," said John.

"I don't know if I would want to go into a cave," said our mother.

"Mum, they are more like a warehouse than a cave, and they have light," John replied. We all went down to the caves as we passed the cave with hazardous materials, and people were working there. The accountants were working in the gold section of the first cave, but we went in anyway, and everyone was shocked at what they saw. Bars of gold were stack as high as the ceiling, and you couldn't see the end of the cave. It was the same with the platinum and silver sections. The excitement at what they saw in the jewel section was much more than in the other caves.

"Go ahead and take a piece of jewelry if you want something; there is plenty of it," I said. They went among the boxes with the excitement of a child at an amusement park. When they got what they wanted, we went into the cave with paintings, statues, vases, books, scrolls, and other things. "In this room, please don't touch anything; the oils on your hands could damage these items," I said. We went back to the house; John and I sat on the porch with my father and brothers while Charles stayed with his family.

Admiral McDonald came up to us and sat down, then said, "That hazardous material cave has a lot of material that has radiation." "It also has other material that we don't know what it is." "Is it worth anything?" asked my father.

"Oh, yes, a lot, if I'm not mistaken."

"I'll want use to it if I choose," I said.

"What for?" the Admiral asked.

"John and I will get into something that will interest us, to keep our minds occupied, and we may need it," I said.

Over the following week, we started loading the cargo ships with our valuables. We also loaded the Black Pearl with food and water and personal valuables from the house, including a computer that contained everything in the library. Valuable books in the house we also took and all the inventions and discoveries that the Hooker family had. Three days before we were to depart, John and I were sitting on the porch; I was looking at the stars and said to John, "We will have to do something that will interest us when we go back."

"Yes, you're right," he replied.

"Do you have anything in mind?"

"No, what about you?"

"We will see most of this world, and after that, then what?" "I think we should get involve in things that we are good at." "I'm interested in astrophysics; I want to see what is up there."

"I would like to do things to help people," said John.

"I would think what I have in mind will do just that."

"Perhaps," John said.

"Why don't you think about it in detail what you want to do, and I will do the same so that we can do something together."

"Alright."

We gave our mother enough medication so she wouldn't get sick. We let the Pongo know we were leaving, also everything that was going to happen, they were alright with it. They were delighted with Jane Goodall, and she was happy with them. We showed the military the defense systems. We also made arrangements to get secured warehouses to store the valuables to be changed into cash when we returned to America. What we had on the Black Pearl would be stored at our parent's house if we could store it all. It was time to leave; Admiral Mc Donald gave us a sailor to help with instructions to do as we said. Charles's parents wanted him to stay with him, and I believe he also wanted to be with them. We slipped out of the channel and sailed towards San Francisco.

T E N

HARD TRANSITION

THE WATERS AND WEATHER were good. We found all we need was our sails because the rest of the fleet couldn't move fast enough. The sailor concerned John and me because we got the impression that he thought we were just children and didn't have to listen to us. He wasn't a joiner; he preferred to fix his meals and sleep on deck or in the medical room instead of with us. We had been at sea for about a week when John and I were on deck. I decided to check the radar and sonar, and from the north, I saw many ships coming toward us from about two hundred miles away. "You didn't see those ships coming towards us?" I growled to the sailor at the wheel.

"They are far away, and we have plenty of ships to protect us, sonny," he replied, annoyed.

"You fool, get away from the ship's wheel I'm taking over," I said. The sailor smirked and ignored me, so I grabbed him and said, "I told you to leave." I lifted him and threw him over my head, and he landed on the deck against a mast. "John, man the weapons," I said. I got on the radio and said, "Get me, Admiral Mc Donald, quickly it's an emergency."

"Admiral Mc Donald here."

"Admiral, it's Peter; there is a large naval fleet coming towards us about two hundred miles away."

"Do you know who they are?"

"They look like Russian."

"Where are they?"

"About five points port side." "Sir, we will attack."

"Understood, Peter."

When they were Seventy-five miles from us, I put up our shields as two Russian jets flew over us. The jets circled and flew back over us, and John tracked them but didn't fire. I had an idea and radioed the ship that Admiral Mc Donald was on. "Yes, Peter, what is it you wish?" the Admiral said.

"I have an idea of how to protect the fleet." "If you can move them closer to us, we can extend the shields over everyone."

"How close do we have to be?"

"As close as you can get?" The ships moved, and I extended the shields over everyone except for the navy ships, which consisted of British and American ships. I didn't know the sixth fleet in Hawaii got informed, and they were on their way. It was an hour since the Russians' flyover when our carrier was putting jets into the air. The Russian jets came and attacked our ships, so I said, "John open fire on them." John not only knocked down the Russian Jets but attacked the Russians ships sinking two of them. Three Russian submarines came, and I let John know, and he fired harpoon torpedoes at them, destroying all of them. The Russian jets were taking a beating when the American sixth fleet showed up, taking care of the rest of the Russians.

John secured the weapons, and I lowered the shields; then, I radioed Admiral Mc Donald. "Yes, Peter, what is it you wish?" asked the Admiral.

"Get this sailor you gave me off my ship."

"Why, what did he do?"

"For eight hours, he knew the Russians were coming and said nothing." "When I demanded the wheel, he refused to give it to me; I had to throw him off of it." "He has been doing and saying demeaning things to both of us." "And frankly, Admiral, I don't need a reason to get rid of him." "So, you either get him off my ship, or I will throw him overboard."

"I will send a transport for him, and he will get punished, Peter." "Do you want another man?" the Admiral asked.

"No, John and I will take care of this ship by ourselves."

John and I went over to the sailor, and John said, "Get your belonging and stand by the rail you are leaving this ship." He was about to say something when John interrupted him. "My brother Peter is beyond angry with you; my feelings are worse; I will throw you overboard if you say anything." About an hour and a half later, he got taken off the Black Pearl in handcuffs. It took about another two weeks before we entered the San Francisco Bay, and we docked in the same port as we did before. John and I went down below and got dressed in the same clothing we had when we went on board back in Neverland.

Navy guards got posted around our ship, and military police came on board and came down below as we dressed. "We are here to protect you from the press and people wanting to see you," said one of the M. Ps.

"Are there a lot of people?" I asked.

"Yes, maybe more than five thousand people."

"You realize we are not leaving until our cargo on the Black Pearl is loaded on a secured lorry with an escort as agreed," said John.

"It would also be nice if you could have Admiral Mc Donald join us here," I said.

"We will contact him," the M. P. man said.

About an hour later, the Admiral showed up with our family, and they all came on board. "I didn't think you would bring our family," I said to the Admiral.

"Yes, and your valuables are being stored in warehouses on the base under heavy guard."

"How long do you think it will take to convert it to cash in the bank?" my father asked.

"By the end of the week, the minerals will get converted. Then three weeks after that, the jewels should get converted." "In the next three months, the rest of the things should get converted." "The boys already have several trillion in the bank for the things he has given the three governments."

Two trucks showed up, and we started to unload the ship, and the items got loaded up in the trucks. "Well, Admiral, do you think we have been a pain in your ass?" asked John

"No, not at all," he replied.

"I'm glad you said that Admiral; I think we got you a promotion," I said.

"Yes, I'm sure you did."

"Mr. Reno, you will have help unloading the trucks back at your house, and security will be at your house around the clock."

"Thanks, I just hope I can find a place for everything," our father said.

We all went into a limousine, and everyone went to my parent's house. "How big is your house dad?" I asked.

"It's not as big as the house on Neverland, and I think it will be somewhat smaller with all the things you have."

"Peter and I have a thought about that we will discuss with all of you when we are alone with all of you," said John.

"I've studied much about America and how the whites had destroyed much when they settled this country." "Do you think they will destroy Neverland too?" I asked.

"I don't know, but you got a good deal from what I got told, and I also got told you have a lot of control of that island," replied my father. We drove up to the house, and we all got out. John and I looked around, then John and I went to the limousine trunk to help carry things into the house. Shortly after we unloaded the limousine, the trucks came with military support. Items got moved around in the basement, and we moved everything down there by stacking boxes. The trucks left, and our father talked to the military security and what appeared to be local police. We joined them and found out that they would rent the property across the street and use the back trailer.

"It will not be for long; those items in those boxes are mostly items of value, and we will be selling." "The things we will keep are things to do further research on," I said. We went into the sitting room. I felt awkward and strange, and I'm sure John felt the same way. We both sat next to each other in front of the fireplace.

"We will start to go through the boxes tomorrow if we can get the tools to open them," John said.

"What do you need?" asked our father.

"Hammer and pry bar," I said. "We have toolboxes in one of those wooden boxes."

"You two need haircuts," said my mother.

"We prefer long hair, but you can shorten it up, I guess," said John.

"I've talked to dad about this; we have gotten altered; we have pointed ears." "James Hooker liked us looking like elves, so we need our hair over our ears." "We are also not used to the cold in the winter here too, so our hair keeps us warm." "Besides, I think we look better with long hair, at least for now," I said.

"When was the last time you two had a bath?" asked our father.

John smiled and said, "We bathe differently; when we are on the ship." "Usually, Peter and I bathe together; we take a bucket of water from the ocean and pour it over our head." "Then we soap up, and we take turns throwing water at each other with the bucket until the soap is off."

"What about when you were on the island?" asked Jerry.

"We swam a lot in the bay, or we bathed in one of the rivers." "There is a plant on the island that is like soap we used also," said John.

I could see they thought the way we bathed wasn't right, so I said, "We also used the bathtub and showers in the house too." They were relieved about that, but I said, "I'm curious, do we smell?"

"No, you don't smell, but I think both of you should take a bath," my mother said.

"Okay," said John.

We started to strip out of our clothing when our mother stopped us, "You better take your clothes off upstairs." "Who goes first?"

"We bathe together," I said.

"Alright, do you want a bath or shower?"

"Whatever you want," John said.

"Bath, then, there will be more room for both of you." We stripped, and our mother filled the tub with water. We got into the tub, John sitting between my legs. "Do you two need toys?"

"No," I said.

"There are the soap and shampoo," She said, pointing to them. "I'll be back to wash your hair after I put your clothes in the laundry." John grabbed the soap and started washing his front, and when he finished, he gave me the soap and started cleaning. Our mother came in and started to shampoo our hair. She told us to rinse the soap out of our hair, so John stood up, and I dunked my hair under the water, and John did the same after me.

I finished washing my front, and then I said, "John, stand up, and I'll wash your back, then you can do me." We finished washing, then got out and dried ourselves and each other. Our mother gave us some clean clothes, and we got dressed. We had a brush for our hair, and we brushed each other's hair.

Our father had left to buy takeout food for everyone; we got asked what we wanted, for which we said, "We eat anything."

When our father brought home the food, we got shown where to sit to eat. He bought a hamburger for my brothers and me, and he had roast beef, and my mother had fish. A conversation got started at the table; our father said, "It sure feels good to be home."

"You can say that again," said our mother. David and Jerry said they thought it was nice in Neverland, but they were happy they were home.

John and I didn't say anything, but when everyone looked at us, I said, "We feel awkward here." "To tell you the truth, if it weren't that we knew Neverland would get found and the problem we had of buying food and supplies, we wouldn't have come back with you."

"What Peter has said is true." "I would also say our biggest reason for coming with you is our memory coming back," John said.

"We are hoping that we can adjust and that all of you can adjust to us," I said.

"If you can't adjust, are you going back to that island?" asked my mother.

John and I looked at each other, then, John said, "No, we would make a life for us here someplace or England, I would think; Neverland isn't the same anymore."

"Well, we will have to get both of you registered in school soon," said our father.

"I can see a problem with that," I said.

"What is the problem?" my mother asked.

"Our knowledge is far ahead of someone our age; to be exact, far ahead of most if not all adults," John said.

"Let's let the school people decide that and see what they want to do," said our father. Both John and I nodded, yes.

It was time for bed; we were to stay in Jerry's room. Jerry was going to move over to David's room, but when I saw that the beds in his room weren't wide enough for two people, I said, "No, John and I sleep together." "I couldn't sleep without him; we can sleep on the floor."

They let us sleep on the floor for now, and it was a surprise to everyone when John and I took everything off before laying down. Once we laid down, it wasn't long when we were sound asleep. The next day we were up before David or Jerry; our mother said, "I'm making pancakes."

"What are pancakes?" asked John.

"I think they are like crepes," I said.

As we were eating, Jerry came downstairs and sat at the table. When we finished eating, we brought our dishes to the sink, and I said, "We will help you clean up if you wish."

"No, I'll do it myself," said my mother. As we went downstairs, David still hadn't gotten up; we grabbed the tools to open the boxes. We lifted one box down and worked on the lid, and opened it, and it was full of books. We took them out and started on the next box, which was full of books also.

John said to me, "We need to bring these boxes out of here as we unload them."

"Yes, you are right," I said. "The wood in these boxes are constructed with good wood; I'll go and see what we can do with them."

"They would make good bookshelves," said John. I nodded and went to find our father.

I found our father in the garage, and I asked him, "We need to remove the empty wooden boxes." "They are made from redwood and would make excellent bookshelves, I would think."

"Let's go see them," he said. We went down to the basement, and our father said, "They are too good to throw away."

"One of us could disassemble them while the other opens the boxes," John said.

"Alright, I'll get you another hammer and prybar, and I will find a place to put the wood." John went with him, and I got busy unloading the box, and then I got another box down. When John came back, he started disassembling the boxes and stacking the wood. We had about a dozen boxes unloaded just before noon, and John had disassembled about nine boxes.

Our mother came downstairs and said, "You better get cleaned up; you're going to the school to get registered." We left everything where it was and went upstairs to wash. When we finished, we waited in the sitting room to go. We loaded up in the automobile with our father. We headed for the school we would be going to according to our age.

"After we finish with the school, we will go to the store to get both of you warmer clothing," said our father. We got to the school, got out, and then went to a room where a lady was working. Along the way, we saw many boys and girls our age milling around. We did get some stares from the children that were there, but none approached us.

The lady in the office asked our father, "How can I help you?"

"I've come to register my boys for school."

She looked at us, smiled, and said, "Alright, I'll get you the paperwork."

"Dad, you better explain to her the problem of us being here," I said.

She turned around and said, "What problem?"

"James, maybe you or William should explain."

"We will both explain, dad," I said.

"James and William are our birth names, but my name is also Peter the Pan Hooker, and this is my brother John," I said.

"We are symbiotic and have an IQ higher than most humans," said John.

"We also have the strength of many adults." "As you can hear, we have an English accent; we have gotten educated in the English way," I said.

"So, we don't see any benefit in going to any school."

She smiled and said, disbelieving us, "I'm sure there are a few things you can learn here."

John and I looked at each other, and I finally said in French, "She is another fool who is going to waste our time; what do you think we should do?"

"We could refuse to go, I suppose," John said in French. "You know what will happen if some of these boys and girls see our ears; there will be violence when we defend ourselves."

Our father was about to fill out the papers when a man came out of an office and said, "Why don't you come into my office and let's see if we can resolve some of these boy's concerns." We all went into his office, and he said, "I'm the principal here; my name is John Turner." "You should also know that I am fluent in French." "I wish to know why you think you won't learn anything here; we have some fine teachers here."

"Sir, I would suggest you test us." "For us to be here, your students who tried to harm us would get hurt, and we don't want to hurt anyone," said John.

"Why would you think you would have trouble with the other students?" asked Principal Turner.

"As you can tell, we have an English accent, but that is a minor thing." "Look at us; we have elfin features," I said. Both of us showed him our ears, and I said, "Our ears are another problem we have."

"You two are those boys who were kidnaped and live on an island, aren't you?" the principal asked.

"Yes," we both answered.

"There is a law that says children must go to school," the principal said.

"With every law, there is an exception, and we are the exception," I said.

"I'll tell you what, let me give you two a test; if it tells me you this school won't benefit both of you, then we will explore other options." "As far as other students harming you, I have a few ideas about that also, so will you give this a try?" asked Principal Turner.

"What do you think, Peter?" John asked in German.

"I can't see where it would hurt?" I answered in German. "We will give it a try, Sir," I answered him in English.

"How many languages do you two speak?" Principal Turner asked.

"Six fluently, we can read Minoan also," John said.

"I'll set up a test tomorrow for both of you." "Mr. Reno, you can bring those papers back tomorrow," he said. We got up and left, and we went shopping for clothing. When we got home, we brought our things upstairs and then got busy with the boxes downstairs; we got five more boxes done before dinner. After dinner, we got back on the boxes. In the second box, we found several logs, and journals were given several tarps to cover them.

The next morning, we got told we would be going back to the school. We were taken into a large room at the school and given a pencil and a booklet, then we were told we had three hours to complete the test. We had a proctor, and when we started, we started giggling. The proctor asked, "What's so funny?"

"This is not very hard; we should get done in less than an hour," said John.

She nodded; we both knew she thought we were mistaken. Within an hour, we put down our pencils, and I said, "We finished."

"You finished all of it?" she asked, surprised.

"Yes, and checked our answers," said John. She took our test, and we followed her into the office.

The principal came out and said, "Well, you finish early; let's go visit some of the classes; we have an assembly after lunch in which both of you will be the main topic." We went first to the science room; the principal introduced us to the science teacher Mr. Roberts. He was teaching astronomy, and I said in French to John, "There are errors in what he is teaching."

"I can see that, Peter," said John. "Perhaps he doesn't have the knowledge we have," John added. The principal knew what we said but didn't say anything until we left.

"John, I would guess you're are right; Mr. Roberts doesn't have the knowledge both of you have."

"I can see this might bring conflict with him and us," I said. On the chalkboard was a simple math problem with a sign saying that if you can solve this problem, you will get extra credit.

The teacher noticed John and me looking at the math problem and said, "You two think you can solve that problem?"

"We have already solved it," John said.

"Alright, write the answer on the board and show how you got it," the teacher said.

I went to the board, and within two minutes, I had the answer written down and how I got it. Both John and I looked at the teacher for his confirmation.

He got his briefcase out and pulled out a piece of paper with something written on it. He looked at the paper, then the board, then back at the paper and said, shocked, "That's correct."

We visited two other classes, and then it was time for lunch. We got a tray full of food and looked for a place to eat; there was a nearly empty table we sat down at away from everyone. It wasn't long when others sat around us, and one boy asked, "Who are you two?"

"I'm John Hooker, also known as William Reno."

"I'm Peter the Pan Hooker, also known as James Reno."

Some of the boys and girls were giggling, and the boy who sat next to me brushed my hair aside at the same time, saying, "You got pointed ears, Peter Pan?"

I grabbed his hand in a vice grip and said, "Don't touch me anymore." Everyone around us was shocked at seeing my ears, and John and I got up and left for the office.

An adult tried to stop us from going, and an angry John said, "We are not students here; if we stay, there will be violence; we are going."

We went into the office and sat at a bench until this assembly. Principal Turner knew something happened during lunch but didn't say anything when we went into the lunchroom with him again. We stayed at the far end of the room with him as students started filing into the room.

When everyone was there, Mr. Turner said, "I want to introduce these two boys." Pointing to me, he said, "This boy's name is James Reno, and this is his brother William Reno." "They are very different than you, but none of you are the same, so I don't want you to disrespect them, or you will get punished." "James, William, do you have anything to say?"

"Mr. Turner thinks we are going to school here; I don't think so, so William and I don't see any benefit of us being here," I said.

"You need only to look at our face to see we are different, and we might as well show you our ears," John said, moving his hair and I moving mine, exposing our ears.

"Both John and I were kidnaped and brainwashed, physically and mentally, altered, and enhance." "We got abused in ways I do not wish to mention here," I said.

"Our IQ is far beyond anyone you can think of, and our strength is that of many men." "These things we have told you is only a little of what we could tell you," said John.

Mr. Turner said, "Are there any questions?"

"How high is their IQ?" asked Mr. Boyke.

"I know it is high, but I don't know how high it is," said Mr. Turner. "We did give them a test that should give us an indication of how high it is."

"Boys, what is the highest form of math you have studied?" asked Mr. Boyke.

"We have studied all forms of mathematics." "Peter is studying astrophysics now, and I'm studying biophysics," said John.

"The boys might be right; there might not be much we can offer them," said Mrs. Stone.

Just then, the lady in the office came up to Mr. Turner with some papers. As Mr. Turner and the lady discussed the paper, the same boy who harassed us at lunch said, "If you two are so strong, show us and if you are Peter Pan, let me see you fly."

"As far as being Peter Pan, the book you might have read is a fantasy, however with many fantasies, there is truth," I said. "You can test us in any way to see how strong we are." At that, I jumped up, flew across the room to stand in front of the shocked boy, and everyone else then said, "I am Peter the Pan."

I jumped back to John, and Mr. Turner said, "I have an announcement, according to these test scores, these boys won't be coming to this school." "They answered all the questions correctly; I don't think that has ever happened."

"We told you," said John.

Everyone got dismissed, and as we went back to the office, a boy approached us and asked, "Is your mother's and father's first name Manuel and Marie?"

"Yes," I said.

"I am your cousin Allen Oliveria."

"Nice to meet you: do you live near our parent's house?" asked John.

"Yes, I live near the creek." "Maybe I'll come by."

"That will be fine if you can get by the security." He left, and we went back into the office. Mr. Turner called our father and asked him to come back to the school.

Forty-five minutes later, our father came into the office and said, "Well, boys, how did you do?"

"We did satisfactory other than a few bumps, but I don't believe Mr. Turner thinks it came out the way he thought it would," John said.

"Mr. Reno, your boys, answered all the questions on the test correctly, and for a test that should take three hours to complete, they completed in one hour." "We don't believe we can teach them anything that they don't already know."

"So, where do we go from here?" asked our father.

"Well, Einstein taught at Harvard and also did research; perhaps the boys could do the same," said Mr. Turner.

"Are you saying they are genius like Einstein?" asked our father.

"I'm saying they are greater than Einstein," said Mr. Turner.

"Do you boys want to teach or do research at a university?" asked our father.

"No, we have our plans; we will talk to you about it later," said John. We left and headed home, there was no more talk about school, and we went back working on the boxes. It took us about three days to finish unpacking the rest of the boxes. We set up the two computers we had and a printer on the desk that was down in the basement. We made several bookcases with our father's help with the wood from the boxes, and we placed all the journals, logs, and documents we had on them. Many of the documents we had were copies of scrolls and tablets that we had back on Neverland. The scrolls and tablets are now with our valuables in the warehouses. John and I took a break with all the work we were doing downstairs, and we both had a book to read just for fun in the sitting room.

At the dinner table, the conversation swung to John and me, "Now that you two emptied all the boxes, what are you going to do with the other items such as the books?" asked my father.

"As you know, we kept some of the boxes; we plan to put the books we have read in those boxes along with some of the items we have," I said. "When the boxes get full, I will get an appraiser for those items and then sell them."

"If you want any of those items, let us know, and you can have them," said John.

"Alright, do you need any more bookcases?" our father asked.

"Yes, as many as can be made," said John.

"That would be quite a few bookcases; what are you going to do with them?" he asked.

John looked at me, and I said, "We are going to need to purchase about seven thousand hectares to build a research facility." "This facility will design many things." "We will concentrate on biology and astrophysics, which is John's and my area of expertise." "We will be hiring many people from around the world to help us achieve our goals," I said. "Those bookcases will get used in our personal research rooms."

"I think I can wait to build those bookcases for a while," he said.

"Yes, we will have to get an estate agent soon to find the land we require," I said.

"I'm assuming what you want is a realtor." "We can find one tomorrow after I get back from work."

"Yes," said John.

"How large is a hectare?" asked David.

"A hectare is a little larger than an acre, I believe," said my father.

"I would like to ask you why you are still working?" I asked my father.

"Well, I haven't seen the money yet, and I enjoy working, at least for now."

In the next two days, an estate agent came to our house at three o'clock in the afternoon. "We require about seven thousand hectares of land," I said.

"In acres seven to ten thousand acres," John said.

"I legally can't sell to children," she said.

"It's alright; my husband and I will say okay anything they want."

"That many acres are expensive, but I will find you this land."

"Don't worry about the money; we have a lot of money." "I would suggest you talk to landowners to see if they are willing to sell their land," John said.

"How far away from this house do I have to look?"

"We would like about fifty kilometers or less," said John.

"Kilometers?"

"Yes, about thirty-one, thirty-two miles," I said.

"Alright, I'll get right on it," she said. A week past and an appraiser came to our house, and I showed him the books and things we had. He gave us an estimate of ten million seven hundred thousand dollars for what we would sell at the moment. He said, "I have a buyer for all these items if you would like me to sell them for you."

"Yes, go ahead and sell them, and in a few months, we will have you back for more things to appraise and sell," said John.

Three days after the appraiser, the estate agent came to our house, and since it was Saturday, our father was home. "Well, I've found a little more than seven thousand acres in Livermore, but it will cost you over three and a half million dollars," she said.

"Can we see it?" asked our father.

"Yes, we can go now if you would like."

"Alright, let me get my wallet, and we will go," our father said. We drove for about an hour when we came to a small town and drove out to a dry grassy area with few trees.

John and I looked around, and we notice it doesn't look like much water. We saw a house in a field, and John asked, "Do you think we can talk to those who live here such as that house over there?"

"Yes, if they are home," she said.

We went to the house that we saw, and I asked the lady who answered the door after introductions, "Where do you get your water?"

"We have wells as well as our neighbors." "How hot does it get here, and also how cold?" John asked.

"It can get to about one hundred and ten, and it can get down to the twenties."

"One more question, madam, who controls those roads in front of your place?" asked John.

"The county."

"Thank you," I said. We left, and as we rode back with the estate agent, I said, "We will take the land."

"Alright, I will get the paperwork written up, and you can give me a check for the land."

ELEVEN

INDEPENDENCE

WE GOT THE LAND, and as the weeks and months went by, we could liquidate three-quarters of the boxes we had. We hired an architect for the many buildings we wanted on the land we had. We also, through our father, were able to acquire the county roads into our property. The valuables we had on Neverland had gotten converted to cash in our accounts. We still didn't know what we were going to do with the paintings, statues, vases, and other items we had. We have had many visits from relatives who I knew and some I didn't know; they couldn't believe what I looked like now. What made me happy a few uncles and aunts made a fuss over John, who ate it up.

We were down in the basement one Tuesday afternoon, John had been quiet, and I knew something was wrong with him. I went over to him and hugged him and kissed him, and said, "I know there is something wrong with you; what is it."

"I don't know if I am happy here, Peter."

I walked him over to the sofa, and we sat together, "John, I know what you mean; it's as if we are guests here and not their son," I said.

"They haven't adopted me." "I don't think they want to."

"I will be talking to them about your adoption." "Perhaps there is a problem they are not telling us."

"You know as well as I know it's not just the adoption."

"Yes, everything needs to get discussed; let me handle it."

"Alright, Peter."

At dinner, John and I were quiet, and everyone took notice. After dinner, John and I went into the sitting room to read. John whispered to me in Pongo, "When are you going to say something?"

"I'll know when it is the right time. Be patient; this may take some time, perhaps days." The next morning, we didn't eat breakfast; instead, we went for a walk in the wilderness area near our home. "Why are you remaining quiet and not confronting them?" asked John.

"I want them to approach us first." "If they can't see we are hurting, then they will have a hard time correcting their behavior," I said.

"Peter, I don't want to force them to change." "They must change because they want to."

"Your right John; there is a good chance they will fake liking us, especially our mother."

"I think the problem we haven't bonded with them, and they haven't bonded with us," said John.

"Your right; maybe it is just hard for adults to bond with us."

"Jerry and David haven't bonded with us either, and we haven't even seen your other brother Bob." "Our father, James Hooker, as mean as he got bonded to us quickly."

"You're right again, John." "Maybe it is just not in their nature to bond, or maybe it takes them longer." "I think they should be allowed to explain themselves." We missed lunch also, and our stomach was feeling it. We did find some blackberries that soothed the pain of an empty stomach.

We walked back to the house; along the way, John asked, "If it doesn't work out here, then where shall we go?"

"We could go to England, I suppose."

"Yes, but we would be very far from Livermore and our property."

"Yes, we would; perhaps we should start to build on that property; we can add sleeping quarters for the both of us."

"I think we should start building out there." "I've been worried that the three governments will take credit for the Hooker knowledge and cut us out." "I also think it would be a good idea to build sleeping quarters for us; it could solve a lot of problems we have now." "However, I still want to go over to England sometime."

"We will bring all this up with everyone when we talk to them, and John, we will be going to England." When we got back to the house, we went down to the basement and did some more studying until dinner.

At dinner, we were again quiet as we ate, "What is the matter with you two?" asked our father.

John looked at me, and I said, "What do you mean?"

"You two have been skipping meals, and both of you have been very quiet."

"We have a lot of things on our mind." "Perhaps we should talk about it after dinner," I said.

"Alright, we will talk in the living room," he said. John and I both nodded and finished eating in silence.

After dinner, John and I sat next to the fireplace. After using the loo, our father came into the room with us. "Well, what's the problem?" asked our father.

"Where are Jerry, David, and Ma?" I asked. He called everyone into the sitting room.

When everyone came into the room, our father asked, "Okay, everyone is here."

"We are very different than all of you." "We feel that you are uncomfortable with us." "It is almost like we are a guest than your sons." "We have not bonded with you, nor have you bonded on us; at least we don't feel like you or we have." "The only thing I can think the reason for this is, like I said, we are different; we look different, act differently, and think differently."

"We know you are our son," said our mother.

"Ma, you perhaps know I am your son, but what about John?" "We are symbiotic, which means, at least for now, we are more like twins." "We think alike; we act alike, we feel comfortable together, haven't ever noticed John, or I will say things that the other would have said, or said things at the same time."

"We care about John," said our father.

"You haven't adopted him yet, nor I don't believe you haven't even started the process yet."

"I should have at least started the process and will tomorrow."

"It's just not the adoption, as I have told you."

"What do you think, John?" asked our father.

"As Peter said, we think alike; it is making it uncomfortable for us to stay here."

Our father looked at Jerry and David, and David said, "You haven't made it very easy for us either." "You don't use your real names, and both of you keep to yourselves."

"We told you, you could call us anything you wish, but perhaps you are right, maybe we should call us by our real name," said John. "Mom, will it bother you if I switch to William since your son William died?"

"No, it doesn't bother me; we called him Bill anyway, so it isn't the same."

"Are you saying things around here hadn't gotten better from when you first got here?" asked David.

John and I looked at each other, then John said, "It has gotten better, but not as good as it should have gotten."

"Adjusting takes time; things will get better," said our father.

"James, if you can remember, we have never been a close family or expressed our feelings," said David.

I looked at William and said, "I do remember it being that way." William nodded, and I said, "We must start construction on our property." "It's going to take time to complete everything, and we must get started." "I don't trust the governments; they will use the Hooker inventions and claim they are theirs cutting us out of them." "By doing this, it will keep us in court for years fighting them."

"Does it matter you have a lot of money?" asked our mother.

"Yes, it matters if we don't protect what is ours, we will soon find we are out of money, especially with all our projects we wish to do," said John.

"We can find companies to do the construction," I said.

"Alright, I will help you with this also," said our father. I don't think anyone won that meeting; we still felt uneasy living in the house.

Downstairs I talked to William in French and said, "How do you feel about what happened upstairs?"

"I have mix feelings; I don't think we got everything we wanted," he said.

"Perhaps we should give it a try to see how much things change," I said. Over the weeks, we got a construction manager who hired companies to build our property. We hadn't heard anything about William's adoption, so while we were working in the basement, I went down to our father's office, where he was working. I sat down, and when he looked up, I asked, "Why haven't you adopted William yet?"

"It takes time," he said.

"Have you done anything yet?"

With anger, he said, "I've done plenty of things." I stood up, angry; I nodded and left.

William could see I was angry and asked, "What's wrong, James?"

"We need to be free from these people." William didn't press me for details, and I didn't want to talk about it.

At dinner, I was still fuming and didn't say anything until David said, "What's the matter with you?"

"We are leaving here." "For now, we will go to England and live at William's and my estate."

Our father looked at David and said, "He's mad because I haven't adopted William yet."

"If truth be told, your father doesn't intend to adopt him." "It has been a big mistake for us to come here." For that, our father became enraged, and he swung his arm to hit me, but I was faster than him and grabbed his wrist and said, "You have no right to touch William or me." By this time, John and I were on our feet.

"Since you don't want to be part of this family, I guess you don't need to eat my food," said our father.

"We don't need your food," John said. "I also don't want to be part of your family; I've never felt comfortable here."

We went downstairs while our father was yelling for us to come back. We started packing our things into the wooden boxes we had left. As we unhooked our computer, I could see the tears in William's eyes, and to tell the truth, I had a tear or two dropped from my eyes too. We were hoping for a family, but this family didn't appear to be the right family. While we were unhooking our computer and printer, David and our father came downstairs. William and I had been talking in French, ignoring our brother and father. "Why don't you two go upstairs and eat," our father said.

I asked William in French, "Are you hungry?"

"No."

"We don't want your food; we will be out of your house after we finish packing," I said.

"We don't want you to go," my father said.

"Except it's not you; it's we." "Had you done, what you should have done, all of this wouldn't have happened." "Now it's too late; William doesn't want to be part of this family, nor do I."

"Your twelve years old; what are you going to do for food and housing?" said David.

"James and I don't completely trust anyone; we never have and never will." "We had stored money away since before we came to this country just in case something like this happens," said John.

"We will be getting in touch with our solicitor Jack Bryant to become emancipated." "We are doing this so that we will have total control of all our funds," I said. We could see our father and brother were upset as they went upstairs.

We went back to packing our things when our mother came downstairs. "What are you two doing?" "Your father is upset; you both have hurt him badly."

"It is obvious to us we are not accepted here." "Dad is not Williams's father; he is only my father, technically." "As far as me, I died many years ago to all of you." "You above all are uncomfortable having us around; this whole family is completely dysfunctional."

She started to cry, which shocked William and me, then John said, "Put yourself in our place; this is not mine and James's home." "What do you think we can do?"

"You can listen to your father, work it out, compromise."

I looked at William and asked in French, "What do you want to do?"

"It doesn't hurt to listen," he answered in French.

"We will talk to all of you if you want to talk." She went upstairs, and shortly after she did, everyone started to come downstairs.

"What can we do to keep you from going?" asked my father.

"There is nothing you can do to keep us here eventually; no matter what you do, we will leave," said John.

"What do you think all that construction is for out in Livermore?" I said.

"That is our school, our university; that is our purpose." "We had decided that back in Neverland," said William.

"James Hooker, in altering us and training us made us to be independent; to be able to rely on ourselves." "He wasn't totally successful; William and I rely on each other we don't need other people," I said.

"You see us as two twelve-year-old boys, and in some ways, we are." "However, mentally and physically, we are far beyond twelve-year-old boys," said William.

"Maybe that is why you haven't bonded to us," said David.

I looked at William, and William said, "Perhaps your right, and there is no fix to that." "What are all your excuses for not bonding with us."

"Who says we haven't bonded with you?" said our mother.

"You have a peculiar way of showing it, something we are not used to," I said.

"We don't express our feelings very well; it's the way we got raised," said David.

"And what about William; he is in limbo; he is my brother that is not in question, but William is not your brother, nor is he your son," I said to everyone.

"I will fix that tomorrow," said our father.

I looked at William and said in French, "What do you want to do?"

"We can give it one more try," he replied in French.

"Why do you speak in French?" asked David.

"I would think that would be obvious; so, William and I can speak freely," I said.

"If you want us to stay, there are three things we wish, and there is no compromise." "First and foremost, tomorrow, there must be some major progress towards William's adoption by dinner." "You will give us full access to our funds without us having to go through you or a solicitor." "We need a way out to our property; we could walk there, but it would take too much time."

"I will get ahold of an attorney tomorrow morning, and both of you will get involved; perhaps we can get your Mr. Jack Bryant," our father said. "Also, tomorrow, I will make sure you can get money out of the bank, but I will need to get you an identification." "I will also get you a credit card and a checkbook." "I can bring you out to Livermore, or David can," he said.

"No, we don't want to depend on you or David to take us out to Livermore," John said.

"I think perhaps we should get a full-time chauffeur," I said. "It's just not Livermore we need to go to, but we need to go to several different institutions to do research, and there are other places we would like to go to."

"Alright, we will get you a chauffeur, perhaps security, also," said our father.

"For now, we won't go, just don't procrastinate; let's get these things done, please," I said. The next day in the morning, just as our father said, we got ahold of Mr. Jack Bryant, our solicitor. He had a man in his office draw up the paperwork to adopt William. Our father also called a chauffeur company that agreed to have someone with us every day; he would also double as security. He left to go to the bank to make arrangements for us to get access to our money. By the following week, our chauffeur came, and we first went to Livermore. Our chauffeur was a huge man; his name is Scott Prichard. When we got out of the car, he followed us, which pleased us. We saw some construction vehicles out in the field, and I said to Mr. Prichard, "I want to check out these houses first." We knocked on the first house door, and no one answered, so we looked into the window, and it was empty, and we tried the door, but somebody locked it. We tried the next house with the same results, so we left for the last home near the construction. There were lights on in the house, so we knocked. Our construction manager Rich Mortensen came to the door.

"Mr. Mortensen, we have come to talk to you about your progress," said William. "Why haven't you hired more construction equipment?"

"I'm trying to save you money."

"Money is not an issue with us; quality and speed is an issue," I said.

"Alright, I'll hire more companies."

"Since we brought up quality, who does the quality control of the work getting done," asked William.

"Well, I keep an eye on them."

"You're too busy; why not hire a quality control person for each project," said William.

"Alright."

"The three houses appear to be in good shape," I said. "If I am correct, I want you to save the houses even if you have to move them." "Where are the keys to the other two houses?"

"I have the keys, and I will try to save the other houses."

"Make a copy of the keys for us," William said.

"Alright, I'll have it done this week."

We went back to the car, and I asked Mr. Prichard, "Are you hungry, Sir?"

"I could eat," he said in his deep voice. We went to a Chinese Restaurant call Yin-Yin to eat.

"I think we will go to the University of California in the city of Berkeley." "I understand they have something to do with the radiation lab here in Livermore," I said.

"What are you going to do there?" asked Mr. Prichard.

"Research," said William.

"I would suggest you contact the university to get access to everything."

"Sounds like a good idea, Mr. Prichard; we will call them when we get home," I said. When we got home, I called the university in Berkeley. I made an appointment to talk to the president at eleven a.m. the next day. We also made an appointment to see the president of Stanford University, which was across the bay, at one p.m. the following day.

The next day we headed to the university in Berkeley and the president's office. We stopped at a secretary desk, and William said, "I'm William Reno, this is my brother James, and he is Mr. Scott Prichard, our chauffeur, and our security." "We have an appointment with Mr. Sellers, the university's President."

She got on an intercom and said, "Your appointment with James and William Reno is here, Dr. Sellers."

I whispered to William in Pongo, "He prefers to be called doctor."

William nodded, and the lady said, "I'll take you to his office."

After shaking hands and introductions, William said, "Dr. Sellers, do you know who we are?"

"Yes, you are the boys from that island, Neverland, I believe."

"You're correct, Sir." "If you don't know our, I.Q. is off the scale," said William.

"The school we took the I.Q. Test said there is nothing they could teach us, nor any university could teach us," I said.

"We have a lab being constructed in Livermore about the same size as the Livermore Radiation Lab there," said William. "We would like to use your university to do research and to be able to get access to materials that a normal student wouldn't be allowed to access."

"In what fields?" he asked.

"All areas, but we will start with Astrophysics, Astronautical Engineering, Botany, and Biophysics," I said.

"I'll tell you what we will give you full access to the university." "Are you two willing to teach here?"

"At this time, we can't teach, we have too many projects going on, but we are willing to be an advisory to anyone you wish."

"Alright, my security will give both of you access to all materials and departments." We filled out the paperwork, and she said, "They will mail both the passes to your address." She took our pictures and fingerprints, and we left.

"Mr. Prichard let's eat first; then we wish to see if we can see our friend Charles; I'll give you the address at lunch," I said. We ate and headed to Charles's home about two-thirty in the afternoon.

When we got there, I rang his doorbell, and Mrs. Kahler answered the door. "Mrs. Kahler, we would like to visit with Charles if that would be alright," I asked.

"Who's that behind you?"

"Our chauffeur and our security, Mr. Scott Prichard," William said.

"You're not planning to take another trip with Charles, are you?"

"No, we bought a lot of property in Livermore, and we are turning it into a research center," I said. "Besides, Neverland will never be the same as it used to be."

"Well, Charles isn't home yet from school, but you can come in and wait for him."

Charles and all his siblings came home about forty minutes later. We didn't stay long; he had homework, and we left an hour after he got home. The next day we went to Stanford and were able to get the same deal as we got at Berkeley. Over the weeks and months, construction at the Livermore property was coming along just fine. We gathered a lot of information from the two universities, but most were incorrect or not up to date. We did advise a few professors on a few topics. We did have a few students who had the desire to work at our new research center.

"William, I think we should go out to the Livermore site tomorrow."

"Alright, James, but why?"

"If our construction manager Rich Mortensen knows we are keeping an eye on him, he will make sure everything goes right."

After dinner, our mother brought out a cake, and William asked, "What is this for?"

"Well, it's after your birthday, James, and just before William's birthday, so we thought we would celebrate now, covering both birthdays." The cake was chocolate with chocolate frosting. Candles got put into the cake, and they got lit, then William and I blew them out. We each received a book, both novels William's book got centered around plants and mine around space.

The next day we went out to our property in Livermore, "Mr. Mortensen, how are things going?" asked William.

"They are just fine; everything is on schedule."

"Let take a look at the plans," I said. We looked at the plans and flipped to the page where it showed our property boundaries. I took a pencil and pointed to a section of the property, and said, "We want two hotel towers here with kitchenettes." "Each tower will have five thousand rooms in them for a total of ten thousand rooms."

"That's a lot of rooms; it would be better if we put four towers with twenty-five hundred rooms each."

"Alright, that will be fine," said William. "Put a swimming lagoon in the center of all the towers."

"Alright, is there anything else?"

"Yes, we want a grocery store built here," I said as I pointed to another area.

"Alright."

"We will be back in a few months," said William. Several months went by, and in July, William and I got a letter from the county. The county wanted to know when we were going to construct the new county road around our property.

We drove out to the property; we were pleased to see many of the buildings going up. We found Mr. Mortensen near one of the buildings with the plans. "Mr. Mortensen, we got this letter from the county," William said as he handed the letter to him.

He opened it and read it and said, "Let's look at the plans." "We can put a road to the north and east around the property then connect to the old roads."

"Mr. Mortensen can you make it so when a vehicle drives down the road, they can't look into the property either by digging down or building a berm," I asked.

"I don't think that will be a problem."

"Good, also, will you answer that letter, and we will be answering it also, and get on the road as fast as you can; I don't want a problem with the county."

Back at home, we were in the sitting room reading; our mother came into the room to get the mail when I asked, "Ma didn't you play the piano at one time?"

"Yes."

"I also play the piano, and William plays the violin." "How do you feel if we bought both a violin and a piano?"

"Well, it's okay with me, but ask your father."

At dinner, William said, "Dad, we were thinking of buying a piano and a violin; how do you feel about that?"

"Can you play the piano and the violin?"

"James plays the piano as does mum, and I play the violin," said William.

"I think there is a violin downstairs, but you can get them if you want."

"Can we look at the violin downstairs?" asked William.

"Yes, I'll get it for you after dinner."

After dinner, we went downstairs to the freezer room, and upon a shelf was a violin case. Our father gave it to William, and William open the case and took out the violin. He examined it very closely and then the bow, and afterward, he started to play it. "What do you think, William?"

"It's a student violin, but it will work." The next day we went to a piano store, and I bought an excellent Yamaha piano. Over the weeks, the piano came and got set up in the sitting room. I found my mother was using it more and more every day, which was alright with me.

Our fourteenth birthday came and went; many of the buildings got completed, and I had a landscaper working on the grounds. We were downstairs when William said, "James, when are we going to England?"

"I think we should go this June, William."

"That would be a good time, I think." "We should call and make arrangements to get the estate ready," William said.

"Okay, what about our family here?" I asked

"We can see if they want to go too," William said.

At dinner that night, William said, "As you know, we have an estate in England." "We think it is time we go there, at least for a while this summer; how do you feel about this?" "We were planning to go this June."

"Well, if you want to go, you can go, but what about your property out in Livermore?" our father asked.

"The property won't be ready until next year, and we will leave instructions with our construction manager," I said.

"We would like to know if you all would like to go with us?" asked William.

Our father looked at our mother and said, "Marie, do you want to go?"

I could see she was leery about going, and she asked, "Are we going by boat?"

"Not unless you want to; otherwise, we will go by air," I said.

"To tell you the truth, I don't want to go," she said.

"I can't go either," said David.

"What about you, Jerry?" asked our father.

"I don't care if we go or not."

"Well, maybe you boys should just go by yourselves," our father said.

"We are going to find out if Mr. Prichard will go," said William. The next day we called the staff taking care of our estate in England and let them know we were coming.

Mr. Prichard picked us up at about ten o'clock, and we headed to Livermore. "Mr. Prichard, we are going to England; we would like you to accompany us there," I said.

"I will have to see if my main office will allow this." "How long will we be in England?"

"A month or two, I would think," I said. "How long will it take you to contact your office?"

"I will call when we get to Livermore."

Mr. Mortensen was in his office when we got to Livermore. "Mr. Mortensen, we are going to England for a few months; how are things going here?" William asked.

"We are ahead of schedule; we are doing just fine."

"I hate to set you back, but we have more buildings we want to get constructed," William said. "Let's look at the plans," Mr. Mortensen said.

"We want a petrol station here, and across the street, we want a charging station for electric vehicles," I said.

"I don't think charging station has ever gotten constructed before; I wouldn't know how to build it."

"Build it like the petrol station but instead of petrol, just put electrical lines in it, and we will design it," said William.

"We also want you to squeeze these buildings onto our property," I said.

"Alright, I'll get on it."

"Mr. Mortensen, do you have security out here?" asked William.

"Yes."

"How many security people do you have?" William asked.

"About fifty."

"Hire another three hundred to be posted around the completed buildings and watching the other buildings," William added.

We left for lunch, and as we left, Mr. Prichard said, "My office said I could go to England."

"Do you have a passport?" I asked.

"No, but I will get one; when do we go?"

"About five weeks," William said. We ate and went home, and for the next five weeks, we hung around the house. Mr. Prichard arrived with another driver, and we went to the airport; we got on a TWA jet to Heathrow airport, which would take about fifteen hours.

Surprisingly, the sky was clear when we landed. We took a helicopter ride to Cartmel, which was where our estate was. The home was beautiful; the servants showed us to our rooms. I told the house manager, "William and I would like to have a meeting with you after we rest."

"Yes, my lord."

We stripped out of our clothing and went to sleep after we put everything away. We slept for six hours, bathed, and went downstairs and found our house manager a Mr. Nigel Homes. "Mr. Homes, we have some questions for you," said William. Has there been anyone here that is looking for something such as the government?

"No, my lord."

"Does this estate have any hidden rooms that you know of?" I asked.

"Yes, my lord."

"We will want to see these areas and the whole estate," said William.

"I will show you everything after we get finished here, my lord."

"We will need a financial report," said William.

"Mr. Homes, we need to contact the Queen and let her know we are here; do you have any ideas?" I asked.

"I could have a letter written and sent to Her Majesty."

"That would be just fine," I said. Mr. Homes showed us the house, and by the time we finished, we ate dinner with Mr. Prichard.

"Mr. Prichard, you can go off and enjoy yourself if you want; we won't be going any place other than the grounds for some time," said William.

"Alright."

After dinner, I asked Mr. Homes, "Do we have any construction plans for this house?"

"Yes, my lord, I believe they are in the safe in the library." "The combination is in the desk that's in there, I would think."

"Would you please come to the library?" "I wish to ask you something in private," I said.

"Yes, my lord."

We went into the library; "Mr. Homes, when was the last time you and the staff have had a raise in salary?" I asked.

"About ten years, my lord."

"Give everyone, including yourself, a twenty percent raise," William said.

"That's very generous, my lord."

"Please give us our financials as soon as you can," I said.

"Yes, my lord."

We looked inside the desk for the combination but could not find it. So, we looked around the library and still could not find the combination. William sat at the desk, and he was opening and closing the desk drawers while I rechecked every inch of the library again. While I was checking, Williams slapped the side of the desk and out popped a secret drawer, and William called me over.

I looked inside, and there was a card, key, and another device that was a half-inch thick and two inches wide and three inches long; it also had a button. I put the device in my pocket. On the card were many numbers, and William and I went over to the safe, then William tried the numbers, and the safe opened. There was a lot of cash in the safe. The rolled-up paper with the plans of how the estate got built was what I was interested in seeing. We put the key and card back in the hidden drawer of the desk and closed it. We looked at the plans very closely, room by room, and pointed to several spots where I thought might be a secret room, including our bedroom. "We will look in there tonight to see if this is a secret chamber," I said. We also noticed that there was possibly a chamber or something else around the fireplace in the library. "I think we should put this away; for now, it is almost dinner time; we can check later when no one is around," I said.

We stuck everything in the safe and locked it just as a servant came into the library and said, "It's time to dine, my lords."

Mr. Prichard was not at dinner; in fact, I do not think he was even in the house. After dinner, we retired upstairs to our room; we stripped out of our clothing, and I started looking for a secret room. We knew the general area; it was near the small bedroom fireplace. Both William and I tried tapping, pushing, and sliding everything in the room. We both agreed that it had a hollow sound in the room, but nothing we did seemed to work. I pulled out the device and said, "I wonder what would happen if I pressed this button."

"Go ahead and push it, James," William said. I pushed it and a hidden door opened by the fireplace.

William and I looked in; there was a flight of stairs going down with many cobwebs. "William, we are going to need a torch and something to knock down these cobwebs."

"Yes, your right; it's getting late; we will get something tomorrow and explore where those stairs go," William said.

We shut the door by pushing the button again and went to bed. The next day we ate breakfast and got two torches and a stick to knock down the spider webs, and we went back to our bedroom, locking the door behind us. William pressed the button, and the door opened; we turned on our torches and entered the staircase. William closed the door behind us, and I cleaned the spider webs as we went down the stairs. The stairs led us to a large room where there was a lot of electronic equipment. We found a light switch and turned it on, and it lit up the whole chamber, and we got a better look at what was down there. We noticed three exits from the room, not counting the one we came down. On the walls of the room were bookshelves. We would look at everything in the room when we thoroughly explored all the other areas. We went into a hall, and along the way, we passed a small library and then into a laboratory. The laboratory was smaller than the last room but larger than the one on Neverland. We went back into the Electronics room, and down a long hall off to one side was a large room with jewels and gold. On the other side of the hall was a medium-sized room with documents, scrolls, and books. The corridor continued down for about ten meters until we came to a dead end. "William, turn off your torch," I said.

"Why?" he asked.

"I'm going to turn my torch off too." "I have a feeling this wall is a door, and I want to see if any light comes through it."

We both turned off our torches, and sure enough, a light came through a tiny hole. I was able to look through the whole, and William whispered, "What do you see?"

"It looks like a garage." "I see some vehicles in there," I whispered back.

"Do you see any people?" William asked.

"No, try using that device to see if there is an opening." William pressed the button, and the wall opened, and we walked through. It was the garage; we went to the garage door and could see the driveway. Next, we went to a side door that went out to the garden. We went back into the hallway, and William closed the door behind us, then we went down to the electronics room. We went into another hall and up a short staircase to another wall, and like before, we turned off our torches and seen another light. This time William looked through the hole and whispered, "It's the library."

"We don't need to go in there, William."

"Yes, you're right."

We left and went back to our bedroom, and once in our room, we unlocked the door. "I think we should look at all the books in the library first, and then we need to deal with the treasure room," I said.

"I agree, James." We examined as many books as possible in the following weeks, and at dinner, William asked Mr. Homes, "Have you sent a letter to the Queen, Mr. Homes?"

"Yes, my lord, six days ago."

"Let us know if we get any response," said William.

"Yes, my lord."

Another week went by, and we got about half the library checked out and had about a thousand books that we wanted to bring back to America with us. We ordered several crates to be made and brought to the house; the company also expected more orders.

"My lords, I have a letter for both of you from Her Majesty."

William read it out loud, "Dear, William and James, I'm so happy that you have come to Great Britain it would please me if the both of you could come to Winsor on the fifteen-day of July." "Mr. Prichard, do you think you could accompany us," asked William.

"Of course, I will."

We had called our solicitors Miss Witherspoon and Mr. Greenfield, to let them know we wanted to meet with them on the sixteenth of July, and they agreed. In the days leading up to the fifteenth, several crates got delivered to the estate. William and I gave instructions for them to get stored in the library. On the fifteenth of July, we entered Winsor and got taken to the Queen. Mr. Prichard was not allowed to see the Queen but could wait for us in another room. After the customary greetings, William and I sat down across from the Queen. "How long will you boys be in Great Britain?"

"About another month, Your Majesty," said William.

"The American government has only shared a little of the knowledge they got from you two," said the Queen.

"They haven't kept the agreement they had with Great Britain?" I asked.

"No, I was hoping the agreement could improve the lives of our people."

"As you know, Your Majesty, we have no control over what the United States does," said William. "What has the British government done to resolve the issues with the United States."

"Our government officials are talking to the American officials, and government solicitors have filed a lawsuit."

William looked at me, and I said, "Your Majesty, I wish to reveal something to you, but I need to know if what I say will leave this room?"

"You can speak freely, James; we have complete privacy here."

"Very well, Your Majesty; we are building a large laboratory in the United States, nearly three thousand hectors on it." "We have two main projects going one is a starship, and the other is a way to produce more food for everyone on earth." "There will be a lot of other projects stemming off from the main project." "I assure you that Great Britain will get about half of these jobs, and the other half will get divided out amongst other countries."

"Also, Your Majesty, over a billion pounds into a bank near where we live very soon to hire people to build the things we need for our laboratory," said William.

We finished talking and left for our hotel room with Mr. Prichard. The next day we went to see our solicitors. "We talked to the Queen yesterday." "We got told that the United States is not living up to the agreement with Great Britain, and I assume Australia is this true?" asked William.

"The United States is sharing what they got through you but not very fast, and I think that they thought they would get more than what they have," said Mr. Greenfield.

"I also think that both Great Britain and Australia are slow at developing what they have been getting." "You also need to know this issue has nothing to do with you boys; it's really out of your hands," said Miss Witherspoon.

"We realize that it is out of our hands, but there are other ways we could retaliate if we wish to," I said.

"What we are going to ask you next can't go any further than this office," asked William.

"We are secured here, William," said Mr. Greenfield.

"At our estate here in England, we have a large amount of gold and jewels that we need converted into pounds and placed in a bank near our estate."

"How much do you believe it is worth?" asked Miss Witherspoon.

"It's in the billions of pounds; I am guessing," William replied."

"We will send a reputable person out to your estate who will handle all of that," answered Miss Witherspoon.

"We have another problem," I said. "We are building a laboratory in the United States; the laboratory is just about completed." "We found a lot of equipment and other items that we need to ship to our site in the United States." "These things are secret, and a lot of care needs to place on these crates so that no other country tries to steal them." "What do you suggest we do?" I asked.

"We will get your things transported discreetly and with enough security that it will be well protected," said Mr. Greenfield.

"Thank you," we both said at the same time. We left and headed back home with Mr. Prichard.

Over the following weeks, we boxed all the books and started on all the equipment. Armored trucks picked up all the gold and jewels, totaling over three and half billion pounds. We worked on both labs every day, it was not easy, but we got everything packed away and shipped to our lab in Livermore. We call Mr. Mortensen and told him what was happening and where to put the boxes. Then we called Mr. Jack Bryant and had him hire a reputable security company to watch over all the boxes and buildings at our lab.

TWELVE

LIVERMORE SPACE LABORATORY

WE LEFT FOR THE United States and our parents' home. Mr. Prichard dropped us off and said he would come at eleven in the morning the next day.

As we came into the house, everyone seemed very cold and distant. As William and I sat in the sitting room, I said in German, "Here we go again."

"We better find out what is going on and soon," said William in German.

"Yes, your right," I replied in German.

Our Father came into the sitting room, and I said, "What's going on; everyone seems distant and cold towards William and me."

"Everything is fine; there is nothing wrong," said our Father.

"That's not true; we are not stupid; we noticed it when we first walked into the house," said William.

Our Father gave William a nasty look as our mother came to the door. I said, "What William said is true, and if you don't want to tell us what the problem is, we will stay tonight, but we will leave tomorrow."

At that, both William and I got up and went downstairs; we packed our things.

Most of our things got already packed anyway, so about midnight, we got finished. "Perhaps we shouldn't stay here, William," I said.

"I was thinking the same thing," said William. We left a note on our crates, which read; we left for our lab where we have living quarters. Our boxes will get picked up within the next couple of days. By two-thirty, we were in Livermore, and we headed for a motel. It was not easy, but we got a room, and we both stripped out of our clothing, and we went to bed. We woke up at about ten in the morning, and we called Mr. Prichard and let him know we needed him to meet us at the motel.

"We are moving into the lab today, so we need to go to the lab first, then we need to do a lot of shopping," William said.

"Alright." We got into the car, and Mr. Prichard drove towards the lab. As we went, he asked, "Are you having trouble with your parents?"

"Yes," I said. He did not say anything else as we drove up to the building where we would be staying. We ran into security, but we had our identification cards and showed them to him and went upstairs; there were crates all over the place. We left for a furniture store and bought furniture for our quarters. They were to be delivered that night; we next went to a store to buy towels, blankets, sheets, and so forth, everything we would need. We finally went to a grocery store and bought a ton of food and other items. Our furniture came about nine that night; we set up the bedroom things first and the next day arranged the other items where they were supposed to go. We started moving the boxes upstairs to our lab, and on the third day, we received the crates from our parent's house. In about two weeks, we had moved everything moved upstairs and started unpacking the boxes.

We took a break and went to talk to Mr. Rich Mortensen, "Mr. Mortensen, how much longer will it take you to finish everything?" asked William.

"About another month, then we will get finished unless you have another project for us to do."

"We are going to start hiring people today; we will see if any of the department heads want something extra or to make modifications," I said. Mr. Mortensen went back to work, and we hired a human resource manager to start hiring personnel for all departments. We also told the lady we hired to hire people from around the world. We instructed the manager all must pass a stringent background check that William and I had written up. We did not care if the person had a criminal background. Still, our biggest concern was whether they would be loyal to us or another person or country.

Over the next month, we got our lab up and running, and our library got set up. More people were getting hired. Each person hired was told that there would be a meeting when all departments were complete. Mr. Mortensen finished all the projects, but we kept him on until we could determine if there were any more projects to be done. The grocery store opened as well as the petrol station. About a month later, every department had at least a department head. William and I scheduled a meeting in the conference room. We had Mr. Mortensen with us as the meeting started. "Everything done here is secret; nothing is to leave here without permission from my brother or me." "Everyone will be checked before you leave this campus," I said. "The goal of this lab has two purposes; one to build a starship and two is to increase the capability for this planet to produce food." "Both of these projects have side projects that will support the main projects." "Your motto is "Anything and Everything That You Can Think of Is Possible;" if you do not believe this, then you should not be here," I said.

Then William got up and said, "You may purchase all materials through the procurement department." "All copies of all construction plans will get picked up in building one." "Any problems will get brought to my brother or me." "For security reasons, we will only give you part of the plans." "No work is to leave this campus." "At random, you will be check for passing on information." William then told everyone what their benefits were and asked, "Are there any questions?"

"My name is Fred Malcolm." "Why are we constructing a starship without knowing how it is going to get powered, amongst other things?"

I got up and asked, "You don't think it can't get done?"

"No, we aren't advance enough to do this."

"You aren't, but William and I are." "Let me remind you again of our motto, anything and everything that you can think of is possible." "What we don't know, we will research and find the answers." "We will build this starship from the outside to the inside."

"Well, if you want to waste your money."

"You will never know if we waste our money or not; you no longer work here." "Security escorted him off the campus." As they took him away, I said, "I don't mind questions, but I will not tolerate I can't do attitudes." "Is there another question?" We answered questions for about another hour and a half and left for our quarters in building one. Over the next several weeks, more and more people got hired. Supplies also came to the warehouses and equipment, such as cranes, scaffolding, braces, and other equipment. William had just come back from build two, where he was working to enlarging the yield and gene-altering as to growth and where something could be grown.

Our secretary called and said, "Sir, you and your brother have a visitor."

"Who?" William asked.

"He claims to be your brother Robert."

"Show him to our quarters," William replied. After a few minutes, our front doorbell rang, and William answered it, and Robert dressed in his Air Force uniform was standing there. "Come in, Bob, and sit down." "Would you like something to drink or eat?"

"What do you have to drink?"

"Anything you want."

"How about a root beer?"

William left for the kitchen, and I said, "What brings you here?"

"Well, you and William are my brothers; I just come to visit."

William gave him a bottle of root beer and said, "I think you aren't telling us the full truth."

"I'm here to talk to both of you about Ma and Dad also."

"What there to talk about?" I asked

"Do you hate them?"

"No, I don't hate them; what about you, William?"

"No, I don't hate them."

"Then why don't you move back home?" asked Bob.

"It was they who created the problem in the first place, and we don't even know what the problem was," I said.

"We can't go back; we are too busy here, and besides, I don't believe down deep they want us there; we are just too different for them."

"You would be willing to talk to them," Bob asked.

I looked a William, and he nodded, and I said, "Yes."

"Do you want to stay and eat?" William asked.

"What are you eating?"

I smiled and said, "Shrimp."

He nodded he would stay, and William said, "I'll fix it." Bob and I stepped out on the balcony, and I pointed out what everything was that you could see from the balcony.

"You think you can make a starship?" he asked.

"I know I can, and it will carry about twelve hundred people comfortable, and can in an emergence carry twice that much." "We could build it in two years, but there are other things I want it to have before we feel it is ready." "I feel there will be a new military branch when this ship gets built."

We went in to eat, and as we sat around the table, Bob said, "William, what is your field of study centered around?"

"Botany, I'm trying to get plants to grown in places where they normally don't grow, and I'm trying to increase the yield of a plant."

"How are you doing that?"

"By genetically changing them." "I'm probably going to branch off into animals also."

"Where are you going after here, Bob?" I asked.

"Back to Dad's house, then back to my base." He left at seven o'clock that night, and we cleaned up everything and went to bed. Over the weeks, construction on the starship was progressing, and William had planted several test plots of plants. The first computers got installed in many departments, and we had been stocking the library with many books. The following month we had a visit from David it went about the same as Bob. We walked around the campus and had a hamburger at the restaurant, and afterward, he talked about our parents. We then again explained that the reason we have not reached out to our parents has nothing to do about what happened at our parent's house. We are just too busy, but we accept them if they wanted to come here.

The following week, on a Saturday morning, I got a call that my parents were at the gate, and I told security to have them escorted to my quarter. I was downstairs when security drove up with my parents, and I said to them, "Well, this is a surprise; what brought you out here?"

"We have come to visit you and William; where is he?" asked my father.

"I'm guessing he is working at his lab?"

"I'm surprised you two aren't together," he said.

"No, we have two different projects going on here." "I can take you over to where he is if you wish."

"That would be great," my father said.

"You have quite a place here," he said.

"Yes, we made it so everyone who works here would enjoy themselves." "This vehicle is an electric transport." "It will go at top speed about one hundred and twenty miles an hour, and as you might have noticed, it is quiet."

"I hope you're not going to go that fast," my mother said.

"No, we will travel about fifteen to twenty miles an hour."

"How long does it take to charge the batteries?" asked my father.

"About thirty minutes, but when I get all the materials I need, all the vehicles will not need any charging." I parked in front of building two, and we all went in. We walked up to a receptionist, and I asked, "Where is my brother William?"

"In the lab, Sir," she said.

"We won't go to the lab because we would have to get dressed in special clothing." "We will go to the observation room." We all gathered in the observation room, and I explained everything going on in the lab.

"Which one is William," my mother asked.

I pressed a button and said, "William, can you take a break and come out here."

"I'll be right out," he said. I pointed him out to my parents as he moved to the exit.

A smiling William came into the observation room, and our father said, "How is it going on in there?"

"Very good; we had a couple of breakthroughs today so far."

"I thought we would give them a tour of the campus; how do you feel about that?" I asked William.

"Sounds great; let me shower first; it gets hot in there." We went back to our quarters, and William strip and went into the shower. At the same time, my father and I went out on the balcony to talk.

"How are things going for you and William here?" asked my father.

"For William, he is more patient, things are going just fine, but for me, I want things to move more quickly, but I know with speed comes mistakes, and I can't have mistakes."

"Do you and William miss home?"

"To tell you the truth, William and I are much too busy to be thinking about home." "I can tell you one thing I don't miss the uncomfortable feeling that we are not welcome and the feeling of negativity."

"Do you and William hate us?"

"No, we have talked about the situation between us quite a bit." "We figured because of what William and I went through and how much we are different from you, it is a lot of stress on all of you." "I do want you to understand something; while William and I were on Neverland or at sea, we took care of ourselves." "James Hooker did little to take care of us; to tell you the truth, we took care of James Hooker more than he took care of us, so you can see we are very independent."

"That James Hooker was a bastard, I'm glad he is dead."

"In some ways, you're right, but he did do some things that were good that I don't think would have happened if we had never got kidnapped." I changed the subject and started pointing out things that I could see from the balcony.

My mother and William came out to the balcony, and William said, "We are ready."

We went to the hotel first, and they were impressed. Then we passed the grocery store and where the gas station and electric station, was and I said, "Any of those places you can use if you wish; they are all a lot cheaper than what is off this campus." We passed many other buildings, which I explained what they were until we came to where the starship was getting built, and we got out.

"How big is this ship?" asked our father.

"About the size of four aircraft carriers," I answered.

"When do you think it will get finished?" asked our mother.

"We will be adults when it gets done," I said.

We walked back to the car and went to where William's building was, and we got out and went into a greenhouse; and William said, "Most of these plants in this greenhouse are rare and from Neverland." We went through a hall, and as we did, William stopped and pointed to another greenhouse. He said, "In there are plants from seeds James

Hooker had we don't yet completely know what they are, but we have them isolated just in case they are harmful or very rare we won't be going in there. We went into another greenhouse, and William said, "These plants are items that we have genetically altered to grow more food." At the next greenhouse, William said, "These plants are the same plants as the last greenhouse, but we are trying to change the type of soil and temperature that they will grow."

"What are you planning to do with the plants from Neverland?" asked our mother.

"If we can adapt the plants to this climate, we will plant them here; if not, we will sell them to areas that can use them," said William.

As we are leaving, I said, "Most of the other buildings you have not been in, you have to wear special clothing to go into them; they are for the starship."

"That open field, we will be building another building, barns, and pens for animals," William said.

"When are you going to start that?" our father asked.

"Maybe next year, and we won't start experimenting for another two years after that," said William.

We came back to building one, and my father asked, "What are in those other two buildings?"

"Accountants, lawyers, payroll, employment, insurance, research, and department head offices, and so forth; that far building holds security with a few holding cells. Mr. Scott Prichard is now the head of security," I said.

"Would you like to eat at our quarters where James and I will cook for you or at our world-class restaurant, which is right around the corner?" William asked.

"So, you don't have to cook; let's go to the restaurant," our mother said. William drove around the corner and parked, and we all got out. As soon as the hostess saw William and me, we were all taken to our table, facing a tropical garden window. An older lady played music near the restaurant's center; I had hired several older people to play throughout the day. The waiter came after we had time to look at the menu, and we ordered what we wanted after my mother and father asked the waiter a few questions. Another person came and wanted to know if we wanted something to drink. William told them they could get anything they wanted with or without liquor. William and I usually would have gotten wine, but we found out a long time ago because of our age, we could not get any.

"It seems like everything is going smoothly for you here," our father said.

"It is, but it does get hard because of our age to get things done; we have to go through other people," said William.

"William, I meant to ask you something; while you were in England, did you stop by the town you are from?" our mother asked.

"No, my mother wasn't a very good parent, and we didn't live in a good area."

"She still was your mother," our father said.

"Yes, I suppose you are right, but she was more concerned about the things she wanted than me." "I was an inconvenience to her." We talked about England and our laboratory. Towards the end, we told our parents they could use the hotel, store, restaurants, or gas station as much as they wanted.

As the weeks, then months, and years passed, much had changed on the campus. William and I got our driver's license, and we had our vehicles. The pens, corrals, and barns for various animals got constructed, and William experimented with the animals. William was able to triple the yield of most plants, and he was having great success in areas and climates that plants could be grown. The starship was all framed up, and titanium and another alloy we invented on campus were getting made and turned into the ship's hull. The starship was coming along much slower than William's projects because every weld got doubled and tripled checked. William and I opened several factories across the United States, Great Britain, and Australia to manufacture the things we needed. We had hired millions of people to work in these factories. By this time, we were making a profit, so money was not a problem if it ever was.

The relationship between our relatives and us was cordial, but we did not join in; we were too busy in any activities they were having. Our aunt Dorothy did visit several times, and for some reason, we felt comfortable with her. We offered her to use the hotel swimming pool, which she did, and we swam with her at times.

We had turned eighteen, and I had noticed William had been spending less time with me, and he told me, "I ordered a twin size bed for you and me."

"Why?"

"I think it is time we had our separate beds."

"Alright, if that is what you want." Summer came, and William cut his hair a lot shorter than what it was. I asked him, "Why did you cut your hair so short?"

"I'm not a boy anymore; you don't like it?"

"I think it is alright; I'm just not used to seeing it being so short."

"Maybe you should cut your hair short too."

"Yes, maybe." A week later, I cut my hair, and it felt funny, but I got used to it. Over the next few months, I saw William less and less. At first, there were days when he did not come home; then it was weeks at a time; I finally asked him, "William, you go away for many days, why?"

"It's private."

"From me?"

"I have my own life."

"We have never had secrets between us."

"There is always a first time."

"You don't love me anymore?" William got up without a word and left. I was devastated; he did not come home that night nor the next. I occupied myself with work to keep my mind off William. I was stressed so bad that I was not eating nor getting any sleep. I had never been sick before, at least from what I could remember, but I still went to work. We just had a meeting with department heads; when I got up, everything started spinning, I took two steps, and I collapsed. I got rushed to the hospital in Livermore, and there I stayed until William finally came back home.

"Where is my brother James," William asked our secretary.

"You don't know, Sir; he is in the hospital."

"No, what happened?"

"He collapsed and got rushed to the hospital; he has been there for three days so far."

"Was he sick?"

"I don't know, but he had been looking bad for weeks." "He had lost a lot of weight, and he was disheveled."

Tears flowed down William's face, and he said, upset, "It's all my fault." William rushed to his car and headed to the hospital. "Where is my brother James Reno," William asked a lady sitting at a desk.

"He is in room three twenty-six." "Take the elevator to the third floor; he is in room twenty-six."

William walked into my room, and I was unconscious, and I looked terrible. William was shocked at my condition; he kissed me and held my hand. He was with me for two hours when a nurse came into the room, and he asked, "I'm William Reno James's brother; how bad is he?"

"He is not in good shape, but he is better now than he was when he came in here."

"What's wrong with him?"

"You will have to ask the doctor that; I can't say."

"When will the doctor come here?"

"He is due here in another hour, I believe."

William waited for over an hour, but the doctor did show up, and William said, "I'm James brother William; what is wrong with him?"

"I'm Doctor Cellars; he came in here extremely malnourished and dehydrated, but there is something else bothering him; he seems given up in life."

"It's my fault, we are very close, and I abandoned him."

"You're here now; maybe he will come around."

Several hours had passed; William called our parents and let them know what happened. Mom and dad showed up around an hour and a half later. "How bad is he, William?" asked my father.

"I don't know; the doctor said he has given up." "He came in he passed out from being extremely malnourished and dehydrated." "It's all my fault; we had words, and I abandoned him."

"You're here; you haven't abandoned him," said our father.

They stayed a couple of hours then left; the hospital gave William something to eat and drink while staying with me. It was the next morning when I woke up and saw William's head on my chest. I stroked his head and bent down, and kissed him. "James, you're awake."

"Where am I?" I whispered.

"You're in the hospital; you're very sick, and it's all my fault."

"No, it's my fault," I said, shaking my head. "You have the right to your own life."

"I should have told you why I've been gone so much." "I've been dating someone."

I smiled and said, "Why were you secretive about it?" "I'm your brother, not your wife."

"James, my date is male."

I stared at him for a minute, then said, "You are my brother; if you love him, that's alright with me."

"Do you prefer males?"

"I never thought about it." "I love you, but you are my brother, and I love Charles, but he is like a brother, as you know."

"You don't have any experience with females."

"No, I've been too busy; I just don't know."

"Well, we can talk about this later." "You need to get yourself better; they need you back at the lab."

"How long have I been here?"

"About a week."

"And you, how long have you been here?"

"Two days."

"You need to go home and get some rest." "I'll call you when I need a ride home."

"Alright." "By the way, mom and dad came back to see you."

I nodded and said, "Make sure you tell my project manager that I will be home in a few days."

"Alright." He kissed me and left.

Two days later, I got released from the hospital, and William picked me up. "It's good to be out of the hospital," I said.

"How do you feel?" asked William.

"A lot better."

"You need to take time off every once in a while and enjoy yourself as I do," said William.

"I'll see what my project manager has done and then make my decision." It was three o'clock in the afternoon when I walked into our apartment in building one. William had cooked for me, and after I ate, I went right to bed.

The next day I got up at about nine o'clock and went out to the starship. I could not push myself for a while; I was still weak and did not want to take a chance. "Nice to see you back, Sir," said the project manager.

"Thank you; stick with me, Fred, while I inspect the work on the starship." Everything looked good; after the inspection, I said, "Let's go to the restaurant."

"Alright."

We sat down and ordered what we wanted, and I said, "Fred, I have been overworking myself

since you have been doing well, I'm going to take off some time."

"I have been concerned about your health for some time," said Fred. "What got you to take some time off?"

"My brother." "After we get the other side welded, we need to do a pressurized smoke test to see if there are any leaks."

I went back to the apartment and took a nap for several hours; later, I got woken by William, "You want to eat?"

"Sure, I'll get dressed."

We did not eat on campus but went into Livermore and ate Chinese food. As we were eating, I said, "I would like you to develop a way to be able to carry a large amount of food and for an extended amount of time that doesn't use too much room."

"That's a big order and will take time to do."

"Do you think it is impossible?"

"No, but do you have any ideas?

"Possibly breaking down the food to the molecular level."

"Breaking it down to that small, I don't think will be a big deal, but bring it back to what it was will be a problem, but I will give it a try."

"When am I going to meet this friend of yours?"

"Do you want me to bring him by?"

"Yes."

"I might be traveling for a while."

"Where are you going?"

"I don't know." We went home, and I got on the computer and looked at areas that I might want to visit, and I decided to at first travel around the United States. I would not go for a while; I wanted things here going right before I went.

William was spending more and more time with his friend. I did meet him and was not impressed with him, but I did not say anything to

William. The project I gave William was going slowly, but it was moving forward since William was not around much. I talked to Fred, my project manager, and asked him, "How long until you finish the outer welds on the starship?"

"By the end of next month, we should get finished with the outside; then we will start with the inside that will take about a year and a half, I would guess."

"I'm going to travel around the United States. I have your telephone number as well as all the other departments." "I'll be back to inspect all the welds and the smoke test and if there are any problems." "Don't try to take shortcuts with the welding; everything must be perfect."

"Yes, Sir." "When are you leaving?"

"As soon as William comes back."

William had not come back for another three weeks after being gone for more than a month. He came with his boyfriend, whose name was Scott, and I said, "I'm going away for some time."

"Where are you going?"

"I'm just going to travel around the United States and then to Europe."

"I was planning to go to our estate in England with Scott."

"Well, before you go, will you light a fire under those working on the food project?" "Also, will you give me a call every so often in case there is a problem, and I know where you are," I said, not so happy.

"What is the matter; you sound mad?"

I looked at Scott and said, "Perhaps we should talk privately."

"You can talk in front of Scott."

"Alright, Have you lost interest in what we are doing here?"

"Yes, I want to have a little fun in my life."

"And you want to distance yourself from me."

"Are you jealous?"

"No, you're just not the same William as you use to be." "If you don't want to be here anymore, I will take over your department; just tell them that I'm in charge of your department."

"I still love you."

"Sometimes I wonder," I said as I went out the door. I was upset, but I was resigned to the fact that William was going down his path, and I could do nothing. I went over to the starship site and checked out the work that had gotten done.

"I thought you were going on a trip, Sir?" said Fred.

"I am, but I need to get the lawyers busy stopping the government from drafting me into the military." After talking to the lawyers, I went over to building two to light a fire under them. While I was there talking to the project manager, William entered the office. "I'll be taking over the projects dealing with food," I said.

"I didn't say I gave up this department," said William.

"You're too busy with your personal life."

"It's not for you to decided."

"Then get your site in order." I left for our apartment, and once there, I packed my things, withdrew a large amount of cash, and headed to Aunt Dorothy's first.

THIRTEEN

FINDING MYSELF

"I'M SURPRISED YOU'RE HERE; you have been so busy with that ship of yours."

"I'm going to take some time off and travel the country." "I'll come back from time to time to make sure everything is going well." We talked for about an hour, and I left for my parent's house. As with my aunt, my parents were surprised to see me and wanted to know where William was. I told them about William, and they were surprised but did not think much of it. I let them know I would travel throughout the United States, and I then left to visit Charles Kahler.

Charles was working on his car in his garage, and when he spotted me and said with a smile, "You come to kidnap me again?"

"Kidnap, you came willingly." "What are you doing?"

"Working on my car."

"Why?" "I gave you enough money to have someone do it for you."

"I haven't gotten that money."

"Why?"

"My father wants me to wait until I am older and after I go to college."

"You're the same age as me."

"Yes, I know." "What are you doing here?" "Aren't you busy at your laboratory?"

"Yes, I've been swamped." "I worked so hard it put me into the hospital, so I'm going to take some time off and travel around the United States at first."

"By yourself?"

"Yes, unless I can talk you into going with me."

"I can't; I don't have the money." "Why don't you take William with you."

"William is involved with someone; his name is Scott." "You don't need money, and when you come home, you will have more money than you need."

"After you told me about William, what will our relationship be?"

"I love you anything you want."

He thought for a few minutes and then said, "I'd like to go with you, but I better not." "I will be attending a university in a couple of days, and I don't want to upset my parents again."

"I'm disappointed, but I understand." After a bit, I left and headed east; when I got to Winnemucca, I stopped for the night. The next day I went to Aurora, Colorado, and stayed there also overnight. I knew I mainly wanted to roam east of the Mississippi, but I thought of stopping in Missouri to visit my aunt. I stopped overnight in Clinton, Missouri, near my aunt's house, near Ellsinore, Missouri. The next day I arrived at Ellsinore at about ten-thirty in the morning. I stopped at an old fashion gas station and asked if they knew where my Aunt Adeline Kornack lived.

"Go down that dirt road about three miles, and you will come to a white house with a red barn," said the attendant at the station. I thanked him, and headed down the road, and came to a place described by the gas station, man. On the mailbox was Paul Kornack, and I went into the front yard and knocked on the door.

"Hello; are you my Aunt Adeline Kornack?" I said.

"I don't know; who are you?"

"Oh, excuse me, I'm James Reno."

"Manuel's Jimmy."

"Yes."

"You're blond, and you don't look anything like your brothers."

"My parents didn't tell you about me."

"I know you got kidnaped."

"I've gotten altered; it's a long story if you want to hear it."

"Well, come into the house and tell me." For the next hour and a half, I told her everything, including William. "That's quite a story."

"It's all true." I then brushed my hair away from my ears and showed her what Jim Hooker did. She believed me then, and we talked about what I was doing now. Some of my cousins came home, and I spoke to them also. I got invited to have dinner there, and I accepted, and as we ate, I talked. "When I lived on Neverland, my name was Peter the Pan." "My brother William had the name of John the pan." "Our father was James Hooker."

My cousin Tom smiled and asked jokingly, "Could you fly, and did Tinkerbell live with you?"

"I hadn't flown for a long time, but I could fly as well as John could." "Tinkerbell lived in a village near my home. I was very close to her." Everyone was noticeably quiet and staring at me, so I added, "My mother was Windy; she lived in the same village as Tinkerbelle." "Unfortunately, my mother Windy died." "I know it is hard to believe, but it is all true." At that, I showed them my ears.

"Peter Pan is novel, it's a book, it's not real," said my cousin Ray.

"Yes, I know, but all novels have some truth." "My grandfather Peter, the Pan Hooker was the first Peter Pan, and he was friends of James Matthew Barrie who wrote about him." "I have been told I am more like the Peter Pan in the book."

"We will have to see you fly after we eat," said my cousin Mike.

"Alright, I will give it a try," I said. We went outside, and I ask if it would be alright to strip down.

"To your shorts, it's alright," said my uncle.

I strip and ran and then jumped up about twenty feet and about forty feet out and landed on the ground. I turned around and saw all my relatives looking at me in shock. I walked over to them and said, "I told you I could." I was offered to stay with them for a while, but I said, "I don't want to impose any more than I have; I should be going; besides, I need to make a few telephone calls tomorrow to California."

"Well, it's getting late; no use of leaving now, and you can make your calls from here," said Uncle Paul.

"Alright, I'll stay, but tomorrow I'll have to leave."

The next morning, I went into the kitchen where my aunt was, and she asked, "Did you sleep well?"

"Yes."

"Are you hungry?"

"Not really."

"Well, you need to eat something." She gave me some cereal to eat, and after I ate it, I sat in her living room with her.

"May I use your telephone in about a half-hour?" "I have to call my project manager and head of security."

"Yes." "Where are you heading after here?"

"Up north, then I'll cross the Mississippi River and head east." "I'm thinking about going to the New England states first, then head south."

"James, what are you looking for?"

"I don't know; the only thing I do know when I find it, I'll know it." I made my calls, and everything was fine. I left first to Poplar Bluff, and I went to a bank. "I would like to speak to the bank manager," I said.

I got directed to the office of Mr. Biel, and I said, "My name is James Reno." "My Aunt and Uncle Kornack live in Ellsinore." "Do they have an account here?"

"Yes, they do."

"I would like to deposit a million dollars into their account and pay off any loans they may have through you." "Then I wish you to send them a letter stating how much is in their account and that the loan is paid off; do not let them know it was me who did this for them."

"How would you like to deposit the money?"

"Bank transfer." I gave him all the information he needed, and after about twenty minutes, he gave me a receipt, and I left the bank. As I was getting into my car, my uncle spotted me and stopped to talk to me.

"James, what were you doing in the bank?"

"I got some money to travel."

"You are heading out then?"

"Yes, thank you all for being so kind to me."

"You're my nephew; you don't need to thank us." We talk for a few minutes, and I drove away. I ended up in Hicksville, Ohio, and decided to stay for a few days. Hicksville was a nice-looking town, but the people were not very friendly, and from what I got told, Hicksville gets windy and very cold in the winter. I moved on to Wellsboro, Pennsylvania, and I stayed for two days also. I liked Wellsboro; the people were more friendly than in Hicksville, but I did not care for their winter either, so I decided to leave. I was at a restaurant where truckers ate, just off the highway. A young child who looked nine or ten came into the restaurant. I assume the child was a boy but looked and sounded more like a girl. He was asking truckers if they were going to California, and most said no.

One fat and balding trucker said, "I'm eventually going there."

I knew that look, and I knew that the boy would be in great danger. I got up and said to the boy, "Come with me; you don't want to go with him."

"Say, mind your own business."

"The boy needs someone to defend him."

"You could get yourself hurt."

I gave him a threatening look and said, "So could you." At that, I grabbed the boy and brought him to my table.

"He was going to hurt you badly, maybe kill you."

"How do you know?" asked the boy.

"I was once your age and saw that look before, and I could tell by the way he was talking." "I'll get you something to eat, and we will talk about what you want to do." He had a hamburger with fries and a large coke. As we were eating, I noticed that trucker was eyeing us, and he had an angry look; I knew there would be trouble. For now, I just ignored him and started asking the boy questions. "My name is James Reno; what is your name?

"Kevin." He hesitated then said, "Kevin Jones." I knew his last name was not Jones, but I did not say anything right then.

"How old are you, Kevin?"

"Eleven, but I will soon be twelve," he said, wanting to be older.

I was about to ask Kevin why he wanted to go to California when I notice the trucker angrily pay for his meal by throwing the money at the waitress. Then as he came storming towards me, he said, "I'll see you outside."

"I'll come now," I said. I turned to the waitress and said, "I'll come back to finish eating and pay my bill; you better call the authorities, tell them to send an ambulance." Kevin followed me out to the parking lot, as did some other truckers and two waitresses. I said to Kevin, "If anyone asks, you are my nephew." "I've come to take you to California, and you were asking the other truckers if they ever been to California because you wanted to know what it was like, understand?"

"Yes, Sir." As soon as I got outside, the trucker rushed me, but he was too slow, and I was able to jump over him, which surprised him. He tried to take a few swings at me but kept on missing, and I finally smacked him with a hard punch to the nose, which immediately broke and bled. He grabbed a tire iron from his truck and tried to swing at me with it, but I blocked his arm and broke his arm with my other hand. I then swept his feet, and he went down, hitting his head on his truck. By this time, the police showed up, and I stepped back from him.

"Put your hands behind your back," said the officer. I did as he said, and he handcuffed me. The officer went over to the trucker and checked him out as the ambulance showed up. A separate police car showed up with two officers, and they talked to the officer checking out the trucker. Meanwhile, the one officer who had me asked me, "What's going on here?"

"That trucker wanted to harm my nephew." "I pulled my nephew away from him, and he took offense to it and wanted to fight me."

"What is your name?"

"James Reno."

He stared at me and then asked, "You got an ID?"

"It's in my back pocket."

He took it out and looked at it and then asked, "You use to be Peter Pan, am I correct?"

"Yes."

"We talked to the witnesses, and they back this man," said another officer who just came over. "We also ran that trucker's name and description, and it appears they want him in several states." I was uncuffed and said I was free to go.

I walked over to Kevin, and one female officer asked, "Why is your nephew so dirty?"

"I just got him; his parents didn't take care of him very well." "That's why I'm taking him back to California." Kevin and I went back into the restaurant; we finished eating and left. After driving for about an hour, I went off the highway and parked to talk to Kevin, "We need to talk before we go any further."

"Alright."

"You need to start telling me the truth." "I believe you when you said your name is Kevin, but I don't believe you when you said your last name was Jones." "What is your real last name?"

"Miller."

"What is your real age?"

"I'm almost eleven; I didn't lie about that."

"I'm glad you didn't lie about that, but now tell me about your parents; where are they?"

"They both died."

"Are you telling me the truth?"

"Yes."

"You don't have any other relatives."

"No, none that want me."

"Why did you leave your foster parents?"

"They didn't like me, and they were mean." "They wouldn't feed me very much, and I was kicked out of the house early in the morning and couldn't come back until night." "If I had to go to the bathroom, I would have to find some bushes to go in."

"Why didn't they like you; you're an easy person to love."

"I prefer boys to a girl, and they caught me with another boy." "Are you still going to take me to California?"

"Nothing has changed if you want to go with me; I'll take you." "We do need to talk about why you want to go to California."

"It's a long way from here, and I thought about maybe getting into movies or TV."

"You're almost eleven years old; you are not old enough to get into the movies or TV without an adult signing a contract." "You also need an agent; most actors get hired through agents." "You have nowhere to live nor have any money for food."

"I hear it's warm there." "I could sleep on a beach or in a park, and I know how to get money for food," he said, not so sure of himself.

"I think I know how you would make money, and you wouldn't survive a month before you were dead." "If a chicken hawk didn't pick you up and make you a male prostitute, then a police officer will get you and send you back to New York."

He had his head down and had a hopeless look on his face. I could see tears coming down his cheeks, and he said, "What am I going to do?"

I stared at him for a few seconds, then said, "I'll take you with me and take care of you." "I'll protect you from harm; you will never be hungry, and you will have nice clothing." "I will even help you get into the entertainment industry if you want, but I don't think that is what you want." "I think you just want a normal life and to be loved, am I right?"

"Yes," he said, sniffling.

"You will have to follow my rules." "Are you willing to do this?"

"Yes, but what are the rules."

"You obey what I say, no lying to me, no secrets between us." "I want you to express your feelings, and to protect you and me, you keep private what we do, talk about, and especially what you see." "Where we live have many secrets things there that no one can know about." "Do you understand, and will you follow these rules?"

"Yes."

"I will go into more detail about the rules later, and then we will seal the rules." "We won't be going through New York; instead, we will go south when I legally get custody of you, then we will go North, okay."

"Yes."

We headed out going south, and when we got into another state, I said, "Kevin watch for a mall so I can get you some clothing." Twenty minutes later, we found a mall, and we went into a Macy's store. Before we got out of the car, I checked the size of Kevin's clothing. I got him two packs of briefs and four shirts. I then got some pants that I thought would fit him and took him into the dressing room. Fortunately, the pants fit, and I got him three pairs of pants. I got him also bib overalls and another button-down blue shirt. I got him two packs of socks at the shoe department and a new pair of sneakers, which excited him. I got him a jacket in case he needed it and a suitcase to carry everything. "Do you want some toys?"

"Yes," he said excitedly, "but can I get into my new clothes first?"

"No, I want to clean you up first before you wear them." We got some toys and left looking for a place to sleep. We stopped at a nice Super Eight motel, and I got a nice room. After bringing everything into the room, I closed the curtains, and stripped down to my briefs, and removed Kevin's clothing, and his clothing reeked. I threw everything into one of the bags from the mall. I ran his shower, and when the water was suitable, we got in. I shampooed his hair; I had to do this three times, then I put hair conditioner on his hair. I washed the rest of him good then wash the hair conditioner out of his hair. I bathed myself and got out. I told Kevin to sit down, and I ran his bathwater. Then I said, "Stay there until I come to get you."

"Okay."

I dried myself off and shaved, then I got Kevin out of the bathtub, dried him off, then dressed him in his bib overalls with a blue shirt and his new tennis shoes. After combing his hair, I pointed to the mirror, and he checked himself out, admiring how he looked. "Let's go get something to eat," I said.

"Okay, I'm getting hungry anyway," Kevin said with a smile. After we ate, we went back to our room, and we stripped out of our clothing, and I let Kevin play with his toys while I read. At nine o'clock, we went to bed, and Kevin snuggled next to me. The following day, we showered and headed southwest, not going anyplace in particular. We ended up in Blackstone, Virginia, and we got a room in a motel. Blackstone was alright, but I wanted something more. Kevin wanted to take a bath instead of showering, so I let him; I figured he wanted to play in the tub. We just stayed overnight, then headed south to North Carolina and ended up in the lovely town of Hendersonville. Hendersonville was a pleasant town, and I decided to stay there for a couple of days. Kevin was becoming close to me, and he started to call me daddy; I did not say anything; I would talk to him about that later. After looking at some houses, I almost bought a home here.

"Would you like to live here, Kevin?"

"I will live anywhere you are, daddy, but maybe we should look at a few more towns."

"Alright, we will head west tomorrow." He grabbed my hand, looked up, and smiled at me as we walked down the street to a restaurant. That night we were in our room, and about nine o'clock, he crawled up on the bed and snuggled next to me as I put my arm around him.

He leaned into me even tighter and asked, "Daddy, do you love me?"

"More than you can understand." "Do you love me?'

"Oh yes, ever since you beat up the bad trucker."

"You need to let me know you love me from time to time." "I notice you keep calling me daddy; do you want me to adopt you."

"Yes, will you?"

"I do love you; I'll see what I can do."

The next morning, we headed west, and we ended in a town called Laurel, Mississippi. I liked the town, but I had two concerns: hurricanes and tornados, so after we got our room, we went to eat at a small restaurant. There was no one in the restaurant except Kevin and me, so I asked the waitress to stay and talk to us. "I can't, but the owner could."

"That would be good," I said. A heavy-set black woman came out from the kitchen.

"Mable said you all wanted to talk to me."

"Yes, please sit down." She sat, and I said, "My name is James Reno, and this is my son Kevin."

"Well, it sure is nice to meet you." "My name is Tizzy Jenkins; what is it you want to know?"

"I'm thinking of buying a home here, but I'm concern about hurricanes and tornados."

"Oh, you shouldn't be too worried about them." "When there is a hurricane, we get a lot of rain and a little wind, but we don't get much damage from it." "Tornados, we occasionally have them." "They are generally out of town; we have never had any damage here."

"How do you think we would get treated here?"

"Everyone is friendly here." "May I ask you what you do for a living?"

"My brother and I own a laboratory in California; however, we have so much wealth; we don't need to do anything."

We finished eating and went to a realtor. I told him what I was looking for, and he said tomorrow he would take Kevin and me around looking at houses. After Kevin and I took our bath, I let him play on the other bed as I made some calls back at the lab. I let my project manager know after I leave here, I would be heading back home. I also talked to my security, who told me he had not seen William in some time; this concerned me. I then called my lawyers and spoke to them for some time, telling them about Kevin, and they said they would start working on it.

The next day we found a four-bedroom craftsman's house in an excellent neighborhood. I told the realtor that I wanted it, and I signed the paperwork. I then went to a designer and a contractor to remodel the house the way I wanted it. We stayed there another day and then left for home. As we traveled back home, Kevin became even more closer to me, and he was affectionate. We stayed in the town of Norman, Oklahoma, overnight. The next day we stayed in Gallup, New Mexico, and we went to dinner there. Kevin was noticeably quiet at dinner, and I asked, "What's the matter, Kevin; are you tired of traveling?"

"Yes, daddy."

"We will be home in a couple of days." Kevin nodded and leaned next to me, and shut his eyes. I took him back to our room and put him to bed. We left late after I bathed Kevin. And we ended up in Barstow, California. Kevin had been sleeping except when we ate in Flagstaff, Arizona.

When we pulled into a motel, I woke Kevin and said, "Time to wake up and get cleaned up."

"Where are we?" Kevin asked.

"Barstow, Barstow California."

Kevin looked all around and said, "It's not what I thought California would look like, daddy."

"It will change by the time we get home tomorrow."

After breakfast, the next day, we headed north towards Livermore. Kevin was wide awake, looking all around at the landscape. Finally, after about an hour, he asked, "Daddy, where is the ocean?"

I pointed left and said, "About seventy-five miles that way." We traveled for about another three hours and came to the Altamont Pass, and I said, "At the other end of this pass is Livermore." Forty-five minutes later, we left the freeway and entered the starship laboratory campus. It was good to be back home; we drove up to building one, and I parked in my space in the parking garage under the building. I noticed that William's car was missing, and I assume he still had not come back. Kevin and I unloaded the car and brought our things to the elevator and up to our apartment. "I'll show you everything we have here tomorrow, especially the starship," I told Kevin. I called all departments for a meeting down on the second floor for tomorrow at ten. At the meeting, there will be security and my lawyers also. As I was hanging up our clothing, I noticed that all of William's things were missing. There were no notes or anything as to what was going on. I checked our account activities, and the last transaction got done yesterday, and it got done at a nightclub in the Los Angeles area.

F O U R T E E N

WILLIAM

ALL DEPARTMENT HEADS AND all others showed up for the meeting. The first subject that I brought up was my military deferment and Kevin's adoption. "Because of your great wealth, I've been able to get the state to approve your adoption of Kevin," said Mr. Leland Walter. "You adopting Kevin has helped with the deferment." "Also, the fact that you run this facility, the government feels that you are best at working here than going into the military, at this time."

"Get me all the paperwork I need to make Kevin legally my son." "When was the last time that someone has seen my brother William?"

"I haven't seen or heard from him since shortly after you left, which is unusual," said his department head.

"Mr. Scott Prichard, please see if you can find William; I have a bad feeling." "The last time he withdrew cash was two days ago at a nightclub in the Los Angeles area." "I have a picture of his boyfriend at my apartment; after this meeting, I'll give you the information."

"Yes, Sir."

"Meanwhile, William's department will take direction from me."

"Yes, Sir," said the head of William's department.

"How is the starship coming along?"

"We are still welding, Sir." "Everything looks good; when will you come and inspect?"

"Tomorrow." The rest of the meeting went on for another hour, and I went upstairs with the head of security, Mr. Scott Prichard.

When we went into the apartment Kevin, who was in his underpants, came running into my arms when he spotted me. I kissed him and said, "This is Mr. Scott Prichard; he is the head of security here." "Mr. Prichard, this is my son Kevin."

"Nice to meet you, Kevin."

"Nice to meet you too," said Kevin.

"I'll get you what I have, Mr. Prichard." I gave him a bank statement and a picture of William and his boyfriend. He said he would get right on it and keep me posted if he finds out anything.

After he left, I sat down with Kevin and said, "We will go tomorrow to see the starship and other things going on here." "Would you like that?"

"Yes."

"You don't have to worry about someone taking you away from me; I have full custody of you." "As soon as we can get a court date, I will be adopting you, if that is alright with you."

Kevin became excited, and he said, "How long do you think it will take, daddy?"

"I'm not sure, maybe two or three weeks." "Why don't you get dressed, and we will go to the mall for some clothing and other things." He rushed to get his clothes on, and we went downstairs to the parking lot, and we drove off to the mall.

After getting a ton of clothing, a swimsuit, and toys, I asked Kevin, "Are you hungry?"

"Yes." We ate and went back home, and the next day we went to see the starship. Kevin was amazed when he saw the starship. I spot-checked the welds, and they looked good; I informed my project manager of what I wanted. After the starship, we checked out other areas, and Kevin was fascinated with everything.

The next day I got a call from Mr. Prichard; he asked me, "Would you freeze William's and your account, so no one but you can get into the account?" "Yes, I will take care of it today." Kevin and I went down to the bank. I talked to the manager and put a freeze on all our accounts, but not until I open another account with a large sum of money to keep everything operational. I had also hired a tutor for Kevin to get him caught up with his studies, and they were to start tomorrow. That afternoon, I took Kevin swimming at the hotel, and after we ate lunch, Kevin was tired, so we went back to our apartment. While Kevin was playing with his toys, I called my parents and let them know about Kevin and my concerns about William.

Over the next six weeks, the welding on the starship hull got completed to my satisfaction, and I approved a leak test to be performed. The test would take about two weeks to complete, so in the meanwhile, I ordered all the materials to apply the same coatings that were on the Black Pearl. We had to make our panels and sealer, and that took a lot of time. Mr. Prichard tracked me down one afternoon while I was at the starship, and Kevin was studying with his tutor. "James, we need to talk in private."

I knew something was wrong because he never addressed me by my first name. "Alright, let's go to the restaurant."

Mr. Prichard ordered a coffee, and I ordered some tea. "We found your brother's boyfriend; we found him hopped up on drugs." "We held him for a few days until he was sober enough to answerer some questions." "At first, he wouldn't answer any questions about William, so we knocked him around, and he talked fast." "He had left him in an abandoned building." "We found him in terrible shape, barely alive." "The ambulance took him to Linda Vista Community Hospital, where they don't know if he will live." "The San Diego Sheriff Department arrested the boyfriend."

I stared off into space, and tears seeped from my eyes. "I'll be flying down there as soon as I make arrangements for Kevin."

"Yes, Sir." "I would suggest you let me accompany you."

"Alright." I got up and left for my apartment. At the apartment, I explained to Kevin about his uncle and asked him, "Do you want your grandparents to stay with you, or you can stay with them?" "If you don't want your grandparents, I can get some other person to stay with you."

"I want to go with you."

I thought a second then said, "I wouldn't advise it; I don't know what your uncle looks like."

"I don't care, daddy; I want to go with you."

"Alright, Mr. Prichard is going too." After I informed my parents what was going on, we packed and left with Mr. Prichard to the airport.

After a little more than an hour, we landed in San Diego, and I said, "Mr. Prichard, would you get us a car rental."

"Yes, Sir."

Mr. Prichard got us a small compact car, and I said, "Take us to the hospital." With Kevin in the back seat, we headed to the hospital, which took about an hour to get there. We found out that William was in intensive care, and after much discussion, Kevin and I could go into his room. They did not want Kevin in at all nor more than one person at a time. William looked terrible, but he was still alive. I hoped that he would recover; he was strong because of what James Hooker did to him, so maybe he would get through this one. He was not awake, so after about twenty minutes of holding his hand, I found his nurse and started asking her some questions. "What is the chance my brother will recover?"

"I can't say I will find his doctor so that he can talk to you."

"Thank you."

Ten minutes later, an older man came to William's room and said, "Mr. Reno, I have gotten told you wanted to talk to me?"

"Yes, is there someplace we can go to talk about my brother?"

"Please come with me." After I told Kevin to stay with his uncle, I followed the doctor to a small room. "Mr. Reno, your brother is in terrible shape." "He had a cocktail of drugs in him, and it has done a lot of damage." "He has also been assaulted and abused." "We do not know if he will survive; it's amazing, he is still alive."

"If you haven't figured it out already, he has been altered and enhanced much like me." "I want the best of everything for him; we have more than enough money." "Not to disrespect you, but best of doctors too."

"Alright." "I'm interested in learning more about this enhancement."

"Anything you want." I stuck my hand into my pocket, handed him two bottles, and said, "Give him this; it will help him." "Three equal shots per vile." "The second vial is for you to check, which I'm sure you were going to do."

"What is it?"

"My stepfather was a genius when it came to medical things." "William and I have a background in medicine." "Check out who we are, and you will understand I know what I'm talking about." I knew he had no intention of giving William the medication, but I had a plan if this happened. I had a third vile in my pocket and plan to give it to William regardless.

"I'll have to think about giving this to your brother," the doctor said.

I nodded and went back to William and asked Kevin, "Has there been any difference with your uncle?"

"No."

"Mr. Prichard, I'm going to give my brother some medicine; please make sure no one sees me."

"Yes, Sir." Mr. Prichard went to the front of the room and said, "Go ahead, Sir."

I pulled a needle out of my pocket and gave William a shot, then replaced the needle in my pocket. "We will come back tomorrow morning; there won't be any change before then anyway," I said.

I went up to a nurse and said, "We are going to get a room; what number can I call to find out the status of my brother?" The nurse gave me a number, and we left to find some lodging.

That night late while Kevin slept, I called ICU and asked the condition, "He seems to be resting comfortably, Mr. Reno."

"We will be in to visit him tomorrow late morning." At that, I hung up and went to bed.

The next morning after breakfast, I fixed a shot and placed it into my pocket. We went to the hospital and got there at about eleven in the morning. Right off, I could see William looked better, and I knew the medication I gave him was working. "Sir, when are you going to give him his next shot?" asked Mr. Prichard.

"I will give it to him about one o'clock."

About twenty minutes after we got there, a team of doctors came into William's room, and we had to step out. When they stepped out, William's doctor said, "He looks excellent today; perhaps we won't have to use your medicine." I smiled, and at that, the doctors left, and we went back into his room.

At one o'clock, I had Mr. Prichard watch as I gave William another dose of medicine. About twenty minutes later, he started moving around; he opened his eyes and then closed them again. "I think we will get some lunch now." "By the time we come back, he may be awake," I said.

We got back to William's room at about a quarter after two in the afternoon, and I was happy to see William was awake. He smiled at me, and I bent down and kissed him and said, "You made me very worried; you almost died."

"I'm sorry I didn't mean to upset you."

"I'm alright now." "Do you know what happened?"

"No."

"It turns out that your boyfriend drugged you and physically abused you." "He left you in an abandoned building; it was Mr. Prichard who found your boyfriend and got him to tell them where you were." "Your boyfriend is in jail now on a million-dollar bond." "He has been charged with several drug charges, kidnapping, attempted murder, and larceny."

"He was demanding more and more money from me, and he was trying to dominate me, but he wasn't strong enough," William said.

"The fact that you hadn't contacted me or the lab and some suspicious transactions with our accounts, I sent out Mr. Prichard to find you."

"Thank you, Mr. Prichard." Mr. Prichard nodded and smiled, and William asked, "Who is this boy?"

"He is your Nephew, my son Kevin." "It's a long story; I'll explain when you are back home."

"Kevin, come over here and say hello to your uncle William."

He bent over and kissed his uncle and said, "I'm happy you are getting better, Uncle William."

We were talking another ten minutes when the doctor came into the room and said, "It's amazing that you are recovering so fast, William." "James, here are your two vials; we won't need them now." I looked at William, smiled, and winked, and he giggled. He knew that I did something, and I would tell him tomorrow. After talking to him a bit longer, I told him I would be here tomorrow, and we left to get some dinner and then back to our lodging.

The next day we found out that William was doing so well that they moved him to a private room. We went in and saw a smiling William, and I said, "Well, you look better."

"Thanks to you," said William.

"I'm going to have Mr. Prichard take Kevin to Marine World and San Diego Zoo tomorrow while I'm with you." "Then the next day, I'm going to go back home so Kevin can resume his studies, and I can get back to work." "I will also leave one of Mr. Prichard's men with you until you and he can come home."

"Alright, James."

"Mr. Prichard, contact one of your men and have him stay down here with William until he can accompany William back home."

"Yes, Sir."

About an hour later, I said, "Mr. Prichard, kept guard while I give William his last shot."

"Yes, Sir."

"Is that one of Fathers elixirs James?" asked William.

"Yes, in part, it's his and the Pongos." I gave William a shot and then told William, "You need to rest now; try to get some sleep."

"Alright."

William closed his eyes, and we all left for lunch. "Mr. Prichard, tomorrow while I'm with William, I want you to take Kevin to the San Diego Zoo and Marine World also, find a beach so he can see the ocean."

"Yes, Sir."

"Tonight, I will be going to visit William; there is no need for Kevin or you to be there, so would you watch Kevin while I'm with William?"

"Yes, Sir."

"When do you think your security man will be here."

"She is a female, and she should be here tonight." I was just about ready to go back to the hospital when a Mary Trumbo showed up at Mr. Prichard's room, and Mr. Prichard introduced me to her. "Sir, this is Mary Trumbo; she will stay with William until he can come home."

"I believe I have seen you on the starship campus," I said. "I'm going to visit William." "Would you like to go with me?"

"Yes, but just give me a few minutes to get my room."

"Alright." We took Miss Trumbo's rented car to the hospital and went up to William's room. When William spotted us, he had a smile ear to ear, and I said, "This is Miss Mary Trumbo; she will be accompanying you home when they release you."

"Hello, William." "I hope you are feeling better," Mary said.

"I do, thank you for asking." We stayed until about ten o'clock and then left at the urging of the nurse.

The next day Mr. Prichard took Kevin to do the activities we talked about, and Miss Trumbo and I went to see William. I noticed that

William spent a lot of time with Miss Trumbo, and I thought that was odd because William preferred males. At one point, I asked Miss Trumbo to go down to the cafeteria to get me something to eat. While alone with William, I asked him, "Do you have feelings for this woman?"

"Yes."

"How?"

"How what?"

"Well, you prefer males, don't you?"

"I thought I did, but I was just confused; besides, I would like a child, as you have someday."

"I'm adopting Kevin; you could adopt too."

"You don't want me to pursue Miss Trumbo?"

"I want you to do what will make you happy." "If you want to have a relationship with her, then do it." "I just want you happy."

"Thanks; since you are asking me about my love life, what is the story with Kevin?"

I smiled and said, "As I was touring around the United States, I came across a filthy Kevin who was running away from an abusive foster home." "He wanted to go to California to be a movie star." "I told him the truth about his chances of getting a job in the entertainment industry." "It turns out he didn't want to get into acting; he just wanted to be loved." "He became closer to me, and by the time I bought a home in Mississippi, he wanted me to adopt him." "The adoption should be finalized soon."

"You bought a house?"

"Yes, after you rest for a while, Kevin and I will take you there." When Miss Trumbo started to interact with William, I stepped back and let William and her interact. I even left his room for a few hours so that William and Miss Trumbo could have some private time together. By the end of the day, I rejoined them and said my goodbyes to William and instructed Miss Trumbo to take good care of him and bring him straight home.

"Yes, Sir." I kissed William, and Miss Trumbo drove me back to my lodging. As we were traveling, I said, "I think my brother likes you."

"I'm sorry if you are offended."

"On the contrary, if it were my son, I would, but it's William, and what makes him happy makes me happy." "How do you feel about him?"

"I'm very fond of him."

"He is very good looking once he gains his weight back, much more than me," I said.

"You love him a lot, don't you?"

"Yes, he is the best brother I could have."

"Don't you have other brothers?"

"Yes, but they are very different than William and I."

"You think you will ever marry?"

"Yes, when I find the right one for me."

Kevin was excited about his day with Mr. Prichard, and he could not wait to tell me about his day. "Daddy, you should have seen what I saw today." "The zoo must have had every animal there is in the world." "At Marine World, I got to pet a whale and got wet by a killer whale."

"It sounds like you had a lot of fun today." "Mr. Prichard, was that your first trip to the zoo and Marine World."

"Yes, Sir."

"Did you enjoy yourself?"

"Very much so, Sir." We all talked into the night about their day, and Kevin and I went to bed.

After we bathed and ate breakfast the next day, we went to the airport and flew back home. At home, I called the teacher to resume Kevin's studies. I had built another bedroom in our apartment for Kevin. I also called my parents and told them about William. I checked all departments and was satisfied with their progress. William came home after three weeks; he seemed to be in a great mood. I had built another bedroom in our apartment for Kevin. He was not happy sleeping alone, but I told him he would not be sleeping alone all the time, and he could decorate his room the way he wanted it.

Over the next several days, William mainly stayed home; he did interact with Kevin more than he had. I came home from working on the starship one day the following week, and William was not home, "Kevin do you know where your uncle went?"

"Not really; he said he needed to get some air." "He got dressed up nice and put on some of that smelly stuff you put on after you shave."

I had an idea where he went, and I said to Kevin, "I'll be gone for a while; I'll be back." I was about to go over to security when I noticed our electric car was over at the restaurant, so I went over there first. When I walked in, William with Mary Trumbo spotted me, and William called me over to them. "I was wondering where you went."

"I had to get out of the apartment and get some air; besides, I wanted to see Mary."

"Well, I came to get dinner for Kevin and me." "Are you going to eat at home?"

"No, I thought I would take Mary into San Francisco for dinner if I can use your car."

"You know where the keys are; you two have fun."

"Thanks, James."

That night I slept with Kevin, but I woke up about one-thirty in the morning when William came in. I did not greet him, thinking he might have Mary with him. I will find out how it went at breakfast. At ten o'clock in the morning, I was up in the kitchen making breakfast. I checked in on William and seen Mary there, so I made breakfast for everyone, consisting of pancakes and bacon and orange juice and tea. I had Kevin sit at the table just before eleven. As I was serving Kevin in walks, William half asleep and with nothing on, he said, "You have any more of that food."

"Yes, there is more than enough for you and Mary."

"Oh, you know she is here."

"Yes, I checked in on you this morning." "I take it things went well last night."

"Oh, yes," William said with a smile.

"Go get Mary, and I will serve the both of you."

I served everyone, including me; William asked, "Do you think when we go visit your house, we could take Mary?"

"I assume you asked Mary already?"

"Do you want to go, Mary?"

"Yes, I would like to go anywhere you go."

"Then I don't see why we couldn't, but I think we should talk to Mr. Prichard first."

"I'll do that myself; when do you think we will be going?"

"About two weeks, I would think."

Two weeks passed quickly. William was looking good, and his involvement with Mary was going well. Mr. Prichard gave Mary time off to go with us to Mississippi. I had told Mr. Prichard where this was heading, and he was aware of it and was looking for a replacement for Mary. All departments were making breakthroughs with what they were doing. The starship had its outer skin completed, and a special paint was getting applied to the hull. The ship's inside got worked on at a fast rate. The only exception was the engine room and a few other places with much more to do. William's department had a breakthrough with the problem with food was solved. We still had a water problem, so I had part of William's building converted to solve that problem. We flew to Mississippi instead of driving and rented a car when we got there. We went straight to the house. People were still working on the house, but it was nearly finished, for the most part. We toured the home; I felt it was remodeled very well; William and Mary were excited by the house. We toured the town and William, and Mary thought the town was charming. It was a little past noon when we went to eat. William said, "I wouldn't mind living here; everybody is so friendly, and it's just beautiful here." "What do you think, Mary?"

"It would be a wonderful place to raise a family?"

"Alright, this is what I could do after we eat and get a room; we will get a realtor and find another house." "While that second house is getting remodeled, you can stay in my house when the second house gets finished; we can decide who gets what house." "How does that sound?"

"That would be great; what do you think, Mary?" asked William.

"That sounds great, but what about work?"

"I don't need to work, James, and I have more money than we could ever spend." "Of course, I wouldn't want to put all the burden of the lab on your back, James."

"Don't worry about that, William." "I've been doing the work for some time now, and we have good people." "If I need you for something, I can give you a call, and you can come back for a few weeks."

"You wouldn't mind?"

"No."

"William, have you forgot something," said Mary.

"What's that?"

"We are not married."

William became beet red in the face, and Kevin giggled; then William said, "I was going to talk to you about that when the time was right."

"And when will that be?" asked Mary.

"When we are alone."

"We will be getting our rooms after we finish eating," I said. We got our rooms after we ate; I had told William to let me know when you want to look for a realtor. About an hour later, Kevin and I got a knock at the door, and it was William wishing to search for a realtor. I drove, and as we were going, I asked, "Well, you two getting married?"

"We have decided to go back to California and have a wedding there." "After the wedding, we plan to fly to England for a honeymoon for a month, then come here to live."

"Sounds like a good plan; you need anything from Kevin and me, let me know."

We found a house near my other home; it was much bigger than my first house. I signed the papers and paid for the house, and then we went to talk to the remodelers. After we finished with the house, we ate dinner and went back to the motel; well, Kevin and I did. I don't know where William and Mary went. The next day we flew back home.

FIFTEEN

TROUBLES BEFORE THE WEDDING

WILLIAM AND MARY WERE busy planning the wedding while Kevin was busy with his tutor and getting ready for school. I was spreading my time between the interior of the starship and the engines; that afternoon, we would test the engines. I had talked to the school principal about a bodyguard for Kevin. Because of who we were and the chances of kidnapping him or harming him, they allowed me to always have a bodyguard with him. I contacted Mr. Prichard's office and told them to have him meet me at the starship. At eleven o'clock in the morning, Mr. Prichard showed up. "You wanted to talk to me, Sir?" asked Mr. Prichard.

"Yes, have you hired another person to replace Mary Trumbo?"

"Yes, Sir."

"Hire another person; I need someone to be with Kevin all the time, especially when he is at school and activities, so pick someone."

"Yes, Sir."

"He starts school in a week, so if you can find someone before that time, I can tell that person exactly what I want."

"Yes, Sir."

We had the new engine's first test-fire, which shook the ground, but it was not quite what I wanted. We did see what was wrong, and the engine went back to the lab to be corrected. That night I received a bodyguard for Kevin, and I told him how I wanted him guarded. Two weeks passed; Kevin was attending school with his bodyguard, which he thought was neat. I kept Kevin's tutor to help him through the first year. I got a letter from the government wanting to speak with me, so I called them, and it got decided that the meeting to be held here at the lab. Something about the letter bothered me, so I went over to security to talk to Mr. Prichard. "Mr. Prichard, I have a feeling that the government is up to something."

"Why would you say that?"

"Well, here is the letter; read it, and tell me what you think."

"Mr. Prichard read the letter and said, "You think they want to take over your labs and starship?"

"Yes, or at least take control of it."

"What do you wish me to do?"

"Are you aware of the forcefield I have around the perimeter of the campus?"

"What is a forcefield?"

"It's a barrier like an invisible fence; no one on the planet can penetrate it." "What I want is when everyone is here at the meeting, I want the forcefield activated." "I want all security people armed and ready in case of invasion." "I want you at the meeting."

"Are you sure this is legal, Sir?"

"I have an agreement with the government to be able to work independently without interference." "I think I should get ahold of my solicitor."

"Solicitor, Sir?"

"Lawyer." I finished talking to Mr. Prichard and called the lawyer that represented William and me when it came to the American government.

"This is Jack Bryant; what can I do for you?"

"Mr. Bryant, this is James Reno." "Do you remember me, Sir?"

"Yes, what can I do for you?"

"I believe I require your services." "The American government wants a meeting with my brother and me over what we are doing at our lab." "The tone of the letter has me concern; I think they want to take over our lab." "What we are doing here is highly secret, and I don't want them to know, at least not right now."

"When is this meeting?"

"Friday afternoon about three-thirty."

"I will make arrangements to be there."

"Don't worry about lodging; we have a five-star hotel here."

"That would be just fine." "I will be there Thursday."

"That would be great, thank you." Thursday came, and I got Mr. Bryant a room and a vehicle. He came to my apartment late in the afternoon. I presented him with the letter I had and the American government contract.

After reading the document for a half-hour, he said, "The government doesn't have a leg to stand on." "I'll be back tomorrow, and I will study these documents very close."

The next day, one hour after Kevin came home from school, the government people came into the starship campus. After they entered, the gates were closed, Mr. Prichard sent out all security, I turned on the forcefield. I waited until everyone was seated, and both William and I walked into the meeting. I had told William I would be doing the talking with William adding to the conversation as needed. "Gentlemen, I think everyone should introduce themselves first, then we can get into this meeting," I said.

"I'm John Forester from the Federal Bureau of Investigation."

"I'm Tom Benedick, also from the Federal Bureau of Investigation."

"I'm Senator Bill Morton."

"Bob Sorenson, I work for OSHA, which is Occupational Safety and Health Administration."

"Terry Farnsworth, Occupational Safety and Health Administration."

"Rich Blevins, Occupational Safety and Health Administration."

"I'm Dr. David Springer; I'm an aeronautical engineer."

"I'm Jack Bryant; I'm the boy's lawyer."

"I'm Scott Prichard, head of Security."

"Joe Summers, Security."

"I'm William Reno.

"I am James, and this property and lab are William's and mine." "Senator Morton, what brings you here today?"

"We have come here to inspect the safety of your workers."

I stared at him for a few seconds, which made him uncomfortable, and then said, "I don't think you are telling me the whole truth." "I think you want to see what William and I are doing here."

"What you are doing here isn't important to us; it's the safety of your workers we are concern about."

"Senator, you don't need the F.B.I., an aeronautical engineer, and you here to check on our workers," said William. "You want to spy on us."

"They are secret not only to protect my brother and me but our people who work here." "They are also secret to protect the United States, England, and Australia if not the whole world."

"Nevertheless, we want to see what you are up to," said the Senator.

I started to talk in Pongo, "What do you think, William?" "Shall we show them?"

"I think if we show them, there should be no cameras or note-taking while we are touring."

"I think we should talk to Mr. Prichard first."

"Yes."

"We wish to talk to the head of security in private first, Senator," I said. He nodded smugly, and Mr. Prichard, William, and I left the room.

"Mr. Prichard, what do you think, should we show them everything?" asked William.

"It would defuse the situation, I would think."

"Alright, send in a half dozen of your men fully armed," I said.

"Senator, this is what we will do; we will show you everything, but no weapons, no cameras, and no note pads." "My brother, myself, and Mr. Prichard with a half dozen of his men fully armed will accompany you," I said.

"I don't think that is acceptable," said the Senator.

"Senator Morton, I believe James and William are very generous with you," said Mr. Bryant. "Legally, they don't have to show you anything."

"It's in the country's best interest."

"Then the country shouldn't have signed the agreement," I said. "It will be my brother's and my way, or you won't be able to see what we have been doing." Just then, six-armed security personnel came into the room.

"Looks like I have no choice but to follow your rules," said the Senator.

"Gentlemen,would you please relinquish your weapons, cameras, and notepads," said Mr. Prichard.

"James, I'm going back to be with Mary," said William.

"Alright."

We went directly to the starship first. The Senator was in total awe at what he saw, as was everyone else in the Senator's group. "Can that thing fly?" asked the Senator.

"Yes, it will fly faster than the speed of light."

"That's kind of hard to believe."

"It was kind of hard to believe Howard Hughes's Spruce Goose could fly, but it did." We went inside and toured the starship amongst the busy workers inside. As we left to go to the other buildings, I said, "There are a lot of things still to be done before we take it out to space."

"You are near the town of Livermore; don't you think you might cause damage to the town?" asked the Senator.

"No, it will sound like a large jet taking off when it goes out into space." "This next building, we are going into, you will need to put on protective clothing so nothing gets contaminated."

We went through the rest of the buildings, and everyone was overly impressed. We ended up at the restaurant, and we gathered in the banquet room. "I feel the government should have control of the facility," said the Senator.

"That isn't going to happen, at least not until my project is finish and my brother and I are paid very well for it."

"I could send troops here to take over this project," said the Senator.

"Try it, and they will die, and I will declare war on the United States." "Don't misunderstand me; I don't want to harm anyone, but we will defend ourselves."

With much anger, the Senator and his people left the campus. Mr. Prichard turned to me and said, "I don't trust him; he will try to take over your lab, Sir."

"He is right, James," said Mr. Bryant.

"What do you two suggest?"

"I think we should stay on high alert, and if the Senator does something, act with appropriate force."

"Go ahead and do that, and meanwhile, double security around Kevin."

"Meanwhile, I'll take care of the legal end of it; I have some friends in Washington," said Mr. Bryant.

I found William and Mary and explained to them what happen and what I intend to do. Later that night, I sat down with Kevin and explained what was going on, and the next day I sent a memo to all the employees. Two weeks passed, and nothing happened. At the start of the third week, Saturday, a convoy of military trucks rolled up to the main gate at ten-thirty in the morning. The campus went on full alert, and the perimeter got locked down. All security got armed with advanced weapons, and the experimental energy lasers got posted around the campus. All departments got notified, and when William got word, he joined me at the front gate. "What are you going to do, James?" asked William.

"Let them make the first move, then respond with the same force." "I have Mr. Bryant working on this problem also." As the military trucks approached the main gate, they had gotten stopped by the campus shields.

William and I waited at the gate to see what would happen next. A group of military people and the Senator came forward. "We come to take over this facility," said the Senator.

"By what authority do you try to do this?" I asked.

"By my authority," he replied angrily.

"Who is the head military person here?"

"I am Colonel Mark Preston."

"Colonel, I have nothing against you or your men and don't want to harm anyone." "You need to know our defense system here is far beyond anything this world knows; if you attack, many of your people will die." "The Senator knows this but doesn't care; he wants to intimidate us in hopes to take over this facility, and in doing so, making a name for himself."

"The research you have done here, I am told, is vital to America."

"It's vital to the whole world, but even so, the Senator knows that once everything is finish and working properly and we get compensated, it will get turned over to the government." "You should also know we have a contract with the governments of the United States, Great Britain, and Australia protecting us from people like the Senator."

"I have my orders, Sir, and they come not only from Senator Morton but other Senators too."

"Enough of this take over this facility; that's an order," said the Senator with anger. They all returned to their vehicles, backed up, and started to fire, and everything they threw at us bounced off our shields.

"Mr. Prichard, do you see that empty truck over there?" William asked.

"Yes."

"Hit it with an energy laser." He did what William said, and the truck vaporized to the shock of the military and the Senator.

The Senator yelled to the Colonel, "Call in the jets."

William and I laughed, and William asked, "Shall we bring out the shuttles?"

"No, not yet; let them try to attack us, then we will show them what we can do," I said. "We will try not to harm them, just damage their jets a bit." William smiled, and we went back to watching what would happen next.

Jets and helicopters came about a half-hour later, and they did fire on us with no effect. William and I walked over to the shuttle hanger; as we walked, I said, "Make sure you have your shields up and only hit areas of the aircraft that will force them to land; I want no one killed."

"I will be careful."

We both flew up; the shields got dropped in our area long enough in the sky to let us out. A dog fight started with the jets and us, but we were too fast and could maneuver much better than they could. I radioed the jet, and I said, "Prepare yourself; I'm going to damage your jet."

"You can try," he responded. At that, I fired a laser cannon and clipped his tail wings. He went down at the Livermore airport, as did another jet that William got. William went after another jet while I went after one of the helicopters. I hit him in an area that did not damage the helicopter very much, but he had to land, and I went after another. William must have got another jet because I saw another one head to the airport in Livermore. After a short time, the jets and helicopters retreated, and we flew back to our facility. We had our people check over the shuttles, and William and I headed back to the main gate. The Senator was hopping mad everyone at the gate was laughing at him. He yelled some more threats to us, but that did not last long because a convoy of vehicles drove towards us and stopped. The first person to get out of the lead car was Jack Bryant, our lawyer.

"James, William, you can drop your shields now it's over." "Senator Morton has gotten arrested," said Mr. Bryant.

I turned to William and Mr. Prichard and said, "I will go out by myself; if this is a trick, raise shields and attack them with everything we have." They both nodded, and the shield at the front gate got lowered, then I walked out holding a weapon.

"James, you don't need that weapon anymore; these men I brought with me are from the F.B.I. they have arrested Senator Morton."

"I don't trust anyone."

"Not even me?"

"They may be tricking you."

"No, this is real; the Senator didn't get authorization to do this."

"What about the Colonel and his people?"

"He didn't know what was going on; he had to follow the Senator's orders." "He will most likely get a note in his record, but nothing else."

I walked over to the Colonel with Mr. Bryant and said, "Were any of your men or pilots harmed in the exchange we had with you?"

"No, it's amazing that no one was hurt or killed."

"We tried not to target any of your personnel." "We just wanted to show you what you would face if we chose to attack you." "What do you think will happen to you?"

"Reprimand and a write-up my career have ended, so before all this happens, I will retire."

"I'm sorry this will happen, but I did warn you."

"Yes, I know, and I should have listened to you." "There was something about that Senator I didn't like."

"Good luck with whatever you want to do." At that, I turned around and went back to the facility with Mr. Bryant.

"Is everything alright, Sir?" asked Mr. Prichard.

"Yes, Mr. Prichard." "You can lower the shields and put everything else away." "We will want to keep the standard security procedures."

"Yes, Sir."

One week went by, and William was married and went to England for a honeymoon. Senator Morton was removed from congress and had to spend some time in jail. The Colonel did retire from the Army, but at least he did not go to jail. Things were going back to normal for the most part at the facility. One day I was on the balcony of my apartment at night. I had just put Kevin to bed, and I wanted to get some air. I looked up at the stars when I spotted a strange aircraft. The facility had a no-flyover rule, and besides, the craft was hovering, and it was not a helicopter. I called security, and they went out to investigate what I saw. When I went out to the balcony, the craft was gone. About an hour later, I got a call from security, and they said, "We didn't see anything, Sir."

"I know it left."

The next day it was cloudy, and I thought I saw something in the clouds. I went over to the hanger and told the people working there to have one of the shuttles ready for me for tonight and make it fully loaded. That night I looked out the window and saw the craft again, and I called security and told them to send someone to my apartment to watch Kevin and someone meet me at the hanger. Mr. Prichard joined me into the shuttle, and I headed for the spacecraft. As soon as the craft spotted me, it took off rapidly, but I was faster and gained on the craft. The craft went into space, and I followed it. When I was close enough, I tried hailing the craft, but it would not answer. I next fired a warning shot with my laser cannon, and that got its attention. The craft slowed to a stop and then turned, and I hailed the craft again. This time the craft answered with what looked like a laser cannon of its own, and they hit us with no effect on the shuttle. I hailed the craft again; when there was no answer, I fired at it, damaging the craft, and I got a hail. "Please do not fire on us; we mean you no harm."

"Who are you, and why were you spying on us?"

"My name is Sorcha." "We are called Damari; we come from a planet called Damar." "It is in the part of the sky you call Vela." "We were not spying; we were curious and wanted to learn of your progress?"

"You could have asked." "My name is James."

"We apologize and will not bother you anymore."

"I accept your apology, and if you want to know something, just ask." "Do you have much damage; I could tow you to where you are going, or you could land at my facility, and we could help your repair your craft."

"We do not need your assistance in repairing our craft; it should get repaired shortly." "We do have a question about your larger craft." Does your craft have light speed?"

"We have warp speed which is much faster than light speed." "We wish to be friendly with you and carry on an exchange of information if you will consider it."

"We will consider an exchange of information." "When will your larger craft be ready for space?"

"It is ready now, but we are adding things to the craft." "It is easier to work on the ground for us at this time than in space."

"Do you plan to build more craft?"

"I do not, but my people will." "Are you concern because of my people's violent nature?"

"Yes, we are concern."

"Do not be concern; before we make more craft, we will have a rule not to be violent to others in space unless we get threatened."

"You attack us."

"The first shot was a warning shot at getting you to stop; it meant no harm." "When you fired at me and hit my craft, you became a threat, and I responded the same way."

"I understand."

"Now I have a question for you; are there other planets beside your planet populated with sentient beings?"

"Yes."

"Please contact us when you want to exchange information."

"My people or I will." "I would advise you not to let your people know of our meeting; it might cause panic."

"I don't think I need to; I think many already know of you."

"Perhaps we underestimated your people." "Our repairs got completed; we must be going now."

"Alright then, until we meet again." The craft took off at a high rate of speed, and we headed back to our facility. I could see Mr. Prichard was in shock at what just happened. So, I said, "Are you alright, Mr. Prichard."

"Yes, Sir." "I'm just a bit shocked at what just happened."

"I can assure you we had the upper hand, and they knew it." "At least you can say you flew out into space," I said with a smile. We landed near the shuttle hanger, and the people inside took care of the shuttle.

Three weeks past and my secretary came into my office and said, "There is a Dr. Stromsburg from NASA who wishes to talk to you."

"Have him come in." I stood up and shook Dr. Stromsburg's hand, and we both sat down." "What can I do for you, Doctor?"

"We at NASA would like to be involved with your ship."

I nodded and said, "Correct me if I'm wrong; the government controls NASA."

"Yes."

I thought a minute and said, "There are two other governments that are involved with this project, Great Britain and Australia." "They would have to be also involved and perhaps other countries as time goes on." "So maybe the American government needs to form a federation with these other two countries, with my brother and me in a controlling position."

He nodded and said, "That would be fine." "How close is your ship to being completed?"

"About a month, but I won't fly it into space until I train a crew."

"I have another question for you." "Did you fly a smaller craft into space about a month ago?"

"Yes, it was a shuttle." "We intercepted a spacecraft from a planet they call Damar; they are from the Vela constellation."

"Are you telling me you encountered a UFO?"

"Yes, and I talked to them."

"I think we should have a meeting with the government and military also representatives from the other two countries here." "Do you agree?" said Dr. Stromsburg.

"Yes, will you make the arrangements?"

"Yes." I gave him a number to contact me directly and warned him to keep this quiet for now to the public, and he left to make the arrangements.

About ten days later, I got a message from the doctor telling me the government, NASA, Great Britain, and Australia will come for a meeting. It would be held here on the twelfth of next month if it were alright with me. I contacted William and told him about the meeting, but he was not interested in being there. I sent a message back to Dr. Stromsburg that the twelfth of next month would be alright for the meeting. The twelfth of September came, and all who would be at the meeting came, and I gave them lodging at the hotel. Dr. Stromsburg and Dr. T. Keith Glennan were there from NASA. Mr. Henry Kissinger from the American government was there, Sir Denis Spotswood from

Great Britain and Sir Frederick Scherger Australia. The meeting started at ten o'clock in the morning with everyone introducing themselves. "Gentlemen, Dr. Stromsburg told me you have a desire to be part of my brother's and my project." "We've always said that once this project got finished, we would share this project with the three governments represented here as long as we had control of what goes on with our ships." "We at present have one Star Ship and twelve shuttles." What we lack is personnel to man the ship and shuttles; except for my brother and myself, we need to staff every position." "I have a list of positions we need to get filled." "Are there any questions so far?"

"I think we have to discuss how we are going to act in space first," said Henry Kissinger.

"I would agree," I said. "There are many things we need to do first also."

"Perhaps we should see this starship and maybe take a ride in one of its shuttles," said Sir Denis Spotswood.

"Does everyone agree?" I asked. Everyone agreed, and I called down to the ship. Then we were all transported to the starship, much to the shock of everyone.

"What just happened to us?" a shocked Dr. Keith asked.

"You all have gotten transported to the starship," I said. Dr. Keith and everyone else looked confused so, I said, "You were disassembled down to your atoms and reassembled here."

"How could this be done?" Dr. Stromsburg asked.

"I would like to know that too," said Sir Frederick Scherger.

"The same way I built this starship; pure science." "I have all the specifications that you will be able to see."

We toured the starship for a couple of hours, with everyone asking questions. In the end, Sir Denis Spotswood stated, "I'm surprised that you claim something this big could fly into space." "I'm an expert in aeronautics, and it goes against everything I know."

"Sir, it can fly in space, and once in space, it will move many times faster than light." "When we get into the shuttle, you will see how advance we are here." After we toured the starship, we went into the hanger, and I got into the largest shuttle. I piloted the shuttle out of the hanger and up into space. "Where would you all like to go?"

"Let's go to Mars," said Dr. Stromsburg.

"Mars it is." Twenty minutes later, we were orbiting Mars.

"Can we land," asked Dr. Keith.

"We can land, but we can't leave the shuttle; if someone did, we would all die." We landed near the equator, and everyone had a chance to see what was outside the shuttle. After a short time, we headed back to earth and my campus for lunch and then continue with the meeting.

"Just how much do you and your brother want for sharing your information with us?" asked Mr. Kissinger.

"The cost my brother and I put into this project plus ten percent; also, fifty-one percent control of the project for now." "Later, we will give up total control, so you won't have to deal with us anymore."

"You possess more money than the United States has, perhaps more than all three countries represented here have," said Henry Kissinger. "I don't think any country could afford to pay your brother and you what you want."

"We could work something out later instead of money."

"That's good," said Sir Frederick Scherger. The meeting went on for three days, and it got decided how we would conduct ourselves while traveling in space. The mission for the starship will be to first explore and for science purposes, and second if we get threatened for protection. There was an agreement from all three countries that a training camp would get set up to train to man the starship. The first candidates to man the starship would mostly have on-the-job training. A name for the starship would be Neverland. Finally, my brother and I would go with the new crew to train the personnel and exploration.

After everyone left, I called William at his home in Mississippi. "William, how have you been doing?"

"Just fine; I've meant to call you."

"Oh, what about?"

"No, you go first; I know how you are; you wouldn't call if what you have to say wasn't important."

"I love you; I would call just to talk to you." "However, I have opened the starship to Australia, Great Britain, and the United States." "They are to pay us back in services and money plus ten percent." "We will have fifty-one percent control for now." "They will supply the personnel to man the ship." "I said I would go out into space to train the people that will man the starship and said that maybe you too."

"Do you want me to go?"

"Of course, but it is really up to you."

He was silent for a few seconds and then said, "I'd like to go with you, but one of the reasons I was going to phone you is Mary is pregnant." "I don't think it would be a good thing to go now."

"That's great!" "How far along is she?"

"About two months."

"Do you know what it is going to be?"

"It's too soon to know."

"Well, it would be safe to take her alone we will have some of the best doctors, but if you don't want to take a chance, I will understand." "Besides, this is your first baby." "I can understand if you want to play it safe."

"I think if you can do this without me, I will play it safe."

"So, how is it living there in Mississippi?"

"It's great; people are amicable here." "By the way, the other reason I was going to call you is your house is ready." "When are you coming here to live?"

"I'm thinking in about a year or so, but Kevin and I will visit before then."

"Then this will be wonderful."

"I love you, William, and always will."

"I love you too."

"I'll let you go, William."

"Goodbye, James."

SIXTEEN

GOING HOME

THE NEXT DAY AND the following week, people from NASA started to show up. I housed them at the hotel and had security check them out and show them the shuttles and the starship. Over the next month, some who were building the starship were working with the crew, as was I. After about a month, Kevin and I took a trip to my brother's home. Kevin was entering Junior high school, and he had other interests, primarily sports, which surprised me. While we were in Mississippi, we visited the Junior High School. Kevin decided, and I agreed he would stay with his Uncle William until I moved to Mississippi myself so Kevin could start and finish his high school there. I went back home, gathered Kevin's things he wanted, and flew back to Mississippi in one of our shuttles. I stayed another week and reluctantly flew back to the starship campus. To keep my mind off my family in Mississippi, I kept busy. Of course, I had family here in California, but they seemed distant to me, maybe because I had gotten changed during my time on Neverland. From time to time, I did have visits from some family members, particularly my siblings, parents, and occasionally aunt or uncle. The following week I had a meeting with all the workers, and I said, "I am going to allow everyone to be part of the crew of the starship." "Now, if you choose not to become a crew member, you still have a job here creating a new starship, more shuttles, and everything else we need." "For those who wish to be a crew member, contact personnel." "After everyone has had a chance to sign up, we will have a meeting of the benefits and hazards about being a member of the crew of a starship." "Are there any questions?"

"Charles Duncan, I would like to go, but I have a family; what can I do about that?"

"Perhaps your family can go also; we can talk to you about that."

"You said there are hazards; what are they, Sir?" asked Manuel Gonzales.

"Explosions in space, radiation, unknown anomalies, but what concerns me most are sentient beings that are out there." "The Neverland starship is very powerful; however, I believe there are other beings that might be more powerful." "I, with the help of one of the shuttles, encountered an alien craft." "With some effort, I was able to communicate with the aliens; they were friendly once they knew of my intentions." "I was lucky that day the shuttle was faster, stronger, and more powerful, but the outcome could have been quite different with another being." "Of course, there is a chance something significant could happen to the ship, but the chances are low."

"I would assume we would be exploring other worlds and perhaps people; what do we do about viruses, bacteria, or other dangers."

"The ship's computer is very advanced and has medical advancements that will help." "Everything else, we will do what has always been done, research and apply a cure that fits the symptom." "Of course, we will also take precautions until we know what is out there." "The same applies to other beings, but I believe even though other beings might be different looking than us in general, they are the same as us." More questions got asked for another half hour, and then everyone went back to their jobs while a team was set up to interview everyone who wanted to become part of the crew.

As the crew was being trained and people were building more shuttles, I went to Mississippi to talk to Mary, William, and Kevin. When I got to William's house, Kevin spotted me and flew into my arms. "Daddy, I missed you a lot; are you going to stay?"

"Not quite yet, but I will be here for some time."

"How are things at the lab, James?" asked William.

"The training is going slower than I figured it would go." "I keep forgetting most people are not like us."

"When do you think the starship crew will be able to take the ship out into space?"

"About another year, but even then, they will be green."

"That long, are they that bad?" asked Mary.

"No, they aren't that bad but flying a starship is quite different than what NASA has."

"The government wants to build a second starship after this one goes into space."

"How much are you going to be involved with it?" asked William.

"Very little, just as an advisor; it's time I spent more time with Kevin."

"And maybe to settle down and find a wife too," said Mary.

"Yes, you're right, Mary." "When is that baby of yours due."

"Any time now, I've already had some false labors where I was rushed to the hospital," said Mary.

"There is something I want to discuss with all of you, but later on." I brought my bags to Kevin's room then sat down in the sitting room.

"Tell me what you want to talk about?" asked William.

"I think we need to take a trip to Neverland to see the Pongos."

"Mary is pregnant."

"I don't mean now; maybe a month or so after the birth, we would take the shuttle."

"What are your concerns with the Pongos?" asked William.

"We haven't heard about the Pongos since we left Neverland, and they were supposed to keep us apprised of their welfare." "Everything might be just fine, but you know how the countries involved say one thing and do what they want." "For the welfare of the Pongos, we need to see how they are."

William was quiet for a few seconds, then asked Mary, "How do you feel about this?"

"You need to go, I wish to go with you, but I need to know how long the flight would be?"

"Under an hour," I said.

"If I go, I will need to bring a lot of things."

"You can bring as much as you want; the shuttle has a lot of room."

"If everything goes alright with the birth, then we all can go," Mary said. A week later, Mary and William had an eight-pound seven-ounce healthy baby girl.

I had been stocking the shuttle with enough food and items for the baby. I had hired a nurse who would go with us in case something happens to the baby.

Five weeks after the baby Kathern was born, we headed to Neverland. We flew up slowly to the photosphere then back down slowly because I did not want to upset the baby. It took about forty-five minutes when I leveled out; Kevin was excited about the whole trip. As we approached the island, we noticed the cloud wall seemed less dense than it used to be. We flew around the island, and we saw many large ships; what upset me was one of those large ships was going through the channel. The only way that a large ship could have passed through the channel is by widening the channel, which was strictly forbidden. As we headed to the compound, we saw many new buildings, and again they were erected without permission. As we landed, several armed people came running towards us. William and I put the screens on and fired a warning shot, and they stopped in their tracks. We walked outside the craft armed with energy pulse rifles and waited. With caution, they approached us, and then one of the armed men yelled, "You are trespassing leave."

I looked at William, shocked, and said, "What do you mean trespassing; this is our island?"

Now it was they who were confused. After several minutes of discussion, one of them said, "Who are you?"

"This is my brother William, and I'm James Reno."

They talked among themselves and then radioed someone. A few seconds later, two men came running towards us. One of the two men said, "I'm John Warner, the Island manager; this is Michael Cruz." "You said that you are William and James Reno?"

"Yes," William said.

"Can you prove it?"

"Have you ever seen a ship like this or weapons as we have?" I said. "Where is Jane Goodall; she can vouch for us?"

"I threw Jane Goodall off the island; she was too pushy in what she wanted for those animals."

"What happened to the Pongos?" I asked.

"They became hostile after Goodall was thrown off the island, so they were forced to a remote part of the island." "Some wouldn't go, so we had to shoot them before they would move."

"You murdered some of the Pongos because they wouldn't move when this is their island," said William.

"All of you will leave this island now," I growled.

"I won't go anywhere, nor will any of my people; we control this island now; by this time, we attracted a lot of attention from many people on the island.

William looked at me, and I at him, and I said, "This means war." I raised my rifle and vaporized John Warner; some of the other men started shooting at us, and we fired back, hitting some with the same effect that John Warner received. At that, the rest ran back to the buildings while William and I went back into the shuttle and used the loudspeaker, telling all, "We are going to find the Pongos if you are here when we get back, you will die." At that, we blew up a building that we could tell was empty and flew to find the Pongo. We first flew up above the island and radioed our lab by bouncing a signal off the moon, and we got Mr. Prichard. We informed him what happened and to contact the lawyers.

"Do you wish me to send help?"

"Yes, if they can fly the shuttles, send extra men everyone armed with energy pulse rifles," I said.

"They should be there in about thirty minutes."

"Make sure you lock down the lab."

"Yes, Sir."

It was not hard to find the Pongo, and they were not in good shape. At first, when we landed, they were overly cautious about approaching us. It was not until William, and I spoke to them in their language that they came to see who we were. They did not know who we were because we had grown before William or I could explain who we were; one of the Pongo said, "Who is this that knows our tongue."

"This is William once known as John the Pan, and I am James once known as Peter the Pan."

They talked amongst themselves, and then the same Pongo said, "We remember John and Peter; they were much loved by our people and great warriors; you don't look like them."

"We grew up; when you knew us, we were children; we are adults know." One female Pongo came up to us and looked at us very closely. There was something familiar about her, and I said, "Tinker, is that you?"

"You remember me?"

"Of course, I love you."

At that, she turned around and said to her people, "They are the Pans." At that, the Pongos gathered around us.

Our nurse was a bit nervous, as was Mary and Kevin, but William and I assured them that they would not get harmed. I told all the Pongos, "Assemble all your elders; we have much to talked about." As we walked to their village, the Pongos took great interest in Kathern and Kevin. Kathern seemed to eat it up, but Kevin did not know what to make of it, much to the amusement of William and me. In about a half-hour, the elders assembled, and William and I sat in front of them. Macoute, one of the elders, said, "What is it you have to tell us?"

I stood up and said, "We have heard terrible things that have happened to the Pongo; is this true?

"Yes," said Macoute. "Many have died by those that live in your father's home."

"What happened to the woman who we left with you?" asked William.

"She was helping us, then one day she came to us no more."

"Would you like her back?"

"That would be good; she is our friend."

"The one who killed many Pongo is no more, nor is some of his friends; John and I killed them."

"This is good, but there are many of them."

"We have powerful friends who have flying boxes like we; they should be at my father's house now making sure those terrible creatures leave this land or die."

There was much talk among the Pongo, and finally, Macoute asked, "What do you want of us?"

"Your happiness and love," said William.

"Love you have and always will; happiness will come with time."

"We wish you to send runners to all the villages to inform them of what is happening and make preparations to move back to your home by the big river."

"This we will do."

"We must go to our father's house," I said.

"You will not stay and eat?"

"We can't; we must make sure that those evil creatures are gone," I said. At that, we went back to the shuttle and flew to our house. As we flew to the house, we saw three shuttles on the ground with eighteen-armed security guards from the lab on the ground ushering some people into boats. Among those from security was Mr. Prichard directing the rest of the guards.

We landed near the house, and Mr. Prichard walked over to us, and he said, "All should be off this island in about an hour," he said to all of us.

"Make sure you do a sweep of the compound area, especially the caves, which is about a quarter of a mile above the house," William said, pointing.

"Yes, Sir."

We all walked into the house, and it was a mess, so William and I started to clean it up while Mary sat in the sitting room with the baby talking to the nurse. About an hour later, we did well enough for the time we would be here.

We were on the porch when Mr. Prichard and the rest of the men came up to us. "Everyone has been cleared off this island, Sir," said Mr. Prichard.

"Good; do all you pilots know how to use a tractor beam?" Everyone said yes, and I said, "Go around this island, and also these smaller islands near here lift boulders off those islands and drop them into the reef channel leading into this island."

Everyone said yes, Sir and William said, "If someone wants to get on the island, they will find a way to do it channel or no channel." "Are you planning to live on the island?"

"No, I don't plan to live on the island, and yes, I know someone might find a way to get on the island; I just need some time to find the Pongo a new home."

"I think we need to find live coral to plant into the channel," said William.

"You're right; we will go and search for some live coral to plant into the channel."

"Mary, will you be alright while we are gone?"

"We will be just fine."

As soon as all the other shuttles came back, I had a few securities to stay with Mary, Kevin, and the nurse. The rest of the shuttles I sent back home, then William and I went to other islands to find some live coral. It took us seven trips to various islands to retrieve enough coral for the channel; by the time we got back to the house and landed, it was dark. I got everyone to agree to spend overnight at the house to see the Pongos one more time.

The next day early in the morning, William and I went to see the Pongos for the last time. We found them still traveling back to their original village near the river. We landed just ahead of the Pongos, and they all gathered around the shuttle. The elders came forward, and William and I started talking. "All those horrible creatures are gone; you are safe for now," said William.

"You are safe, and we must also leave and go far away to another land," I said. You must know that although those horrible creatures are gone someday, they might find a way back here."

"What can we do about this?" said one of the elders.

"You can do nothing but hide in the woods until I come back." "I will come back and take all Pongo someplace away from these creatures, and they won't be able to harm you anymore."

"Where will you take us?"

"To the points of lite in the night sky."

There was much discussion about what I said, and one of the elders said, "In the before time, the sky people took us from our home and brought us here." "Will you take us back to where we came from?"

"That is what I hope." "Did the sky people say why they brought you here?"

"The air was dirty and too many Pongo." "They said too much Pongo war."

We said our goodbyes, headed back to the house, then loaded up and flew back to the lab. We found out through our lawyers no one wanted to press charges against us. They said they investigated why the island had gone so wrong and came up with a criminal group that took over the island and fooled everyone about what was going on. Of course, William and I did not believe them and told all the island was off-limits to all or there would be hell to pay.

Everyone went back to Mississippi except me, and the starship was finally ready to take off. At first, we took the minimum amount of crew and me just in case something happened as we lifted off. I took the captain's seat, and we lifted off; everything went off smoothly, and when we achieved orbit, I had each department check out the condition of their department. After about an hour and a half, all appeared to be working as well as expected. There were some overturned tables and chairs and a few things thrown to the floor, but there was no significant damage. We started to transport the rest of the crew into the starship, and when the captain came aboard, he met with me before taking over his command. His name was Captain John Rogers, and I said, "I won't bother you as far as everyday command, but I will tell you where we are going and tell you what to do if we encounter anybody."

"Yes, Sir."

"Now, let me show you where we are going." I pull up a star map on the computer, and I pointed to where we were going. "Before we head there, we will go to Mars for a shakedown with the crew then Pluto."

"We should travel at sub-light speed, don't you think, Sir?" Captain Rodgers asked.

"Yes."

"If your settle into your quarters and everything has been brought on board, we shall leave," I said.

"I'm ready now, Sir."

"Alright, make the announcement to your crew where we are going."

"Yes, Sir." "Attention, this is Captain John Rogers; in a few minutes, we are going to go to first Mars for a shakedown cruise, then to Pluto at sub-light speed."

"Good, but you don't have to be so detailed." "If the captain says something, they should just accept it." "Also, Captain, relax; you're doing just fine."

"Yes, Sir."

"Captain, I'm getting a message; there are six people who wish to come aboard," said the crew member that was manning communication. "They are from England, Australia, and the United States."

The Captain looked at me, and I said, "I think we better find out what they are up to."

"Bring them aboard," said the Captain.

As the Captain got up, another crew member took his place, and we went to the transporter room. We got to the transporter room before our guest arrived, we had two from security with us as they arrived, and at the captain's orders, everyone got escorted to a conference room. "So, who are you and what has brought you here today?" asked Captain Rodgers.

"Captain, we represent the three countries that have interest in this project." "We are all scientists, and we were asked to come here." "I'm William Smite from England; my interest is in geology." "This is Edward Partridge, also from England; he is interested in Biology." "She is Helen Morgan, who is a zoologist; she is from Australia." "He is Benjamin Carter, also from Australia; he has a background in bacteriology." "This is Mary Steward; her field is astrophysics, and she is from America." "He is Charles Tate his field is astronomy; he is also from America."

The Captain looked at me, and I asked, "Your government ask you to come here to keep an eye on us; am I right."

"Yes, Sir," said Charles Tate.

"Why, since we would give them a full report anyway?" I asked.

"I guess they just want to hear it from someone who is not part of your crew, and I would say I am very interested in what you will find out there."

I looked at the Captain, and he said, "What do you think?"

"Captain, it is your decision, but I see no harm as long as they understand we have scientists here in their field of study that they will be under and subject to their rules." "Also, they will be subject to our rules," I said.

"Are you all willing to follow our rules and the rules of your department heads?"

William Smite looked at his fellow scientists, and they all nodded, and he said, "Yes, we are willing."

"Let me warn you all, your loyalties are to this ship and its crew, not your governments; if you break the rules, you will be placed in the stockade and be sent back to Earth," the Captain said. Everyone nodded, and the Captain said to the two security people, get these people quarters and then take them to their departments."

"Yes, Sir."

We went back to the bridge, and the Captain and I took a seat, then the Captain said, "Alright, helmsman set the setting for Mars."

"It's already set, sir."

"Then proceed." We proceeded towards Mars, and though we never made it to lite speed, we still made it to Mars in less than twenty minutes. When we got to Mars, we went into a high orbit around Mars. This was all done at the direction of the Captain. As the Captain did checks of all departments, he was asked by some of the scientists if they could do some exploring down on the surface. The Captain said they could do a limited exploration if they come under the control of security which will be going with them.

I whispered to the Captain, "All information discovered on Mars will get added to the ship's computer." He nodded at what I said and informed the scientists. I got up and went to my quarters, leaving the Captain to figure everything out for himself, but I told the Captain to call me if he needed me.

I was either in my room or the social room for a day and a half. I assume that everything was going smooth because the Captain had not called upon me. I was sitting in the recreation room having something to eat and drink when the Captain came in, "May I sit with you, Sir?"

"Please do."

"We will be heading to Pluto in a few hours."

"That's good; how did the exploration go down on Mars?"

"Good, they got a lot of samples of soil and rocks and tested the atmosphere." "They said they would post it on the computer when they have everything typed up."

I finished eating and told the Captain that I would join him on the bridge when we start for Pluto. I headed back to my quarters and took a nap for a few hours. I was awakened when I heard over the intercom the notice of departure of the starship to Pluto. I headed for the bridge and got there as the ship moved out. I sat next to the Captain, and he said, "We should arrive at Pluto in about three hours."

"Yes, be careful of the asteroid belt." "You might want to raise shields."

"Raise shields." We passed through the asteroid belt without any trouble and headed towards Pluto; after about three hours, we came into sight of the planet. The Captain placed the ship in orbit and again asked each department to do a diagnostic. The scientists wanted to go down to Pluto's surface also, and the Captain allowed them to do so under the same precautions as they went down on Mars. The Captain then turned to me and asked, "Where do we go next after Pluto?"

"Back to Earth to do a full diagnostic of the ship, take on more supplies, and let off our scientist friends." "Then we will go into deep space to another system look for life and categorizing each planet."

"Anywhere, in particular, you want to go to?"

"Not sure yet; I have to check my notes first and check with the astrophysicist."

"How about Alpha Centauri?"

"It is near, I know, but there isn't any life there and can be checked out later."

"How do you know there isn't any life?"

"The red star shot out a solar flair throughout the whole system." "If there were anything there, it would have been fried by the flair."

"I didn't know that."

"Not many did, but at the lab, we have powerful instruments that detected it."

I went back to my quarters, went over my notes, and noted the entry of the beings from the Vela Constellation and thought that would be an excellent place to start looking for habitable planets. I next went to the astrophysicist lab and asked them to pull up the Vela Constellation. I studied the constellation closely, and finally pointed to a star, and said, "That star is similar in size to our sun, am I right?"

"Yes, Sir," said an Astrophysicist by the name of Cecil Bowman.

"Do we have any additional information about that sun?"

"Let me check." Dr. Bowman got on the computer and looked and said, "There is not much information about it." "Your right; it is similar to our sun." "The sun is about eight hundred light-years from us." "From what we can tell, it is stable." "You should know that the Vela Constellation main star went supernova about twelve thousand years ago."

"I didn't know about the supernova, but at least one star wasn't affected that much, and it has a planet around that sun that has life on it."

"Then it must be thirty light-years from where the main star was to have survived."

"Well, let's check; approximately where would that main star be?"

"About there, Sir."

"Calculate how far away it is to the sun we are going to."

"About thirty-five lightyears." "It could have survived the supernova." I thanked everybody in the department and went back to where the Captain was.

I found the Captain in his quarters and asked to come in. He showed me to a chair, and I sat down and said, "I know where we will be going after we go to earth."

"Where is that?"

"The Vela Constellation."

"The Vela Constellation, I believe that is eight hundred light-years away." "If I'm not mistaken, there was a supernova there."

"You're right, and I'm surprised you know."

"My major at the university was astronomy."

I nodded and said, "It should take us about eight or nine days to get to the Vela Constellation." I know there was a supernova, but the solar system we are going to should have escaped the damage of the supernova." "Let me explain why I want to go there, and perhaps you will understand."

"Please do."

"Do you know about the UFO I encounter some time back?" He nodded, and I said, "When I talked to the beings, the person I assume was the captain said they were from the Vela Constellation, and they were called Damar." "I assume Damar is the name of their planet."

"You want to talk further with the Damar?"

"Yes, because I am looking for a new home for the Pongo's on Neverland."

"A place where they can be the dominant people."

"Why, aren't they happy on Neverland?"

"At one time, they were happy, but man is determined to make them go extinct." "There is no place they can go to get away from humans on Earth."

"So, you want us to transport them to a new planet."

"Yes." We stayed at Pluto for another day and a half, then headed back to Earth. Along the way back, I said, "When we get back to Earth, do a full diagnostic of the ship and store enough supplies to last a few months." "We may not need them, but it's better to have too much than not enough."

"Yes, Sir."

"After we find a place for the Pongos and we'll transfer them there, I will be turning the ship over to you and leaving." The Captain smiled, and I said, "Don't be too happy about it." "I'll be coming back on occasion."

"I wasn't smiling because you were leaving; Sir, I was smiling because I will have full command."

"You always had full command." "I wasn't going to interfere with whatever you did unless it harmed someone."

"Yes, Sir."

"If it were me, I would give leave to as many of the crew as you can spare." "Also, I think you better write up a report for the government." "They will want to know how well everything went."

"Yes, I plan to do just that, Sir."

We got to Earth, and I took a shuttle. Instead of going back to the lab, I went to Mississippi to my brother's house.

I landed in front of William's house as I usually do, and as usual, people came out of their homes to stare at the spectacle of my landing. I had expected someone in the house to come out, but no one did. As I walked up to the house, one young boy of about ten said, "Mr. is that a spaceship?"

"No, it is a shuttle; the spaceship or starship is orbiting over the United States."

My answer seemed to satisfy him, and I went up on William's porch and rang his doorbell.

I heard footsteps coming to the door, and when the door opened, it was Kevin, "Daddy, you're back."

"Yes, where are your uncle and aunt?"

"They went to the doctors for a baby check."

"Is the baby alright?"

"Oh yes, he is fine." "It's something you're supposed to do when you have a baby."

"When are they coming back?"

"I don't know, maybe an hour, maybe less."

"Good, I'll wait."

"Are you going to stay?"

"No, not quite yet." I could see the disappointment on his face, so I said, "Do you want to come with me?" "We are going to planets in another solar system."

"Yes," he said excitedly.

"I want to see if your aunt and uncle want to go too."

"They most likely don't."

"I think you're right, but it's polite to ask."

Kevin got me some lemon aid, and we talked about a lot of things. I apologized for not being around much, and he said it was alright, but I could tell he had missed me. I told him my absence is ending and that he would be with me from now on; a little after an hour entered Mary, the baby, and William with big smiles on their face. "Are you finished roaming around space?" asked William.

"No, not really; I've come to get Kevin and talk to the both of you."

"What do you want to talk to us about?" asked Mary.

"I just got back from going to Mars and Pluto, and everything went smooth." "I'm taking Kevin with me; I don't want him away from me anymore." "I was wondering if all of you want to go to; it would be a great adventure."

"How long would we be gone?" asked William.

"I'm not sure it could be a month; it could be longer." "Your quarters would be about the size of a large hotel room, very comfortable." "There would be other families there; we also have medical and everything you would find on earth."

"Where would we be going?" asked William.

"To the planet Damar, they are in Vela Constellation." "It is about eight hundred light-years away."

"Can your ship move fast enough to get there in a month?" asked Mary.

"First, it's not my ship; it's our ship, and yes, it can go that fast."

Mary and William looked at each other for a few seconds, and finally, Mary said, "Alright, James, we will go; I know down deep William wants to go; besides, I'm a bit curious." It took them more than an hour and a half to get everything they wanted to take, even though I told them half that stuff they would not need.

We all loaded up in the shuttle and headed to the starship, and when we got near, I radioed the starship, "Shuttle, Wendy ready to enter the dock."

"Wendy, we read you proceed to dock," was radioed back from the starship.

We landed, and some of the crew members helped unload Kevin's and William's family things onto a cart to be taken to their quarters. I had already arranged for William's quarters; it was large with a window. I showed William and Mary how everything worked and showed a map of the ship on the computer. Kevin and I left for our quarters, and as we went, Kevin was all excited about things he saw as we proceeded, but I must admit he was already excited when he first got to fly on the shuttle. I showed Kevin how everything worked then told him, "Stay here until I come back." I called William and said, "William, are you ready to meet me on the bridge?"

"Yes, but how do I find the bridge?"

"Just ask the computer in the hall, and it will guide you."

"Alright, I will meet you."

I was on the bridge with Captain Rodgers when William came on the bridge. "William, this is Captain Rodgers, Captain Rodgers my brother William." They both said, "Nice to meet you," and shooked each other's hands.

"We will be leaving in about an hour," said Captain Rodgers.

I leaned over to William and said, "I'm going back to my quarters and taking Kevin over to your quarters to keep Mary company."

"Good idea," said William.

When I came back into my quarters, I said to Kevin, "I think it would be a good idea to keep Mary company for a while." "What do you think?"

"That is alright with me." As we walk over, Kevin asked, "Daddy, when is the ship going to go?"

"In about an hour."

Just when I was about to sit down back on the bridge, the radioman said, "Sir, there is a message coming in from NASA wanting to talk to Admiral James."

"Admiral James?" William questioned with a smile.

"We will take it in the conference room."

William and I left, and when we got into the conference room, I said to William, "We have to have some rank to be in control." "By the way, you're an Admiral too."

William nodded, and I pressed a button, and a man came on a screen. "Admiral, I am Terry Wells, director of NASA."

"Hello Mr. Wells; this is my brother William also an Admiral." "What is it you want?"

"We wish to start building another starship and shuttles at your facility, as does Britain and Australia jointly."

I looked at William, and I could tell he was letting me handle it, "Yes, we will let you use the facility, as long as you pay us back what it cost to develop the starship and shuttles." "You understand we have fifty-one percent control and the starships as we agreed on with our last meeting with the governments."

"This will be fine."

"I will contact our security at the facility." "I would suggest you create a school to train men and women to man these ships."

"Thank You, and we will be starting up a school soon." "We figure with your starship plans; we should be able to build a ship in half the time as you did."

"I would assume you are right." "I have two more flights with this ship, and then my brother and I will turn it over to you." We finished talking and headed back to the bridge. I had the radioman contact the head of security and inform him of NASA.

Ten minutes after contacting NASA, we left for the Vela Constellation. William and I left the bridge to Captain Rodgers after telling him to contact us if you encounter another ship or an emergency.

We both went to Williams quarters so I could collect Kevin. "They have a place here where they serve food and drinks." "Do any of you want to go?" I asked.

"Maybe in about an hour; I want to clean up and feed the baby," said Mary.

Kevin and I went back to our quarter to clean up, and a little after an hour, we went back to William's quarters to pick everyone up to go down to the social room, which was like a lounge and restaurant. We sat next to a window I had given Kevin a handheld game to play with so he would not get bored but looked out the window at the star and an occasional planet as we passed it. We ordered food and drinks and talked of Mississippi and other things. The conversation swung towards me when William asked, "James, you ever planning to get married?"

"I would guess eventually when Kevin and I find someone we both love."

"That might take forever, James," said William.

"What else can I do; you're more experienced at this than I am."

"You have to put your guard down and talk to someone you're attracted to," said Mary with a grin.

"Yeah, daddy, I could use a mom," yearned Kevin.

"You think so, uh."

"Yep."

"There is a nice-looking girl over there; why don't you introduce yourself and try to get a date," said William.

"I don't know if she is involved with someone or married."

"You're not going to know unless you ask, or are you afraid to ask?" said William.

"Me, Peter the Pan Hooker afraid." I got up and started walking over to her; my heart was pounding. "Hello."

"Hello, Admiral Reno."

"You know who I am."

"Yes, everybody knows you."

"I wish to ask you a personal question."

"What is it?"

"Are you married or seeing someone else?" "I would like to date you and see if we are compatible."

"Compatible," she smiled.

"Sorry if I offended you; I'm not used to dating nor talking to females other than business."

"You haven't offended me, and no, I'm not dating anyone or married."

"Oh, well, would you like to go out with me?" I said with a smile.

"And where would you take me?"

"Well, I can give you a tour of the ship, and perhaps we could have dinner here."

"Alright, but I think the next time you should ask me who I am."

"Oh, excuse me; I told you I hadn't done this much; what is your name."

"My name is Nancy, and I would be happy to go out with you."

"Where are your quarters, and what time do you wish to go out?"

"I share a room with a friend; it's 204." "I get off my shift at five; how about six?"

"Well, how did it go, James?" asked Mary.

"I have a date with her at six tonight."

"That's wonderful, James," said Mary.

"I feel awkward."

"You will do fine," Mary replied.

I cleaned up and put on something comfortable as I was doing this; Kevin was teasing me. At five-thirty, I took Kevin down to Williams quarters kiss him, and said to William and Mary, "How do I look?"

"You look fine," Mary said with a smile.

At that, I went to Nancy's quarters and buzzed her door. The door opened with another female there, and I said, "Do I have the right quarters?" "I'm looking for Nancy Fuller?"

"You do, Admiral, come on inside." "Nancy will be right out." "I'm her roommate Kathy Stromberg."

She was beautiful also, but I was only interested in Nancy right now, and as I waited, the more nervous I got. I hoped the nervousness did not show I did not want to make a fool out of myself. A moment later out walked Nancy, and I went to her and said, "You look beautiful."

She smiled, as did Kathy, and Kathy said, "Have fun."

"Have you had a tour of the ship before?" I asked.

"No, not really."

"Well, let me know if you get bored." "Perhaps we should start with the bridge."

"I didn't think I was authorized to go there."

"Normally, you wouldn't be able to, but you are with me, and we won't be staying long."

When we entered the bridge, the captain was not there, but another officer named Lieutenant Commander Howard Stiles was. "Sir, can I help you?"

"No, Howard, I'm just showing crewmember Nancy Fuller what the bridge looks like; we will be leaving shortly." I explained to Nancy everything on the bridge, "Commander Howard, are we still in our solar system."

"Yes, Sir, we are just about to enter the Kuiper Belt."

"Nancy, do you know what the Kuiper Belt is?"

"No."

"It's an Asteroid belt beyond the planet Pluto." "After we passed the Asteroid belt, we will be out of our solar system."

We left the bridge and headed to engineering; when we got there, we were greeted by another lieutenant commander. After I explained how the power for the starship worked, I thought it best to go to the conservatory. I figured she would like that, and we could relax and talk before we went to get something to eat. "I have heard of this place and planned to visit." "It's beautiful here and smells wonderful," said Nancy.

"These plants come from all around the world, and when we find plants on different worlds, we will add them to our collection," I said. We found a bench and sat down together, and started talking. "Tell me about yourself," I asked.

"Well, I'm from Pennsylvania; I lived in a small town called Meadville."

"Is it a nice town?"

"Oh yes, it is a charming town." "My family still lives there."

"What brought you to work on a starship?"

"Well, I'm interested in animals, not as a veterinarian, but as a zoologist."

"Are you interested in the field of Anthropology?

"I plan to minor in it at Penn State."

"Have you ever heard of a Pongo?"

"No."

"They are a humanoid species; at least some people consider them humanoid others think of them just as animals." "Their whole population will be coming on board this starship, to be transported to a habitable planet so they can thrive."

"Why not just leave them on Earth?"

"Too many want to kill them or put them in cages even though they are sentient." "What about your family?"

"I have two other sisters who still live with my parents." "My parents are wonderful people who welcome all."

"I wonder how they would treat me?"

"I would think they would treat you like one of the family." "They aren't too happy about me going out into space; they think I should find someone to marry and raise a family."

"You don't wish to be married and have children?"

"It's not that; it's not many men want to be around me once they know me because I can be peculiar."

"I'm pretty peculiar myself."

"Tell me about yourself, James."

"You may not want to know, but let's go get something to eat, and I will tell you everything."

We went to the social room and found a quiet place to talk and eat. A waiter came to our table; Nancy ordered, then I ordered something lite since I had already eaten earlier. "Would you like something to drink?" the waiter asked.

I looked at Nancy and said, "Would you like wine?" She nodded, and I said, "A bottle of your best Green Hungarian."

"Yes, Sir." The waiter came back with two glasses and a chilled bottle of Green Hungarian, and he served us.

Nancy tasted it and said, "This is very good."

"Yes, my stepfather, who preferred fine wine, had William and I drink wine at an early age, and this is my favorite."

"Tell me about yourself, James."

I told Nancy the whole story of my kidnapping and William's kidnapping and what James Hooker did to both of us. I told her about our wealth, why I bought a home in Mississippi and an estate and title in England. We talked about how the starship came about and what it took to build it. In the end, I asked her, "Are you shock and not want to see me anymore?"

"No, I'm not shocked, but I would say you were raised a bit more peculiar than I was." "Tell me about Kevin."

"Kevin was a runaway; he left his foster home about the time I was looking to buy a house." "He had been abused, but with me, he has adjusted just fine." "He loves William's and my peculiarity and fits in just fine." "He is thirteen, but he acts and has the maturity of a nine or ten years old, and he fits in well with children at that age." "He thinks he is a homosexual, but I don't think he is; I think he is just gendered-confused."

"Why do you think he is gender-confused?"

"Since he has been with me, the way he talks is different, and I've noticed him looking at girls a lot different now." "So, would you like to go out with me again?"

Before she could answer in walks her roommate, and she winked with a smile at Nancy. "Is this date over?"

"I don't want it to be; what do you have on your mind?"

"How about coming over to my quarters for some drinks, and who knows?"

I smiled and said, "Well, in your quarters, your roommate might come back, but in my quarters, my son is staying at his uncle's quarters." "Which shall it be?"

Now she smiles and says, "I would assume your quarters are a lot better than my quarters; let's go to yours."

When we got to my quarters, I put on some soft music and asked her if she wanted anything to eat or drink. "Oh, you pick a drink for me." "I don't know the names of many drinks."

"I'll order a Piña Colada for the both of us."

"This tastes good."

"I'm happy you like it." She liked it so much she and I drank several more. I tried kissing her, and that did it; the kissing led to bed, and we became intimate. The next morning, we both showered, and then with a kiss, she went back to her quarters with a promise of another date tonight. I ate breakfast then went to William's quarters.

"You're glowing, James," William said, chuckling.

"Yes, my date went quite well last night."

"Daddy did you get any last night?" asked Kevin.

"Your uncle said I glowed; what do you think?" We talked, and I took Kevin home but not until I got permission from William and Mary for Kevin to stay another night.

Over the next few days, Nancy and I went to some live entertainment, and we had several rooms on the ship that had a virtual reality device in it, and a few of those times, we had a picnic in a meadow and at a beach. We took Kevin with us on the picnics, and he got along well with Nancy. Kevin took off all his clothing at the beach and went into the water, which got me nervous because I did not know how Nancy would react until she, with a giggle, did the same and joined Kevin in the water. Of course, I joined them, and when finally, we were all tired, we walked out of the water, Kevin holding both my hand and Nancy's hand. As we sat on the beach, Kevin asked, "Nancy, are you going to be my mother?"

"Do you want me to be your mother?"

"Yes, I love you, and it would be nice to have a mother."

Nancy smiled and said, "Your father hasn't asked me to marry him." Kevin gave me that look that says, what are you waiting for, daddy.

"Why don't you go back to our quarters and get cleaned up," I said to Kevin. He got dressed quickly and left for our quarters, and then I turned to Nancy and said, "I am falling in love with you, but I don't truly know how you feel about me as I told you I'm not used to dating."

"I'm in love with both you and Kevin."

"I have to talk to Kevin about the changes he will have to get used to."

"Changes?"

"Yes, for example, he likes crawling into bed with me at night, and when he is home, he doesn't like to wear clothing."

"Well, I feel comfortable in the buff too, so I don't think I'd object too much, but perhaps we should date a few more times, so people don't talk." I kissed her passionately, then we got dressed and went back to my quarters.

When we got into my quarters, Kevin was sitting on a couch with nothing on, not paying too much attention to Nancy and me other than a smile; I said, "Don't you think you should put clothing on when we have company?"

"Why, Nancy is going to be my mother."

"It's alright, James, I might just join him," Nancy said as Kevin giggled. Nancy stayed that night; I did not bother sending Kevin to sleep at his uncle's quarters; he knew what was going on. Then next morning, when I got up late, Nancy was gone, and Kevin was curled up beside me. I assumed that Nancy went back to her quarters to get ready for her work.

As I dressed to go on the bridge, Kevin woke up and said, "Daddy are you going to see Nancy?"

"No, I assume she went back to her quarters to get ready for work." "I'm going to the bridge; you stay here when you get up, eat something and then get busy with your schooling using the computer as I showed you; you have been away from it too long."

"Alright."

"When did you crawl in bed with me?"

"When Nancy left, she told me to sleep with you."

"How long ago was that?"

"Not long, a couple of hours, I guess." "She kissed me before she left; she kissed you too."

"How do you feel about that?"

"Who you or me?"

"Both."

"I like being kissed." "She kissed me when I went to bed too." "You are going to marry her; that's what moms and dads do, so it's alright that she kisses you; it means she loves you as she loves me."

I kissed Kevin just before I went up to the bridge; when I got there, William was already there. "I haven't seen you for a while; how are things going?" asked William.

"Alright, I guess I would like to talk to you and Mary."

"Alright, we will go to my quarters after we leave here."

"How fast are we going, Captain?" I asked.

"About light to the power of five."

"Why so slow we need to be at least light to the power of eight?"

"I felt it better to increase the speed gradually to see how the engines take it."

"And how are the engines doing?"

"The engines are fine, just like everything else."

"When do you think we will be at light to the power of eight?"

"By the end of the week, I would think."

"That is going to put us back for another week and a half."

"Well, I could increase it to light to the power of eight if you want me to."

"No, this is your ship; if you think you need to be cautious, then do what you think is best." "Just remember there may be times where you need to take chances." "And remember, don't be afraid to challenge William or me if you think you are right; we won't take it against you."

"Yes, Sir."

I turned to William and said, "This will put us back about a week and a half." William nodded, and I asked Captain Rodgers, "Has the school opened up yet?"

"Yes."

"Do you know what grades they are teaching?"

"Kindergarten to ninth, I believe."

"I will need to get my son in rolled."

"I was going to ask you about that, Sir." "I also heard you been dating Nancy Atkins."

"Yes, do you object?"

"No, what the crew does in their spare time is their business." "From hearing what you said to your brother, it sounds like it is getting serious."

"Yes, I might just marry her." "Do you know how to do a marriage?"

"I've never done one, but I have a book that will show me how; just let me know when you want to do it." I nodded with a smile, and I saw many on the crew who heard our conversation smiling also.

When William and I left the bridge, we went to his quarters. "I won't stay long." "I want to talk to you about Nancy." "I'm thinking about proposing to her, but I don't know if I'm rushing things." "Perhaps I should wait longer to get to know her better, although I know a lot about her now." "I just don't know about this; I don't want to make a mistake."

"James, do you love her?" asked Mary.

"Yes, I love her very much."

"William didn't date me for very long either."

"Yes, but your very special if William didn't marry you, I would have," I said with a smile.

"You are going to have to make a decision," said William.

"I think I will date her a few more times and then talk to her about it."

"I think that would be wise," said Mary. I thanked them and left to my quarters, and when I got there, Kevin was not dressed, but he was working on the computer doing schoolwork.

"Kevin, get dress and clean up." "I'm taking you to school."

"But it's summertime."

"Not on the starship besides, you will make friends, and your schooling won't hurt you." Reluctantly he did as I said, and we went down to the school. I told the teacher his grade, name and he got told to sit next to another boy about his age; then I left. I went to get something to eat in the social room, and Nancy was there.

"You can't wait until tonight," Nancy said with a smile.

"I can't; I miss you too much."

"I have a break in a few minutes, and I will sit with you."

"That would brighten up my days."

"What can I get for you?"

"Breakfast anything you get would be fine with me."

"It's past noon; you sure you don't want lunch."

"No, I prefer breakfast." Twenty minutes later, she came back with breakfast, and she sat down with me.

"I have heard rumors that you are going to ask me something."

"It seems like gossip goes around this starship quick; I was going to wait until I pick you up after work."

"Why wait?" she said, smiling.

I hesitated for a minute, then said, "I was going to ask you to marry me, but I don't know how you feel about that since we hadn't dated long."

"How long do you need to date to know it's time?"

"I don't know; this is all new for me."

"James, just ask me."

By this time, everyone in the social room was staring at us with a smile, but I did not care; I said, "Will you marry me?"

"Now was that hard, of course, I'll marry you."

"You will?"

"Yes."

"I think we should talk to Kevin about this; I think he will be thrilled when he hears."

"Yes."

"Why are you willing to marry me, your very beautiful you could have any man?"

"James, I've dated other men, and most just want to get me into their bed." "Most were jerks and belittled me, and a few were very mean." "Most of the men my parents met didn't like them because of the way they were, and my parents and others warned me about them; of course, they were right." "You're different; I suspect you hadn't dated much, so I know you won't run off with some other woman." "You also treat me like an equal, and I believe we can be both peculiar at times which makes it nice, I believe for the both of us." "You're also not too bad looking; I'm almost sure my parents will love you and Kevin."

"I'm sure I'll love your parents too, but I'm not marrying you for your parents."

"Nor am I."

I went back to my quarters, and after several hours Kevin came home. "How was your day in school?"

"Good, I have some reading to do."

"So, you like school?"

"It's not like school back home on earth; it's a lot better."

"Have you made any friends?"

"There were two boys about my age."

"How about girls?"

"There is one girl who is nice; her name is Sarah," Kevin said softly.

"Do you like her?"

"Yes, I didn't think I would ever like a girl, but she is different," he said with a little more conviction.

"You love your Aunt Mary and Nancy, don't you?"

"Yes, but that's different; they are adults, and Mary is my aunt."

"Nancy isn't your aunt."

"She is special, and I think she will be my mother someday."

"Perhaps, you need to get cleaned up; Nancy is coming over after work."

"Okay, you're not going to talk about Sarah, are you?"

"Why would you care?" "You said she would be your mother someday?" "Who else would be better to talk to about girls than your mother or your Aunt Mary."

"Yes, I guess it would be alright, but not yet; besides, it should be me talking to her, not you, Daddy."

"Okay." Kevin stripped out of his clothing and went to clean up. A few hours later, Nancy showed up.

"Have you told him yet?" Nancy asked.

"No."

"Told me what?" asked Kevin.

"Well, Nancy and I are thinking of getting married, and we want to know how you feel."

"You are going to be my mom, Nancy?" Kevin asked excitedly.

"Yes."

"Well, do you want us to get married?" I asked Kevin.

"Yes, when?"

I looked at Nancy, and she said, "Anytime you want James."

"What about your siblings and Parents?"

"They will want a church wedding; we can have that when we get back, but we could get married now." "I think I would also want to adopt Kevin too."

"I'll talk to the Captain."

"I'm going to go and tell Aunt Mary and Uncle William," said Kevin.

He started to go, but I stopped him and told him, "Perhaps you better get dressed first."

Two days later, we got married, followed by Kevin's adoption. My brother's family and Nancy's roommate were there, and many of the starship crew. Three days later, a ship from what we assume was from the Damar approach us. William and I were summoned, and I said, "Captain, let me handle this," I said.

"Alright."

I got on the ship-to-ship communication and said, "We are the Starship Neverland from Earth; we mean you no harm, are you the Damar?"

We waited for what seemed forever, then from the other ship came, "Are you the same person who contact us on a smaller ship."

"I am."

"We are the Damar; what do you want; you are in our system territory."

"We want to talk to you about a friendship pack and a trading pack." "Also, we have a problem back on Earth we are hoping you can solve."

We waited for a long time; we assume they were discussing it back on their planet. The Damar finally said, "Follow us to our planet, and we will talk."

I looked at Captain Rodgers, and he said, "Raise the force field." We followed the craft to their planet. Their sun was not that bright; it is a red dwarf, most likely why they had large eyes.

"What is it you wish?"

"We would like to negotiate a friendship pack and trading pack with you." "We also wish you to help us with a problem we have on earth."

They talked among themselves and then said, "Where would you like to talk?"

"We are scanning your planet to see if the atmosphere is compatible with us."

I looked at the Captain, and he said, "The planet is a little richer with more oxygen than Earth but its breathable."

"Sir, it appears we can breathe your atmosphere, so I will let you decide where to meet, either here on this ship or your planet."

"Perhaps it would be better to meet on your ship."

"That would be fine sir, when do you want to meet?"

"We will contact you in one period of time."

The screen when dark, and I turned to the Captain and said, "I think a period-of-time is an hour." "Perhaps we should offer them something to eat."

I don't think that is a good idea, James; we don't know what they eat," said William.

"You're right; perhaps we could ask them if they would like to try some of our food."

William nodded, and nearly an hour later, they contacted us. "If they ask us how many starships we have, we should tell them three and more are being constructed."

"I would agree with you," said Captain Rodgers.

"Earth people, we will fly to your ship now."

"There is no need to fly to us; we will transport you."

"How will you do this?"

"You will see, are all your people who are going with you now?"

"Yes, all in this room."

"Stand by; transporter room; bring our guests aboard."

"Yes, sir." Captain, William, and I all went down to the transporter room to greet our guests. There were eight of them as they appeared on the transporter platform.

"Welcome to the Starship Neverland," I said. "Would you please follow me to the conference room?" We all went into the conference room and sat down. "Would you like to try some of our food and perhaps a beverage?"

"No, that won't be necessary."

"My name is Admiral James Reno, this is my brother Admiral William, and this is Captain Rodger."

"You don't captain this ship?"

"No, my brother and I are in authority here, but he captains this ship."

"Interesting, my name is Vere, this one is Iao, he is Uzi, and she is Porta; we represent our government." "It is my understanding you wish a friendship pack."

"Yes, and a trade pack."

"We have studied your people and found them violent."

"We do have violent people, but we are getting better." "I am guessing, but I would think you think we aren't as far advance as we are."

"You are correct, Admiral."

"We know you have to be cautious with us, and we will be cautious with you until we know each other."

"Then, if you understand this, we can accept a friendship pack with you." "I think a trade pack will be on the same agreement as our friendship agreement until we know each other we will trade some things, but not all things."

I looked at the Captain, and he nodded his head, and I said, "That is an agreement, perhaps we both could write this agreement down, and later others of our people can make a more detailed agreement."

"This will be good." "It is our understanding you have a problem you want us to help solve."

"Yes." I called up the first picture on the screen. "These people are called Pongo." "I call them people because they are sentient; they have high intelligence and a language which my brother and I can speak."

The Damar were shocked when they saw the picture of the Pongo. "They are sacred to the Damar; we thought none existed anymore." "Before the supernova in what you call the Vela Constellation, we rescued the people you called Pongo." "We tried to settle them on our planet, but they weren't compatible with us, so we transported them to your Earth at a time your people were few and primitive." "We will help you with anything you need."

"They are now not compatible with us either, and if they stay on Earth, they will not exist anymore." "We need to find a planet they can thrive in peace." "There is a planet that would be good for them." "It has a good sun and plenty of food and water and no other intelligent beings."

"Do you have a star chart you can show us?"

"Yes, I will call down to my planet to give to you."

"Captain, have someone from Astrophysics meet with the Damar, so we know for sure where to go."

"Yes, sir." The map got sent up to us, and an astrophysicist from Damar came to assist our astrophysicist. I asked why Damar or other people have not colonized the planet. They said there are many planets to inhabit, and this planet is well in their area of control. The Captain, William, and I gave the Damar a tour of our ship. Then when the two astrophysicists understood where this planet is, everyone left, but not before Vere said, "When you come back with the Pongo, please come by Damar so we can greet them and send a crew with you to help them settle on the planet."

"We will do this," I said. We left Damar, and in two weeks at high speed, we were back on Earth. I took a shuttle with Kevin and Nancy and headed to Neverland, William, Mary, and the baby went back to Mississippi. The captain went and reported what happened with the ship and with the Damar people.

We landed in the Pongo village that I was accustomed to, and I spoke to the elders and explained what I wanted to do and why I wanted to do it. It took some convincing, but they agreed to go to this new planet. I had to do the same to all the other tribes, but in the end, they decided to go, and they wanted to meet the Damar. With all their belongings, they were transported to the ship, in all, there were a little over five thousand we housed them in all the hangers and virtual reality rooms. Then we left for Damar again with some government people who had gifts for the Damar, and they wanted to negotiate a more detailed agreement with them. Nancy spent a lot of time with the Pongo; fortunately, we had a voice translator so she could talk to them. Two weeks later, we orbited Damar and Vere and some others who would negotiate with our government people joined me on the starship.

"I would like to see and speak to the Pongo," requested Vere. He and a female named Quirt joined me as they met the Pongo, and they were in awe. What surprised me is they both could speak Pongo even though they did not need to. The Pongo was enthralled with the Damar; the elders from all tribes met the Damar, which is a great honor.

The planet was thirty-five light-years from Damar, and it took us five days to reach the planet because we matched the speed of the Damar spacecraft. All decided to name the planet Pongo since each tribe had its name, but the species was Pongo. The Damar had been all this time instructing the Pongo about the wildlife, resources, climate on the planet.

The elders were shown from the starship what their world looked like, and they were impressed. The Damar ship would stay on the planet for some time to get the Pongo used to it. Captain Rodgers, some of the crew, Kevin, Nancy, and I went down with the Pongo to the surface and to bring back some of the fauna, plants, water, soil, and rocks of the planet. After being there for two days and saying our goodbyes to the Pongo, we headed back to Damar with some of the Damar people. We spent one day at Damar; our government people negotiated an excellent agreement and an agreement for both planets to protect each other from other hostel species. We headed back to Earth and were home in about a week. I turned total control of the starship to Captain Rodgers; then Kevin, Nancy, and I headed for her parents' home.

We drove up to Nancy's parent's house in a rented car, and Nancy knocked on the door then opened the door and yelled, "Mom, Dad are you home?"

"Nancy!" yelled Mrs. Fuller excitedly. Nancy went into her arms a few seconds later in came Mr. Fuller, and Nancy went into his arms. Kevin and I were both bewildered at the way Nancy's parents showed her affection. "You must be James, and you are my grandson, Kevin." She went over to hug us both, much to the delight of both of us. Then my father-in-law did the same, and we got shown to their sitting room. "Your sisters should be home soon, and we can discuss the wedding plans then."

"It sure going to be nice to have a couple of men in the family for a change," said Mr. Fuller.

"A couple of men, who is grandpa talking about Daddy?" asked Kevin, confused.

"He is talking about you and me, Kevin."

"I'm just a boy."

"You're a male Kevin, and that's all that matters," said his grandpa. "James, would you like a cold beer, and how about apple juice for you, Kevin?" Nancy, Martha, do you want something?"

"Beer would be fine for me, Bill," said Martha Fuller.

"The same for me, dad." We talked for hours, much to the boredom of Kevin.

"Kevin, why don't you go into the backyard?" "There are swings and slides there you might like the door is through the kitchen," said my mother-in-law. Kevin looked at his mother and me, then Nancy nodded, and he got up and left.

Nancy's mother started making something to eat, and I said, "You're not cooking for us, are you?"

"Yes, I am," said Martha.

"That is not necessary; we need to be going; we need to find a room," I said.

"You're not going to stay at a motel, James; you're staying with us," said Bill.

"That's right," said Martha.

"We couldn't impose on you," I said.

"We insist you stay," said Martha.

"But," I started to say.

"No use to argue with them you will lose James," said Nancy.

"Alright, I know when I won't win, we will stay," I giggled.

"You and Nancy can sleep in her old room, and Kevin can sleep in the guest room," Martha said.

"Oh, yah Kevin, he isn't bashful; he might walk around with nothing on," I said.

"James, nudity is no big deal here, hasn't Nancy told you?" said Bill.

"Yes, I believe she said something about that," I said. Nancy's sisters, Betty, and Susan, came home, and they fussed over us and drove Kevin crazy, but I think he ate it up. Nancy, her sisters, and her mother worked on the arrangements for the wedding. I called William and Mary to invite them and my parents and other siblings. I also call a few other relatives and friends at the lab. My father-in-law Bill took Kevin and me to see the sites of Meadville while the women worked on the wedding.

We told the guest that no gifts were necessary; we had or could get everything we needed or wanted. Some did give gifts, primarily antiques and family heirlooms which we were happy to receive. A few days after the marriage, we said our goodbyes and left for our home in Mississippi. Over the weeks, months, years, Nancy went to the University of Southern Mississippi and got a degree in Zoology and Biology was teaching in the local college. Kevin graduated high school and entered the same University that Nancy went to; he wished to be an Astrophysicist. By the time Kevin graduated, there were five starships; Kevin wanted to be on one of them as an officer. The lab got enlarged, and besides being a place where starships got built, it was also an Academy for officers and crewmembers for the starships; Kevin will be going there before he works on a starship. William and I collaborated and wrote books about the hooker family and us. We also wrote science books dealing with what we had learned or had gathered from the Hooker family. William and Mary had three more children, two girls, and a boy. Nancy and I had two more children, a boy, and a girl. If you wanted to find William or me, we would be fishing someplace or doing charity work, and if we are not doing that, we are doing some new project somewhere.

Lightning Source UK Ltd.
Milton Keynes UK
UKHW012000160921
390713UK00008B/445/J